ECSTASY

ALSO BY *Beth Saulnier*

Reliable Sources

Distemper

The Fourth Wall

Bad Seed

AN ALEX BERNIER MYSTERY

ECSTASY

Beth Saulnier

Published by Warner Books

An AOL Time Warner Company

Copyright © 2003 by Beth Saulnier
All rights reserved.

 Mysterious Press books are published by Warner Books, Inc., 1271 Avenue of the Americas, New York, NY 10020.

Visit our Web site at www.twbookmark.com.

An AOL Time Warner Company

The Mysterious Press name and logo are registered trademarks of Warner Books, Inc.

Printed in the United States of America
First Printing: March 2003
10   9   8   7   6   5   4   3   2   1

Book design by Fearn de Vic.
Library of Congress Cataloging-in-Publication Data
Saulnier, Beth.
    Ecstasy / Beth Saulnier.
      p. cm.
    ISBN 0-89296-750-1
    1. Women journalists—Fiction. 2. Universities and colleges—Fiction. 3. Music festivals—Fiction. 4. Drug abuse—Fiction. 5. LSD (Drug)—Fiction. 6. Hippies—Fiction. I. Title.

PS3569.A7882 E28 2003
813'.6—dc21   2002026519

Dedicated to the memory
of *Wall Street Journal* reporter Daniel Pearl,
a fellow alumnus of the *North Adams Transcript*
who died in the line of duty

ACKNOWLEDGMENTS

With many thanks to:
Sara Ann Freed,
my beloved editor

Jimmy Vines,
agent extraordinaire

Miss C. A. Carlson,
weaver of diabolical plots

Seth Adelson and Jackie Cerretani
for "Melting Rock" insights

Susan Bloom
for coming up with the title

Mark Anbinder,
iMac wrangler and man-about-town

&

special thanks, as always,
to David Bloom
for being himself

ECSTASY

I still wonder what it was like for him in those last minutes—lying there alone, the nylon walls close against him in the dark, the only light coming from the kaleidoscope in his own head. I wonder if he was scared; did he know what was happening to him was the *end*, or was he just too out of it to realize? And if he did know, did he kick himself for it?

His death, after all, can in great measure be chalked up to his own stupidity. You can argue all you want about the fundamental nature of justice, you can point out that the punishment didn't really fit the crime, but the bottom line is that although other people were obviously responsible for his death, he damn well helped; somehow, this clueless seventeen-year-old boy managed to be both victim and accomplice.

I barely knew him, so it's probably nuts even to speculate, but at the moment I can't seem to stop. Maybe that's because lately I've come across so many kids just like him, or because I've spent so many hours trying to walk in his patched-up Birkenstocks. Either way, right now his last hour or so on earth is incredibly vivid in my imagination. And I'll tell you the truth: I really, really wish it weren't.

But it is. And I picture it like this:

He crawls into the tent, strips down to the childish white underpants they'll find him in. He's full, probably uncomfortably so; the coroner will find a gigantic amount of food in his stomach—falafel and veggie chili and peanut butter cups he put away a couple of hours before, probably in an attack of the munchies from all the grass he smoked that afternoon.

A different sort of guy might want company, but later his friends will say that wasn't his style. He likes to be by himself, savor the moment—open his mind to new realities, I suppose he'd say. He prefers to lie by himself in the dark and wait for the universe to open up and swallow him, to take him on some dopey journey of the imagination; the next morning (or more likely afternoon) he'll tell his friends all about it over a whole wheat bagel with extra honey.

So he pins a sign to the tent that says—no kidding—TRIPPING, DO NOT DISTURB. He zips up the flap and lies on top of his sleeping bag mostly naked, since the late-August heat is all but unbearable, even if you're in your right mind. He pulls his long corkscrew curls out of their usual ponytail and wraps the elastic around his flashlight. He lights the candle on the milk crate beside him, but only long enough to let the scent of sage waft over to him. He blows it out after a minute or so, not only because he craves the dark but because he knows you're never supposed to have an open flame inside a tent; later, when his friends are called upon to eulogize, they'll say he was a kick-ass camper.

He's happy, at least that's the way I imagine it. He's utterly in his element, a skinny little fish gliding in his favorite pond. Within a few hundred yards are most of the people on the planet who really matter to him—guys he's been skateboarding with since he was ten, girls he's danced with and gotten high with and screwed, and no hard feelings afterward.

The night feels alive around him; it's loud with laughter and bits of conversations, all of them important—some pondering the next band on the playlist, others the fundamental meaning of the universe. There's music everywhere, coming from so many sources and directions it's impossible to separate them, innumerable voices and bass lines and drum beats going *thump-thump-thump* inside his chest.

He closes his eyes, because even before the candle goes out there's no need for vision. His other senses are on overload, and he likes it. If he's feeling this much even before the drug really kicks in, he knows he's in for one hell of a ride.

This is the moment he likes best, when it's just starting and he's not quite sure which world he's in. At first, the sensations are slow, sneaky, subtle—fictions masquerading as fact. The beginning of a trip is like crossing a river, he's always said; you can try to stay on the rocks of reality, but the closer you get to the other side, the wetter you're going to get.

I have no idea how long he balances in the netherworld between here and elsewhere; for his sake, I hope it's a while. But eventually, he segues into something infinitely wilder—and since my personal experience with mind-expanding drugs is essentially nil (my head being kooky enough without the addition of psychotropics), I have a hard time imagining it. When I ponder the usual stereotypes—shooting stars and melting walls and talking rhinos and such—it just seems pathetic, and I know he didn't see it that way. To him it was something profound, something worth stretching yourself, maybe even scaring yourself, just for the sake of the experience.

But was it something worth dying for? That much I seriously doubt. But there's no arguing with the fact that that's precisely what happened.

At some point, quite when I don't know, things start to go wrong. His mouth goes dry. He gets a raging headache. Maybe his stomach starts to hurt; then it starts to hurt *bad*. He can barely breathe. Eventually, he can't breathe at all.

I wonder if he thinks it's all just part of the experience—that he's taking some dark spirit journey to the edge of his own demise. (And, okay, I know that sounds like your typical druggie-hippie crap; it just goes to show you how much time I've been spending with these people.) How nasty a surprise must it have been to realize that it wasn't a fantasy version of death, but the real thing?

But there's another possibility—one that's even more unpleasant, if such a thing is possible. From what I've been told, physical well-being is essential to the enjoyment of your average acid trip. The symptoms he must have experienced, then, could very well have sent him spiraling into the same mental purgatory that keeps cowards like me limited to gin, Marlboro Lights, and the (very) occasional joint.

This seventeen-year-old boy, in other words, may not have died in just physical agony; he may have died in mental agony as well. *Serious* mental agony. Through the magic of chemistry, his was an anguish not necessarily bounded by the normal limits of the human mind. It's a horrible thing to contemplate, to tell you the truth. There's plenty of pain in the conscious world, after all; how much must there be when the pit is well and truly bottomless?

When they finally found him, he was in the fetal position—curled up tight, knees against his chest, stringy arms wrapped around each other. The doctors say this doesn't necessarily mean anything about his last moments, but frankly, I don't buy it. As far as I'm concerned, it means he didn't go peacefully.

Because, after all, neither did any of the others.

CHAPTER *1*

August in a college town is its own special brand of torture. The living is easy, the weather is still gorgeous, and the students have been gone so long you have a hard time remembering what the place is really like nine months out of the year. You have these vaguely distasteful images of crowded restaurants and SUV-driving frat boys and gaggles of tummy-shirted coeds, but none of it seems real. You soak up the delicious moments—when you get a parking place right smack in front of the multiplex, say, or you go out for a drink without having some postadolescent moron comment on your cleavage—and you fantasize that maybe, just maybe, they're never coming back. Maybe the leaves will stay on the trees forever, and the streets will always be open and empty, and the new semester will never come.

But deep down, you know it will. Damn it all, it will—and it always does.

It used to be that October made me feel wistful, what with impending winter and the smell of decay in the air and the knowledge that you weren't going to get to wear shorts again for a very long time. But since I moved to Gabriel five or so years ago, my wistfulness threshold has been pushed back a good two months. Maybe it's just because people around here are too smart to ever really be happy, but we townies tend to start feeling blue three weeks before Labor Day, and we don't really shake it until graduation.

I mention all this by way of explaining that although late summer/ early fall in this ZIP code can be a tough pill to swallow, by all that's holy, last August should've been comparatively jolly. I was, after all, celebrating the fact that I had recently avoided being killed on three separate occasions within a matter of weeks—rather a nifty accomplishment, if you ask me. The newspaper where I work was, for the first time in recent memory, fully staffed. And—here's the cherry on the sundae—my boyfriend, who I'd been fearing was about to move away and break my little heart, showed every sign of staying put. Even the imminent return of fifteen thousand undergraduates couldn't put the kibosh on my good mood.

If I tried to put my finger on when everything went to hell, well . . . it wouldn't be too hard. That would be when I walked into the newsroom around eleven on a Wednesday morning in mid-August. I'd walked out of there precisely ten hours earlier, after covering a particularly pissy county board meeting that went until nearly midnight, then scrambling to slap together three (mercifully short) stories by my one A.M. deadline. Then I'd gone home to hold the crying towel for my roommate, Melissa, whose boyfriend had recently—you guessed it—moved away and broken her little heart.

So it was without a whole lot of sleep that I went back to work, toting a bagel with diet olive cream cheese and blissfully unaware of how much my life was about to suck. I poured some coffee into my big Gabriel Police Department mug, one of several recent gifts my aforementioned boyfriend had proffered to celebrate the fact of me not being dead. Then I sat down at my desk and tried to figure out which of the county board stories was going to need a follow-up for the next day's paper.

I'm not sure how long it took me to figure out something weird was up. I do recall that my first clue was that I was the only reporter on the cityside desk; come to think of it, I was the only reporter in the entire newsroom. It was way too early for the sports guys, but there should've at least been someone else around *somewhere;* as it was, though, the owner of every single *Gabriel Monitor* byline was nowhere to be found.

To round them up: There's Jake Madison (aka "Mad"), the science writer and my best buddy; Cal Ochoa, the cops reporter and one moody hombre; Lillian, the elderly-but-steely schools reporter; Marshall, the Dixie-born business writer; and—both last and least—Brad, an ambitious, scandal-mongering young fellow who's on the towns beat, and whom I avoid whenever possible.

Where was everybody? In a word: hiding. And if I'd known better, I damn well would've been hiding too.

But there I was, sitting at my desk with the kind of clueless-but-doomed expression you see on a cow peeking out of the airholes in a livestock truck. At some point, my catlike instincts must've registered the fact that someone was breathing down my neck; when I looked up, there were three of them.

Three *editors.* As any reporter can tell you, there was no way this was going to end well.

"Alex," one of them said, and way too brightly. "You're here."

This from the shorter and rounder of the two women. Her name is Sondra, and she's the editor of (among other things) *Pastimes,* the paper's deeply mediocre arts-and-leisure magazine. Except for the weekly processing of my movie review column, I don't have a lot to do with her; she mostly lives in her own little universe, eternally beset by underpaid freelancers.

She was already making me nervous.

Standing next to her were both of my bosses—Bill, the city editor, and his own overlord, the managing editor. Marilyn is not short, and she's in no way round; in fact, she has a black belt in tae kwon do.

"Um . . . ," I said, "where is everybody?"

"My office," she said.

"They're all in your—"

"Come *in*to my office," she said, and turned her well-exercised tail on me.

I followed, with Bill and Sondra bringing up the rear. In retrospect, they were probably trying to make sure I didn't make a run for it.

"Um . . . ," I said when we'd sat down, "so where is everybody?"

"Alex," Sondra said, sounding even more scary-friendly than before, "what are you doing for the next few days?"

"Huh?" I looked to Bill, who was taking a passionate interest in the pointy end of his necktie. "You mean, what am I covering?" Sondra nodded and leaned in closer, so I had a clear view right down her blouse to her tattletale-gray minimizer bra. "Today? Maybe a couple follows from last night's board meeting. Tomorrow . . . I think another stupid Deep Lake Cooling thing. Why?"

"And do you have any plans for this weekend?"

Uh-oh. Say something clever. Say . . . you have to donate a kidney to homeless mental patients.

That's what one side of my brain told the other. But I wasn't quick enough on the uptake, so all I said was, "Um . . . No."

Sondra squeezed my upper arm, harder than I would've thought she could. "That's *great.*"

"Huh?"

"Alex," she positively cooed at me, "I was hoping you could do me this teeny-tiny favor. . . ."

Now, at this point my hackles well and truly hit the ceiling. Because when an editor asks you for a *teeny-tiny favor,* it generally means you're about to get screwed without so much as a box of chocolates.

"Listen," I said, "I'm actually pretty busy at the moment, so—"

"You're covering Melting Rock," Marilyn said, sounding nowhere near as nice as Sondra, but considerably more genuine. "Starts today. So—"

"What?"

"Haven't you heard of it?" Sondra chirped at me. "You know, the official name is the Melting Rock Music Festival, but lots of people just call it—"

"Hell yes, I've heard of it. But what do you mean I'm—"

"Freelancer flaked out," Marilyn said into her mug of terrifyingly black coffee. "Chester says we gotta deliver the goods. So go."

Chester is our publisher—and there are guys in the pressroom with better news judgment. Things were not looking up.

"Go where? You mean go *now?* And where *is* everybody, anyway?"

I must've sounded either very desperate or very pathetic, because

Bill finally took pity on me. "Here's the deal," he said. "You know Sim Marchesi?"

"Er . . . I dunno."

"He covers pop music for me," Sondra offered. "I mean he *covered* it. Right now I wouldn't hire that miserable—"

"Listen," Bill said, "Marchesi pitched us this story, and when Chester got wind of the thing, he ate it up—promoted it up the wazoo. Then Marchesi bailed."

"Bailed how?"

"He was gonna cover the days and nights of Melting Rock, camp out there with the rest of the freaks and send us dispatches from the front. It was on the budget at the cityside meeting yesterday. Remember?"

"Vaguely."

"So the thing starts today. He was supposed to get there last night to cover the setup—was gonna file right before deadline for today's paper."

"And he blew it off?"

"Blew it off?" Marilyn growled with a whack of mug onto desktop. "Little prick flew the coop."

"You mean he hasn't filed yet? But maybe he just—"

Sondra waved me off. "He never even came by to pick up the laptop or the cell phone we were lending him. I tried his apartment and the number's disconnected. Then I tracked down the fellow in charge of the Melting Rock campground and . . . it looks like he never showed up yesterday."

"So spike the story," I said. It turned out to be a poor choice of words.

"What are you, deaf?" Marilyn said, segueing to something resembling a snarl. "We *can't* spike it. Don't you think I wish we could spike it? Chester's really got his undershorts in a twist. He thinks it's gonna be the goddamn miracle cure for our circulation with the under-thirty crowd. He's been flogging this thing all over cable commercials and house ads and mother-humping rack cards. . . . Don't you even read the paper?"

"Er . . . Yeah, sure I do. I guess I've been kind of busy."

"Okay, here's how it is," she said. "Chester's been promoting this package like it's the Second Coming, you got it? Marchesi's AWOL, so somebody else's gotta cover it. And that somebody would be you."

"Why me?"

Another arm squeeze from Sondra. "Because," she said, "you're a really good feature writer. I mean, I know you mostly cover news, but you always have lots of great color in your—"

"Give me a break." I glanced out the window, which is not the kind you can open. Leaping to my death did not appear to be an option. "Listen, like I said, I gotta do some follows on board stuff, so—"

Marilyn didn't even blink. "Give it to Brad."

"*Brad?* You gotta be—"

"Anything else?"

"Um . . . Yeah. There's gonna be another town meeting for Deep Lake Cooling on Friday night, so I really have to—"

She turned to Bill. "Who's weekend reporter?"

"Madison."

"Perfect. He's been covering the science end anyway. Hand it off to him." She turned back to me. "That all?"

"Er . . ." I racked my noggin for something good enough to spring me, and came up short. "I guess so."

"Super. So be a good girl and go put on your love beads and get the hell out there."

"But why can't we just—"

"Stop whining and hop to it," she said.

I'm not kidding. That's actually what she said. I decided to get the hell out of there before she told me to shake my tail feather, or worse.

Bill, being no fool, beat a hasty retreat to his office. I followed Sondra back to the arts-and-leisure desk, which is at the opposite end of the newsroom from Marilyn's domain. The commute took ten seconds, during which Sondra said, "This is going to be just great!" more times than I cared to count.

Sometimes I think that journalists, like double agents, should be issued a suicide pill.

You may be wondering just why I was being such a baby about

this. To put it succinctly: The Melting Rock Music Festival is my idea of hell. Until I was conscripted by the *Gabriel Monitor*'s editorial staff, I'd been there exactly once, and for a grand total of four hours.

It was the summer I'd moved to Gabriel five years ago, back when I didn't know any better. Melting Rock sounded kind of charming, and . . . well . . . this cute Canadian grad student in materials science asked me to go with him. So I put on a flowy skirt and a tank top to get into the spirit of the thing, and proceeded to experience what was, at least at that time, just about the worst day of my life.

First off, the guy's primary purpose for attending the festival proved not so much to be rocking to the groovy beat but hunting down his ex-girlfriend, whom he'd met there the year before. He didn't actually inform me of this at the time, though I had a sneaking suspicion something was up since I spent most of the afternoon looking at his back as he dragged me from stage to stage.

You might think, therefore, that my negative feelings toward Melting Rock amount to sour grapes. But the fact remains that the whole event gave me both a stomachache *and* a migraine. I'm not quite sure what my personal "scene" is, but I can tell you this much: Whatever it is, Melting Rock is the opposite.

So what's it like? To start with, it's hot as Satan's rec room, and sanitary facilities consist of overtaxed Porta-Johns and rusty taps sticking out the side of a barn. Consequently, the whole place stinks— not only of urine and sweat but also frying foodstuffs, incense, stale beer, and veritable gallons of patchouli. It's also one of the most crowded events I've ever had the misfortune to attend, so there's no escaping the aforementioned aromas. You're constantly elbow-to-elbow with young ladies who've never heard the words *brassiere* or *disposable razor* and gentlemen who equate their shoulder tattoos with the goddamn Sistine Chapel.

The music is okay, I guess, though I can't say I paid much attention to it. It all kind of blended in together to make this incredibly tedious, drum-heavy soundtrack that was impossible to escape; within an hour I felt like the guy from "The Tell-Tale Heart" who goes stark raving nuts because he can't get the beat out of his head.

After about four hours of this, I decided I'd had enough. I told my quote-unquote date that I needed to go home, whereupon he said that was fine with him and went back to searching for his erstwhile lady friend. Which might not have been so bad—if Melting Rock weren't held in a little village ten miles outside Gabriel.

I walked home. Honest to God. It was either that or hitchhike, which is something my mother would not approve of. I got back to my apartment after midnight and jumped into the shower with my stinky clothes on.

These memories were, shall we say, plenty vivid as I sat at the leisure desk listening to Sondra prattle on about what a humdinger of an assignment I'd just been shafted with. To summarize the various points of my misery:

- I was not only going to the goddamn Melting Rock Music Festival, I was going there for the next *five days*.
- I was actually going to have to talk to people who frequent such events. Then I was going to have to write down what they said and churn out stories that presumably made it look like I gave a damn.
- I was going to have to eat a lot of greasy carnival food. (Okay, maybe this part wasn't so bad.)
- Any plans to spend the weekend in the boudoir of a very attractive policeman named Brian Cody were out the window.

And, worst of all:

- I was going to spend the next four nights in a tent. *Four*. In a *tent*.

I was pondering this litany of misfortune when my newsroom compadres finally started filing in. I was on the point of unloading on one Jake Madison when I realized that—big surprise—he was already very much in the know.

"So you guys knew she was gonna sandbag me and you didn't even give me a heads-up? Thanks a lot."

"Hey, every man for himself."

"Lovely."

Mad took a seat on the edge of my desk and unwrapped his tuna sandwich. "Human nature."

"Yeah, maybe *yours.*"

"Come on, you know," he said, "it's like that story about the two guys and the bear."

"What the hell are you talking about?"

"Two guys are walking in the woods and they see this bear, right? So one of them pulls his sneakers out of his backpack and puts them on. And the other guy says to him, 'What are you doing? You know you can't outrun a bear.'"

"And?"

"And the first guy goes, 'Hey, man, I don't have to outrun the bear.'" He smiled his wolfish Mad smile and poised to take a bite. "'I just have to outrun *you.*'"

CHAPTER 2

Jump forward half an hour. Since one of the two men in my life was offering me zip in the way of consolation, I decided to go in search of the other. So there I was, standing in the vestibule of the Gabriel police station, talking to a certain red-haired officer of the law. And, okay, I wasn't just trolling for sympathy; I also needed to ask him to baby-sit my dog and to lend me (*ugh*) a sleeping bag and a tent.

To give you some background:

Detective Brian Cody is thirty-three, as upright as they come, and the most unabashedly nice guy I've ever even considered dating. He married his college sweetheart, then got summarily dumped when she decided she'd rather sleep her way up the chain of command of the Boston P.D. Ours is one of those patented opposites-attract kind of romances; witness the fact that he carries a gun to work *and* actually enjoys spending the night in the woods sans both TV and air conditioner.

"You know," he was saying, "camping out can be really fun. I've been trying to get you to—"

"Come on, Cody. If I never wanted to sleep in a tent with *you*, what're the odds I'm gonna like sleeping in a field full of dancing hippies?"

"Can't argue with you there. I guess you just gotta try and make the best of it."

"Couldn't you just pat me on the head and say, 'Poor baby'?"

"Poor baby."

"What about the head-patting part?"

"Don't want to mess with my macho image. They giving you hazardous-duty pay for this one?"

"Since I'm kind of working night and day, they're giving me a four-day weekend for the next two weeks, which is nice. Just about the only nice thing, if you ask me."

"Poor baby."

"Keep it up," I said, "and you might get lucky on Sunday night, after all."

As it turned out, Cody got lucky roughly fifteen minutes later, when he used his lunch break to squire me over to his apartment to pick up his camping gear. It wasn't until around two that I finally got into my trusty red next-gen Beetle and drove the ten miles out to Jaspersburg, the one-horse town that has hosted Melting Rock lo these thirteen years. Even a festival basher like myself knows that it's the quintessential love-hate relationship: The town fathers love the bags of money that Melting Rock drops on their doorstep and hate just about everything else about it.

I drove down the main drag in search of the so-called VIP parking lot, which proved to be hell and gone from the campground. I, therefore, hauled my tent, sleeping bag, laptop, and backpack full of clothes half a mile through scraggly grass, already starting to sweat and realizing that the only way I was going to get clean was to open my heart to the concept of the communal outdoor shower.

I stomped around like that for a while before I realized I had no idea where I was going. Eventually, a wiry young man walked by toting a load twice as big as mine, and I yelled for him to stop. He did, and when he turned around, I noticed he had a ring in his nose—not a wee one through the side of one nostril but a honking doughnut of a thing right through the middle, like a prize bull.

"Uh, excuse me," I said. "Could you tell me how to get to the campground?"

"Sure, sister. Which one?"

"Er . . . The main one, I guess."

"Main? You sure?"

I dug a piece of paper out of my pocket. "Yeah," I said. "I'm supposed to go to the main campground."

He whistled at me, and probably not because I was a vision of loveliness. "Hey, you're *lucky*," he said. "Slots in Main almost never open up." He gave me an assessing look. "Hey . . . are you, you know, here by yourself?"

"Unfortunately."

"Cool," he said. "How about I crash with you?"

"Excuse me?"

"You know, can I crash in your tent? We'd have a *blast*. I got a ton of buds coming, and they're bringing some really sweet—"

"Er . . . I'm afraid not. I'm kind of, um, here on business."

"Yeah? Whatcha sellin'? You got E? 'Shrooms? What?" His eyes narrowed. "Listen, I don't do Oxy—"

"Oh, er . . . nothing like that." He looked rather crestfallen. "So could you maybe tell me how to get to the main campground?"

"Yeah, okay." He walked ahead for a few paces and stopped. "Like . . . you really don't want me to crash with you? You sure?"

"As sure," I said, "as I've ever been of anything in my life."

MY NEW FRIEND was nothing if not tenacious; he repeated the question at least half a dozen times before we finally got to the campground. At one point I tried telling him that I couldn't bunk with him because I had a boyfriend, but this did no good whatsoever; he just mumbled, "But, come on, this is Melting Rock . . ." and proceeded to tell me I was one freaky chick.

I didn't contradict him.

His name, as it turned out, was Doug—a rather conventional moniker for a guy with a pacifier through his proboscis, if you ask me. And though I tried to shake him once I figured out where I was supposed to be headed, in the end I was just as glad he stuck around; *somebody* had to get the tent to stand up on its own, you see, and that somebody wasn't going to be me.

By four o'clock I was settled in my nylon rathole and beginning to contemplate the awful truth, which was that I was going to be calling this place home for the next hundred or so hours. In a vain attempt to cheer myself up, I went in search of sustenance. You'd think that a place as hippie-dippy as this would be all about macrobiotic tabouli, but a lot of the vendors who come to Melting Rock are the same ones who hit the county fair circuit. And to add insult to atherosclerosis, the stuff is more overpriced than movie theater popcorn. I settled on a pizza slice dotted with a few pathetic mushrooms and a small diet Coke. Although I was plenty thirsty, I was determined to keep my Porta-John trips to a minimum. It cost me five bucks.

Eventually, I couldn't avoid work anymore; I had to file something pretty soon or Marilyn was going to give me a cellular shellacking. Sondra and I had worked out a tentative story budget that had me doing mainbars that would jump off page one on Thursday, Friday, Saturday, and Monday (there's no Sunday paper), plus a couple of daily sidebars on whatever I happened to dig up.

That didn't sound so bad . . . but neither was it the whole story. Chester, who had recently discovered that there's this nifty gizmo called "the Internet," had decided that nothing would be cooler than having dispatches from the festival posted on the *Monitor*'s spanking-new Web site six times a day. This meant that I had to come up with six story ideas a day (mercifully, only three that first night)— which, in turn, meant that I was what we professional journalists call *desperate.*

I decided the first Web piece might as well be on something I was already acquainted with, so I did a little eight-hundred-word story on the vendors. This turned out to be a damn good idea, since it got me a complimentary funnel cake as well as a bag of curly fries and a caramel apple, the latter of which I stashed away for a future moment of emotional desperation.

Once I finished the piece, I figured I might as well file it. I, there-fore, went in search of the so-called "media tent," which I assumed was going to be a pole with a phone line stapled to it. It proved to be an actual army-style green canvas tent containing a cable modem on a folding table and two strapping young fellows checking press passes to make sure nobody else tried to sneak in.

One down. A feature and a sidebar to go before I sleep. But what to cover?

I decided a little aimless wandering was in order. So I strolled from the media tent, past one of the minor concert stages, and toward the much-ballyhooed main campsite; then I looped around to where the Jaspersburg Fairgrounds ended in an abrupt (if climbable) two-story drop to a decent-size creek. I peered down the slope and was greeted by the sight of several dozen human beings engaged in some very enthusiastic skinny-dipping. Then I headed toward the epicenter of the revelry, a pancake-flat space known as the Infield. It was barely a few hours into the first day of the festival and already the place was packed with undulating youth. The Infield stage was set off to one side of the oval of trampled grass; on the other was the geological freak-out that gave the festival its name.

The Melting Rock is maybe fifteen feet tall and looks like a blackish-grayish wedding cake that's been left out in the sun too long. It has four tiers, which (in kind of a Mesozoic version of *American Bandstand*) a few of the aforementioned undulators were using as a perch to boogie and watch the musicians howling from the other side of the field.

One of the fans—a guy of about thirty with a bushy beard and an equally bushy ponytail—was wearing a homemade T-shirt that said ASK ME ABOUT THE ROCK. I did. He turned out to be a Benson University geology professor, and once he filled me in on the origins and composition of the thing, I figured I had a sidebar on my hands.

That was all well and good—but I still had the next day's mainbar hanging over my head. I decided my next mission was to track down someone in charge, if such a person existed. I managed to grab a girl in a tie-dyed T-shirt with the Melting Rock logo on the front and STAFF on the back, and she told me I had to talk to some guy named Joe. As it turned out, I had to talk to some *woman* named *Jo*—a person so womanly, in fact, that she had one fat baby in a sling on her hip and another one threatening to pop right out of her midsection.

Jo—short for Joelle—had been in charge of Melting Rock since I'd been in junior high. I interviewed her about how the festival had changed over the years, yadda-yadda, and at one point she let it slip that she was in a "committed relationship" with the drummer for Stumpy the Salamander, the roots-rock band that was the festival's headliner.

Jo proved to be a veritable gold mine of story ideas; after sitting on a tree stump with her for half an hour, I found my budget was filled to bursting. There was one about a couple who'd met at the festival two years before and were getting hitched that weekend; the guy who'd had the festival's ever-changing logo tattooed somewhere on his corpus every year since it started; the bunch of friends from Jaspersburg High who'd been coming to Melting Rock together practically since they were old enough to walk—et cetera, et cetera.

I didn't have a strong feeling about which story to hit first, so when Jo told me that the high-school kids always had a picnic by the rock on the first night of the festival, I figured I'd check it out. And there they were, eight teenagers decked out in the Melting Rock uniform of grubby T-shirts and baggy shorts (for the boys) and flowery tank tops and foofy skirts (for the girls).

They seemed to be having a hell of a good time, kicking back on blankets, smoking cigarettes, and munching on a combination of homemade snacks and vendor food. Normally, I would just have walked up to them brandishing a notebook, but something made me hang back and watch them for a minute. Maybe these kids were a breed apart from the mainstream, I decided after a while, but adolescent group dynamics were universal; this crowd definitely had a caste system.

Maybe because (like most of my friends) I'm a refugee from the high-school unpopularity wars, I'm often acutely aware of who sits where on the food chain. At the top of this one was a pretty, round-faced brunette with glitter on her cheeks and a clove cigarette between two fingers. She wore her hair loose, with a tiny blue flower stuck over one ear; the hand that wasn't holding the butt had a ring on each digit, including the thumb. She sat in the center of the ragged circle like she was holding court, barely paying attention to the guy who had an arm draped loosely around her shoulders.

Like half the menfolk at the festival, her prince consort had his hair pulled back in a droopy ponytail; when he let it down, it must be even longer than hers. He kept peeking at her out of the corner of his eye as the conversation ebbed and flowed, but there was something unpossessive about the way he was touching her, and I got the feeling they were just friends.

Sitting around them in uneven clusters were three girls and three boys who kept their mouths fully occupied at all times—with food, tobacco, chitchat, or a combination thereof. At least half of them had visible tattoos, which kind of astounded me; if I'd been fool enough to get myself branded before I was old enough to vote, my dad would've made me get it removed and cheerfully tithed the doctor bill out of my allowance.

When I got tired of watching, I sidled up to the group and gave my standard journalist's mating call.

"Hi, my name is Alex Bernier, and I'm a reporter for the *Gabriel Monitor*. Would you mind if I asked you guys a couple of questions?"

Unsurprisingly, it was the girl in the center who fielded the query. "Um . . . You mean you're, like, from the newspaper?"

"That's right."

"And you want to talk to *us?*"

"Yep."

She raised a dainty eyebrow at me, though not obnoxiously. "How come?"

"Jo Mingle said you guys might make an interesting story for the paper—about how you've been coming here together for a while and all."

"And you want to put us in the paper? Like, with our picture and everything?"

"Yep."

A smile overtook the lower half of her face, revealing the results of a relative fortune in orthodontia. *"Cool."*

"You mind if I sit down?"

She scooted over and made room for me in the midst of the gaggle of adolescents, then stuck out a ring-covered mitt. "What's your name again?"

"Alex Bernier."

"I'm Lauren Potter." She turned to the guy next to her. "This is Tom Giamotti." I shook his economy-size hand, and he favored me with wide eyes and a goofy grin; the overall effect was of an adolescent Saint Bernard. Then Lauren proceeded to go around the circle introducing the six others, who waved at me with varying degrees of understated coolness. I wrote all their names down, with descriptions so I could match them up with their quotes when I put the story together. At first glance, they'd all seemed to be cut from the same batik cloth, but once I got a closer look, I realized they were sort of a Rainbow Coalition of high-school hippies, drawn from all the stereotypical social subgroups.

Since I spent over an hour with them, I had time to take a lot of notes. Here's a rundown of the eight kids, translated from my bad handwriting:

- Lauren Potter—long legs, pretty, confident, "the queen bee"
- Tom Giamotti—bushy hair, sweet, STONED
- Alan Bauer—Gap T, clean-cut, major muscles, "the jock"
- Cindy Bauer—Alan's younger sister, purple hair, nice, kinda sad
- Trish Stilwell—super thin, rose ankle tattoo, gawky, quiet
- Billy Halpern—big stupid sideburns, bigger ego, "the hunk"
- Dorrie Benson—crew cut, many piercings, "the freak"
- Shaun Kirtz—glasses, goatee, acne, pot-leaf T-shirt, "the nerd"

The kids may have been vaguely freakish, but they were plenty gracious. Over the next half hour, I was offered home-brewed beer, chocolate-chip cookies baked by Tom's mother, umpteen cigarettes, Kool-Aid, dried apricots, limp sweet-potato fries, and a pan of very inviting double-chocolate brownies. I was just about to go for the latter when I realized they weren't *hot brownies* (as in warm from the oven) but *pot brownies,* as in laced with marijuana. I took a pass.

"What are you," said buzz-cut Dorrie, "some kinda Nancy Reagan?"

"Huh?" I was distracted by the metal tongue stud that flicked out of her mouth with every syllable.

"Are you, like, all 'Just say no' or something?"

"Me? Not on principle. I just don't, um, get stoned too often."

"Oh."

"You know, I'm kind of surprised you guys've even *heard* of that Nancy Reagan thing. That stupid 'Just say no' campaign dates back a—"

"Hey," Alan said as he absentmindedly flexed a well-developed bicep, "we take history."

"So how come?" This from Billy, who was stroking his sideburns with what seemed to be great enjoyment. I had a feeling a lot of teenage girls might enjoy stroking them too.

"How come what?"

"How come you don't get stoned too often? Don't you dig it?"

The truth was, I'd indulged in such things a lot more often when I was dating a guy for whom ganja constituted a leafy green vegetable. Now that I was with Cody—a straitlaced law-and-order type if ever there was one—ingesting illegal substances didn't exactly make for a typical Saturday night.

"I did a little when I was in college," I said. "I guess I just kind of lost interest."

Billy stopped playing with his facial hair long enough to skewer me with a goggle-eyed gaze. "How old *are* you, anyway?"

"Twenty-seven." The assembled masses looked at each other and then back at me, their expressions equal parts horror and pity. *Wonderful.* I decided not to bother mentioning that Billy's pointy-lapelled polyester shirt had probably been sewn when I was in elementary school. "How old are you guys?"

They were all seventeen, except for sixteen-year-old Cindy; Shaun, whose knobby knees and bad skin made him look like the youngest of the bunch, was turning eighteen on Sunday. All but Cindy were about to start their senior year at Jaspersburg High. One of them (Billy) had been at every single Melting Rock since its inception thirteen years earlier—originally brought by his parents who, he reported with some relief, no longer had any interest in boogying on down for the weekend.

"So how come you guys come here every year?" I asked.

This time, they looked at me like I was the one who'd stuck a damn earring through my tongue. Since the rest of them appeared speechless at the sheer idiocy of the question, it fell to Lauren to answer. "Like . . . it's Melting Rock," she said.

"Yeah," I said, "but what does that mean?"

More pitying looks. "You know," said Tom, "it's the *Melting Rock Music Festival*." There was an earnest tone in his voice, like he really cared about sparing me the embarrassment of my own ignorance. I decided on the spot that, high as a kite though he may be, Tom Giamotti was my favorite of the bunch.

"I got that. But what I mean is, what is it about this thing that makes you want to come back year after year? Is it just that you guys all get to see each other? But you all go to the same school, so you probably see each other all the time, right? So why is this place so special?"

Momentary silence, punctuated by the munching of Fritos and the lighting of yet another American Spirit. "You know," Cindy said finally, "I think that's a pretty cool question."

"Yeah?"

"I guess we just, like, never thought about it before, you know? Why do we like it here? . . ."

She chewed on her bottom lip, and I took a good look at her. Her spiky hair was an alarming shade of violet, which contrasted badly with her pale skin; the effect was something approximating the walking dead. But she had wide blue eyes, and (as my mom would say) if she'd fixed her hair and lost twenty pounds, she could've been a pretty girl. On the other hand, I wasn't entirely sure she wanted to be.

"I guess," she went on, "I'd have to say Melting Rock is . . . It's like our touchstone."

She immediately realized what a lousy pun she'd made, and some life blushed into the pudgy cheeks. Then everybody else figured it out too: Shaun made a gagging noise and threw some corn chips at her. She stuck her tongue out at him, then turned back to me. "I didn't mean it like that. Don't write that down, okay?"

"Don't worry about it."

"What I meant is, like, Melting Rock is the thing we always come back to, you know? And we all promised that we always will—no matter where we go, we'll always come back here. Right, Laur?"

Lauren favored her with the zillion-dollar smile. "You betcha."

"Even if we, you know, get married and have kids and all, we'll bring them here and they'll play together and stuff," Cindy said. "It's this tradition we're gonna have for, like, forever."

Tom shot her a salute and said, "You said it, sister." He was starting to slur his words, like he'd had one brownie too many. "We're like the sparrows going back to Castipano."

Shaun tossed some Fritos at him. "That's the *swallows* returning to *Capistrano,* you shithead." He shook his head and smirked at me. With his little wire-rimmed glasses and vaguely Germanic features, he kind of looked like one of the Nazis from *Raiders of the Lost Ark.* "Dude don't pay attention in class."

"Yo," Tom said, "you're the one who wants to go to MIT, bro. I'll be psyched if I get into SUNY."

"And we're not just visitors," Lauren continued after a vaguely exasperated glance at the two guys. "We, like, sort of help organize it too. Tom volunteered to do paperwork in the Melting Rock office over in Gabriel, and Billy and I sat at the promo table on the Green this year. Shaun even helped redesign the Web site. Have you seen it?" I shook my head. "It's really cool."

"Okay," I said, "but what is it about the festival in particular that you really enjoy—I mean, besides just being together? Is it the music?"

"The music *rocks*," said Billy, and nobody contradicted him. "You got Stumpy, the Blowflies, Seven-Fifty-One Man, Krönk, Missy and the Moguls. . . ." He ticked off the bands on his fingers. "You're talkin' a shitload of talent, yeah?"

I scribbled down the names, whereupon he instructed me not to leave the umlaut out of Krönk. "So a lot of it is about the music, huh?"

"Yeah," Lauren said, "but it's not just that. It's also . . . kind of an oasis, I guess." She wrapped her arms around her knees, like it helped her focus. "Sort of . . . a special place that's apart from everywhere else." She looked around the circle. "You guys know what I mean, right?"

Dorrie nodded, running a hand over her nearly naked skull. The only one clad in long pants, she was wearing gray Carhartts and a long-sleeved T-shirt—chemistry apparently having made her immune to the heat. "I think it's sort of like, you know . . . kind of another dimension."

Shaun hooted the theme to *The Twilight Zone,* though no Fritos went aloft. Cindy smiled at him and joined in, and from the way she glanced at him in those two seconds, I could tell that—despite Shaun's status as a Stri-Dex poster child—she had quite the crush on him.

"Anything goes," Trish mumbled, and I realized it was the first thing she'd said so far.

"How do you mean?" I asked.

She turned her attention to her toenails, which were painted metallic blue. "Um . . . Kind of like, it's free here. No rules, you know? Anything goes."

The girl was skinny as a greyhound, her pointy knees poking out of what looked to be cutoff army pants. She might be seventeen, but—well, I'd had more of a bosom by the third grade.

"And you like that?" I said. "The freedom?"

She shrugged her bony little shoulders, and Billy jumped in. "It's kind of like . . . Melting Rock is this island where the laws of the universe don't have to apply, see? Nobody gets bogged down by petty, stupid shit like they do the other three hundred sixty days of the year." He was really getting into it; I could tell from the flush that was spreading inward from his sideburns. "The rest of the world, it's just out to judge you all the time. You get graded and hassled and all. But at Melting Rock, it's not like that. Get it?"

Cindy nodded her grape-colored head. "It's like you just get to be yourself," she said. "You don't have to pretend to be somebody else, like some fake person society wants you to be."

"Yeah," Lauren said. "It's kind of like"—she glanced around the circle, her long hair swooping in a chestnut cascade—"You guys are gonna totally laugh at me for saying this, but it's like . . . Last summer my mom dragged me to this play in Gabriel, *The Prime of Miss Jean Brodie*. And there's this part where the teacher talks about 'the common moral code,' how it doesn't apply to her because she decided she wants to live outside it. And I remember thinking, 'That's kind of like Melting Rock.' Nobody gets bogged down in that stuff, you get it?"

I flashed back to Doug, my aspiring tentmate. "I think so, yeah."

"Cool," she said, and leaned her head back to lower a pale orange French fry into her mouth.

"Hey, Laur," Shaun said from the blanket where he was lying flat on his back. "That's right on, what you just said. 'Common moral code.' Screw it, huh?"

"Screw it," Dorrie offered, and a few of the others joined in. This inspired me to entertain myself by contemplating the headline possibilities: DISAFFECTED DRUGGIES DAMN DECENCY.

"So," I said, "do you guys usually spend the whole weekend together?"

Alan shrugged, still taking what seemed an unnatural interest in his flexing muscles; he'd started with his biceps, moved on to his forearms, and was now working on his quads. I was half afraid he was about to start reciting love poetry to his own abs. "Kinda," he said.

"Not like we make a big deal about it or anything. Everybody just sort of does their own thing. I mean, that's the whole point, right?"

Tom offered me the brownie pan for the fourth time, and I waved it off. "The guys hang with the guys," he said with his mouth full, "the girls hang with the girls, we all hang together. . . . And, you know, we make some friends. . . ."

From the way he said it, I had a feeling these blossoming friendships involved a fair amount of latex. At least I hoped they did.

"And do you all camp out together?"

Another shrug from Tom. "Not like all in the same tent or anything, but we're all in Main 'cause we've been coming here so long. Pretty cool, huh?"

"I've heard it's a big deal."

"It sure as hell is for Shaun here," Billy said, and not particularly nicely. "How else is a skank like him gonna get laid?"

"Fuck you, man," Shaun shot back at him—but wearily, like he was used to his role as the alpha male's punching bag. "At least I don't hafta pay for it." He turned to Tom, who high-fived him.

Billy made some condescending kissy noises at Shaun, which I took as some sort of manly provocation. "Hey," Billy said, "I never paid for it in my life. Chicks dig me."

Frankly, the guy *was* the dreamboat of the group, what with his movie star chin and well-sculpted bod; I got the feeling he was used to getting female attention wherever and whenever he felt like it. But the Steve McQueen sideburns were downright ridiculous—and since I've never been remotely attracted to younger guys, he didn't exactly make me wild with desire.

"Yeah, bullshit," Shaun was saying. "What they dig is the E your fucking cousin sends you."

"Hey, man," Billy said with a grin, "whatever gets your rocks off."

For the record, I wasn't writing any of this stuff down; there was no way their sexual escapades (real or imagined) were going to make it past my editor. "Okay," I said, "let me ask you another couple of—"

"Hold up a second," Alan said. "I kind of feel like maybe you're getting the wrong idea about us. We're not all a bunch of wasted drug addicts or anything."

He seemed to want a response, but I had a hard time coming up with anything conciliatory. "Er . . . You're not?"

"No way. I mean, I wouldn't even touch that shit. I'm on three-season varsity—soccer, basketball, *and* baseball. I'm probably gonna get a scholarship too."

"So you—"

"Lauren's practically valedictorian at JHS. Last year she won this big science award. Billy made all-state in swimming and he was vice president of the junior class. Shaun's got a kick-ass summer job working on computers at Benson. Tom can play, like, five different instruments. So it's not like we're just a bunch of losers, okay?"

I glanced at the brownie pan and realized I hadn't seen Alan take one—or, for that matter, even smoke a cigarette. "You mean you go through the whole festival without doing any drugs?"

His face twisted into a particular look, one I was starting to get used to. "Well, the rest of the year I wouldn't touch it," he said. "But hey—this is Melting Rock."

CHAPTER *3*

You might be wondering why these kids were so cheerfully telling a reporter about their consumption of illicit substances. So was I. And the answer wasn't what you might think—that they were too stupid to know any better. Rather, they were smart enough to know that since the *Monitor* is that bourgeois entity known as the "family paper," nothing about their recreational activities was going to end up in print anyway.

So I had two choices: I could forget about doing a story on the Jaspersburg Eight (as I was starting to think of them), or I could pound out some sanitized version depicting them as wholesome youth who liked to hang out and listen to a little rock and roll music.

Since I was desperate, I gritted my teeth and opted for the latter. I even called Melissa—who in addition to being my housemate is a *Monitor* staff photographer—to come take a picture, for which they smiled nicely and hid their cigarettes under a blanket.

The story ran in the next day's paper—where the aforementioned wholesome youth wound up as the page-one feature package. I ran into some of them Thursday afternoon as I was wandering the vendor booths for yet another sidebar—interviewing purveyors of open-backed halter tops, beeswax candles, handmade drums, and the like. When I ventured over to a stand selling fabric hats, the four girls trying on the floppy fashions turned out to be Lauren, Cindy, Trish, and Dorrie. They each had on a version of a jester's cap, complete with garish colors and jingle bells, and they were jostling for a peek in the lone hand mirror.

Trish noticed me first. "Hey," she said, "it's you."

The other three turned around, heads all ajingle.

"Hey," Lauren said, "how ya doin'?"

"Okay," I said.

"Really?" Dorrie offered. "You don't look so good."

"I'm just tired. I only got five hours of sleep last night."

Dorrie pulled off the (extremely hideous) cap, which would've been an improvement if she hadn't had the coiffure of a West Point plebe. "You got five hours?" she said. "That's, like, twice as much as we got."

"Melting Rock's not about sleep," Lauren said. She snagged another look in the mirror before handing it back to Cindy, whose violet hair clashed mightily with her magenta hat. "Never was, never will be."

"No kidding," I said. "Between all the drumming and the drunks screaming all night—"

"Hey," Dorrie said, "didn't you say you were supposed to write about the real Melting Rock? Well, you got it, huh?"

"Great."

The four of them were in the midst of debating precisely how little sleep they'd gotten when they were favored with a lengthy wolf whistle.

"Yo, ladies," said the whistler, a long-legged guy of maybe twenty with a giant scab on his left knee. "Lookin' *good.*"

He was standing there with his arms crossed, clearly attempting to look as cool as is humanly possible; hovering next to him was a compadre of about the same age, a stockier fellow with a shaved head and four—no, five—earrings shinning up the curve of his left ear.

"Hey, Axel," Dorrie said with a wave, and the others followed suit. "How's it goin'?"

"Mighty fine," he said, wandering down the aisle toward a table selling a variety of pipes that would never know tobacco. "Mighty damn fine."

His friend followed, looking the girls up and down like he was trying to decide whether to have them roasted or grilled. When he was done, he winked at them, so exaggeratedly it almost looked like there was something wrong with his eye; none of them seemed to notice. The lack of response seemed to piss him off, and he turned his attention to the wares at the House o' Highs.

"Is it my imagination," Axel said as he wandered off, "or do you ladies get more sexalicious every year?"

The girls swapped a set of gooney, wide-eyed looks and, being a member of the female persuasion, my crush radar went off for the second time in two days. It took me another half second to figure out which one had a thing for Mister Giant Knee Scab, because Lauren turned to Dorrie and mouthed *Go talk to him*. Dorrie shook her head and mouthed *No way*, but Lauren gave her a shove in his direction; Dorrie resisted, but barely. Then she giggled—the sound was a weird contrast with the crew cut—and jogged after him. "Hey, Axel," she yelled, "wait up. . . ."

Lauren turned back to the mirror and doffed the jester's cap, trading it for a cloche made of a half-dozen different fabrics that made me think the seamstress needed residential treatment. "You know," she said, "that story you did on us was pretty cool."

"Glad you liked it."

"It was *way* cool," Cindy said. "My mom wants to buy, like, ten extra copies. You think she can do that?"

"Yeah, she can just call the circulation department."

Lauren stopped futzing with the hat and turned to her. "When'd you talk to your mom?"

Cindy became the dictionary definition of *mortified*. "Uh . . . a while ago."

Lauren rolled her big brown eyes. "She still making you call in? I thought you were gonna tell her to get over herself."

"I tried, but it was totally no go. I mean, you know, she's always gonna think of me like the baby in the family. It was, like, 'Take the cell phone and call before noon every day or you're not going, period.'"

Lauren's eyes bugged out even farther. *"Cell phone?"*

"Er . . . She didn't want me saying the lines at the pay phones were too long."

"*Whoa.*"

"Hey," Trish said, "at least you've only gotta call *once* a day, okay?"

The other three offered up suitably pitying looks. It fell to Lauren to translate.

"Trish's dad is, like, really strict," she said.

"Well," I said, "he let you come here, didn't he?" I'm not sure why I suddenly found myself sympathizing with the parental side of things; maybe it's because I'd let a kid of mine go to Melting Rock over my dead body.

"Wouldn't look too good if he didn't," Cindy said.

"Yeah," Lauren said, "that'd be like saying it wasn't safe, right?" After they nodded amongst themselves for a while, she noticed I had no idea what they were talking about. "Trish's dad is a cop."

"In Gabriel?" I cast about for which of Cody's colleagues might qualify and came up empty.

Trish shook her head. Then she took off her jester's cap, like all the jingling was suddenly giving her a headache. "I wish. He's the Jaspersburg chief of police."

"Oh."

"'*Oh,*'" Trish mimicked back at me. "That's what everybody says. 'Oh, your dad's a cop. *Oh.*'"

"What's so bad about that?"

Trish looked at me like I was a bona fide fool. "It totally changes the way people think about you, that's what. 'Don't do anything bad around Trish, she might tell her dad. . . .'"

Cindy put an arm around her. "Hey," she said, "your dad's not so awful."

Trish hung the hat on a wooden peg. "As Nazi storm troopers go."

"Well," I said, "for what it's worth, from what I saw yesterday, nobody felt too inhibited around you."

"They're my *friends.*"

"I see," I said, though I didn't. "Does your dad hang out around here during the festival?"

"You gotta be kidding."

"Don't the local cops have some kind of presence, you know, just for safety's sake?"

Lauren plucked a paisley skullcap from a peg and plopped it on my head. "You've never been here before, have you?"

"Once, a long time ago. Just for a couple of hours."

"Figures. Listen, like we said yesterday, Melting Rock is its own thing. As long as nobody gets hurt, everybody kind of looks the other way."

"And why is that?"

Lauren shrugged. "I dunno. Tradition, I guess."

After twenty-four hours of quasiflackery, my journalistic instincts finally kicked in. "Do you think it's maybe about the bottom line? I mean, how many people are gonna show if there're cops all over the place?"

Trish looked at me like maybe I wasn't such a moron, after all. "Not a whole lot," she said. "I sure as hell wouldn't."

I LEFT THE three of them closing their deals with the mad hatter and went in search of lunch. I was closing a deal of my own (with the makers of a black-bean burrito with extra guacamole) when I ran into the last person I expected to see at Melting Rock—a guy who did me the favor of making me the *second* most miserable person there.

"What the hell are you doing here?" I said, as it was the first thing that came to mind. "And why in God's name are you wearing a tie?"

"I'm working," he said.

"Well, I didn't think you were here for the food."

"That's for damn sure."

"Want a bite of my burrito?"

"Yeah."

The unhappy bastard in question was one Gordon Band, the up-state correspondent for the *New York Times* and my former colleague at the *Monitor*. Gordon is officially the most ambitious person I've ever met, and though he works for the journalistic equivalent of the

Yankees, he's not what you'd call happy on a day-to-day basis. Or, come to think of it, ever.

"So what *are* you doing here?" I asked, once he'd demolished half my lunch. "Wait, let me guess. Your editor made you do it."

"I *hate* my editor."

"You say that a lot."

"And I mean it every time."

"You here for the whole weekend?"

He reclaimed the burrito, took another bite, and talked with his mouth full. "Are you out of your mind?"

"I ask myself that every day."

He made a deeply unattractive snorting sound. "Anyway, I'd fucking *kill* him if he tried to make me spend another day at this freak show. I'd rather have my guts dug out with a—"

"I'm here the whole weekend." He stared at me for a minute, then launched into a laughing fit. It continued for some time. "Jesus, Gordon, would you be nice?"

"Do you have to sleep here and everything?" I didn't answer. "Tell me you don't have to sleep here. . . ."

I cleared my throat. "On the advice of counsel, I choose not to answer."

More insane chuckling. "Are you living in a *tent?* Oh, my God, that is priceless. . . ."

"Hey, at least I'm not sleeping in my car."

He gave me a sour look. "It's a van."

"Whatever."

"A *tent.* Alex Bernier in a goddamn tent. Christ, I wish I had a camera with me. . . ."

"You know, some people think camping out is fun."

"What are you now, the goddamn queen of the forest?"

He finally caught his breath and reached for a napkin to wipe his little round glasses—but since it had previously contained my burrito, he only managed to smear grease all over the lenses. He swore under his breath, yanked the hem of his undershirt out of his pants, and tried to clean up the mess.

"Serves you right," I said.

"I'm still hungry."

I waited while he scored a hot dog, and the two of us took refuge under a scraggly tree. He handed me a diet Coke, then ruined the gesture by saying he'd bought it out of pity.

"So," I said, "how've you been, anyway?"

His face immediately twisted into the scowl that constituted one of his four major expressions.

"Have I mentioned I hate my editor?"

"Yeah."

"Well, I do."

"Are you any closer to getting yourself back to the Big Apple?" No response. "Come on, Gordon. It's not so bad up here. Some of us even consider it home."

"Ugh."

"So what've you been covering out here?" I gestured toward the grooving masses. "You just doing a general-feature thing?"

He nodded. "Running in Metro with some big stupid picture. Monday, I think. How'd you get shafted with this shitbag assignment, anyhow?"

I told him. He laughed, again in a not-very-nice way.

"Madison's a smart son of a bitch."

"I'll be sure to tell him you said so."

We parted ways fifteen minutes later, with Gordon still making nasty remarks about my sleeping accommodations. Having no choice in the matter, I made a visit to the third circle of hell, aka "the Porta-Johns." Then I spent the next hour trying (and failing) to track down the guy with all the Melting Rock tattoos.

The festival was definitely in full swing then, with revelers filling every square inch of trampled grass. As I passed the main stage, I noticed that what appeared to be a genuine mosh pit had formed in front of it. Live human beings were getting passed over people's heads like sacks of flour, and they actually seemed not to mind. People were dancing so close they might as well have been wearing each other's undershorts. From the fact that the crowd was screaming "STUMPY!

STUUUUMPEEEE!" I deduced that the band was Stumpy the Salamander.

There were five of them—lead singer, drummer, two guitarists, and a keyboard player. And although the singer was front and center, it was fairly obvious that the drummer was running the show. The other band members seemed to be taking their cues from him, checking back over their shoulders every once in a while. The guy was wearing a cutoff shirt, whacking on the drum set in a blur of spidery white arms. The lower half of his face was covered in a scraggly black beard; poofed atop his bullet-shaped noggin was a multicolored Rastafarian cap.

He looked, in a word, ridiculous.

The song they were playing seemed to have something to do with a dog who liked to chew up shoes, cast as some sort of romantic allegory. I managed to catch a snippet of the lyrics:

She's got my heart inside her jaws.
She holds the world between her paws.
I tell her no, but she just won't quit.
O doggie, don't you love me just a bit?

It must've been a favorite, because the crowd was going wild, stomping and hooting and whirling each other around. There was no denying that there was a lot of energy pulsating through the fairgrounds, the beat binding the people and the band together in some funky symbiosis. For a second I thought I could understand what people loved about Melting Rock—the sheer, mindless camaraderie of it. Then somebody stepped on my foot, hard, and I decided they could all go to hell.

Reverting to my former state of journalistic desperation, I wandered around for a while looking for something to write about. Just when I was ready to conduct another interview with the funnel-cake salesman, I happened upon the Melting Rock equivalent of a blood sport: a cadre of young men engaged in a Hacky Sack tournament. Hallelujah.

I filed the story two hours later, along with a little profile of the winner. As it turned out, this beanbag he-man was Axel Robinette— the older, scab-kneed fellow whom Dorrie Benson had been mooning over a few hours before. And there she was: stapled to his flank and basking in his reflected glow.

I hit the sack early, determined to make up for the previous night's sleep deprivation. No go; if anything, the Thursday-evening festivities were even more bacchanalian. I tried plugging my ears with cotton balls, a vain stratagem if ever there was one. The drumbeat was deafening, as were the screeches and howls of several hundred drunks. I lay sweltering in my tent, cursing everyone who'd been remotely involved in dragging me there. I read my *New Yorker* until my flashlight died; then I spent some quality time wallowing in a swamp of similes, comparing Melting Rock to everything from a Stasi torture chamber to a special-ed class reunion.

I finally fell asleep around four, only to get up before seven. That would've been bad enough, but what woke me was way worse.

It was the sound of a girl screaming.

Screaming, as they say, to wake the dead.

CHAPTER *4*

I'm not sure how I knew something was really wrong—that this was something other than the usual drug-addled hijinks. I mean, it wasn't as though people hadn't been hollering all night long, a few even shouting "Help" at the top of their lungs. But there was always some mitigating factor in their voices, a layer of laughter or irony or plain-old inebriation that told you that everything was okay.

This time, the cry that streaked across the field of tents was 100 percent pure; it contained horror and nothing but. It started off with a shriek, piercing and awful and long enough to wake me up in time to hear the rest. "Help me," it said. "Oh, God, please, somebody help me. . . ."

The campground was silent for a few beats before voices erupted all around; people were trying to figure out whether the screams were for real, and if they were, where they were coming from. I was about to scramble out of my tent when I realized that I was wearing nothing but a tank top and a pair of pink cotton panties that said TUESDAY. Half-zombified, I rooted around in the half-light for some shorts and a sweat jacket; once I found my clothes I did another Braille search for my glasses.

By the time I found them and got out of the tent, there were dozens of other people standing around trying to figure out what they were supposed to do. A couple of seconds later, there was another shout from the same direction, this time a man's voice. It was a lot calmer, though still fairly freaked out. "Somebody get the EMTs," he said. "Does anybody have a cell phone? Somebody needs to call an ambulance. Come on, somebody's gotta have a cell phone. . . ."

I did, but before I could yell back, someone else beat me to it. So I followed the scraggly crowd toward the epicenter of the distress, which turned out to be a battered blue tent festooned with blinking red lights shaped like chili peppers. There were a couple of folding chairs by the open flap, and lying on the ground in front of them was the body of a young man.

I say *body* because even from a distance—even peeking through the gaps in the crowd—I could tell he was dead. His eyes were glassy and staring, like the vacant expression you see on a deer lashed to a car hood during hunting season.

The girl was still screaming, grabbing the front of his T-shirt and yanking it toward her as though the motion could wake him. But all it did was roll him from side to side—not much, but enough so his head rocked back and forth in some awful parody of being alive.

In a weird way, neither one of them looked human. She was shrieking like an animal; he was lying there like some sort of horror-movie prop.

Maybe that's why it took me so long to recognize them. But after a couple of minutes—once an older woman had wrapped her arms around the girl and gotten her to calm down a little—I noticed that she had purple hair. Even at Melting Rock, it was pretty damn distinctive.

The girl was Cindy Bauer.

That made me take a closer look at the corpse. It had a wispy goatee, but no glasses—another reason why the face hadn't seemed familiar.

But it was. The dead guy was Shaun Kirtz.

KEEPING AN AMBULANCE parked at the entrance to the fairgrounds is the town of Jaspersburg's major contribution to Melting Rock public safety. In this case, though, it didn't do much good. Although a pair of EMTs came jogging over with their bags and stretcher within a matter of minutes—while I was still standing there reeling at the fact that I actually *knew* these two kids—it was obvious the victim was way beyond saving. They messed with him a little, but you could tell it was just for show—whether for themselves or for the crowd, I wasn't quite sure.

Before long, the woman EMT shook her head and her partner, a guy barely older than the one they'd been working on, pulled a walkie-talkie off his belt and spoke into it. They sat there on their haunches for a few seconds; then the woman noticed Cindy, still whimpering and sobbing in the arms of a middle-aged lady with a gray-flecked ponytail and a Fifth Dimension T-shirt.

The female paramedic went over and guided the girl back to one of the folding chairs so she could check her vital signs. She must not have liked what she saw, because she got a concerned expression on her face and pulled out her own radio. Then she called to her partner to help her get Cindy on the stretcher—not a big one with wheels but the hand-carried kind with fabric strapped to a metal frame. I figured they'd whisk her off, but the woman just knelt by Cindy and covered her with a thin blue blanket, alternately saying vaguely soothing things and checking her watch.

After a few minutes of this—just when she'd unzipped her bag like she was going to administer something—another pair of EMTs showed up. They stood over the body with a distasteful sort of detachment, like a couple of DPW guys assessing a pothole. The woman went over to talk to them, and when she was done, she and her partner picked up Cindy and hauled her away.

The two new EMTs had clearly been given the job of baby-sitting the body and weren't happy about it. They stood there look-ing uncomfortable, crossing and uncrossing their arms, periodically glancing in the direction they'd come from. The collective shock was wearing off, and the crowd was starting to bug them—wanting ex-planations for what had happened to the poor kid, even though the two of them had just gotten there and obviously hadn't the slightest clue. They kept having to ask the crowd to stand back, to "keep the area clear," but shock was turning to agitation and the EMTs were severely outnumbered. Eventually, a trio of volunteer firemen showed up, all wearing baseball hats and yellow jackets over blue jeans. They joined the other two, who looked decidedly relieved to have reinforcements.

"What's going on?" The voice came from behind me, so close it made me jump. I turned around, and there was Lauren Potter. "Hey," she was saying, "what's all the buzz about? Did somebody get sick?"

She tried to peer through the thickening crowd, though by now neither of us could see much. "What's up, anyway?" she said again, her voice tinged with classic rubbernecker's relish. "Are they taking somebody to the hospital?"

"Um . . . I think they already did."

"No way. You know who?" She looked over at me, and I realized she hadn't recognized me before. "Oh, hey, hi, Alex. So what's going on? Somebody get sick or something?"

"Listen, Lauren. . . . Are any of your other friends around here anywhere?"

She looked thoroughly flummoxed. "Uh . . . I dunno. Why?"

"Is"—I grappled for the name—"Tom around here maybe?"

"I don't know where he is. I've been looking for him for a while. Why?" Now she was starting to get worried. She looked from me to the crowd and back again. "What's going on?"

When I didn't answer her—mostly because I had no idea what to say—she made a move toward the commotion. I grabbed her arm and held her back. "Wait," I said. "You don't want to go over there."

She stared at me for a second, then tried to break free. I held on. "Hey, what the—"

"It's . . ." I chickened out, if only briefly. "It's your friend Cindy."

She stopped struggling. "What happened to her? Is she okay?"

"She kind of collapsed. They took her to the hospital."

"Oh, my God. Is she gonna be okay?"

"I'm sure she'll be fine."

"But what *happened?*" She started chewing on a pinkie nail. "Oh, man, her mom is gonna freak. Does Alan know?"

"I'm not sure. I don't think so. I didn't see him around here."

"I gotta find him. . . ." She started looking around, then seemed to realize there was still something major happening at the epicenter of the crowd. "What is going on over there, anyway?"

Damn. "I . . . It's Shaun."

"Shaun?"

"Yeah."

It was only one word, but apparently it was enough for her to get the drift that something was seriously wrong. She gave me a look that was both confused and hostile, then blew past me and elbowed her way through the crowd. I was too short to see what happened next, but I could hear it; for the second time in one morning, the tent city echoed with a young girl's scream.

As a reporter, I've been compared to a vulture more times than I care to count. Also a leech, and a vampire . . . and a parasite too.

All the aforementioned creatures prey on the misfortune of others; they can't survive without somebody's lifeblood to suck or corpse to ravage.

Now, this certainly isn't nice, but occasionally it's true. Like the members of many other professions—doctors and cops are the obvious ones—we journalists tend to do our best work when other people's lives have gone all to hell.

Personally, I've never been a big fan of covering major tragedies, or minor ones, either. Being the stereotypical newshound who sticks a tape recorder in the face of some woman who's just lost her daughter in a plane crash and asking, "So how do you feel?" makes me sick to my stomach.

Still, there's no arguing with the fact that my life got a whole lot more interesting after poor Shaun Kirtz, as his hippie mother would later put it, "crossed over to a friendlier realm." Suddenly, I wasn't just covering a music festival that had gone off pretty much unchanged for the past dozen years; I was covering a music festival during which a teenage boy had—as the rumor mill instantly reported—died from an overdose of some unspecified recreational substance.

I called Bill as soon as I was sure Lauren was okay. He made no particular pretense of being bummed out by the young man's demise. When I told him that Melissa had previously taken the guy's photo, he was positively gleeful.

But to go back to what happened during the event itself: From the time the EMTs left with Cindy, it took the Jaspersburg cops the better part of an hour to show up—and mere seconds to piss everybody off once they got there.

First they sniped at the firemen for letting the crowd get too close to the body; then they declared everything within a ten-yard radius off-limits, which meant that about fifty people were forbidden from entering their own tents. I expected them to cordon off the area with crime-scene tape, but apparently they didn't have any—or if they did, nobody could find it. Eventually, one of the volunteer firemen left, returning a few minutes later with a yellow roll that, when unfurled, turned out to say WET PAINT.

I tried to get some information out of the cops, but they weren't in a talkative mood. One of them told me to back off until the chief got there; he proved to be the charmer of the two, since the other told me to back off or get arrested.

"Arrested for what?" I said.

"I'll think of something," he said.

I backed off.

News of the death was spreading through the festival at light speed, the crowd getting bigger (and the cops more ornery) by the minute. I was navigating my way through the sea of agitated humanity, not sure where exactly I was going, when I ran into two other members of the Jaspersburg Eight: Billy Halpern and Dorrie Benson.

I was fully prepared to turn tail and run—there was no way I was breaking the news to more of Kirtz's friends—but they caught sight of me, and one look in their eyes told me they already knew.

It wasn't that they were crying or anything, just standing there looking totally helpless and sucking on cigarettes like the butts supplied oxygen instead of carbon monoxide. When I got over to them, I realized that Trish Stilwell was standing on their far side, so small and slight I hadn't seen her. She wasn't crying, either, but she'd obviously just stopped; her eyes were dazed and red, lids puffy and lashes clumped together.

"You heard?" Billy asked.

"Yeah," I said. "Do you know if Lauren's all right?"

"She went to lay down in her tent." He reached up to take another drag on the cigarette, and I noticed his hands were shaking. It was hard to reconcile this version of Billy with the hipster from the day before; he came off as a whole lot younger and way less cocky. "She asked us to look for Tom and tell him to come stay with her. You seen him?"

"No. Sorry."

"I just can't believe it," Dorrie said, wrapping her arms around herself so tightly the cigarette seemed to sprout from her left shoulder. "This is like some nightmare, you know? Poor Shaun. . . ."

"Poor Cindy," Trish whispered.

"Poor Cindy," Dorrie echoed. "You think she's gonna be okay?"

"I'm sure she'll be fine. She was probably just in shock."

"Of course she was in shock," Dorrie said. "Can you imagine how awful that was, watching Shaun—" She cut herself off. "Of course she was in shock," she said again. "Wouldn't you be?"

Billy shrugged, then parked his eyes on my reporter's notebook. "You gonna put this in the paper."

"You mean Shaun dying?" He nodded. I nodded back. "It'll be in tomorrow."

"You mean, like, with his name and all?"

"I assume so. The only reason we wouldn't run his name is if the cops can't notify his family in time."

I girded myself for a lecture about how much newspapers suck, but none of them seemed particularly pissed about it. Dorrie tilted her head so she could take a drag off the cigarette without unfolding her arms. "You mean, you won't say his name if they don't tell his mom first?"

"Nobody wants somebody's family to find out they're dead from reading the newspaper."

"Oh," she said. "That's good, I guess." The other two nodded vaguely.

"Listen," I said, "I hate to ask you this, but I'm gonna have to write a story about Shaun for the paper. Do you think you guys would mind talking about him?"

Billy looked at me like I'd just grown a pointy nose. "I thought you said you weren't running his name unless—"

"We're not, but my guess is his folks have already been notified. Unless they're out of town or something—"

"It's just his mom," Dorrie said. "She's probably at her store in Gabriel. That's where she usually is."

"Oh. So listen, you don't have to say anything if you don't want to. It's just that I have to write what we call a news obit, talking about Shaun and what kind of person he was, what he liked to do and everything. . . ." I was starting to feel like a ghoul, a title I arguably deserved. I decided to plow ahead anyway. "It's better if I can talk to his friends than somebody who barely knew him, you know? That way you get a realistic picture of a person."

Billy didn't look convinced. "And you want to do that now? Like, right here?"

"Not necessarily, but I figured you guys would be leaving soon and I didn't want to bother you—"

"Huh?" He looked to Trish, who'd been staring at the ground for the past few minutes. Then he tried Dorrie, who rewarded him with a mirror image of his own cluelessness.

"Leave?" she asked. "Why would we leave?"

"Um, I just figured that with . . . what happened to your friend, you probably wouldn't want to stay."

"But what good would leaving do?"

"Don't you, you know, want to go be with your parents?" The looks I got reminded me it had been a decade since I was seventeen. "So . . . I guess you're staying?"

"That's what Shaun would want," Dorrie said, and turned to Billy. "Don't you think?"

"Yeah," Billy said. "You could write that down if you want. We're staying at Melting Rock because that's what Shaun would want."

It was as good a quote as any, so I jotted it down. "But don't you think they might cancel the rest of the festival?"

Now the two of them looked genuinely horrified. Dorrie recovered first. "Are you serious?"

"I'm just guessing."

"But why would they do that?"

"Well, for one thing, the police might be worried that if Shaun really died from a drug overdose, maybe somebody else'd do the same thing."

Dorrie unclasped her arms and ran the butt-free hand through her spiky hair. Then she just said, "Oh."

"And listen," I said, "I'm not trying to be your mother or anything, but if you guys have any . . . you know . . . If you've got any drugs on you, for chrissake, don't take them. Flush them down the toilet or whatever, okay?" Dorrie and Billy offered a pair of shrugs by way of response. "Trish?"

She looked up from the ground, though her eyes didn't quite meet mine. "Okay. Whatever."

Billy pulled out another cigarette and offered the pack around. This time, I took one—not so much to ingratiate myself with them as to calm my nerves. I still couldn't shake the memory of Shaun Kirtz's vacant eyes.

Billy produced an expensive-looking windproof lighter, and I leaned toward the flame. "So what do you want to know about Shaun?" he asked.

"Well, first off, how long have you guys known him?"

He lit his own butt and pocketed the lighter. "Since, like, fifth grade. He and his mom moved here from San Francisco."

"What about his dad?"

"Shaun never met him," Trish told the grass. "Never even knew who he was."

"Yeah, but it isn't like it bugs him or anything," Dorrie said. "He and his mom are really tight."

"Really? What's she like?"

"She's really cool. She lived in Haight-Ashbury back in the day, when she was our age. And when she got older, she decided she wanted to have a baby, so she had Shaun—even though she wasn't married. Don't you think that's cool?"

"You said before she had a shop in Gabriel. Which one is it?"

"You know the yarn store on the Green?"

"The one that sells all the homespun wool? Sure."

"That's his mom's place. She raises her own sheep—shaves them and spins it and dyes it and everything."

"Where do they live?"

"You know Eco-Homeland?"

I did. It was a latter-day commune a couple of miles off the main road between Gabriel and Jaspersburg, a clutch of modernish buildings where people who earned incomes in the mid-to-high five figures could live in environmentally conscious comfort.

"So what kind of things was Shaun interested in?"

Billy fielded that one. "Lots of stuff," he said. "He's a huge skateboard freak, for one thing. That and computers—he's a total whiz. You ever see that movie *Hackers*? He *loves* that movie. He's always saying he wishes he lived in a big city so he could hang with guys like that."

I noticed he was still talking about Shaun in the present tense—understandable, since the guy's body was barely cold. "So . . . he's that good at computers, huh?"

"He's *amazing*," Dorrie chimed in. "Like, he never paid for a long-distance call—he had some system he figured out to do it for free and—"

Billy put up a hand to interrupt her. "You can't put that in the paper. I mean, his mom didn't know that he—"

"Don't worry about it."

He exhaled smoke in a relieved plume. "Cool."

"Listen," I said, "this can be off the record too if you want, but I was wondering . . . What do you think he took?"

He eyed me, suddenly wary again. "You mean, like, what drug?"

"Yeah."

"What difference does it make?"

"I'm just wondering."

Dorrie shrugged. "I dunno." My expression must've told her I didn't buy it. "No, really," she said. "I don't know. It could've been anything."

"Well, what was his, you know, drug of choice?"

She didn't answer, just looked at Billy with a knowing sort of smile. "Pretty much anything," he said with a grin. "That was Shaun for you. He'd try anything once."

Trish offered up a mirthless laugh and looked me straight in the eye. "I guess last night," she said, "that was one time too many."

CHAPTER 5

The three of them were still standing there chattering about what an adventurous drug taker Shaun had been when Melissa showed up and started snapping pictures. This pleased the Jaspersburg cops not at all, though there wasn't a damn thing they could do about it. She took photos of people who were weeping and exhausted; of others who looked strangely jazzed up; of cranky policemen; of the chili-bedecked tent surrounded by the banner of WET PAINT that made the local constabulary look like a bunch of idiots.

And speaking of the tape: Two minutes later, it was ripped down by a burly fellow in a green windbreaker and jeans. I barely had time to wonder who he was when Trish said, *"Daddy!"*

The man stopped gathering up the tape and just let it drop. Trish came rushing through the crowd toward him—which, considering that she'd recently described him as a Nazi storm trooper, rather surprised me.

If I expected him to shy away from a show of fatherly affection in the middle of a crime scene, I was off base there too. He wrapped her in his arms, each of which appeared to be roughly the circumference of a telephone pole, and held her in an extended bear hug. She must've burst into tears, because I could see her slender back shaking up and down. He rocked her gently from side to side, his jaw set in a grimace that told me he couldn't stand to watch his little girl cry.

They stayed like that for longer than you'd think, and when they finally let go of each other, they both looked kind of embarrassed. After they talked for a few more minutes, Trish gestured toward the three of us; then her father sized me up just like I've seen Cody do with a potential perp. He leaned in as if to ask her something, and her reply consisted of several shrugs of her bony little shoulders.

He took a step toward us, then stopped and reached into his coat pocket to produce another big yellow roll—thus deflating what I'd mistaken for a moderate beer belly. He whistled to one of his underlings and tossed the roll to him underhanded; voilà, some genuine crime-scene tape.

"You're from the newspaper," he said, once he'd crossed the space between us in three strides.

"That's right. The *Gabriel Monitor.*"

"I didn't think you were from the *Jaspersburg Shopper.*" His delivery was so deadpan I wasn't sure whether or not I was supposed to laugh, so I didn't. "Let's go over here."

He commuted a few yards away from the teenagers, and I scampered to keep up with him. "I'm Alex Bernier. I've been covering the festival for the paper."

We shook hands, and when we were through, I was worried I might have to go to the emergency room and get fitted for a cast.

"Chief Stilwell. Only one *L* after the *I.* First name Steve."

"Steve spelled the normal way?"

He fixed me with another Cody-like look. "Are you being smart with me, young lady?"

"Definitely not."

He cracked the suggestion of a smile, which went a long way toward making him something less than terrifying. "Let's keep it that way."

"Absolutely."

"I take it you're the one who did the front-page story on my daughter and her friends."

"That's right."

"I see." His tone said he wasn't thrilled with the coverage, but he didn't elaborate. "And I assume you're doing a story on"—he looked back toward the tent, now being reencircled—"this."

"Yeah."

"I also assume you know who the victim is."

I told him I did, and he gave me the standard speech about not ID'ing the kid until they'd notified his next of kin. I said I knew the drill, though in terms considerably less snarky than that.

"Any idea when you'll have a cause of death?"

"As you can see, the coroner hasn't even arrived yet. And as I'm sure you know, that's the kind of question you'll have to ask him."

"Any idea what it was he took?"

"Are you being willfully obtuse?"

"Um . . . no."

"Then I'd think you'd be aware that if we don't know the cause of death, then we damn well don't know what he took."

"I was just asking."

"You're not the regular police reporter, are you?"

"I usually cover government—common council, county board—"

"And the Melting Rock Music Festival?"

"I was sort of a last-minute substitute."

"I see."

"So . . . what's going to happen next?"

"Meaning?"

"Is the festival going to stay open?"

"Of *course* the festival's going to stay open," somebody chirped, and it definitely wasn't Chief Stilwell.

No, the voice belonged to a lady who looked like she'd leaped off a box of cake mix—a portly, Midwestern-mom type in a flowered jumper and a straw hat. "Of course it'll stay open," she said again. "What would make you think otherwise?"

The woman in question was somewhere on the near side of middle age. Her lipstick was coral pink and not very accurately applied to her kisser; her hat, perched atop a bottle-blond mane, was big and floppy and had a blue grosgrain bow.

Stilwell eyed her, and I saw his jaw tighten. The woman, meanwhile, stood there looking from the chief to me and back again. She was clearly salivating for an introduction, while he was just as clearly savoring the act of not giving it to her. Eventually, he gave in.

"Mrs. Rosemary Hamill, this is Alex Bernier from the *Gabriel Monitor*. Mrs. Hamill is the president of our town council and head of the Melting Rock Community—"

"I'm just so *pleased* to meet you," she said, aiming a doughy paw my way. "So you're the one who's been doing all those *lovely* stories. I have to say, the council was just pleased as punch to hear that the paper was doing a special section on the festival. . . ."

I gaped at her, wondering what Emily Post would think of uttering "pleased as punch" within spitting distance of a corpse.

"I hope you're having a good time so far," she was saying. "Are you? Hmm?"

Who was this crazy person? And was she, by any chance, high as a kite herself?"

"Er . . ." I fumbled for something resembling a response. "It's definitely been . . . interesting."

"Of course it is," she said. "Melting Rock is *always* interesting; that's what we say around here. Melting Rock weekend is the most *interesting* weekend of the year. Don't you think so, Chief?"

I wouldn't have thought his jaw muscles could get any tighter without snapping, but they did.

"Alex here was just asking if we're planning on shutting down the festival," he said, and I could tell he was taking a fair amount of pleasure in it. "Do you have any comment on that you could give her?"

She pursed her hot-pink lips. "I believe I already have." She turned to me. "But in case Alex didn't get my meaning, I'll say it again. There's no reason this unfortunate incident should ruin a very important occasion for everyone." She waved a matching fingernail toward my notebook. "You may write that down if you wish."

It was pretty much what Shaun's friends had told me, albeit crafted like a goddamn press release. I was starting to think there was something funny in the Jaspersburg water supply. "You see, Mrs.

Hamill, the reason I'm asking is that the conventional wisdom around here is saying Shaun Kirtz died of a drug overdose, and—"

"Your point being?"

"Well, aren't you worried that whatever killed him could kill somebody else?"

She looked at me like I'd just run over her poodle. "Are you trying to stir up trouble?"

"It's just a question."

"A very irresponsible question, if you ask me."

"Why is that?"

"There's no need to get everyone all upset over nothing."

Stilwell finally had enough. "Rosemary, for chrissake, it's not nothing. A boy died. A friend of Trish's, as a matter of fact."

Now those neon lips made a vaguely conciliatory smooching sound. "And it's a terrible tragedy. But these things do happen."

I was wondering how she'd feel if she wound up reading her own idiotic comments in the next morning's paper: *These things do happen," town council president Rosemary Hamill said of the rapidly stiffening corpse off to her left. . . .*

"And besides," she was saying, "who's to say that the poor boy didn't die of natural causes? Perhaps he had some sort of heart defect, poor thing."

"I suppose that's true," I said. "But in case it *was* drugs, aren't you worried that other people might be at risk?"

I could tell I was starting to bore her, but she tried to hide it by making her tone even more icky-friendly. "That's a very important issue," she said. "And I'm sure I speak for the entire council when I say that I'd hope that after what happened this morning, people would have the good sense not to . . . not to partake of any dangerous substances."

I wrote that down, partly out of spite.

"Are you going to try to spread some kind of safety message around or something?"

I'd addressed the question to Mrs. Hamill. She immediately turned to the chief with a look that said *that's your problem.*

"We're already running some flyers," he said.

She raised an eyebrow at him. "Flyers?" Somehow, she made it sound like a dirty word.

"Reminding people that if they get caught with controlled substances they're going to get arrested."

Hamill looked downright horrified. "Really," she said, "there's no need to be so"—she cast about for the right word—". . . adversarial, now is there?"

"Rosemary, drugs are against the law."

"I realize that," she said. "But it's not as if it's any sort of widespread problem."

"Are you kidding me? For chrissake, Rosemary, wake up and face reality for once in your life."

Apparently, the two of them had managed to forget there was a reporter roughly two feet away. Then they remembered.

"The flyers will educate people about the potential dangers of drug consumption," she said, suddenly sounding like she was giving a speech to the Revolutionary Daughters of Jaspersburg. "That should more than suffice, don't you think?"

She didn't stick around to hear his answer, just favored us both with her "ladies' club" smile and walked away. That left me and the chief, a Mutt and Jeff pair if there ever was one—him topping six feet of hirsute machismo, me at five feet three and all of 120 pounds.

"Chief," I said, "can I ask you something else?"

"From what I know of reporters, that's what I'd call a rhetorical question."

"Is that a yes?"

He looked like he was getting a headache. "If you make it quick."

"What's your policy on drugs at Melting Rock?"

He glanced over at the spot where what was left of Shaun Kirtz lay on the encircled grass. "My policy is if you take them, you're an idiot." He shook his head. "And you're welcome to quote me. But I guess you probably meant the department's official policy."

"That's right."

"Well, you heard me before. Drugs are illegal."

"Look, Chief, I don't mean to be disrespectful or anything, but I've been here for the past two days, and, well . . . A lot of this stuff seems to be going on pretty much out in the open, but hardly anybody ever gets busted for it."

"We arrested three people last year for possession with intent to sell."

"Right, but three out of how many?" He opened his mouth, then closed it again. "Again, no disrespect, but it definitely seems like it's not in the town's best interest to bust people. Would you say that's true?"

"Now you're putting words in my mouth," he said, though he didn't seem particularly annoyed.

"I'm just trying to understand the situation."

"That makes two of us," he said. "And that's off the record."

The coroner showed up then, and Stilwell looked plenty relieved to see him. He excused himself and went back to the crime scene, and I stood there for a while wondering why he'd spent so much time talking to me in the first place.

It was pretty obvious that any efforts he made to police Melting Rock were going to be hamstrung by the town, which (as I mentioned) is deeply in love with all the cash the festival generates. And though I didn't know a damn thing about the guy, he struck me as one of those men-of-action types who didn't take kindly to that sort of thing. Admittedly, my perceptions might have been colored by the vast hours I spend inside a movie theater. Stilwell, in fact, reminded me of a middle-aged Burt Reynolds, mustache and all.

Once he left, I realized I was, well, starving. I was headed toward the coffee tent when I passed a pale young woman in a flowing purple gown, doing some sort of interpretive dance all by her lonesome. I probably should've kept walking, but she seemed vaguely familiar. I stood there and stared in a way that my mother would have told me was impolite. She had her eyes closed, but after a minute she opened them and stared back at me.

"Wow," she said. "It's you."

Her voice had an oddly deadpan, distinctive singsong inflection, and I definitely recognized it—though from where, I still had no idea.

"Um . . . Do I know you?"

She smiled a sad sort of smile.

"You know everybody, man. We all know everybody."

It was the "man" that jogged my memory. The first (and last) time I'd seen her was a year or so ago, when she and a bunch of other local psychics had tried to convince the Gabriel police to let them help in the search for a serial killer. The cops, as you can imagine, had been less than inviting.

"Guinevere, right?" She nodded and kept dancing. I realized she was wearing exactly the same outfit as when we'd met before, a medieval robe that put her bosom front and center. "You come to Melting Rock a lot?"

"Every year, man. Every year."

Shocking. "You like it a lot, huh?"

"I just live for the Rock, man. Just *live* for it."

"Um . . . Can I ask you something?"

"Absolutely," she said. "Knowledge is power."

"How come you're dancing when the music hasn't even started up again yet?"

"I'm reading." The word's first syllable came out in a long note: *reeee*-ding.

"Er . . . Reading what?"

"The air," she said, arms waving like snakes above her head. "The wind, the sky, the elements. It's all there."

"What's all there?"

"Everything. You just need to know how to listen."

"Oh. And, uh, what're you listening for?"

She stopped undulating all of a sudden, dropping her arms and looking at me. The expression on her face was dead serious. "How many?"

"Huh?"

"That's what I'm asking. How many?"

"How many what?"

"How many *boys*. How many will there be?"

"You mean—"

"We've lost enough already," she said. "How many more will there be?"

"Look, I know what happened to Shaun Kirtz is terrible. It's a total tragedy. But what makes you so sure there'd be any others?"

She closed her eyes and recommenced the dance. "I asked the air," she said, "and it told me there already are."

AFTER BEING THOROUGHLY FREAKED OUT, I went in search of an overpriced bagel from the coffee tent, then did a few more color interviews and checked in with Bill. Predictably, my story budget had been totally overhauled; he and Marilyn had decided that my coverage was now going to be All-Shaun-All-the-Time. And although this was considerably more interesting than being on the handmade-sandal beat, it was also a lot more work.

For starters, they wanted pieces on how Shaun's friends were coping with his death; on the mood of the festivalgoers in general; on how the event's organizers were dealing with the safety issue. And although the print deadline was hours away, they wanted all this for the Web site ASAP, with continual on-line updates and fleshed-out versions for the paper edition.

Meanwhile, Mad's duties as a weekend reporter now included pulling together a sidebar on past Melting Rock deaths, of which I could recall two off the top of my head—one drowning and a heart attack that had felled a fried-dough vendor a few years back. And yes, dragging Mad into it did feel rather good from a revenge standpoint.

As I raced around the Jaspersburg Fairgrounds trying to cover all this stuff, it definitely seemed to me that the mood of the place had changed. Maybe it was my imagination, but the music seemed quieter, the dancers shaking their collective booty with a lot less enthusiasm. Many of the people who'd been running around laughing like hepped-up fools were now engaged in earnest conversation, and every time I got close enough to eavesdrop, I found they were talking about the same thing. Although, in the Melting Rock version of telephone, the facts were starting to get wildly distorted.

> . . . And then he, like, had this huge seizure right in the middle of the drum circle, and this one dude just totally fainted. . . .
> . . . This chick he was with, she's in the hospital, and they're pretty sure she's not gonna make it. . . .
> . . . I heard he got bit by a spider, like a tarantula or a black widow or something, but now the powers that be are trying to cover it up so everybody doesn't get all freaked out. . . .
> . . . Truth is, he was doing this, like, primitive ceremony, man, but he didn't know what he was messing with. . . .

I filed my stories by six, after seeking out Chief Stilwell for another interview and getting the brush-off from one of his officers on the grounds that he was too busy. Shortly afterward, when I was consoling myself with a potato pancake topped with sour cream and to hell with the fat, I ran into Dorrie, Billy, and Trish. They'd bought matching ears of roasted corn on the cob, and though it looked quite tasty, none of them were eating. The ears just sat in the grass in their little paper boats, a bright yellow flotilla bound for nowhere.

"You guys doing okay?" I asked. They shrugged en masse. "Have you heard anything about Cindy?"

"My dad says she's not bad," Trish said. "I guess they took her to the hospital in Gabriel and gave her some tranquilizers or something. Alan's with her."

"That's good," I said.

Dorrie rolled her corn with her index finger, then licked the butter off. "They told Shaun's mom," she said. "She's pretty upset and all."

I tried to think of something comforting and came up short.

"Hey," Dorrie said, "can we ask you something?"

"Sure."

"What do you think we should do?"

"You mean, do I think you should go home?"

"No, I mean . . . with Shaun's mom. What do you think we should do?"

"Oh. I guess . . . I'm not really sure."

"But you, like . . . You've done stuff like this before. I mean, my mom says you're pretty famous in Gabriel."

"What?"

"I . . . Uh, I talked to her a little while ago, to say I was okay and everything, and she saw your name on that story you did about us. She told me, um, about how you've had some friends die and all, so we thought maybe . . ."

She was starting to blush, the redness all the more obvious due to her extreme lack of hair.

"I see."

All three of them were staring at me like I was supposed to know the secret handshake.

"I guess . . ." For the second time in as many minutes, I grasped for something profound. Still no go. "When you get the chance, I don't know . . . just tell her you're sorry."

They looked vaguely disappointed. Billy compensated by stroking his sideburns. "That's it?" he said.

"Hell, I don't know. . . . I guess, maybe . . . try and figure out when she needs company and when she needs to be left alone, when she wants to talk about Shaun and when she wants people to shut up about it."

"Tricky," Dorrie said, and the other two nodded. Then she picked up her corn and took a bite.

I left them there like that, nibbling on their dinner and contemplating the proper etiquette for dealing with your dead friend's mother. And what they didn't know at the time was this: Inside of twelve hours, two of them would still be pondering the same question.

But only two of them.

CHAPTER 6

To this day, I cannot possibly comprehend why he did it, not really. Some people say he was trying to play chicken with the universe, others that he actually believed the tarantula story (though, frankly, I think that's absurd). The most popular theory was that he was so freaked out about his friend, he desperately needed solace—and being a kid, he didn't contemplate the consequences. If you ask me, that last one is the only explanation that comes anywhere close to making sense.

But whatever the reason, at some time past twelve on Friday night, Billy Halpern sat on the highest tier of the Melting Rock and dropped the same acid that had killed his friend the night before.

And by two A.M., he was just as dead.

He was found by a couple who wanted to perform certain intimate acts at the top of the rock—one of the festival's lesser-known traditions—and decided the spot was wasted on the sleeping Billy. They tried to wake him, and when he didn't respond, the girl shook him harder than she'd meant to. He went tumbling down from tier to tier until he landed on the hard ground, where he lay so still it was obvious he wasn't going to move again, ever.

Then she started screaming.

Her cries drew the Jaspersburg cop who had been stationed there overnight by Chief Stilwell, in defiance of both the town council and the overtime budget. The guy was the force's rookie—a kid barely eight weeks out of the state academy who, when I met him the following morning, didn't seem entirely clear on how to button his uniform shirt.

That this was the first dead body he'd ever seen went without saying; that he threw up would be both a hoary stereotype and the honest-to-God truth.

Since I was so exhausted after two nights of crummy sleep, it took more than shouting to wake me up; it took the piercing shriek of an ambulance. Still, I tried very hard to pretend I couldn't hear it—and when that didn't work, I tried equally hard to convince myself I was dreaming. Flunking there as well, I hauled myself up and out of the tent. In what felt like déjà vu all over again, I fumbled for my glasses and made my way toward the source of the commotion, stomach knotted and notebook in hand.

After what had happened to Shaun Kirtz, I have to say I half expected to find exactly what I found—a crowd gathered around the prostrate body of a teenager. That being said, I'll admit to being intensely surprised that, for the second time in two days, it was someone I knew.

Unlike with Shaun, I recognized him instantly; chalk it up to the oversize sideburns that had been Billy's defining feature. Even though his face was obscured by the paramedic who was trying to revive him, the sight of one of those bushy parentheses told me exactly who it was.

There's not much lighting at the Jaspersburg Fairgrounds, and the scene was being illuminated by a combination of headlights, flashlights, and torches that an enterprising few had brought over from the campgrounds. It added up to create a surreal mood, with some places as bright as Fenway Park while others were pitch black, the spots in between flickering in and out of focus according to the whim of the flames and the motion of people's wrists.

I stood there gaping at the body, one hand over my mouth and the other clamped around my notebook. I knew I should snap out of it, that I should act like a reporter and do some reporting. But for the life of me, I couldn't move. For some reason, why I couldn't tell you, it struck me that between them Shaun and Billy had been on the planet a grand total of thirty-five years—roughly the age of most of my drinking buddies. I hadn't particularly liked either one of them, mostly because I have a low tolerance for clueless teenage boys. And now neither one of them would ever be anything else.

As soon as the first orange strips of daylight hit the horizon, I called Cody. Being the virtuous sort who actually exercises before work (we don't have this in common), he was already awake. I told him about all the fun I'd been having at Melting Rock, and the first thing he wanted to know was just why the hell I hadn't called him sooner. I mumbled something about being busy filing stories, which was only marginally accurate. The truth was that although I'd been dying for some boyfriendly sympathy, I was also sick of blubbering to him every time I ran into something nasty.

"So you actually talked to these kids?" he was saying. "You mean *both* of them?"

"Yeah, in that story on their bunch of friends I did for the Thursday paper."

"You want to tell me what you saw?"

"I already told you," I said. "Two dead kids. Consecutively."

"Yeah, but you and I both know there are bodies and there are bodies."

"True."

"And?"

"And . . ." I thought about it for a minute. "All things considered, I guess this wasn't so bad."

"Then tell me."

"First kid was worse. Eyes were still open and everything. This girl was with him—she was completely freaked out. Seeing her was almost worse than seeing him, if you can believe it."

"I can believe a lot of things."

"Name's Cindy. Youngest in the bunch."

"How's she doing?"

"Not so good. She ended up in the hospital on sedation."

Deep sigh. "Goddamn self-destructive idiots."

"The follies of youth, I guess."

"Hey, you and I were both teenagers once, and we managed not to take drugs and die."

"Yeah, but it's not like they deserved what they got. Being young and stupid isn't a capital crime."

"For them it was."

I thought about it for a while. "True enough."

"Listen, baby, you want to get the hell out of there? Because if you want, the dogs and I can come get you in twenty minutes."

"That's extremely sweet, and completely not necessary. I'm fine, really. And anyway, I'll be home tomorrow."

"Good."

"Listen," I said, "do you know this guy Steve Stilwell?"

"The J-burg chief? Sure."

"Nice guy?"

"Yeah. Solid. Why?"

"I just met him today . . . I mean yesterday. His daughter was tight with the guys who died."

"Rough."

"Anyway, she was telling me what a fascist her dad is, but when he showed up, she went running for him. It was kind of sweet, actually."

"Teenagers are an up-and-down proposition."

"How would you know?"

"I arrest a lot of them."

"Oh. So, do you like Chief Stilwell? Is he, you know, a buddy of yours?"

"Not like I'd go out for a beer with the guy, but I've met him a few times."

"What can you tell me about him?"

"Not much. Seems like a decent sort. Can't say what kind of cop he is. Wife died a while back—about five or six years ago, I think. Did a hitch in the army, then served in the Gulf as a reservist. We talked about that a while."

"The Gulf War?"

"Yeah."

"What about it?"

"Just comparing notes."

"You mean you were there?"

"Um . . . yeah."

"Jesus. How come you never told me?"

"You never asked."

"Oh. Right."

"Why is that, anyway?"

"I . . . Maybe I didn't want to know."

"You asked me once if I ever killed anybody."

"That's true."

"And I told you I did. In the navy and on the force."

"Yeah."

"Well, where did you think I did it? Basic training?"

"Fine. Have you been in any other wars you'd like to mention?"

"Nothing you would've seen on CNN."

"Christ, Cody, this is the weirdest conversation I've ever had."

"No offense, baby," he said, "but I kind of doubt that."

BY TEN O'CLOCK the word had come down. The Melting Rock Music Festival was over—not forever, mind you, but definitely for this year. By order of the Jaspersburg police, the bands were to pack up their instruments, the campers to unstake their tents, and the vendors to empty their fryers. The resulting atmosphere was how I'd imagine a retreating army would look, picking up and moving away without an ounce of joy, and an overarching sense that they'd been robbed.

The festival's organizers seemed to take it fairly well; when I interviewed Jo Mingle about the situation, she seemed much more worried about the deaths of two teenagers than the loss of one day of Melting Rock.

"This is totally out of control," she said, looking so haggard and drawn as to be in danger of premature labor. "This place has gotten so goddamn far out of control. . . . Melting Rock just isn't what it used to be."

"What did it used to be?"

"Something else."

She turned her back on me and resumed packing up more crates of unsold merchandise—bright green T-shirts with dissolving musical notes on the front, compilation CDs of festival regulars entitled *Melting Rock Mojo.*

I was about to walk away, then changed my mind. "No, really," I said, coming around to her spherical front. "I want to know. What was it like?"

She took a deep breath, exhaled, and put down the stack of T-shirts. The back turned out to say MELTING ROCK—LUCKY #13.

"You never came before? Back in the day?"

"Just once, five years ago, and not for very long."

"Then I'm not sure I can explain it right," she said. "The first year it was, like, maybe a hundred people. Somebody brought an Airstream and the bands set up in front of it and that was the stage. The food was free, just this guy who baked a ton of bread and gave it all away. It was like . . . Man, it was like *heaven.* I know you're gonna think that's a bunch of crap, but it's true. Everybody was just so mellow, you know? People just wanted to hear music and have a good time."

"So what happened?"

"I don't know. I guess maybe it was inevitable, right? Every year more and more people showed up, and since it got bigger and bigger, it had to get really *organized*—parking permits and vending licenses and liability insurance and sales tax, all that junk. Past couple of years, it hasn't really seemed like Melting Rock anymore. I mean, it's still better than most festivals—way better than those goddamn rip-off Woodstocks they did—but I know a bunch of people from the old days who won't even come anymore."

"Because it got too big and . . . what? Establishment?"

"Yeah, that, and . . ." She reoriented her attention somewhere over my shoulder, her face breaking into a wide smile. "Hey, babe."

I turned around, and there was the drummer from Stumpy the Salamander. Up close, he looked even taller and scrawnier than he had onstage—a great, tattooed arachnid of a person with an air of such studied casualness, I wondered if he had a B.A. in nonchalance.

The guy came over and gave Jo a sloppy whopper of a kiss, their bodies at an odd angle because of her protruding belly. When they came up for air, she said, "Babe, this is Alex from the newspaper. Alex, this is Trike Ford, my life partner. He's the drummer for Stumpy."

I stuck out my hand. "I caught part of your show."

"Cool," he said, then kissed Jo again. "Hey, I gotta go help the guys pack up."

"But . . . I thought you were gonna take the chicklet," she said, gesturing toward the infant sitting in a shaded baby seat.

"Sorry, babe," he said. "Busy."

With that, he headed off toward the main stage. If Jo was upset, she didn't show it.

"Um, you were saying before, about the festival getting to be too big . . . ?"

She shook her head, either at Trike or at Melting Rock in general. "Christ, I'm gonna sound like my dad, but these kids that come now . . . I mean, I was their age when Melting Rock started, but we just had a whole different attitude. We just kind of went with the flow, you know? But these kids, it's like they're on a mission or something. Like they gotta do the fest to the nth degree—get no sleep and party till they drop—" She clamped a hand over her mouth. "I can't believe I just said that."

"It's okay. I know what you meant."

"I guess what I'm trying to say is, the beauty of Melting Rock used to be that it was so low-key. People did their own thing, hung out, soaked up the sound, you know? Nobody had anything to prove. Nobody had any kind of agenda. They just wanted to hang out and have a good time and hear good music."

"And you don't think it's like that anymore?"

"For some people it is. But for a lot of them, it's all about 'Where did you get to camp? Did you get in Main? How much goddamn jewelry did you sell? How many times did you get fucked up?'" She shook her head and settled heavily on a milk crate, which disappeared beneath her maternal bulk. "I probably sound like a grumpy old lady, don't I? But I'll tell you, it makes me sad. It really does."

"How do you think what happened is going to affect next year?"

Heavy sigh. "Next year. Good question. Tell you the truth, I can't even think about it. And what's more," she said, "I can't even *think* about thinking about it."

I left her there packing up official Melting Rock water bottles (five dollars a pop) and went in search of more color for my story on the festival's premature end. If anybody was happy about it, I couldn't find them. I interviewed a dejected couple who'd come all the way from Myrtle Beach for the Melting Rock experience, and a home-grown Gabriel band whose festival debut had lasted exactly one set, and a portly potato-pancake vendor who complained bitterly of all the inventory he was going to be stuck with. ("Ya want 'em?" he said, pointing to a mountainous vat of shredded spuds. "They're yours.")

Although the assembled masses seemed disinclined to go anywhere fast, the Jaspersburg cops were having none of it. The festival was over, and everyone was expected to get out of Dodge posthaste. A few Yuppie types tried to argue that they'd paid for their campsite through Sunday afternoon and weren't about to be displaced, whereupon they were directed to the fine print in the program that said there'd be no refunds if the festival were canceled in case of "emergency, inclement weather, or act of God."

The deaths of Shaun Kirtz and Billy Halpern had also mobilized the Walden County Health Department, not to mention a cadre of other local social-service groups dedicated to saving adolescents from themselves. They wandered the fairgrounds distributing flyers and buttonholing people as they hauled their belongings to their cars, the messages varying according to the agency's political bent, from "Don't take drugs" to "Don't take drugs from people you don't know real well."

I was getting quotes from one of the shaggy-haired members of Unitarians for Social Sanity when somebody grabbed me by the elbow. It turned out to be Lauren Potter, and she looked like hell. Her eyes were bloodshot, and her moon-shaped face was stained with tears. When she spoke, she sounded so manic I thought the Unitarian was going to perform an intervention right then and there.

"Have you seen him?" she asked.

"Seen who?"

"*Tom.* Have you seen Tom? It's been days. It's been two days. I've been looking for him for two days. Have you seen him anyplace? Because he isn't home. I called his folks and they haven't seen him since he left with us. Since he left to come here. And I've been looking for him everywhere. . . ."

She seemed about to walk off, so I grabbed her by the shoulders. "Hold on a sec. Calm down, okay? Try and breathe—"

"But I can't find him. I've been looking since before . . . since before Shaun. . . . And now there's Billy and I still can't—"

"Wait. Just listen to me for a minute. When's the last time you saw him?"

Both her eyes went off to the left, like she was trying to access the information from a balky database. "I . . . Wednesday night."

"And where was he going then?"

"His tent. Everybody split and he went off by himself, and now I can't find him anywhere. I've been looking and asking around to everybody I could—"

"Is his stuff still in his tent?"

"I . . . I don't know."

"What do you mean you don't know?"

"It's new, and I don't know what it looks like."

"Don't his parents?"

"No, I . . . They're not really into outdoor stuff. I asked them, but they weren't even sure what color it was."

"But don't you even know where he was camping?"

"He . . ." She stopped and stared at the ground. "You're gonna think it's stupid."

"No, I'm—"

"But it's *not* stupid. It's just this thing he likes to do, okay?"

The urge to throttle her was growing, and fast. I tried to ignore it. I also tried to sound soothing. "Okay, Lauren, what does he like to do?"

"He . . . He has this thing where he likes to move his tent around, crash in a different spot every night if he can find a place. He says it makes for"—her eyes darted left again—". . . for a more varied experience. He says it makes it so it's like a different Melting Rock every night."

"And you're not sure where he's camping now?"

She shook her head. "It was just this *thing* he did, and now I can't find him. . . ."

She started to cry, fat tears streaming down her face like something out of a comic strip. She'd obviously been crying plenty of late, because she didn't even bother to swipe at them.

"Have you talked to the police?"

"I tried, but they're all busy, and everything's so crazy with the festival getting canceled and everybody leaving. . . ."

"Did you talk to the chief? To Trish's dad?" She shook her head again, and this time one of the tears that had been poised on the edge of her cheek flew off and landed on my shirt. "Who'd you talk to?"

"I don't know . . . some deputy or something."

"What about Melting Rock security?"

"They said he'd probably turn up once everybody got moved out. And I tried to tell them I hadn't seen him since Wednesday night, but—"

"You haven't seen him since *Wednesday?*"

Her drowning eyeballs took on a wounded look. "I told you that already. We had our first-night thing at the Rock and then we all split off to do our own thing, and Tom—"

"Has anybody else seen him since then?"

"Nobody. And I've been asking and asking. . . ."

"Come on. We're going to find Chief Stilwell."

"How . . . How come?"

"If nobody's seen him in forty-eight hours," I said, "then Tom's officially a missing person."

MY MOM HAS A FRIEND who's so disorganized, she'd lose her head if it weren't physically attached to her neck. She's gone through at least twenty pairs of eyeglasses in her lifetime, and once (no kidding) managed to fly to Europe without her purse. On more than one occasion, she's gone to a classical concert at Tanglewood and completely forgotten where she parked her car—and then had to wait until the other five thousand people went home so she could find it, the only one left in the lot.

I mention this for no particular reason, other than to explain what was on my mind when they finally found the tent. One by one, several hundred others were collapsed and folded into bright piles of nylon, and by the time dusk fell, there was only one left standing. It was forest green, brand new, with a rain fly expertly staked above it and a DO NOT DISTURB note pinned to the front flap.

And inside, as you've probably already guessed, was the corpse of a skinny young kid named Tom Giamotti.

CHAPTER 7

I didn't actually see the body; whatever gods govern such things must've decided that two dead boys in as many days was enough for this girl. But since it was my job to describe the scene to the paper-buying public, I did gather a fair amount of details: the fact that by the time they found him, he'd been dead so long that rigor mortis had come and gone; that he had his knees up to his chest, his arms wrapped around them in a pose that sounded both defensive and childlike; that, nature being what it is, several generations of insects were born and died with his body as their entire universe.

By the way, we didn't print that last one.

I finally left Melting Rock just as night was falling on Saturday. Although the bosses would probably have loved to have me file more updates for the goddamn Web site, I decided they could go screw themselves. After failing to get in touch with Cody either at home or on his cell, I went to my house and made haste to the shower. Lacking the melodrama of extreme youth, however, I opted to take off my clothes first.

Although crawling into bed definitely had its allure, I was in severe canine withdrawal; there's nothing like viewing corpses to make a girl long to snuggle up with her dog. So I got myself dressed and went over to Cody's, where I found two excellent pooches but no boyfriend. Both dogs—my Shakespeare and his Zeke—jumped all over me, which (for me, at least) was a pretty good substitute.

I spent some time rolling around on the living-room floor with them, then tried to figure out what to do with the rest of my evening.

I could stick around at Cody's and watch TV with the dogs until he showed up, but despite the recent Melting Rock mob scene, I wasn't craving solitude. When I really wanted, I decided, was an old-fashioned debriefing—preferably one that included copious amounts of alcohol. So I left Cody a note to call me on my cell when he got in and headed over to the Citizen Kane.

The Citizen is located on the Gabriel Green, a pedestrian mall that (despite its name) has not a single blade of grass within two blocks. The bar itself is located toward the middle, so its window seat has an excellent view of the various freaks and slackers who congregate on the concrete at all hours and in every kind of weather.

Sure enough, the plate-glass window framed its usual occupants: Mad, Ochoa, and their third musketeer, sports editor Xavier O'Shaunessey. The three of them make one hell of a motley crew: Mad is six foot four and resembles an ad for either Norway or the Ab-dominizer; Ochoa is Mexican American, wiry and dark like I used to like them in my pre-Cody days; O'Shaunessey tips the scales at around two hundred and fifty flabby pounds, never cleans his glasses, and is as white as a nurse's panty hose.

They might've seen me coming, but they were too absorbed in whatever they were arguing about. When I got within hearing range, I realized Mad was holding forth on his familiar diatribe about how Joe Cocker sang Beatles songs better than Lennon and McCartney. I was glad I'd missed it.

"You got room for one more?"

Mad stopped in midtirade. "Hey, Bernier. Made it out of that place alive, did you?"

I pulled a chair out from under his feet and sat down. "Hardy har-har." On the table were three beer mugs and a nearly full pitcher. It was undoubtedly not their first, though at least the evening hadn't yet degenerated into tequila.

"Girl needs a drink," O'Shaunessey said. "On me. Whatcha want?"

"Tanqueray and tonic. A really big one. Two limes."

"You got it," he said, and headed for the bar.

Mad stood up too and announced he was going to "the head." That left me with Ochoa, who hasn't always been my biggest fan. That's partly because he's been damn possessive about the cop beat since he got to the paper a few months back. Unfortunately, it's also because (for reasons beyond my ken) his long-distance girlfriend decided we had the hot potatoes for each other and dumped him on his attractive Latino ass. Lately, though, things had thawed a little— possibly because he hasn't seemed to have time to make any other friends.

"So it was pretty wild out there, eh?" he was saying. "Must've been a blast to cover."

"Oh, yeah? Then why did you two head for the hills when Marilyn was looking for somebody to send out there?"

"Hey, come on. I never said I wanted to cover the damn thing *before* those kids went and got themselves dead."

"Yeah, well, it was kind of a drag."

"You ladies are so sensitive. . . ."

"Jesus, Ochoa, you've been hanging out with Mad too much. You're starting to sound like him."

"Ay, *pobrecita* . . ."

"And would you stop with the Speedy Gonzalez thing?"

"Hey, I'm a proud Mex—"

"Give me a break. You're about as white bread as they come, *Calvin.*"

He shushed me and looked around to see if anyone was in hearing range. "Hey, you promised you wouldn't tell anybody."

"Tell them what? That *Cal* is really short for *Calvin* and you went to boarding school and your father's a brain surgeon and you're—"

"Would you shut up?"

I was starting to feel better already. Then O'Shaunessey showed up with a giant gin and tonic, and my life improved even further.

"Okay, Bernier," Mad said once he'd returned from the loo, "tell us just what the hell happened at that freak show."

I filled them in on all that had gone down since Wednesday night. It took me the entire first G & T and halfway into the next.

"So let me get this straight," Mad said. "You did a feature story on eight kids. Now three of them are dead."

"Yeah."

"Just goes to show you," Ochoa offered. "You talk to Bernier, it could cost you your life."

"Nice," I said. "Really nice."

O'Shaunessey topped off his mug. "So what are the cops doing about it? Or . . . what, the county health department? I mean, if these kids are OD'ing on something, it's—"

"It's what I call natural selection," Mad said with a lupine smile.

I rolled my eyes and turned back to O'Shaunessey. "To answer your question, I'd say they're going out of their gourd. It was bad enough after the first kid died, then after the second . . . And Jesus Christ, once they found Tom Giamotti . . ."

Ochoa leaned in. "So what did they take?"

"Damned if I know. Jaspersburg cops sure aren't talking, and neither's the coroner. Can't blame them for flipping out—this is probably the worst thing that's happened in the village since . . . well, since ever."

"Come on," he said. "You hung out with these kids. What's your guess?"

"Honestly, I've got no idea. I can barely tell one drug from the next."

Mad raised his mug in my direction. "You mean there's more than one?"

"Out there, there were plenty. Like, I'd barely been there five minutes when some guy with a goddamn ring through his nose took me for a dealer. And by the way, what the hell is 'Oxy'?"

"Oxycontin," Ochoa said. "Heavy-duty prescription painkiller. People grind it up and snort it and get addicted in about ten seconds."

"Wonderful."

"So what was up with these kids?" O'Shaunessey asked. "You get the vibe they were a bunch of—"

"Self-destructive morons?" Mad interjected.

I punched him in the shoulder. "Look, I agree with you. What they did was idiotic. But like I told Cody, it's not exactly a capital crime, okay?" Mad opened his mouth. "And don't say it was this time, because Cody already beat you to it."

"Smart guy."

"Whatever. So to answer your question . . . Hell, I don't know. These are definitely not the kind of kids I would've been friends with in school. They're too messed up and way too cool. I was pretty much a big square."

"Hard to believe," said Ochoa. I decided to ignore him.

"Oh, hey, I forgot something," I said. "Three guesses who I ran into out there."

"The Doobie Brothers?" Mad offered. I shook my head. "Ghost of Jerry Garcia?"

"Not even close."

"Timothy Leary?"

"I think he's dead too."

"Oh. Who then?"

"Try Gordon."

"Band?"

"The one and only."

"Wait. You mean before the kids started keeling over or after?"

"Before. Long before."

"Jesus," Mad said, "poor bastard must've been suicidal."

"Yep."

"I'd have paid money to see it."

"It was the high point of my weekend."

"He find out you interviewed those kids before they died?"

"Only if he looked at my Thursday story and put two and two together," I said. "Which, knowing Gordon, he probably did."

"And which must be driving him nuts with envy."

"I can only hope."

"So who are these kids, anyway?" Mad asked. "Damned if I can tell them apart."

"Well, like I said, there were eight of them all together. Four boys and four girls. Now only one of the guys is still breathing."

"Whoa," said O'Shaunessey. "When you put it like that, it sounds pretty bad, eh?"

"Jesus," I said, "how else is it supposed to sound? So the first one who died, his name was Shaun Kirtz. I guess he was some sort of a computer genius, had a summer job at Benson. Kind of the least hunky of them, but this one girl really seemed to like him—this girl named Cindy, who's the only junior in the bunch. The rest were all seniors.

"Next was Billy Halpern. One of those kids you see walking around who looks like he just dropped in from the seventies—really big sideburns and all that. Kind of arrogant, obviously thought of himself as a real ladies' man. Picked on Shaun, but so did everybody else.

"The last one was this kid I only met once, but I thought he was really sweet. That was Tom Giamotti—sort of looked like he hadn't grown into his own feet, you know? I think he was best friends with the girl who basically ran the group, Lauren Potter. Kind of the queen bee."

"Son of a bitch," said Mad. "You need a scorecard to follow all these kids. How did you even keep them straight?"

"They're kind of all different, actually. The group's a goddamn Breakfast Club. In fact, I was just thinking how this is probably the only time in their lives they'd really be friends."

"High school makes strange bedfellows?"

"Exactly. Take the guy who's still alive—Alan Bauer, who's Cindy's older brother. He's a big jock, says he's getting a college scholarship. Seemed like a pretty decent kid, kind of the Melting Rock version of a Boy Scout. Then there's Dorrie Benson, who's got this hideous crew cut. . . ."

Mad put down his mug with a whack. "Dorrie Benson? You gotta be kidding me."

"Don't tell me you know her."

"Not exactly, but . . . Jesus, Alex, you cover the university as much as I do. Didn't you recognize the name?"

"Benson? It's not exactly an unusual . . . Holy shit. You mean she's one of *those* Bensons?"

His Nordic skull bobbed up and down. "If I remember right, her real name is Constance Dorchester Benson, or something equally obnoxious. Direct descendant of Simeon Benson."

"As in the founder of the college."

"You got it."

"Yikes. Go figure."

O'Shaunessey reached for his Beer Nuts, housed in a helmet-size bowl kept behind the bar for his personal use. "So that's"—he counted on his meaty digits—"seven. Who's the last one?"

"That would be Trish Stilwell. Her dad is the Jaspersburg chief of police—"

"Sucks to be her," said Mad. His companions nodded.

"She seems like a nice kid, kind of quiet. So skinny it hurts to look at her. I think she and her dad are pretty close, actually, though she tries to make herself out to be the rebellious teenager. Cody told me her mom's been dead a while, so I guess he pretty much raised her."

"Tough," O'Shaunessey said. More nodding from the peanut gallery.

"So," Mad said with a familiar waggle of eyebrow, "which one was the foxy babe who ran on page one? You know, the one with the long hair and the perky little gozongas?"

"Jesus," I said, "you ever heard of the term *jailbait?*"

"Hey, she's seventeen. You ever heard of the term *age of consent?*"

"I swear to God, Your Honor," O'Shaunessey said at top volume, "she told me she was sixteen. . . ."

The three of them howled and pounded the tabletop, which was structurally unsound enough to make beer slosh from Mad's recently filled mug. He grabbed a napkin and wiped up the stinky brew with a surgeon's precision.

"To answer your question," I said, "that would be Lauren Potter.

Kind of the cruise director of the bunch. Really good manners for a seventeen-year-old, though I got the feeling she might be a bitch if you crossed her." Mad made a meowing sound. The other two found this the height of cleverness. "Seems like a pretty smart kid, though. I guess her parents are both profs at the Benson med school."

Mad stopped yowling. "Must be Mike Potter's kid. He's in pediatric oncology. So's his wife. Linda . . . no, Lindsay. Lindsay Sherman. That's *their* kid?"

"I don't know. If you say so. Why?"

"Neither one of them is much to look at."

"Call it a genetic mutation. So I take it you guys've heard about the emergency edit meeting?"

"Yeah," said Mad, and turned to the perplexed Irishman at his left. "Don't worry," he told him, "it doesn't have fuck-all to do with you."

"Fine thing," O'Shaunessey said, and stood up. "Who's for another round?"

Hearing no dissent, he toddled off in the direction of the bar.

"You got any idea what Bill's got going?" Ochoa asked. "Like, are we each getting assigned to a kid or something?"

I drained my second G & T in anticipation of a third. "I wouldn't be surprised. I mean, think about it. We've got a shitload of stuff to cover."

"Yeah," said Ochoa, "you've got your standard teen memorial service, times three. . . ."

Mad rolled his eyes. "Crying chicks, autographed coffin, blah-blah-blah. If they play the theme song to *Titanic,* I'm gonna hurl."

"I think that time is mercifully past," I said. "But you're right about covering all the funeral stuff. Plus, there's the news obits. I already filed a profile of the first dead kid before all hell broke loose. Now I gotta come up with something on Billy and Tom by deadline tomorrow. Which, hopefully, you guys are gonna have to help me with."

Mad put up a hand like a cop stopping traffic. "Hey, I'm gonna be all over the public-health stuff. County must be going crazy trying to warn everybody off taking this shit, whatever it is. You can bet your ass they're gonna want to be getting the word out. Plus, maybe the CDC'll get in on it. Christ only knows how much of this stuff's floating around out there, and it don't exactly respect state lines, if you know what I mean."

I turned to Ochoa. "Fine. You can help me out with the—"

"Not so fast, *chiquita*. I'm the cops reporter, remember? I already got my hands full."

"With what?"

He stared at me like I was playing dumb, then realized that I was being straight with him. "What are you, dense?"

"Apparently."

"Jesus, Alex," Ochoa said. "Three kids are dead from bad drugs. Don't you think the cops might be just a little bit interested in who sold it to them?"

CHAPTER 8

I'm not sure why it hadn't occurred to me; I'm guessing it had a lot to do with the fact that I'd had roughly ten hours of sleep in four days, topped off by a liberal amount of Tanqueray. But Ochoa was right. The fallout from the three Melting Rock deaths wasn't just going to involve keeping other psychotropic aficionados from killing themselves. It was also going to mean tracking down whoever was responsible and (figuratively, at least) hanging them from the nearest tree.

Luckily, this wasn't my problem. What very much *was* my problem, however, was covering the grieving rituals of several hundred adolescents. I was aided in this endeavor by two other reporters, one of whom I didn't actively despise. Lillian has covered local schools so long she's interviewed the grandchildren of some of her early subjects, and although she comes across as a sweet little old lady, she's actually the deadliest interviewer in the newsroom. I've always liked her, probably more than she likes me. Brad, on the other hand, is a journalist of the bull-in-the-china-shop variety; his bottomless appetite for *National Enquirer*-style headlines has alienated just about every town father in Walden County. Come to think of it, though, it might be kind of amusing to see him go head-to-head with that awful Mrs. Hamill from the Jaspersburg council. . . .

"*. . . and we remember him not only as a fine athlete, but as a hardworking student, a loving son, and a proud member of the community . . .*"

I'd let my mind wander, and I came back to the here and now with a thud. There I was, in the back pew at St. Anthony of Padua, momentarily unable to remember just whose funeral I was covering. Lest

I come across as horrifyingly callous, let me assure you that I remembered in due course—even before I peeked down at the program I was holding and saw Tom Giamotti's face staring up at me.

And it really wasn't that I couldn't tell the kids apart; in fact, they were more distinct to me than ever. The point of obituary writing is to make your subject come alive to the reader. My pieces on Tom, Shaun, and Billy had made them seem even more like red-blooded human beings than they had before—well . . . before the aforementioned blood was replaced with embalming fluid.

I'm sounding flip again, and I'm sorry; chalk it up to the stress, the lack of sleep, and the fact that a snarky sense of humor has always been my primary coping mechanism. The truth is, the three deaths had gotten to me way more than I'd expected. I'd covered plenty of fatalities, from car accidents to suicides to out-and-out murders, but these felt especially awful. And because I've been known to be the brooding type, I can tell you precisely why.

First off, there was the sheer volume; we're talking not one death but three.

Then there was the fact that I'd met them, so their lives were automatically more vivid to me, greater than the usual sum of details and quotes.

Also that their deaths were so blatantly senseless; if they hadn't opened up their veins (or their lungs or whatever it turned out to be) and ingested some recreational poison, they'd be off skateboarding somewhere as we speak.

And the kicker, the thing that really got me, was simple: They were just so goddamn, heartbreakingly *young*.

Billy had been the last to die, but the coroner released all three bodies at the same time. For whatever reason, his funeral was held first; it happened on the Wednesday after Melting Rock, in the tiny Jaspersburg Lutheran Church on Main Street. So many people attended that their cars overflowed the parking lot and glutted the streets. For once, though, the local cops didn't seem inclined to give tickets.

There was a similar scene the next day at Shaun Kirtz's service, held at the hippie-dippy Congregation of Consciousness, located in what used to be a carpet store in downtown Gabriel. By the time it was Tom's turn to be eulogized, his parents must've realized space was at a premium. They moved the service from their small Jaspersburg parish to the biggest Catholic church in the county.

So there I was in the back row, taking notes and (catechism dropout that I am) trying to remember when you were supposed to stand and sit and kneel. In front of the altar was a white metal coffin that, sure enough, had been scribbled all over with farewell messages in black Magic Marker. From a distance the writing was a blur, but I'd seen it at the wake the night before, and a picture of it would run in the next day's paper. *Love ya, Tommy,* some girl had written, with the *O* in *love* in the shape of a heart. *Keep on rockin' in heaven,* someone else had scrawled, and so on. Honestly, it was all just too damn depressing.

Four of the five surviving members of the Jaspersburg Eight had attended the services—all except Cindy, who'd been in the hospital until Sunday and was reportedly still deeply freaked out. But her brother, Alan, was there, looking stoic as he guided Lauren, Dorrie, and Trish up the church steps. He seemed older all of a sudden, or maybe just miserable. Chief Stilwell was at all three funerals too, sitting with several other uniformed cops and firemen. I also noticed Rosemary Hamill, who wore another bulbous hat (black this time) and positioned herself smack behind the immediate family.

The teacher doing the eulogy for Tom Giamotti came off like he'd rather have his toes chopped off than speak in front of a crowd. His talk was stilted, a passel of platitudes that made Tom sound like some kind of cardboard cutout of a high-school student: good son, good friend, kind to children and small animals.

It was a damn shame, because from what people had told me, he'd been a hell of a lot more interesting than that. For one thing, he was a talented musician who'd taught himself to play a half-dozen instruments. And he seemed like a genuinely nice guy. When he took up drums, one of his teachers told me, he'd spent extra to get an electronic set so he could listen through headphones and not bother the rest of the family. He was also crazy about his much-younger brother and sister, whom he baby-sat every day after school; he'd insisted on doing it. When his parents offered to pay him, he'd turned them down flat.

Okay, it's not that anybody goes out of their way to say something nasty about a recently deceased seventeen-year-old. And, granted, nobody told me tales of Tom leaping tall buildings in a single bound. But there was something about the breadth and depth of Tom's little kindnesses that really got to me—everything from helping his sister learn to ride a bike to giving blood on the first day he was old enough. He just seemed like, well . . . like if he'd had the chance to grow up, he would've been one of the good guys.

I got out of the church ahead of almost everybody and waited on the sidewalk in case some decent color happened by as everyone filed out. Nothing seemed worth writing about, though I did notice that four of the six pallbearers were too young for facial hair. Tom's parents came out last, and they looked as devastated as you'd expect. His mother seemed able to walk only because she had her husband propping her up on one side and her priest on the other.

A boy and a girl of around eight were near them—Tom's twin siblings, being shepherded by an older woman who, I assumed, was their grandmother. The kids weren't crying, exactly; they looked absolutely dazed, as though what was going on was just too awful for them to process.

I was standing there watching Tom Giamotti's mother being helped into a limo—and contemplating all the times I've argued the pro-legalization thing, railing about individual rights and how drugs are a victimless crime—when Dorrie appeared at my elbow. The other three were standing a few feet away; all of them had been crying, Alan included. Lauren, who had looked merely distraught at the other two services, now seemed in danger of collapse.

"Are you going to the cemetery?" Dorrie asked. "You can ride with us if you want."

"Um . . . Thanks, but I've got my own car."

Just between you and me, the idea of being trapped with four sniffling teenagers was downright unbearable.

"But you're going, right?"

"Yeah. I have to cover it for the paper."

"And you're coming to the house afterward?"

"What?"

"The Giamottis are having, you know, a get-together. At their place. His dad said to invite whoever we want."

"Oh, God, no." It came out stronger than I'd intended, but . . . Jesus, even I know that invading a family's privacy by sending a reporter to the private reception is out of bounds.

"I'm sure it'd be okay," Dorrie was saying. "You're kind of our friend now, right?"

I wasn't quite sure how to answer that. "Er . . . Thanks, that's really considerate of you, but I can't. I have a deadline for tomorrow's paper."

I gestured toward the weeping mother by way of emphasis, though this probably wasn't in the best of taste.

"Well, okay."

Dorrie fumbled in the pocket of her black trousers, then took out a tissue and blew her nose with a honk.

"You know," she said, "I never went to a funeral before this week. Never even one. Isn't that weird?"

THE WALDEN COUNTY CORONER has always been something of a slowpoke when it comes to determining a cause of death, but this time he had a fire under his derriere. Within two days of the festival's premature end, he'd announced that the three young men had died from ingesting tainted LSD—though what it'd been tainted with, he wasn't saying.

A source told Ochoa it might be some chemical that's used in the manufacturing process, but frankly nobody seemed too obsessed with the particulars. The important thing was that the powers that be knew what kind of drug the kids had taken, and therefore what drug they had to warn the rest of the world about.

The story had hit the airwaves on Monday, three apparently being the magic number of corpses that merited the attention of CNN and its ilk. The *Times* put the story on page three of the Metro section, the dead reduced to a list of names and ages within Gordon's larger story about the potential dangers of a batch of killer acid.

"Nobody brews up just three doses of LSD," one talking head from the CDC was quoted as saying. "We know there's more out there, probably a great deal more. We need to get the word out about how dangerous this is before more people lose their lives."

The investigation into where the drugs had come from was, by all accounts, going nowhere. It didn't help that the Jaspersburg cops, being in a mighty rush to get everybody off the festival grounds, hadn't gotten names and contact numbers from any of them. Neither did the Melting Rock management offer much help in figuring out who'd shown up. The festival doesn't take credit cards, and although people can send in checks for five-day passes, the volunteers don't keep records after they fill the orders. The closest thing to an attendance roster that organizers could come up with was a list of the people who'd reserved campsites—without phone numbers, hometowns, or (in some cases) first names.

So finding people for the cops to talk to was no easy task; it was also a job that the Jaspersburg police seemed determined to do by itself. Although a few Walden County sheriff's deputies had been recruited to help track down campers, offers of advice or manpower from the G.P.D. had been rebuffed, though politely. The word on the street was that Chief Stilwell was taking the case personally—very personally. Three of his daughter's friends had died, and he was damn well going to find out who'd sold them the drugs that'd killed them.

I heard a lot of this from Ochoa, who was enjoying the typical cops reporter's unseemly glee at the prospect of covering something more serious than jaywalking. But I also got some of the details from

Lauren, who kept wanting to talk—but, to Ochoa's eternal vexation, seemed willing to speak only to me.

She dropped by the paper four days after Tom's funeral, arms laden with the booty of a back-to-school shopping trip, and every male eye in the newsroom looked up from their computer screens to check her out. She was wearing a dark blue Indian-print sundress, the kind you can buy in half a dozen stores on the Green and whose thin straps, sadly for yours truly, do not permit the wearing of a brassiere. Her long hair was swept up in a chunky bun, fastened with two black lacquer sticks that formed an X at the base of her skull. She wasn't wearing a molecule of makeup, and she didn't need to.

"Lauren, this is our science writer, Jake Madison," I said, because I had no choice; Mad was standing there with his hand extended and a shit-eating grin on his face. "Jake Madison, Lauren Potter. Lauren"—I cleared my throat for emphasis—"is a student at Jaspersburg *High School.*"

"Nice," Mad said. "What year?"

"I'm a senior," she said. She hadn't let go of his hand—but then again, he didn't seem particularly inclined to let go of hers.

"Nice," he said again. "So you must be . . . what? Eighteen?"

"In a couple weeks."

"Interesting."

I picked up my backpack. "Lauren and I were just going out for coffee." I'd offered to take her for frozen yogurt—my second of the day—but she'd turned up her nose at it in favor of an espresso. "So, okay, let's go."

Neither one of them moved, though they did have the decency to stop shaking hands. "You want to come with us?" Lauren asked him. I narrowed my eyes at him in an attempt to say *don't you dare.*

"I'd love to," he said. My eyes reduced to slits. "But I've got an interview on campus in twenty minutes. Gotta go."

Now, don't get the idea that Mad was trying to behave like a decent person; I'd been at the edit meeting, and I knew he actually did have an interview.

"Maybe some other time," Lauren said, favoring him with her very expensive smile.

"Sounds great," Mad said, and I got her out of the newsroom before he could say anything else.

We went over to Café Whatever, the Green's newest purveyor of caffeine and overpriced cookies. She ordered a double espresso with a twist of lemon, whereas I went for a big latte with a shot of almond syrup. We settled at one of the tables, with Lauren's packages overflowing the adjacent chairs.

"So did you get everything you need for school?"

She surveyed the bags. "Huh? Oh, some."

"You went shopping by yourself?"

She shrugged. "My mom was supposed to meet me, but she got stuck in the lab. Big surprise."

"She's at the Benson med school, right?"

She nodded. "My dad too. They're, like, totally brilliant."

"Are you going to go into medicine too?"

"Maybe. I'm pretty good at science stuff, chemistry and biology. Must be genetic."

"So, Lauren . . . how come you came by the paper today?"

Another shrug. "You said I could."

"You didn't want to talk about anything in particular?"

She stirred three sugars into her espresso with a dainty little spoon. "Nah, I . . . I was just down here, so . . ."

She's lonely, I realized all of a sudden. *Despite being the alpha female of her social group, the kid's just plain lonely.*

"What are your friends up to—Trish and Dorrie and Cindy?"

She bit her lower lip. "Cindy's . . . She hasn't really seen anybody since . . . since what happened. Alan said he's not even sure if she's gonna come back to school."

"Really? What's she going to do?"

"I don't know. Maybe go someplace different. A private school maybe."

"But Dorrie and Trish are doing okay?"

"I guess. Dorrie . . . Well, Dorrie's just Dorrie. Mainly, she likes pissing off her parents with her hair and stuff."

"Yeah, I heard that they're—"

"Multigazillionaires? Yeah. And they've been taking her to Benson alumni stuff since she was born. Drives her nuts."

"And Trish?"

"Trish? She kind of keeps to herself a lot. She doesn't hang out as much as she used to."

"Since the festival?"

"Since a while."

"Have you, you know, been interviewed by the police yet?"

She rolled her eyes. "Are you *kidding?* They've come over, like, five times since the fest. My folks told me to tell them everything I know, but I can't. I mean, I don't *know* anything. What am I supposed to tell them?"

"You really don't know where the guys got their drugs?"

"I didn't even know they had any." I gave her a look that said I didn't buy it, and she blushed into her demitasse. "Okay, I mean . . . I knew they had some shit. We all did. But I didn't know they had anything new."

"Did you have any acid yourself?"

She shook her head with surprising vehemence. "Me? No way."

"How come?"

"I had, you know . . . a bad trip a while ago. I don't do that stuff anymore. Just pot and a little E and some 'shrooms once in a while. That's it."

"Sounds like plenty."

"Come on, you're not going to get all judgmental on me, are you? I get enough of that from my mom and dad. I mean, it's not like they didn't smoke dope when they were—"

"Jesus, Lauren, think about it. Three of your friends are dead. You can't blame your parents for worrying about you. I'm surprised they didn't confiscate your stash."

"Are you kidding? Of course they did. They made me hand over everything I had and they flushed it down the toilet."

"Good for them." She gave me a beleaguered look. "What about Dorrie and Trish?"

"What do you think I'm going to do, narc on them?"

"If it could save their lives, you bet your ass."

Her demitasse stopped in midair. "You know," she said, "you don't sound like most grown-ups I know."

"Yeah, well, the jury's still out on how grown-up I am in the first place. So, do they have any acid or don't they?"

"Nah. It was kind of a guy thing."

"So does Alan?"

"He says . . . He told me Shaun offered to get him a tab, but he said no. And later he offered to split one with him, but Alan still didn't feel like it. I think . . ."

"What?"

"He won't really talk about it, but I think it has him really freaked out—wondering whether maybe he would've died too, or maybe if Shaun's tab had been split in half, they both would've been okay, just maybe got a little sick or something."

"And do you know where the guys got the stuff they took?"

"At Melting Rock? Could've been from a million people."

"Well, who did they usually get their drugs from?"

"Different places. I don't know."

"Where do you get yours from?" She stared at the tabletop. "Come on, Lauren. Just tell me."

"I don't know if I should."

"Why not?"

She extended an index finger and traced the shape of the question marks embedded in the glass tabletop. "Because."

"Because why?" I was starting to feel like a twelve-year-old myself.

"Because . . . you're not supposed to, you know, speak ill of the dead."

"You got it from one of the boys?" She nodded. "Which one?"

"Shaun."

"Shaun Kirtz? He was a dealer?"

"Oh, God, nothing like that. He just knew what to buy and where to get it."

"And what about now?"

"I haven't . . . Since it happened, I haven't done anything."

"Because your parents threw it all away?"

"That," she said, "and because it just doesn't seem like fun any-more."

CHAPTER *9*

After the first round of stories about the effort to track down the source of the drugs, things died down. There just wasn't that much to write about. Since no new cases had been reported, no other jurisdictions had gotten involved. And when a bunch of drunken students got into a bloody brawl during a Freshman Week party at Bessler College—the tiny liberal-arts school that languishes in Benson's shadow—Melting Rock wasn't even the most recent example of youthful self-destruction.

The deaths did continue to inspire a commotion from the Gabriel activist corps, which mounted an educational campaign warning of the various dangers of LSD. But, like at the festival itself, those efforts varied widely, from "Just say no" to "Just make sure your drugs are kosher." I hadn't realized it until then—mostly because I'd always been wildly uninterested in such things—but apparently LSD still has quite a following. For some people, it's a recreational matter, while for others it's positively messianic.

San Francisco is, naturally, known as the LSD capital of America. But there are still plenty of sixties holdovers in Gabriel, some of whom (literally or figuratively) participated in the Electric Kool-Aid Acid Test all those decades ago. This may be a small town, but it's a pretty funky place.

And as far as I'm concerned, nothing demonstrated said funkiness quite as pointedly as the two informational tables that cropped up on the Green after the three kids died. One was sponsored by the fire department and offered cautionary literature complete with skull and crossbones; the other touted LSD as a potential cure for everything from alcoholism to criminality.

"You know," one fellow from the latter table was telling me and my notebook, "acid's gotten a way bad rap."

The guy was around sixty, sporting a gray ponytail pulled together over a balding pate. His first and only name was Sandy, which he said was short for "Sandman," and though he was the only person sitting at the table, he wasn't exactly alone. Standing off to his left was Joe Kingman, a Gabriel alderman and Benson law professor who was there to protect Sandy's right to free speech. If the cops tried to get rid of him, he told me, he had an injunction request all ready to go.

Although Sandy was (unsurprisingly) doing a brisk business, he was more than happy to take time out to educate me. LSD's ability to treat various disorders had only begun to be explored in the sixties, he said. And although a number of bona fide doctors and psychologists thought it had terrific potential to help humanity, he told me, "their work was quashed by a small-minded government afraid to have its citizens fully aware of their mental and emotional power." Then he gave me a copy of *The Varieties of Psychedelic Experience* and a homemade granola bar, which he told me was, quote, "clean."

I'd happened upon the tables on my way to lunch, which meant that when I returned to the newsroom I had both a gooey slice of white pizza with broccoli and the makings for an equally tasty news story. I dispatched the two inside of twenty minutes, thanking the journalism gods that I'd been coming back out of the Center Gabriel food court just as Sandy was calling his counterpart at the other table a "pea-brained fascist drone."

After lunch I had to turn my attention to something a lot less fun: the open house for Deep Lake Cooling.

What, you may ask, is Deep Lake Cooling?

Allow me to begin at the beginning.

Three years and $150 million in the making, Deep Lake (as we hipsters call it) is the largest single infrastructure project in Benson

University history. And though Mad is the science guy, I've covered the thing enough that I can give you the basics.

It all started when an attractive-but-hirsute Benson engineer named Glenn Shardik woke up in the middle of the night and realized that the university was sitting right next to a honking-big body of water. And not only is Mohawk Lake long, it's really deep—maybe four hundred feet—so the water at the bottom stays something like 38 degrees all year round.

Now, although the subject of air-conditioning is not a particularly sexy one, apparently it's rather important. Cooling the campus costs big money, particularly when you're talking about upgrading from all those nasty, ozone-killing CFCs. And although the powers that be may be perfectly happy to let the undergrads swelter, the fact is that computers and labs need to be kept comfy, or else.

So the solution that Shardik came up with was this: If the campus is hot and the bottom of the lake is practically freezing, why not put them together and—like the TV commercial where the chocolate gets jammed into the peanut butter—create the perfect combination? Suck up some cold water, run it alongside the water from the university's cooling system at a so-called "heat-exchange facility" on the shore, and presto: free air-conditioning.

It wasn't a completely original idea; the city of Stockholm was already doing something like it, and Toronto was thinking about it. But such a thing had never been tried in the United States; now all Shardik had to do was get the university to invest millions, talk the city into letting Benson dig a massive trench from campus to lake, and convince local environmentalists that the whole thing wasn't going to make the water turn purple.

On the first two counts, he succeeded handily. That last one, however, proved to be not so easy.

Now, if you ask me, the Gabriel tree-hugging set would've been foursquare in favor of Deep Lake—if it'd been proposed anywhere but here. Sure enough, Shardik was constantly flogging the project's environmental value, how it'd mean a significant reduction in the university's production of greenhouse gases. But local activists decided early on that if Benson was in favor of it, it had to be fundamentally evil.

They argued that it would raise the lake temperature and cause some hideous algae bloom; Shardik hired a team of independent consultants, who found that the overall increase would be roughly equal to one extra sunny day a year.

They worried about the effect on tiny misis shrimp, who could get sucked into the intake pipe; the experts countered that they were so photophobic, all you had to do was put a ten-watt lightbulb down there to scare them away.

And so on, and so on. If you think it sounds tiresome, well . . . you're right. Try covering it for three straight years.

To be honest, when I first heard about the project, I thought there was no way it'd ever go through. But every time the local government or its citizenry put up a hurdle, Shardik and his team jumped over it. Construction straddled two summers, ripping up umpteen streets and making Benson commuters curse his name. The same Tuesday that I took Lauren to Café Whatever, a state judge had refused to grant an injunction barring the system from being turned on; the following afternoon, Deep Lake Cooling was finally being unveiled.

The occasion was an open house at the heat-exchange facility, located behind a high fence on a knoll at the edge of the lake. Space being tight, reporters and local dignitaries were bused there from downtown—a trip that ended abruptly when we got to the protesters blocking the gate.

There were maybe twenty of them, a scraggly bunch carrying signs like DEEP LAKE = DEEP TROUBLE and the far less original IT'S OUR LAKE, NOT BENSON'S. The bus driver honked, but it was no go; the news service flack who'd handed out fact sheets on the project's environmental bells and whistles looked like she wanted to fall under the wheels.

Finally, we all got out and tried to hoof it—whereupon the protesters put down their signs and linked arms to form a human chain. I shook my head and wondered what it'd be like to be a reporter in a town where civil disobedience wasn't considered a goddamn art form; more work, maybe, but a lot less annoying.

I surveyed the members of the impromptu kick line, most of whom I knew. A few months back, several of them had been all fired up about genetically engineered food. Before that, it was . . . Hell, I couldn't remember. I was just about to try to talk one of the usual suspects into letting me by when I realized that the oddly dressed blonde at the end of the line was Guinevere, the air-reading weirdo from Melting Rock. I went over to talk to her, but it was no use; her eyes were shut tight and some vague chanting sound was emanating from her throat. I shook my head and moved on, and two seconds later, I recognized someone else: Axel Robinette, Dorrie's scab-kneed sweetie.

He was wearing cutoff shorts and a black T-shirt with a drawing of a sturgeon on it; on his head was a red bandanna tied Aunt Jemima style. His knee was healing, but it looked like he was going to have a nasty scar. There was already a vintage one around his hairline, and under his lower lip was a little square of fuzz the Gen Yers call a "soul patch." Yuck.

To his left was someone else I recognized, but whom I hadn't actually met: Axel's slightly scary-looking buddy with the shaved head and the surfeit of earrings. The guy was wearing an identical sturgeon T-shirt, though he'd cut off the sleeves to better display a pair of beefy biceps.

Axel didn't seem to recognize me, but I guess that wasn't surprising; I'd only interviewed him briefly, and he'd likely been under the influence of chemistry. At the moment, though, he seemed generally sober.

"Axel, right?" He blinked at me. "I'm Alex Bernier from the *Monitor*, remember? I talked to you when you won the Hacky Sack thing at Melting Rock."

"What? Oh, yeah, I guess. . . ."

I turned toward Jesse Ventura Junior. "And your friend would be . . . ?"

The guy smiled, which didn't manage to make him look much less intimidating. "Robert Adam Sturdivant," he said, aiming his gaze directly at my cleavage. "But you can call me 'Sturdy.'"

I flipped open my notebook. "So you guys want to tell me why you're here?"

Silence, until Axel finally spoke up. "Um . . . We're protesting Deep Lake."

"Yeah, I got that. But why? I mean, how come you're willing to get yourself arrested over it?"

Axel's eyebrows went up. "Arrested? You think, like, the cops are gonna show?"

"You're blocking the entrance to the big party. Of course they're gonna show." The twenty-something woman on his right made noises that said she agreed with me.

Sturdivant raised his eyebrows, which made his forehead go all crinkly. "No shit?"

"I bet you a buck they're here inside of five minutes."

"Whoa," Axel said. He looked deeply contemplative all of a sudden, and I thought he was going to bolt. But then his scruffy face exploded into a wide grin. "Guess if they're gonna come, they're gonna come."

"You're willing to get busted over this?"

He shrugged, pretty comical considering the linked arms. "Doesn't hurt a bit."

"You mean you've been arrested before?"

"Nah . . . but I mean, what are they gonna do? Kick our ass?"

"Not too likely."

"Gotta stand up for what you believe in," he said, then turned to his friend. "Right, man?"

Sturdivant stuck out his chin. "Fuck yeah."

"So come on," I said, "answer the question. How come you feel so strongly about this?"

"About Deep Lake?"

"Of course about Deep Lake."

"Oh . . . I mean, it's just totally wrong."

"How come?"

"For, you know . . . for a lot of reasons."

This was less than quotable. "Could you be more specific?"

His back straightened, like he was about to give a speech. But all he said was, "It's goddamn imperialism."

"How do you figure that?"

"Benson thinks it's like some royal kingdom." He looked to his pal, whose head nodded on his thick neck. "They think they can come down here and fuck up our lake and nobody's gonna stop them."

"Why do you think it's going to fuck up the lake? I mean, to play devil's advocate, didn't all those ecologists sign off on it?"

His expression indicated that he was starting to think I was very stupid. Hopefully, I was managing to conceal the fact that the feeling was mutual.

"That doesn't mean shit," he said. "Benson's got deep pockets. They can get anybody to say whatever they want."

More agreement from his companions, right and left. Farther down the line, Gabriel's own Mayor Marty was trying to talk the pro-testers into packing it in, with no visible success.

"All right," I said. "Let's assume for a second the environmental reports are flawed. What do you think it's going to do to the lake specifically?"

"Jesus," he said in a tone I generally reserve for three-year-olds. "What do you *think* it's gonna do? You dump a whole shitload of hot water into a lake, it's not gonna do it any good, now is it?"

"But according to the Environmental Impact Statement, it's only going to be a couple of degrees warmer than when they pull it out."

"Fuck the Environmental Impact Statement, okay? And besides, what we're talking about here is the *process*."

"What about it?"

"Come on, the process was a joke from the beginning. You think the state isn't gonna do whatever the hell Benson wants? I mean, Christ, they're the biggest employer in the county. You really think the state wants to piss them off?"

I never got a chance to answer, because the Gabriel cops showed up then and hauled the protesters off in recyclable plastic handcuffs in record time. Within minutes we were inside the building, where we were greeted by big tables laden with apple cider, yummy-looking cookies, and chunks of cheese from the university dairy store. The Benson news service definitely knows its way to a reporter's heart.

In the name of research, I availed myself of all of the above. Then I wandered around the rapidly filling building, whose mammoth pipes and flashing indicator lights looked like a combination of the *Enterprise* bridge and Willy Wonka's chocolate factory. A Benson student group was singing a cappella, and it took me a minute to recognize "Cool" from *West Side Story*. Clever.

"What do you think?" said a voice from behind me. "Pretty neat, huh?"

I turned around, and there was Lenny Peterson from the news service. Lenny is a nice guy, but he's not what you'd call a heartbreaker. He's nearly as short as I am and he has a serious overbite, so the overall picture is of a socially inept bunny rabbit. He's had a crush on me for a while, and though it's definitely unrequited, I haven't been above exploiting it if the situation requires. It's not nice, but there it is.

"Hey, Lenny," I said. "What're you doing here? Deep Lake's not in your beat."

"Whole office is here. Putting on the big shebang."

"I'll say. Cookies are good, huh?"

He eyed my plate longingly. "We only get to have some if there's leftovers."

I aimed a double-chocolate chunk his way. "Go ahead, knock yourself out." He looked over at the news service director, who was introducing Glenn Shardik to a reporter from the Syracuse public TV station. "Come on, go ahead. The coast is clear." His hand darted out like a cobra and snatched the cookie, which he folded in half and jammed into his mouth. "Some crowd out there, huh?" His mouth was too full to answer; he just chewed and made rapturous noises. "You guys expecting any protesters?"

He grunted a "no" through the remains of the cookie, and I waited while he finished chewing. "Who'da thought they'd try and block the buses?" he said. "But I guess we shoulda known, huh?"

"It's not exactly unprecedented around here. Those guys been giving you a lot of trouble?"

He shook his head. "Not up at the news service or anything. I mean, nobody but you reporters even know we exist, right?" He sounded vaguely melancholy. "But, you know, security's been pretty tight down here at the site. Didn't want to let anybody throw a wrench in the works."

"Tell me something, Lenny. You're a science guy—"

He started to blush about the gills. "I just cover science for the news service. I write press releases and stuff. I'm no scientist."

"Yeah, but . . . you have your ear to the ground a lot. Tell me the truth. You think all the environmental stuff about Deep Lake was on the up-and-up?"

"Huh?"

I leaned in closer, in case my cleavage might help loosen his lips. "Come on, you know. . . . All the scientific review about how the project isn't going to hurt the lake or the environment or anything; you think it's for real?"

Now he looked vaguely scandalized. "You mean do I think the university doped it?"

"More or less."

"Why? Did somebody say that?"

"One of the guys blocking the gate."

He rolled his bulgy eyes. "Yeah, like *they'd* know."

"Nah, I don't think they probably would know. They're not as smart as you."

It was shameless, but luckily Lenny didn't seem to notice. For a second I thought it was my bodacious bod that was doing the trick, but as it turned out, he was staring down at my other cookie. It was damned attractive, laden with walnuts and M&M's. It broke my heart, but I gave it to him.

I stood there while he chewed, and when he had finally swallowed enough to make his loaded mouth merely indecent, he answered. "Definitely," he said.

"Definitely what?"

"The environmental reports were definitely straight up."

"How do you know?"

"Jeepers, Alex. You're a reporter. Look at the sources. Glenn made sure they got guys who're pro-environment to begin with, so nobody'd say they're biased. Even Charlie Brewster signed off on it."

"Who?"

"He's that emeritus prof they call 'Mr. Mohawk Lake.' I mean, come on. It doesn't get any better than that."

The singers had moved on to "Cool Change," which has always been a guilty pleasure of mine. I listened to it for a minute before I answered. "So that's it? You think the results are solid because you trust the people who did the research?"

"You're making it sound like that's, I don't know, *sordid* or something. All I'm saying is, these guys live by their scientific reputations. If they signed off on the project and then the lake got screwed up somehow, it'd be the kiss of death. So yeah, I trust them."

"Fair enough."

"Where'd you get this crap, anyway?"

"I told you, from the protesters."

"Which one? Or are you gonna give me some junk about protecting your sources?"

"I'm quoting the guy in tomorrow's paper, so no. His name's Axel Robinette. Also his buddy"—I looked down at my notebook—"Robert Sturdivant."

Lenny gave a horsey laugh. "Sturdivant? *Huh.* Reliable source you got there."

"You know him?"

He looked down at his unlaced Docksides. "Kinda."

"From the anti–Deep Lake thing?"

"Look, I gotta get back to work. I'm supposed to be handling the media."

"Hey, I'm the media. Handle me."

He looked me up and down, then made a snorting sound. "Cute."

"Come on, Lenny, what's the big deal? Just tell me how you know them and I'll free you up for Katie Couric."

His eyes lit up for a millisecond. "Is she . . . Oh. You're kidding."

"Come on, don't keep me in suspense. How do you know them?"

"You know, there's something I always wanted to say to you."

"What's that?"

He started to walk away. Then he stopped, looked over his shoulder, and smiled his bucktoothed smile.

"No comment," he said.

CHAPTER 10

I was in the newsroom the next day, supposedly writing a profile of a Benson freshman but really contemplating what I was going to wear to dinner with Cody that night, when my worst nightmare walked up the newsroom stairs.

Okay, to be more specific . . . it wasn't my own *personal* worst nightmare; rather, it was the worst nightmare of journalists in general.

And that would be: grieving relatives.

Because, you see, when somebody dies—particularly when they die suddenly and young—it's all but inevitable that the media is going to piss off the family and friends, or at least dissatisfy them. These people have lost something precious, and there's no way on earth that anything can make them happy, at least in the short term.

Don't get me wrong; I'm not criticizing them at all. Their reaction is only natural—and when someone I loved died a few years ago, I felt exactly the same way.

No obituary is long or worshipful enough. Media attention is intrusive; a *lack* of media attention is insulting. Reporters ask the wrong questions, or they ask the right questions too many times. When the death is covered on the front page, the family is tortured every time they pass a newsstand; when it's shunted to the inside, it's as though the paper is saying their loved one doesn't matter. Asking people to describe what the victim was like is downright cruel—almost as cruel as *not* asking.

You get the idea.

So you can understand why, when Tom Giamotti's parents walked into the newsroom, I tried to slouch behind my terminal and hide. And when I realized that the three people with them were Billy Halpern's parents and Shaun Kirtz's mother, it was all I could do not to crawl under the desk.

They were greeted by the newsroom secretary, who—merciful God—had just come back from a cigarette break. Mr. Giamotti said they were there to see Marilyn, and when Kathie asked him if they had an appointment, he said they didn't. She told him she'd check, but that Marilyn was a very busy person and the odds that she could see them weren't good. I slunk down even farther.

"What's your name?" she asked.

"I'm Vince Giamotti. This is my wife, Nancy. These people are Bill and Janice Halpern and Marsha Kirtz."

"Okay, I'll just—" Then the names clicked. "Oh. *Oh.* Let me see if she can see you." I caught the top of her head bobbing as she sprinted into the office, emerging seconds later. "Please come right in," she said, smiling way too broadly.

She showed them into the office, and when she emerged, she went hunting for two more chairs, which she pinched from behind Lillian and Ochoa's desks. After she delivered them, she shut the door behind her and sat down at her desk with a dodged-that-bullet sort of whistle. I retained my defensive perch for a couple of minutes, and was just sitting up and breathing my own little sigh of relief when Marilyn's door opened a foot.

"Alex?"

Damn. "Um . . . yeah?"

"Would you come in here and join us, please?"

She sounded extremely polite, which put me on guard for something truly awful. As I walked toward the office, Mad whistled the Darth Vader death march under his breath. I was just about to mutter some choice obscenities when Marilyn called out again in the same scary-nice voice.

"Jake? Would you come in here too, please?"

"Jake?" I stage-whispered to him. "We are *so* screwed. . . ."

Mad let me go first, which I in no way mistook for chivalry. When we got in there, we had to stand in the corner next to the door, since Marilyn's already-compact office was packed solid.

"Alex Bernier, Jake Madison," she said. "These are the Giamottis, the Halperns, and Marsha Kirtz." They acknowledged us with nods and hellos, none of them warm. "Jake is the science writer I was telling you about. And Alex"—their attention shifted to me en masse—"is the reporter who covered Melting Rock."

The sentence hung there in the air for a while, laden with all sorts of unspoken ickyness.

Alex is the reporter who covered Melting Rock. Alex was there when your sons died. Alex snuck a peek at their corpses, then skipped over to the media tent to write about it. Then she went dancing and had some curly fries.

Okay, so I was feeling a little defensive. But it was hard not to, pinioned as I was by five pairs of grieving eyes.

"You wrote about our son's funeral," Janice Halpern said in a voice so blank I wasn't sure if she was pissed about it. "I recognize your name."

"Um . . . Actually, I covered all three funerals."

More silence. For the second time in as many weeks, I longed to pitch myself through Marilyn's office window. Finally, the boss took pity on me and said something.

"The Giamottis and the Halperns and"—I caught her glancing down at the notebook on her desk, though I doubt anyone else noticed—"Ms. Kirtz came in to talk about the coverage of their sons' deaths. They feel that—"

"We feel that you people are being incredibly irresponsible."

This from Vince Giamotti, who sounded equal parts angry and exhausted. I girded myself for the standard lecture about how we were exploiting their pain to sell papers—how if another reporter bothered them or their friends, they were going to call their lawyer, yadda-yadda-yadda. Why Marilyn had dragged us in here for this was beyond me.

"As we've been telling Ms. Zapinsky," Giamotti went on, "there's a vitally important story that you're not telling. Now, I don't know why you're not telling it. None of us really want to get into who pulls the strings around here. But the purpose of a community newspaper is to serve the community, and I'll tell you right now that the *Gabriel Monitor* is doing the community a disservice."

I still had no idea what he was talking about; in fact, he seemed in imminent danger of losing it. His words were running together, and the tightness in his jaw said he was trying not to cry.

"The point is," he continued, "there's got to be more of those drugs out there—more of that garbage that killed our boys. Now, I don't know why you don't consider this to be newsworthy, but I can tell you the rest of the community doesn't agree with you."

He was starting to get choked up, and his wife put a hand on his arm. The other hand stayed in a white-knuckle clench around her handbag.

"We're not trying to blame anyone," she said, though nobody in the room believed her. "All we're saying is that we don't want this to . . . to happen to another family. We don't want anyone else to go through what we've been going through."

"We need you to help us get the word out," Marsha Kirtz said in a matter-of-fact way that seemed to come out of nowhere. On second thought, though, it fit; with her graying braids and aging hippie manner, she was a breed apart from the Giamottis and the Halperns. "We can't afford to let people's interest in this wane. We need to have parents talking to their kids about it. Do you understand?" The three of us nodded. "Good. So what do you plan to do about it?"

Marilyn gave her own longing look, at the set of nunchakus hanging on the wall. "As I told you, our coverage has been driven in part by local law enforcement. If they aren't actively—"

"Please don't pass the buck," Kirtz said. "We've all heard of freedom of the press. You don't need the police to give you permission to write about something."

Marilyn was managing to keep her temper in check, which for her constituted front-page news. "I didn't say that we did. All I'm trying to tell you is that if the story isn't there, we can't cover it."

Janice Halpern drew in a sharp breath. "Isn't *there*? How can you say that . . . ? Our children are *dead*. Don't you dare even presume to tell us that—"

Her husband put an arm around her and made shushing sounds, though I got the feeling he was more embarrassed than anything else.

"I'm sorry," Marilyn said. "I didn't mean that like it sounded. Of course this is an important story. It's an extremely important story. And as I'm sure you've seen, it's had a presence in the paper almost every day since it happened."

"But the stories are getting shorter and shorter," Tom Giamotti's mother said.

Her voice cracked at the end of the sentence; since I couldn't bear to look at her, I stared down at my sandals. If Marilyn gave the poor woman a lecture on the structure of the news cycle, I was going to slit my wrists with her Japanese throwing star.

"In your opinion," Marilyn said, "are the police doing an adequate job with the investigation?"

They looked to each other, and I saw Marsha Kirtz give Vince Giamotti some sort of unspoken go-ahead.

"Chief Stilwell is a good man," he said, "and we all appreciate his desire to solve this case himself. All of us . . . I'm sure any one of us would love to get our hands on the person who sold our sons those drugs. And we're all very fond of his daughter, Trish. But we feel as though . . . We're concerned that he's in over his head."

"You think he should ask for help from other law-enforcement agencies?"

"That's right."

"Have you spoken to Chief Stilwell about your concerns?"

"We have, but . . . it doesn't seem to have done a lot of good. He was very nice, but he obviously thinks he can handle this. We disagree."

"And would you be willing to say that on the record?"

"I suppose so. . . . Why?"

"Because," Marilyn said, "that's a story."

•   •   •

THERE WERE, in fact, quite a few stories that came out of that excruciating Thursday morning. Ochoa, who'd missed the meeting by the dumb luck of being out on an interview, came back in time to do the piece that would run the next day under the headline FAMILIES PRESS FOR WIDER INVESTIGATION. Marilyn pushed the drug deaths back up to the top of the story budget, either because she was suddenly intrigued by the subject or (more likely) worried that the grieving relatives were going to take their sob story downstairs to the publisher's office.

As for me and Mad: We got pulled off the pieces we were working on and assigned to put together a huge package on LSD—as the rack cards advertised, "Its science, its culture, its possible dangers."

We spent most of Thursday doing research and setting up interviews. It was around five in the afternoon that the police scanner went off, and the day officially tilted toward the absurd.

Emergency control to Gabriel monitors. Report of a suspicious substance at the Deep Lake Cooling facility on East Shore Drive. Two G.F.D. units with paramedics are requested to respond to the scene with haz-mat gear. Repeat, haz-mat gear is required. . . .

"Haz-mat gear?" Ochoa said. "What do you think is going down over there?"

I looked to the scanner, which provided zip in the way of further information. "Maybe something went *ker-bloowie.*"

Mad shook his head. "That's not supposed to happen. Whole system's set up to be . . . What do they always say? 'Passive and benign.'"

"Yo," Ochoa said with a grin. "I likes my cooling like I likes my women."

I cast about for something to throw at him. "You people are appalling."

Bill came out of his office then, having caught wind of something interesting. "And which one of you appalling people wants to tell me what the hell's going on?"

We filled him in, and he pondered which one of us was going to have the joy of going over to the cooling facility. Since I'd covered the

Deep Lake open house—and since I didn't have a story to file for the next day's paper—I was the lucky winner. But at least I didn't have to go alone; Bill's parting shot was for me to get Melissa out of the darkroom and drag her along.

We got into my wee Beetle and wiggled our way out of the *Monitor*'s minuscule parking lot. By the time we got where we were going, the place was clogged with fire trucks, so we had to park a few hundred yards down the road where there was enough of a shoulder to keep the car from toppling into the lake.

We hiked back, and when we got to the top of the curvy driveway, we saw a trio of firemen in protective suits, their heads encased in oversize helmets with thick glass faceplates. It may sound futuristic, but frankly they looked like they ought to be shilling tires for Michelin. There were also two ambulances and a pair of cop cars, Gabriel's finest never liking to be left out of the party. There were no other reporters in sight, which was no surprise. The local TV news goes on the air live at six, and they're not a big enough operation to deal with a story that breaks at five-fifteen.

At fire scenes, at least in this town, you can usually tell from the gear who's in charge. Regular firefighters wear yellow, while lieutenants and other muckety-mucks wear white. I saw plenty of guys in normal yellow coats, but I couldn't find whoever was supposed to be the commander on the scene.

If there's one thing I've learned from covering this kind of spot news, it's that you don't want to piss off cops and firemen by sticking a notebook in their faces while they're trying to do their jobs. So we wandered around the periphery for a while, keeping our distance from the mob at the cooling facility's front door. This wasn't just a matter of respect, mind you; if there was really some awful chemical blowing around in there, we had no interest in inhaling it.

When fifteen minutes went by without anything exploding, I nosed closer in the hope of finding someone I knew. I didn't recognize any of the firemen, but when I got to the other side of one of the ambulances, I encountered a very freaked-out Glenn Shardik.

The Deep Lake Cooling engineer was pacing around a tiny patch of asphalt, looking like he could use a hefty dose of elephant tranquilizer. If I were a nicer person I might have left him alone, but, hey, I'm a reporter.

"Hi, Glenn," I said. He stopped pacing for a second and squinted at me. "Alex Bernier, from the *Monitor.* Remember me?"

"What? Oh. Yes. Of course."

"So . . . can you tell me what's going on?"

He ran a hand through his hair, which is so bushy his fingers got stuck. It must happen a lot, though, because he didn't seem to notice. "What's going on?" He started pacing back and forth again, so fast it was almost comic. "I'd *love* to know what's going on. But nobody's telling me anything, are they?"

"Well . . . what happened?"

I didn't really expect him to answer, but apparently he was upset enough to overlook the fact that he was talking to a reporter.

"There's something in the system," he said. "And don't ask me what, because I don't know." He looked over at the front door, still blocked by a cadre of firemen. "And I'm not going to find out anything soon, because they won't let me back in. . . ."

He was talking and walking a mile a minute. I grabbed him by the wrist and noticed that he had the hairiest forearms I'd ever seen on a two-legged animal. "Look, Glenn, why don't we go sit down for a minute?"

"Where?"

It was a good question, but I had no answer; there's no place to sit in the Deep Lake Cooling parking lot. "Then how about if we just stand still for a second, okay?"

He'd gone back to staring at the entrance. I doubted he was even listening to me.

"Listen, Glenn, can you just tell me what you saw in there?" He didn't answer. "Glenn?"

"What? Oh, sorry. . . . Look, I can't tell you anything. All I know is I got a call from the shift foreman telling me there was something odd in the intake pool. I came running down here and, lo and behold, he was right."

"What is it?"

"I don't know. There's something foreign in there. The whole pool's bright red"—he made a sour face—"like blood."

CHAPTER 11

The police and firemen stayed at the scene for two hours, during which Melissa snapped innumerable photos of burly guys in space suits. The one that ran on the front page was of two of them emerging from the front door, carrying a black plastic case that looked like it housed some sort of video equipment. As it turned out, what was inside was a sample of the water in the intake pool. When I finally found the scene commander, he told me it was being taken for, quote, "analysis."

"Taken where?" I asked.

"Forensics lab."

He kept walking toward his official SUV. I followed.

"Someone said it might be blood. Is that true?"

"We don't know what it is," he said, and not nicely. "That's why we're taking it for analysis. Get it?"

"When do you think you'll have the results?"

"You'll have to ask the chief about that."

"The police chief or the fire chief?" He looked like he wanted to turn the hose on me. "Come on, I'm not trying to be a pain in the ass. I just want to know who to ask, that's all."

"Fine," he said. "Go bother Chief Hill."

Wilfred Hill runs the G.P.D., which makes him Cody's boss. The guy is occasionally grumpy and he's no great fan of reporters, but he's always been fair. He also seems not to mind that one of his men is schtupping a member of the press corps, which goes a long way in my book.

Once I got back to the paper, I tried calling the chief's office, only to be told he was gone for the day. So I asked for the ranking officer on duty, and the next thing I knew I was talking to my boyfriend.

"Uh . . . hi," I said.

"Hey, baby. What's up?"

"Um . . . I actually was trying to get the chief."

"You dating him now too?"

"Come on, don't joke. This is official business."

"I see."

"And I'm officially not supposed to be covering you."

The sound he made didn't quite jibe with his wholesome image. "Sorry to hear that. Having you cover me would be—"

"You're awful."

"Sorry," he said, though he laughed when he said it. "What were you calling about, anyway?"

"I was just out covering this thing at Deep Lake."

"Yeah, I heard about that."

"Well, do you know what's up?"

"You mean on the record?"

"Yeah."

"No idea."

"What about off the record?"

"No idea, either."

"The fire lieutenant said I should call Chief Hill to find out what's going on."

"Chief Hill went home."

"No kidding. And I've got a deadline here."

"Look, I'll ask around and call you back, okay?"

"Better call Ochoa back, what with the conflict-of-interest thing and all." I gave him the number. "I'll give him a heads-up about it."

"Ochoa's not nearly as pretty as you are."

"You know," I said, "I'm sure there's a compliment in there if I just keep looking for it."

I filled Ochoa in on what was up, and when I dropped the problem on Bill's desk, he decided we should write the story under a joint byline.

Here's how it turned out:

By ALEX BERNIER & CAL OCHOA
Monitor Staff

Gabriel police investigators are still trying to identify the substance that contaminated the Deep Lake Cooling intake pool Thursday afternoon. According to fire lieutenant Paul Soper, the fire department was called to the scene at approximately 5:15 P.M. after workers at the Heat-Exchange Facility, located on East Shore Drive, reported seeing a bright red substance in the intake pool. "They called their supervisor and he was concerned enough to call us," Soper said.

In a press release delivered via fax to the *Monitor* newsroom Thursday evening, a group identifying itself as the Mohawk Warriors has claimed responsibility for the contamination. "We will not allow Benson and its corporate interests to rob us of our natural resources," the statement said. "Mohawk Lake must be protected at all costs."

More than a dozen firefighters responded to the scene, including several in full hazardous-material gear. Testing inside the building showed no indication of any dangerous chemicals or gases, Soper said. Although there is no reason to believe that workers are in danger, he said, the facility has been shut down pending analysis of the pool's water. Drawn directly from the bottom of the lake at a depth of 400 feet, the water remains a constant 38 degrees.

According to Detective Brian Cody of the Gabriel Police Department, the sample, described as a reddish liquid, is being stored at the police forensics lab and is scheduled for testing this morning (Friday). "Until we know what this is, we're taking the proper precautions," he said.

Owned and operated by Benson University, the Deep Lake Cooling facility provides air-conditioning for buildings and laboratories on campus by drawing chilled water from the bottom of Mohawk Lake. Four years in the making, the project is the first of its kind in the U.S. and only the second in the world. It started operation on Wednesday, when it was unveiled at an open house whose start was delayed by a blockade by about twenty protesters.

Glenn Shardik, the Benson engineer who designed the system, declined to speculate on whether the contamination might be related to the protests. "The system will be operating normally as soon as possible," Shardik said.

We filed the piece around eight, then went back to work on the drug stories. By the time we left, we needed a little chemical consolation of our own.

"What I want to know," Mad was saying from our usual window seat at the Citizen Kane, "is what kind of goddamn idiot puts that shit in their body."

He said this, by the way, while raising a shot of midpriced tequila to his lips. No one felt the need to point out the irony.

"Hey, come on," Ochoa said. "Kids like to try stuff. Always have, always will."

Mad turned the glass upside down to demonstrate his successful ingestion of every drop. "You saying you've done it?"

"Tried acid? Yeah, a couple times. In college."

"And?"

Ochoa shrugged. "Everything kinda glowed."

"That's it?"

"Colors were brighter; textures were richer; that kind of thing. I guess I didn't take that much. I never saw any sounds or anything."

I reached past Mad to the Beer Nuts. "What do you mean 'saw any sounds'?"

"It's this thing they say about acid," Ochoa said. "Some people feel like they can 'see sounds,' 'hear colors,' that sort of thing. It's all about altering your senses. That's the name of the game."

I drank my drink. "And you actually got into this?"

"Not really. I just dated this chick once who dug it, that's all. Thought I'd give it a try."

"No way I'd put that shit in this body," Mad said again, rolling up the sleeve of his blue oxford and flexing a bicep for dramatic effect. "I mean, come on. Who needs to mess with perfection?"

"And speaking of which," I said, "who needs to mess with seventeen-year-old girls?"

Mad turned a pair of comically wide eyes on Ochoa. "Oh, hey, perish the thought," he said. "Who'd ever want to do something like that?"

"Hey, not me," Ochoa said. "I insist the chick's gotta be at least a college freshman."

"Too bad, man," Mad said. "You don't know what you're missing."

"Jacob Ebenezer Madison," I said, "tell me you're not messing with that girl."

"Hey, she's just called me in the newsroom a couple of times, okay? I haven't laid a hand on her."

"Yeah, and you better not. The kid's all messed up and grief-stricken. She's not even thinking straight."

Ochoa flashed a crafty smile. "So maybe Madison here can help her feel all better. . . ."

"Mad," I said, "Lauren Potter isn't even old enough to vote."

He smiled back at Ochoa. "She will be in a week or so."

"Jesus," I said, "I need another drink. How about one of you two pedophiles go and get it for me?"

Ochoa rolled his eyes, but stood up. "What are you drinking again?"

"Maker's Mark and ginger ale."

"Sad waste of good bourbon," he said, and headed for the bar.

"Seriously, Mad," I said once Ochoa had gone, "are you actually thinking about screwing a high-school student?"

"Nah."

"Because this would be a new low, even for you."

"I said no, okay? Give me a break. The kid's half my age."

"Two minutes ago, you weren't making that sound like much of a liability."

He shrugged and poured himself a beer from the pitcher. "Guy talk."

"I hope that's all it is."

"Christ, Bernier, what do you care?"

"I have a hard time thinking a roll in the hay would do much good for either one of you."

Again with the carnivorous grin. "Might change her political views."

I started to stand up. "You're giving me a headache."

"Where are you going? I thought you said Cody was meeting you here later."

"I'll catch him on his cell."

"Come on, sit down. I'll be a good boy."

I half lowered myself back into my seat. "You promise?"

"Cross my heart. Besides, I've got a funny story for you."

"One that doesn't involve jailbait?" He stuck his tongue out at me. "Fine. What is it?"

"The crazy, mixed-up history of lysergic acid diethylamide."

"What?"

"LSD."

"Oh. What about it?"

"I found out some cool stuff today. Thought you might be interested."

"Give me a break," I said. "We've been dealing with this stuff all day."

"Yeah, but it's pretty fascinating."

"Science stuff?"

"You bet."

"Spare me. I've had enough with the Deep Lake Cooling thing."

"Speaking of which, what the hell's going on over there?"

"You read the story, right?"

"Yeah, but it didn't say much. Come on, Bernier, what do you think's really in the water?"

"Damned if I know. Shardik said it looked like blood."

"Are you serious?"

"That's what he said."

"What could account for that?"

"Honestly," I said, "I don't even want to think about it."

"Wimp."

"Fine. I think it was the goddamn protesters."

"Who, what? Sacrificed a chicken?"

"Have to be more than one chicken. There's, like, thousands of gallons of water in that pool. And besides, the chicken-sacrificing thing isn't what you'd call politically correct."

Ochoa arrived, carrying my drink in one hand and two tequila shots in the other. "What in the holy hell are you people talking about?"

I reached for my bourbon and ginger ale. "You're back fast."

"No line at the bar," he said. "Sweet."

"Yeah," I said. "Just wait until the upperclassmen get back."

Mad took the shot and dispatched it in one fluid move. "I bet Ochoa here'd like to hear a little bit about where his glowing . . . whatevers came from." Ochoa gave us a confused look. "History of LSD," Mad said.

"Cool," Ochoa said. "Lay it on me."

"Okay," Mad said, "the year is 1943. A Swiss chemist named Albert Hofmann is noodling around in his laboratory, working on synthesizing drugs from a plant-based substance called ergot. Now what, you may ask, is ergot?"

I took a liberal slug of the spiked ginger ale. "I can't imagine."

"Ergot is a fungus that grows on grain, mainly rye. During medieval times it killed a bunch of people—causes gangrene and convulsions, really nasty. Over the years it's had a few medicinal uses, and Hofmann starts working on it as . . . how did he put it . . . a 'respiratory and circulatory stimulant.' You following?" We nodded, and Mad stacked the empty shot glass atop the previous one. "So Hofmann synthesizes a bunch of ergot derivatives. One of them, code-named LSD-25, seems to have no use, so it gets dropped.

"But then, five years later, Hofmann has this hunch that there's more to it, so he whips up another batch. Somehow, he ingests a little of it, and he gets to feeling all funky. He has to go home because he feels really dizzy, starts seeing weird shapes and colors. He wonders just what the hell's going on. And, being a scientist and an all-around nut job, he decides to do an experiment on himself. He takes what he thinks is a minuscule dose of the stuff, a quarter of a milligram, and he just completely freaks out. Has your quintessential bad trip, like—this is my favorite part—he thinks the neighbor lady is an evil witch who wants to kill him.

"After a while, he calms down and starts to enjoy it. Starts seeing the sound of a car driving by, like Ochoa was saying. Anyway, by the time he calms down the next morning, he feels great—says breakfast never tasted so good. And voilà, the birth of LSD."

Ochoa raised his beer mug. "What a long, strange trip it's been."

"Now you gotta admit," Mad said, "that's some interesting shit."

"Yeah, you win," I said. "From rotting rye to freaking in the purple haze. Who'da thunk it?"

Mack, the bartender, appeared tableside then and told us Bill was on the phone for Ochoa. The phone number for the Citizen Kane is, after all, noted prominently on the newsroom call list.

Ochoa went behind the bar and picked up the red handset, whose long cord allows it to reach even to the farthest stool. He talked for all of two minutes before he came back to the table and drained his beer. He didn't look happy.

"This is the most unbelievable goddamn day."

I took my feet off the seat of his chair, but he made no move to sit down. "What's up?"

"I gotta get back to the paper."

Mad refilled his mug. "Come on, have one for the road."

"Better not."

"What the hell's going on?"

"Source of mine called the newsroom looking for me."

Mad leaned back in his chair. "So the hell what?"

"Somebody at the coroner's office. Apparently, they're finally gonna announce what was in the acid that killed those three kids."

"And?"

"I don't know the whole story. I haven't even talked to the source yet."

"Come on," I said. "He must've said something to get Bill's knickers all twisty. What's up?"

"What this person told him," Ochoa said, "was that according to the evidence, it's looking like those accidental deaths were no damn accident."

CHAPTER 12

Ochoa's sentence sent all three of us scrambling back to the newsroom, with me simultaneously jogging and dialing Cody on my cell phone. I told him I had to run back to work and I'd call him when I was done; he said he'd just as soon stay at the station for a while longer. (One of the advantages of dating a cop, by the way, is that they're in no position to complain about you working crazy hours, since theirs are inevitably even crazier.)

As soon as we got up the stairs, Ochoa sprinted for his Rolodex. Mad and I went into Bill's office, where we found the occupant reading a story and nibbling on a dumpling he'd impaled on a chopstick.

"Gang's all here, eh?"

I eyed his take-out carton. "Those things vegetarian?"

He shook his head and smirked. "Pork and shrimp shumai." He finished off the dumpling and impaled another. "Where's Ochoa?"

"Went straight to the phone. Who's this source, anyway?"

"Damned if I know. Lady wouldn't give me her name."

"What did she say?"

"To tell Ochoa the coroner's office finally figured out what killed the kids, and no way was it an accident. Gave him a heads-up on the press conference tomorrow afternoon."

"Which blows our deadline but works just fine for TV."

"What else is new?"

Mad reached for one of the dumplings, and Bill warned him off with a threatening chopstick. Mad then announced he was starving, whereupon Bill told him to go over to Schultz's and get himself a turkey sandwich.

Mad allowed that this wasn't a bad idea; he got back just as Ochoa was getting off the phone. The four of us convened in Bill's office, where Mad made a show of offering around a bag of fat-free potato chips.

"Some people," he said, "like to share."

"Kiss my ass," said Bill, and grabbed up a handful of chips.

Ochoa took some too, balancing them against his chest as he flipped pages in his reporter's notebook.

"Okay, it's like this," he said. "We're screwed."

Bill scowled and chomped a potato chip. "Screwed how?"

"She spilled her guts, but off the record."

"So we confirm it with another source and run it unattrib—"

Ochoa shook his head. "I mean *off*-off. *Way off*. As in not for publication."

"So why the fuck did she even bother telling you?"

"She wanted to give me a heads-up."

"Can't you get her to—"

"Said if she leaked it on the record and it got traced back to her, she'd get canned for sure. I had to swear up and down we wouldn't run anything tomorrow."

"Terrific."

"But I figured if we got the lowdown ahead of time, we could at least flesh out the story a whole lot more. I mean, sure, the TV guys'll have the bare bones on the air tomorrow night, but we'll have the jump on them. We can put together a kick-ass package for Saturday—our first-day story'd come off like a second-day story. You know, not just reporting the coroner's finding but really getting into the—"

"Thanks, man, but I know what a goddamn second-day story is, okay?"

"Hey, don't get pissed at me," Ochoa said. "If it weren't for my source, we wouldn't even know what we were in for tomorrow."

"Yeah, yeah," Bill said, rubbing at his temples with his chip-free hand. "So come on, let's hear it. What did she tell you?"

Ochoa finished chewing and took a deep breath. "All right," he said, "apparently LSD is made from this stuff called ergo . . ." He squinted at his notebook. "Ergo . . ."

Mad offered him the chip bag for a refill. "Ergotamine tartrate."

"That's it." Ochoa shook his head at the chips. "Anyway, I guess it doesn't take a whole lot of it to make the drug. Like—"

"Like a half pound of the stuff is enough for a million doses."

I tossed a chip in Mad's direction. "Show-off."

"Just doing my homework, baby."

"Like I was saying," Ochoa said, "each dose of LSD only contains a very small amount of ergotamine. And that stuff itself is a pretty potent poison. Madison was telling us earlier about how it killed a lot of people whose grain got infected with it or something. . . ."

"Jesus," Bill said, "when was this?"

"Middle Ages."

Bill slumped back in his chair. "Like I care."

"Anyway," Ochoa went on, "nowadays a derivative of it is used to treat migraines. But if you take a whole lot of it, it can cause all sorts of shit—messes with your blood pressure, gives you clots, seizures, coma, you name it."

Bill's eyebrows went up. "And it can kill you?"

"If you ingest enough of it, yeah."

"But you just said each dose of LSD only has a tiny amount of it."

"It's supposed to. But this stuff didn't."

"So why does that mean that it didn't happen by accident? Like, couldn't somebody have just put too much of—"

"According to my source, not too goddamn likely."

"I don't get it."

"Neither did I," Ochoa said, "but she explained it to me like this: If you're baking a cake and you put in an extra cup of sugar, it just means you're a little careless. If you put in two extra cups, you're *really* careless. If you put in an extra garbage can full, you did it on purpose."

"We're talking that kind of ratio?"

"Yeah. Plus, she said that nobody who makes LSD throws around their . . ." He looked back down at his notebook.

"Ergotamine tartrate," Mad said with a grin.

". . . their ergotamine tartrate lightly. It's their main ingredient, and they definitely can't waltz in and buy it at the drugstore. It mostly gets smuggled in from overseas."

Bill leaned back and put his feet up on the desk. "So why did it take so goddamn long for the coroner to come up with this?"

"Apparently, the guy just couldn't believe what he was seeing. He thought his equipment was out of whack or something. I mean, that kind of ergotamine level is totally unheard of."

"So why the hell did they release anything?"

"Well, they knew for sure they were dealing with LSD, so they could announce that much and everybody could concentrate on stopping people from taking it. But when it came to the contaminant, the doc wanted to send it out to a couple of independent labs for confirmation."

"And now it's confirmed."

"That's what they're gonna say at the press conference tomorrow."

"Wonderful. Where's it gonna be?"

"At the G.P.D. station."

That got my attention. "Not out in Jaspersburg? I thought Chief Stilwell was being all protective about the case."

"Probably doesn't have much choice," Ochoa said. "Jaspersburg Town Hall's a little small. Plus, the county coroner's based in Gabriel, so there you go."

"Not to mention," said Mad, "that this guy's gonna need all the help he can get."

Bill took a swig of his iced chai and wiped his mouth with the back of his hand. "So let me get this straight. We're saying that these three kids were killed on purpose."

Ochoa looked at him like he was suffering from the mental equivalent of narcolepsy. "Um . . . That's the general idea."

"Then . . . *why?*"

The question hung there for a while. Finally, I decided to take a bite. "What if it's like the Tylenol poisonings back in the eighties? You know, some kind of random thing by a sicko."

Mad's eyebrow went back up. "A sicko who knows enough chemistry to mess with the levels of ergotamine tartrate in their LSD?"

"I guess that would be the job description, yeah. Some kind of mad scientist maybe."

"Benson's got plenty of those." The three of us stared at him. "Hey, I'm *kidding*."

"Seriously," Ochoa said, "how much know-how would it take?"

Mad shrugged. "Probably not a whole hell of a lot. Most LSD is made in small batches in people's houses, for chrissake. Doesn't seem like a huge leap from there to upping the ergotamine levels—not like you'd need a Ph.D. or anything."

"Talk about sick," Bill said. "Some son of a bitch whips up a batch of this stuff and puts it on the market and just sits back and waits for people to die so he can get his ya-yas off on it. Unbelievable."

"Maybe," I said. "But not unprecedented."

"So like Ochoa said before, we're screwed on the deadline. Only thing we can do is try to come out with all guns blazing on Saturday." He turned to Mad. "You've been doing research for this package of Marilyn's, right?"

"Yeah."

"Great. Now it's running on Saturday. And don't expect Alex to help you. She's going to be busy."

"I am?"

"Those kids' parents want more coverage, fine," Bill said. "They're gonna get it. But I'm pretty damn sure they're not gonna like it."

IT WAS AFTER NINE by the time I finally met Cody for dinner at our usual Indian place, which is fifty steps from the newspaper and maybe forty from the cop shop. The restaurant has a line of booths along the front window, but we never sit there. Although our little romance has been out of the bag for a while now, we figure we might as well not advertise it to everybody who fills up at the Gas 'n' Snack across the street.

"Hungry?" he said, once I'd inhaled half of a giant papadum dipped in mint chutney.

"A gentleman wouldn't notice."

"Ah. My mistake."

"So how was your day, dear?"

He stared down at the menu. "So . . . what do you feel like having?"

"Sly way of changing the subject."

"I'm like a cat."

"Yeah, well, don't bother playing all cool," I said. "I already know."

"Know what?"

"Know the thing you're not supposed to talk about, but you were gonna wind up telling me anyway because we promised each other from day one we weren't gonna play that game."

"Oh, right." He finally looked up, and I could swear there was an actual twinkle in those ridiculously green eyes of his. "That."

"That."

"You want to order first?"

"Cody, I swear I'm gonna—"

"The waitress is hovering."

I stopped glaring at him and looked over. "Oh."

We ordered the vegetable korma for me, chicken curry for him, and assorted vegetarian appetizers to split, plus a double order of nan.

"So," I said, once I'd slurped up the better part of a mango lassi, "how was your day, dear?"

"Stunk."

"Sorry to hear it. And why would that be?"

"That would be because some nut decided to whip up a batch of killer LSD and push it just over the line from my jurisdiction."

"Which means . . . ?"

"That this stuff is out there and there's not a lot I can do about it."

"Chief Stilwell's still being all territorial? You gotta be kidding me."

He shook his head and took a drink of his Kingfisher. From what

I could tell, he was probably going to need several more before the night was over. "Not anymore, no. I think he knows that was a major screwup, but . . . truth is, I can understand the instinct. Cops have been known to be macho."

"You don't say."

"Not that I've experienced this personally"—he winked at me, which is something that only he can get away with without a black eye—"but I think it's been known to occur."

"So if Stilwell's willing to play with the other kids, how come you're on the sidelines?"

"Because the deaths happened in Jaspersburg. That means the Jaspersburg cops have jurisdiction; the county sheriff has jurisdiction; the staties have jurisdiction; the D.E.A. has jurisdiction; the F.B.I. has jurisdiction. . . ."

"Everybody but you." He gave a single nod. "Poor baby. Well, maybe Stilwell'll ask for help."

"Nobody's going to ask the Gabriel P.D. for help when the D.E.A. is sniffing around. We're kind of small potatoes. All we get to do is try and figure out how somebody vandalized the Deep Lake Cooling plant. Very damn exciting."

"It's enough to drive an Irish cop from Boston to drink."

He raised his glass with a grin. "Yeah, well, that doesn't take much."

"Poor baby."

"How'd you find out about all this, anyway?"

"Source of Ochoa's tipped him off. Any idea how the investigation's going to go?"

He shrugged. "Depends."

"Well, what would you do if you were in charge?" He shrugged again. "Come on, don't tell me you haven't thought about it. My guess is you've been obsessing about it for the past two weeks."

He concentrated on his half of the papadum, which indicated I'd nailed him but good. "Well . . . maybe I've been giving it a little thought."

"Maybe doing a little more than just thinking?"

"Okay . . . I did have a couple of conversations with a couple of individuals."

"Which translates from the Cop-to-English dictionary as 'I shook down every drug dealer in town and told them if they know who sold this crap, they better tell me.'"

"Something like that."

"And?"

"And nothing."

"Bummer."

"Yeah. But to answer your question, if I were in charge of this . . . Well, first I'd call Stilwell and his men on the carpet for the botch job they did during the festival, letting everybody take off without getting any names. Then I'd acknowledge the fact that there probably isn't a lot of acid getting made in Jaspersburg, New York, and concentrate on where it most likely came from."

"Which is?"

"A metro area. That's where this junk usually gets made, but there's an exception to that rule, which is big college towns."

"And Gabriel isn't a big town, but it's got a big college."

"Right."

"But I thought you already—"

"I did what I could do to try and keep this garbage out of Gabriel, but it hasn't been much. There's only so far I can go when we're not even officially in on the investigation."

"So you think this stuff was really made in Gabriel?"

"It's a possibility, but I'd say it's even more likely that it was made somewhere else and sold through somebody here. Gabriel's a pretty big market for your softer drugs—mostly LSD, ecstasy, and pot. Practically nothing in the way of coke or heroin. But then again, there were people from all over the place at that festival—your story said some of them had even driven cross-country to get there, right? So the truth is, it could've come from anywhere."

"What do you make of what the coroner's office found—the fact that there was so much ergotamine tartrate in there?"

"I never officially worked narcotics, so I don't have a lot of first-hand experience, but I made some phone calls. Apparently, this is just off the charts."

The appetizers came then, and we each grabbed a samosa. I doused mine in tamarind sauce and ate it with my fingers.

"So what you're saying," I said when I'd come up for air, "is that as far as drug enforcement goes, this is pretty much unprecedented."

"Yeah."

"And there's really no way it could've been an accident? Like maybe some kind of production screwup?"

"Hard to see how. According to the M.E., it's kind of an order-of-magnitude thing."

"I heard that too. So you really think there's any hope they'll catch who did it?"

He shrugged and reached for a pakora. "If an investigation gets screwed up at the beginning, a lot of times it can be pretty hard to salvage it later. If it were up to me, I'd have those kids' friends in the interview room for as long as it takes."

"I think their parents might object. Their lawyers too."

"Yeah, and then what are they going to say if another kid dies?"

"Besides, I heard they'd already talked to the cops more than once—that their parents were making them cooperate."

"That's all well and good, but it's got its limitations. You ask a kid questions in front of his parents, there's only so much you're going to get."

"You think they know more than they're telling?"

"Of course they do," Cody said. "They're teenagers."

CHAPTER *13*

It just so happened that the adolescents in question were supposed to be the focus of my Friday. While Ochoa dealt with the cop stuff and Mad wrote about the freaky details of LSD, I was told to come up with something about youth culture—or, to put it more baldly, *drug* culture.

Now, I know that sounds like a dangerously general assignment, and it was. Frankly, I had no idea where to start, or whether anybody would possibly talk to me on the record.

So . . . I called Lauren Potter and asked if I could take her to lunch. She made noises about wanting to meet me in the news-room—three guesses what the attraction was—but I made some excuse about why I needed to meet her at the sandwich shop instead.

She showed up at Schultz's at eleven-thirty, wearing yet another hippie sundress; this one was lemon yellow with moons and stars batiked onto it. Her hair was up in a bun again, and it struck me that I couldn't remember any teenage girls affecting that sort of granny hairdo when I was her age. Then again, since I entered adolescence in the era of leg warmers and cut-neck sweatshirts, I probably shouldn't talk.

Lauren may have been right on time, but she wasn't alone; Trish was with her, the ugly duckling to offset Lauren's swan.

"Trish was dying to get out of J-burg, so I asked her along," Lauren said. "Hope you don't mind."

"That's okay," I said. "How're you two doing?"

They both shrugged and sat down.

"Okay, I guess," Lauren said. "School starts pretty soon, though."

"You're not that excited about going back?"

"It's just, you know . . . it's gonna feel weird to go back without Tom and Billy and Shaun."

"Right, of course. Sorry."

"We're gonna . . . I talked to some other kids from our class, and we're gonna try and do some big memorial thing. We don't know what yet. We're gonna form a committee."

"That sounds like a good idea."

"I guess."

"Are you hungry?"

Lauren nodded, and Trish copied her without much enthusiasm.

"What's this place all about, anyway?" Lauren looked around the room, festooned with plastic salamis and cheeses. "I've never been here before."

"Schultz's? Best sandwiches in Gabriel. Really good homemade pickles too. And I totally dig the rice pudding, as long as Frau Schultz doesn't throw raisins into it."

"*Nein* raisins," a Teutonic voice bellowed from behind the counter.

"*Danke schön*," I yelled back, then turned to the girls. "I'm kind of a regular."

I ordered my usual Swiss cheese monstrosity on rye with extra honey mustard, while Lauren went for a Reuben and Trish a turkey on white, no mayo. Lauren and I went for the rice pudding. As always, the food came with almost incomprehensible speed.

"Thanks for coming out here to meet me," I said.

"No problem," Lauren said through a mouthful of sauerkraut. "What did you want to talk to us about?"

"Why don't we finish eating first? That okay with you?"

Trish shrugged and took a minuscule bite of her sandwich. "Whatever," Lauren said, and scooped up a handful of potato chips.

"Hey, Alex," she said a minute later. "I was kind of wondering . . . how's your friend Jake doing?"

"Jake?" I was roused from the love affair I was having with one of Frau Schultz's pickles. "Oh, you mean Mad. He's okay, I guess."

"Does he, you know . . . have a girlfriend?"

"He dates."

"Yeah, but is he, like, being monogamous with anybody or any-thing?"

The temptation to invent a jealous fiancée was mighty, but in the end, I couldn't see the point. "Not as far as I know."

"Oh." She looked positively carnivorous, and not just because she was eating corned beef.

"Listen, Lauren, I'm not sure if you know this, but Mad is a lot older than you are. A whole lot older."

Her lips formed a Mona Lisa smile. "That's okay. I like older guys."

"Yeah, but he's something like twice your age. So if you're think-ing you'd like to, you know, go out with him or something, it's prob-ably not a good idea. I mean, I don't think your parents would approve."

Trish snorted. Lauren just kept smiling. "I doubt they'd notice," she said.

"Why do you think that?"

"They're busy. As long as I get good grades, they pretty much leave me alone."

"That's too bad."

"Are you nuts?"

For what felt like the hundredth time, I contemplated the chasm between seventeen and twenty-seven. I didn't have a whole lot of time to think about it, though, because Lauren kept peppering me with questions about Mad, and it took all my concentration to dodge them.

Finally, when she'd finished her sandwich and it'd become appar-ent that Trish wasn't going to ingest more than a quarter of hers, I de-cided it was time to talk for real.

"Listen," I said, "there's something I have to tell you guys."

Lauren looked up from the plastic spoon she'd been denuding of rice pudding. "Um . . . okay. What's up?"

"It's about Tom and Billy. And Shaun."

Trish, who'd been zoning out during the Mad confab, finally seemed to focus. "What about them?"

"There's going to be a press conference this afternoon, and then something's going to break on the local news tonight. I wanted to talk to you about some other stuff too for this story I have to do about youth culture. But . . . I thought you guys ought to have a heads-up."

Lauren looked like she was starting to get testy. "A heads-up about what?"

I took a deep breath. I'm not sure why this was getting to me so much, but suddenly the pudding I'd jammed down on top of the half pound of Swiss cheese wasn't sitting so well.

"It's . . . They're finally releasing the details of the autopsy results. And apparently . . . the feeling is that their deaths weren't an accident."

I'm not sure what kind of reaction I was expecting, but I didn't get it. If anything, they both just looked perplexed. I kept talking.

"What I mean to say is . . . it looks like this happened on purpose. Somebody mixed up the batch of LSD in a particular way so that whoever took it would die."

Lauren laughed, which totally threw me.

"That's completely nuts," she said. "Somebody's gotta be playing a joke on you."

"I'm afraid not. The evidence sounds pretty solid."

She just stared at me for a minute; then her face flip-flopped from comedy to tragedy so fast it was almost funny. Almost, but not quite. "Oh, my . . . That's . . . Oh, my God . . ."

Trish, who was plenty pale to begin with, appeared to have gone a shade whiter. "You mean . . . somebody killed them on purpose?"

"Based on the chemistry of what was found in their systems, there's pretty much no way it wasn't intentional."

Lauren's eyes widened. "You mean some sick freak *poisoned* them?"

"Um . . . I guess that's what it looks like."

"But who'd do something like that?"

"I don't know. Do you think—"

"I mean, what kind of crazy maniac goes and kills a bunch of kids they don't even know?" There was an undertone of fury in her voice. "What kind of person would do that?"

"And you don't have any idea who they might've gotten the LSD from?"

"I told you," Lauren said. "Shaun always got that stuff. We'd tell him what we wanted and he'd know where to get it."

"But you don't know where *he* got it?"

Lauren shrugged. "I didn't really want to know."

"Trish?"

"I . . . I don't know. I never . . . I haven't done it in a long time. I kind of gave it up a while ago."

"Really? How come?"

"Um . . . I had this eating problem for a while."

"You mean . . . anorexia?"

"Yeah."

Now there's a shocker, I thought, but I just nodded and tried to look sympathetic.

"So after I got, you know, diagnosed . . . I had to go to this hospital to get help for it. And while I was in there, I didn't take anything, and once I came out, I just never started again."

"How come?"

"I didn't really want to anymore, I guess."

"That's good, right?"

She shrugged, which seemed to be her all-around expression. "I guess."

"And you guys really have no idea where Shaun would've gotten the drugs?"

"I told you," Lauren said, "I never really asked."

"Do you even have a guess?"

She picked up the plastic spoon again, and the business end went *whack-whack-whack* on the tabletop. "Only that . . . I guess he must've got it from somebody in Gabriel."

"Why do you say that?"

"Well, nobody sells in J-burg, and he didn't go anyplace else." *Whack-whack-whack.* "He was working a lot of hours doing computer stuff at Benson, most weekends too, so he didn't go down to the city or anything."

"And you have no idea who his dealer was?"

"I already told you no," Lauren said. "How many times do I have to say it?"

We spent the next hour ostensibly talking about my "youth culture" story, and they gave me some anecdotes I could use as long as their names were withheld. But let's face it: The deaths were the proverbial elephant in the room. No matter what we talked about, the conversation kept returning to what happened to Tom, Billy, and Shaun.

"Let me ask you this," I said. "When you were taking something, did it ever occur to you that something bad could happen?"

Yet another pair of shrugs.

"Not really," Lauren said. "I mean, people try to shove that 'Just say no' crap down your throat, but nobody takes it seriously. Like, Officer Friendly comes and does the D.A.R.E. thing, and all he's got to say is 'Drugs are bad, bad, bad.' Like, how stupid do they think we are?"

"Meaning?"

"People talk as if alcohol isn't a drug, or cigarettes. Even a cup of coffee is a drug, right? So obviously things aren't as black and white as they say they are."

"So you never worried that what you were taking might hurt you?"

"Like I told you, we never took anything big. Just some recreational stuff—smoked some weed, did some E and some 'shrooms and a little acid." She spoke slowly, purposefully, like she was giving a speech for the debate club. "That stuff's no more dangerous than drinking a beer. No way is it like snorting coke or doing heroin or something crazy like that. People try to lump it all in together, but it's not the same thing."

"So you're saying you'd never try those other drugs?"

"What are you, nuts?" she said. "That stuff'll *kill* you."

NEWS OF THE BOYS' not-so-accidental deaths hit the local airwaves promptly at six. We all stood around the newsroom television and watched the video of the press conference, Ochoa eyeballing a slightly overexposed version of himself as the Nine News camera swung around to capture him asking a question about the progress of the investigation.

The press conference had been run by Chief Stilwell, who looked like he was way out of his league. The guy wasn't what you'd call media savvy; he came across looking impatient and uncomfortable, like the school nerd who'd suddenly been asked to dance with the prom queen. There was a much smoother guy on his right, who turned out to be some regional muckety-muck for the D.E.A., and who definitely knew which way the camera was pointing.

The nadir of the thing came when some lip-glossed minion from the Syracuse FOX station adopted an absurdly empathetic tone of voice and asked Stilwell a whopping sob-sister of a question.

"Chief Stilwell," she said, "can you believe this happened in your town?"

The camera had been focused on a three-shot of Stilwell, the D.E.A. guy, and the county coroner, a gaunt, gray-haired Benson med school professor who rather looks the part. Slowly, they panned in on a tight shot of the chief, who looked like he was debating between answering the question and eating his service revolver.

"No," he said finally. "No, I can't believe it."

"Would you care to elaborate?"

The chief winced so noticeably that even the Nine News low-rent camera picked it up. The D.E.A. officer leaned in and whispered something in his ear, and the chief's jaw clenched. It occurred to me that whoever the reporter was, she'd better not speed through Stilwell's jurisdiction anytime soon.

"Jaspersburg has always been a great little town," Stilwell said finally. "It's still a great little town. But before, I guess we always thought . . . We thought we were immune from some of the things that happen in big cities. We thought we could let our kids go out with their friends and have a good time and they'd come home safe."

His voice cracked a little. The camera panned in closer.

"But now we know that isn't necessarily true. We have to be on guard, to protect our young people from things that might hurt them, things that they don't even understand might hurt them. We have to teach them that . . . that even though it's important to trust people, sometimes too much trust can be a dangerous thing. I guess the bottom line is, we have to admit that the world isn't the same as it was when we were kids. And . . . I guess that's a hard thing to know."

The newscast cut abruptly from Stilwell's last sentence to a shot of the Nine News reporter standing outside the Gabriel Criminal Justice building—editing never having been the station's strong suit. The reporter signed off, and the screen flashed a phone number for anyone with information about the three deaths.

We all went back to staring at our respective computer screens—Ochoa working on his news story, Mad on the science angle, me on the ridiculous color piece. Lauren and Trish had, unsurprisingly, been unwilling to give me specific names of other friends I could interview, but they said they'd ask around and if anyone wanted to talk they'd have them call me. The phone wasn't ringing.

I was pondering crawling into Bill's office to tell him there was no way the story was going to come together in time for the next day's paper when Ochoa's phone rang. He answered it, and five seconds later, it was obvious something was up.

"Holy shit," he was saying, "are you sure? When?" He listened for a while. "And you're positive about this?" Another pause. "When are they announcing it? Not until then?" He grabbed for a notebook and started scribbling furiously. "Don't worry, I can get it confirmed from down there. You're totally out of it. Yeah, I promise. Thanks for letting me know." He listened for another few seconds, and I could swear he was starting to blush. "Yeah . . . I'd like that, but I'm gonna be here pretty late tonight. Really? Okay, how about midnight? All right. See you then."

He hung up, then kept jotting down notes until I threatened to throttle him.

"Come on, man," Mad said, "What the hell is going on?"

"That was my source in the coroner's office."

"The one," I said, "that you're obviously having a drink with later."

"Hey, a guy's gotta do what a guy's gotta do."

"Poor baby. So what'd she tell you?"

"You sure you want to know? Or would you rather break my balls for a while?"

"It's tempting."

Mad wadded up a pink message note and threw it at me. "Would you two just get a room already?" He turned to Ochoa. "So come on, what the hell's up?"

"Okay, so obviously her boss was over at the press conference this afternoon, right? And apparently when he got back, there was this urgent message from some doctor in Baltimore who wanted him to send everything he had on the stuff that killed those kids. And guess why."

He'd addressed the challenge to me, so I answered it. "Because there's another one."

"You got it," he said. "But this one's still alive."

CHAPTER *14*

The girl's name was Norma Jean Kramer. Her mother, as we'd later find out, had given her Marilyn Monroe's original moniker in the hope that her daughter would grow up to be a beauty queen. That hadn't worked out so well, to say the least. At nearly nineteen, Norma Jean Kramer tipped the scales at 220 pounds. It proved to be something of a blessing, though. Her weight, plus the fact that she'd only taken half a tab of the acid, very probably saved her life.

But just barely. At the moment, the young woman was comatose in a hospital in Baltimore. Whether she'd ever come out of it was anybody's guess.

What, you may ask, could possibly have possessed her to take the drug, considering what had happened to the three boys?

The short answer is that she almost certainly didn't know.

She'd left Melting Rock on Friday night, because the next morning she and a friend had tickets to fly to Orlando on a trip that was a high-school graduation present from their parents. She'd spent the next week riding on the Jungle Boat and taking pictures with Pluto. If any stories about the deaths filtered that far south, they completely passed her by. Besides, her friends said later, Norma Jean wasn't the type to watch the news.

Our piece about her hit the paper Saturday morning, a scoop that let us recover a little dignity after the previous day's humiliation. Ochoa had gotten confirmation on the record from the authorities in Baltimore, who didn't seem the least bit inclined to try to muzzle the story. To the contrary, actually: The case proved that more of the killer acid was floating around, and everybody—including Norma Jean's hysterical parents—wanted to get the word out.

Running the story also had some benefit for yours truly: It meant that my color piece got overset to Tuesday. It might've run on Monday, but the paper's overtime budget was already getting blown to hell. The four-day weekends I was promised in recompense for covering Melting Rock never materialized, and there was no way Bill could afford to schedule me to work the weekend.

So after crawling into bed after deadline (and, naturally, a post-deadline visit to the Citizen Kane) on Friday night, I woke up Saturday morning with two days of leisure stretching gloriously ahead. I almost didn't know what to do with myself.

It did occur to me that it might be a good idea to get some exercise, but I ignored the instinct in favor of thumbing through *Vanity Fair* in bed with Shakespeare. I read stories about rich people, murdered people, and rich people who'd been murdered, and while I did it, I ingested several cups of coffee and a giant bowl of Banana Nut Crunch. Eventually, this level of sloth became too much even for me, so I put on some sweats and took that most fabulous of all pooches for a walk around the neighborhood.

It was a gorgeous day, sunny and not too humid, so I forced myself to don my biking gear and go out for a spin. I've never been the type who loves exercise—the concept of a runner's high strikes me as a textbook example of self-delusion—but I do enjoy my feed, and I'd just as soon not turn out like Norma Jean Kramer. So I shake my booty now and again, and lately the mountain bike has seemed like the least agonizing way to do it. Not that I go up any mountains, mind you; the last time I tried that, I found a strangled corpse in the woods and nearly cracked my head open. This girl sticks to the pavement nowadays, thank you very much.

I went for a ten-mile toodle around the periphery of the city, avoiding hills to the extent that it's possible around here. I got back home around one and found Cindy Bauer sitting on my front porch.

She looked surprisingly okay for a girl who was supposedly grief-stricken and traumatized. The reason, however, turned out to be not so much her own innate emotional stability as a hefty dose of Paxil.

Still, she didn't exactly look normal. She'd laid on thick swaths of eyeliner, and they gave her eyes a weirdly startled expression. Her purple hair had grown out, maybe just half an inch, but the contrast with her natural color (pale blond) made it obvious. Said hair was hanging straight down, parted in the middle but unevenly, and the whole effect was of someone who had no idea what they looked like to other people. In short, an adolescent.

"Hi," I said, still panting as I wheeled my bike into the little shed next to the house. "Are you waiting for me?"

"Yeah, I . . . Your roommate said I could wait inside, but I didn't feel like it."

"Melissa's up?"

"I think I woke her. I'm really sorry. . . ."

"Don't worry about it. She stayed out kind of late last night. Do you want to come in?"

"I . . . Um, it's kind of nice outside. Can we stay out here? I haven't been outside a lot lately."

"Sure. Just let me run in and get a drink. Do you want something?"

She shook her head. I went in and got two cans of diet Sprite and some raspberry-filled granola bars, in case she changed her mind. The pair of us settled onto the ancient porch swing, which had been one of the house's major selling points but which Melissa and I rarely had time to use. Shakespeare, who'd followed me back outside, stretched out on the wooden floor and watched us glide back and forth; the expression on her face said humans were strange creatures indeed.

"So," I said, "how come you came by?"

Cindy looked panicky all of a sudden. "Isn't it okay?"

"Sure. I was just wondering why."

The panicked look left her face, but it still took her maybe two full minutes to answer.

"Um . . . I heard Alan talking on the phone with Lauren about how you were writing an article about . . . I guess about kids who take, you know . . . who take stuff. It kind of made me want to talk to you. But I wouldn't want you to put my name in the paper or anything."

Story of my life. "That's okay. I figured a lot of the interviews for this one would be anonymous."

I stopped the swing from moving and stood up.

"Where are you going?"

"I just have to get my notebook."

"Oh."

"I'll be back in thirty seconds." I was. "Okay," I said, "what did you want to talk about?" She didn't say anything, just watched the cars going by as the swing went *squeak-squeak-squeak.* She stayed like that until I couldn't stand it anymore. "Cindy?"

"Maybe I shouldn't have come here. Maybe it wasn't such a good idea."

"Listen," I said, trying to sound as comforting as I could muster, "you obviously have something on your mind. You'll probably feel a lot better if you just go ahead and tell me."

Another excruciating pause. "It's just that . . . I never thought it would be like that."

"Be like what?"

"Be so . . ." Her voice cracked, and tears started running down her pudgy cheeks. "I always thought it was just for fun, you know? I never thought something that awful would ever happen."

"You mean Shaun?" She nodded. "That's what you wanted to talk to me about?"

"My parents . . . They just look at me like I'm *broken,* you know? And all they have to do is figure out a way to fix me and everything'll be okay. But it *won't* . . ."

Her voice trailed off into a sniffle. I waited for her to say something else, but she didn't.

"I heard you might not want to go back to Jaspersburg High."

She spun around to face me. "That's not me; that's *them.* I want to go back, but they don't think it's . . . What do they keep saying? That it's not a healthy environment for me. But I just . . . I just want things to be back the way they were."

She swiped at the tears and dried the back of her hand on her T-shirt. Her eyeliner was running, so she looked like a cross between a raccoon and a circus clown.

"Do you want me to get you some Kleenex?"

She shook her head. "They took me to see this doctor and he gave me some medicine, and I guess it's good for me, but . . . I just keep seeing it."

"Seeing Shaun?"

She nodded, wiping at her runny nose. "It was just so *horrible*. And they don't even want me to talk about it. They wouldn't even let Chief Stilwell interview me like he did with Alan. They keep telling me it's not healthy to think about it. God, I hate that word so much."

I put a hand on her knee. It was covered by the hem of her loose denim shorts; below, her pale legs were covered with blond stubble. "They probably have no clue how to deal," I said. "Do you think, you know, maybe you could talk to a therapist or something?"

"Some people said I should. Like, the guidance counselor from school called and I guess she said that. But my folks don't want to send me to that kind of doctor. They don't want me to go to the kind where you talk about stuff. They just want to send me to the kind that gives you pills. Like I can take a pill and just have everything be okay. . . ."

"What about your brother, Alan? Can he help you deal with your folks?"

"Alan is like . . . He acts like he's all strong and everything, but he's all flipped out too. I mean, you can't blame him, right? He lost three of his friends just like that—one, two, three."

She counted them off on her fingers, then seemed vaguely appalled with herself for doing it. Her moist hand fell to her lap.

"How has Alan been doing?"

"He works out."

"What?"

"All he does is go to the gym, go running, practice soccer. He says it's because he wants to be good this season so he can get a scholarship, but I think it's just . . . what he needs to do. I don't know."

"And what do you need to do?"

The tears started up again. "I don't know. But just . . . not *this*. I can't take it anymore. I can't stand Mom and Dad going around like nothing ever happened, like if they just ignore it and fix me somehow and send me off to some Catholic school it'll go away. But how am I supposed to ignore it? How am I supposed to forget . . . what I saw?"

"Have you talked to anyone about it?"

"Just Lauren, a little. But I don't think she can take it, because . . . well, because the same thing happened to Tom. She can't stand to think about it."

"The two of them were really close, weren't they?"

She snuffled up a great quantity of whatever was running out of her nose, and when she spoke again, she sounded calmer, like she was being tranquilized by the change of subject.

"Lauren really loved him," she said. "Not like in a romantic way— she doesn't go out with high-school boys. But they were best friends. I think if she'd been into it, Tom would've gone out with her in a heartbeat, but he didn't blame her for not wanting to or anything."

"What about Dorrie and Trish? Can you talk to them?"

"They're kind of closer with each other than they are with me and Lauren. But when I heard Alan talking to Lauren about the story you're writing, I thought maybe . . ." Her voice trailed off, and she seemed embarrassed all of a sudden. "Maybe it was a stupid idea."

"No, it's not. Go ahead."

"Well . . . I thought maybe I could talk to you."

"Sure you can."

"And you'd want to put it in the paper?"

"That kind of depends on what you say."

She took a deep breath. "Do you think maybe I could have that Kleenex now?"

I went in to get the box, and I was half afraid she'd be gone by the time I came back out. But there she was, swinging on the creaky bench, her mind obviously two weeks and ten miles away from my front porch.

I gave her the tissues, and she blew her nose into a handful of them. Then she wiped at her eyes, and when she balled up the paper, her hands were smeared with black. I offered her a soda, and she took it and popped it open. But she tried to drink it too fast and spent another minute or so coughing into her fist.

"You probably think I'm a total weirdo," she said, once she'd caught her breath.

"Not at all."

"Really?"

It was only one word, but it was delivered so plaintively I had to quell the instinct to hug the poor girl.

"Really."

"You mean it?"

"Actually, you remind me a little of myself when I was your age."

She stared at me, mouth agape. "But you're so smart and pretty."

Now I *really* wanted to hug her.

"Trust me, Cindy. Being a teenager is the worst. It's all downhill from here. Er . . . I mean in a good way."

"People say it's supposed to be the happiest time of your life."

"Nah, that's a crock."

"It is?"

"The only reason people want to recapture their lost youth is because they forgot how much it sucked."

"You really think so?"

"It's kind of a theory of mine."

She contemplated that for a while. "But Melting Rock was supposed to be different. It *was* different. Until . . ."

"Until this year."

"Yeah."

"How was it supposed to be different?"

"You know. You were there."

"Yeah, but to tell you the truth, I never really got it."

Another deep breath. "Melting Rock was . . . It was like this place where anything was possible. Like this never-never land, you know?"

It was a good quote, so I wrote it down. "Go on."

"It was like this place where nothing bad could ever happen. Sort of like . . . you know, when you go on a roller coaster and you get scared, but it's okay because you know nothing's really going to happen to you."

"Melting Rock made you scared? I mean before this?"

"No, that's not what I meant. It's more like . . . you could take risks and be yourself and do whatever you want, say whatever you want, and everything would still be okay. Nobody would hold it against you later. It was just like . . . ecstasy."

"You mean, like the drug?"

"No, not the drug, like the *word.* Like the *feeling.* Just this total perfect happiness, you know? Just for five days a year, but that was enough. And now . . . now it'll never be the same. I wouldn't ever go back there. Not ever."

"I can't blame you."

"Lauren doesn't understand. She's already planning some tribute thing there next year, like planting a tree maybe, plus some other big thing at the high school. It's like she gets off on it or something."

"How do you mean?"

"I probably shouldn't have said that. It's probably not nice. I just . . . Lauren's always been kind of a drama queen, you know?"

"I thought you said she hardly even wanted to talk about it."

"I said she hardly even wanted to talk about what *happened.* But doing this whole memorial thing, it's like her own little holy mission. I mean, I guess I can understand and all, but I can't even think about that kind of stuff yet."

"So . . . what happened?"

She stared at me, like she wasn't sure she'd heard me right.

"You really want to know?"

"Yeah."

More gazing off into space. "My parents say if you're sick, you go to the doctor."

"What?" I was starting to wonder if somebody'd spiked her Sprite.

"Like I said before, they took me to a doctor. But not the kind of doctor who thinks talking's such a great thing."

"So you haven't really had a chance to get it off your chest."

A quick intake of breath, and she started sobbing all over again—and so hard it made the past half hour look like a sneeze. I just sat there and tried to be nurturing, which I'm not so great at if the patient doesn't have four paws and a tail. Finally, the waterworks ran dry and she started talking.

"We were just hanging out, you know?" she said. "I kind of . . . I always sort of liked Shaun, and I was really psyched he wanted to hang out with me. I mean, I knew he was tripping and everything, but he told me I could be his guide. Like, Shaun knew about all that stuff. He read books about what happened in the sixties, about how this guy'd drive around in a bus and give people acid and open their eyes to all this cool stuff. And I'd never done that stuff before, 'cause I was too scared, but Shaun didn't think I was a loser or anything. He said I could trip with him if I wanted, and he'd split the tab with me, or else I could just stay with him and be his guide and help him deal with all the experiences. And . . . I kind of wanted to try it too, because of the way he made it sound, but I thought it'd be cool to be his guide. I guess I was kind of flattered."

"So you didn't take any."

She shook her head. "Just Shaun. And he said he wasn't sure how long it'd take to start working. He said if it was a regular dose, it might be an hour or two, but if it was a strong one, it could be just like twenty minutes.

"But it was only maybe ten minutes later that he started to feel weird—I mean not *good* weird, *bad* weird. He knew right away there was something wrong. He said he couldn't breathe right and his stomach hurt. And I was going to go for help, but he said he was scared and he didn't want me to leave him alone. And I know I should've gone anyway, but I couldn't . . . I couldn't just leave him there."

"Why didn't you yell for help?"

"I don't know. I thought I did, but it just all happened so fast. We were inside the tent and he sort of crawled out, and for a minute I thought he was going to be okay. But then he started having these awful spasms, like his whole body was shaking and jerking back and forth, and his eyes kind of rolled way back in his head. God, it was so *awful*."

I patted her knee again and said, "It's gonna be okay," or something equally lame.

"But don't you get it? It's all my fault."

"What do you mean?"

"If only I'd gone for help, maybe he'd be okay. But I didn't. I just *sat* there. I just sat there and watched him die."

"I really don't think you could've done anything. From what you told me, it all happened way too fast. There's nothing anybody could've done."

"But Shaun . . . He was so scared. So scared and angry."

"Angry at who?"

She shook her head, like it hurt to have the memory rattling around in there. "When he could still talk, when he thought he was just having, you know, a bad trip or something, he was saying . . . he was really mad at the guy who sold him the stuff."

"What did he say?"

"He kept saying, 'I'm gonna kill him; I'm gonna fucking kill him.'"

"I meant, did he say who it was?" I tried to keep my voice calm. "Cindy, please try to remember. It's really important."

"Yeah."

"Yeah what?"

"Yeah, he did."

"And you told the police?" She shook her head. "Will you tell me?"

"I . . . You know him. I mean, I know you sort of met him once. I was there."

"Come on, Cindy. Who?"

"It's this guy who hangs out with that weirdo with tattoos that Dorrie likes," she said. "His name is Rob Sturdivant."

CHAPTER *15*

When you're talking to a hysterical adolescent teetering on the verge of a nervous breakdown, you're probably supposed to treat her with kid gloves. For one thing, you're probably not supposed to jump to your feet, wave your notebook around, and say the following:

"Son of a bitch, Cindy. For chrissake, how could you not have told somebody about this? Are you out of your mind?"

The expression on her face was blank—so blank, in fact, that I had a feeling the prescription pharmaceuticals had just kicked in.

"Um . . ." The swing was jerking back and forth from the force of my exit. "Nobody asked me."

"*What?*"

"I . . . You know, right after it happened, I was, like, totally in a daze, and then I was in the hospital and my folks didn't want anybody bothering me. . . ."

"Didn't you think it was kind of important?"

"I don't know. I guess I was kind of, you know . . . unplugged."

The temptation to harangue her further was great, but I endeavored to resist.

"What else did he tell you?"

"Who?"

Son of a . . . "Shaun."

"Oh. Nothing."

"You're sure?"

"Nothing."

"You know you've got to tell the police about this."

Her eyes went wide. "Why?"

I realized with a start that—*duh*—she didn't know the deaths hadn't been accidental. Then I figured the kid'd had enough trauma for one day. "They have to track down where the drugs came from," I said.

"Can't you tell them?"

"What?"

"Please?"

"Cindy, I wasn't there. You were."

"Yeah, but I don't know anything." She looked like she was about to start crying again, but when I thought she was reaching for the Kleenex, she grabbed her backpack and stood up. The bag was shaped like a teddy bear, with a zipper down its front like it'd had the Muppet version of open-heart surgery.

"Where are you going?"

"I have to get the bus back to J-burg. My parents'll be home soon."

"Wait—"

"I *have* to," she said, and took off down the sidewalk.

I thought about chasing after her, but I couldn't see the point. So I just watched her hustle down the street toward the center of town, her grape-colored hair flopping surreally over the teddy bear's smiling mug.

I sat back down on the swing, wondering just what the hell I was supposed to do now. Shakespeare, who'd taken a dim view of all the jumping and hollering, gave me a wary look as she settled back into her spot.

"Hey, sweetie," I said. "You got any advice for me?"

She raised an eyebrow. It didn't help.

Now, the optimal course of action may seem obvious to you—make haste to the nearest officer of the law and spill my guts—but for me there was another wrinkle.

Because, you see, I'd suddenly come into possession of a rather awesome scoop. I knew something that, presumably, the cops didn't even know: the name of the creep who had sold the LSD to Shaun Kirtz.

So . . . what to do? Should I behave like a decent human being and go tell the cops? Or should I sit on the information until Monday morning's paper, thereby screwing every other reporter in the state—including, most deliciously, Gordon Band of the *New York Times*—but also, theoretically, setting back the investigation by two whole days?

And what about the fact that if I went for option two and somebody else died in the meantime, I was going to want to jump in the gorge while slitting my wrists with a rock tied around my neck?

I could go to the police, they'd pick the guy up, and goddamn Gordon would almost certainly get wind of it in time for the Sunday paper. Or I could keep it to myself, moral misgivings be damned. I could try to track down Sturdivant for an interview on some pretext— and the odds were that as soon as he figured out where my questions were going, he'd fly the coop. I could try to talk to his friend Axel, and the end result would probably be the same. I could call Marilyn and Bill and just drop the whole thing in their laps, and the issue would be out of my hands. But—let's face it—was that any different from deciding to sit on the story until Monday? What would Mad or Ochoa do? And did I really want to ask them?

Unable to think of anything better to do, I sat there and swung back and forth for a while. It was thirsty work; I demolished both my diet Sprite and the rest of Cindy's, then went back in for more.

At some point, I stopped pondering the question at hand and starting thinking about the creepy dude at the center of it: one Robert Adam Sturdivant, aka "Sturdy."

I'd only run into him twice, but his image was rather vivid in my mind—he was, after all, not the kind of character a person can easily forget. I pictured the bald head and the multiply pierced ear, the bulging biceps and the meaty neck. All in all, he did sort of add up to a drug dealer right out of central casting.

And then there was the vaguely threatening aura he radiated, as though he'd just as soon eat you as look at you. But at the same time, I'd also gotten the weird sense that he was desperate to be liked, at least by the female of the species. Maybe that was one of the perks of the drug-dealing métier; it stands to reason that the guy with the goods can be considered an attractive fellow, physical drawbacks and all.

Unless, of course, your customers start dying.

Okay, I thought, let's look at this logically. Did I really think that Sturdivant had concocted the killer LSD himself? Or had he just gotten it from some supplier, who was either the guilty party or yet another unwitting link in the chain? Was it possible that this bullnecked lug of a guy had launched some diabolical scheme to knock off the better-looking competition? And—more to the point—since I barely knew him, why the hell was I even bothering to speculate about it?

But wait—maybe I didn't just have to speculate. I'd recently run into someone who seemed to know Sturdivant and did not think a whole lot of him, either. So I grabbed the phone book and the cordless, came back outside, and dialed Lenny Peterson's home number.

"Hey, Lenny," I said when he picked up, "remember that conversation we had at the Deep Lake open house about Rob Sturdivant?"

"Yeah," he said, "and I think the words I used were *no comment.*"

"Come on, you obviously knew him. And what I'm wondering is . . . Did you maybe know him because he's the one who supplies you with the green stuff you like to smoke for breakfast?"

"How did you hear—"

"It's what you'd call general knowledge."

Click.

I tried calling Lenny again, but he wouldn't pick up. Thus rebuffed, I spent more quality time wondering whether I felt like being a decent journalist or a decent human being. I'm not sure how long I stayed there, swinging and thinking and sharing granola bars with my dog. I do recall that at some point I realized that all the time I'd spent staring at a computer screen had killed off a few too many brain cells. If I played my cards right, I could probably have it both ways.

I informed Shakespeare of this, and I like to think that the way she raised her other eyebrow at me indicated that she was suitably impressed. Then I put her in the car and drove over to Cody's apartment, too pumped up to bother calling first.

I knocked, and when there was no answer, I let myself in with my key. Zeke, Cody's husky mix, came bounding over to Shakespeare and did the canine equivalent of reciting love poetry. When the two of them finally stopped making ecstatic howling noises, I noticed the shower running.

Now, this was what I call *excellent*.

I made my way toward the sound, and, passing the bedroom door, saw that a T-shirt, shorts, and a pair of white jock-socks were lying on the bed. Since I was similarly clad, I decided it was only fair that I toss my biking shorts, T-shirt, socks, and jog bra on top of the pile. Then I snuck into the steamy bathroom, pulled back the shower curtain, and scared the bejesus out of a naked Irishman.

BY MONDAY MORNING every reporter in New York State was pissed at me—at least that's how it felt.

My colleagues at other papers were irked because a pissant fish wrapper like the *Monitor* had scooped them on a certain story, headlined DEALER ACCUSED IN MELTING ROCK MURDERS. And in my own newsroom, Ochoa was fuming over having a joint byline foisted on him yet again. Never mind that we wouldn't even have had the story if it weren't for my source; Ochoa's a damn good reporter, but he's never been one to play nicely with the other children.

Luckily, he was too busy to stay mad at me for long. Sturdivant being identified as the dealer who sold the drugs had kicked the case into high gear, and Ochoa was running around like a maniac trying to cover it.

Mad and I, meanwhile, were charged with making sure some other news actually made it into the paper. He was doing a piece on how Bessler College was launching yet another initiative to make its science departments something better than moronic, while I was putting together a follow-up story on the Deep Lake Cooling brouhaha, along with yet another Melting Rock piece. This time, it was just a short one on how a bunch of its suppliers were fixing to sue over unpaid bills. Of course, said assignments didn't impede us from soaking up the lunchtime rays on the Gabriel Green, where thanks to a leaky pita I managed to drip a great quantity of baba ghanoush down my cleavage.

"What I don't get," Mad was saying as he bit into his chicken kabob, "is how Miss Journalistic Ethics can rationalize making some sweetheart deal with her boyfriend."

"*Shhh.*" I looked around, but there was no one within earshot. "Would you put a cork in it? Nobody's supposed to know."

"So why'd you tell me?"

"I had to tell *somebody.*"

"Ha. Remember never to apply for a job with the C.I.A."

"And besides," I said, jamming a napkin down my front in an effort to rescue my hundred-dollar Lise Charmel bra, "since when am I the ethics queen? I'm as much of a hack as you are."

"True," he said. "I just wanted to hear you say it."

"Charming."

"So what gives with this Cody thing?"

"I already told you."

"Yeah, but I wasn't really listening."

"*Argh.*" I reached for another napkin. "I told you, this kid—"

"This *unidentified* kid."

"This unidentified kid told me that Shaun Kirtz told her he bought the drugs from Sturdivant. And I didn't think I could just sit on it until Monday, because what if some other kid croaked in the meantime? So then it hits me: What if Cody's my source, and I'm his?"

"How romantic."

"Do you want to hear this or don't you?"

He took another bite. "Do."

"So I went over to his place and made him an offer he couldn't refuse."

"Hubba-hubba."

"The deal was, I'd give him the name of the dealer if he promised to sit on the Melting Rock connection until the paper hit the streets on Monday. That way, he could pick up the guy and start working on getting him to talk, and—"

"And meanwhile make sure he couldn't sell any more of that shit."

"Right. So the cops get their bad guy, and we get to break the story. Everybody's happy."

"Except Sturdivant."

"The poor sweet thing."

"How much did he get caught with, anyway?"

"Um . . . a bunch of pot, some ecstasy, acid, mushrooms, prescription pills, you name it. The guy was a walking drugstore."

"Why don't people just go into a bar, for chrissake? It's cheaper, and it sure do taste good."

"So you're suggesting alcoholism as an alternative to drug addiction?"

"Hey, baby," he said with a wink, "don't knock it till you try it."

Back at the newsroom, I had five phone messages from various members of the anti–Deep Lake Cooling contingent, but zippo from the one person I really needed to reach: Glenn Shardik. I tried Lenny at the Benson news service, but if he had any idea what was up with Deep Lake, he was in no mood to tell me. Benson had yet to hire a replacement for its recently departed vice president for P.R., so I didn't have a lot of options for finding somebody to tell me when and if the cooling system was getting turned back on. Therefore, turning ambitious through sheer desperation, I braved the wrath of the Benson parking police and drove up to campus.

Shardik's office is in an aging facilities-maintenance building on the far side of the vet school. Square and squat, it seems to have been designed for maximum ugliness, and on this point it succeeds spectacularly well. It's always been amazing to me that out of what looks like the bureaucratic equivalent of a medieval oubliette sprang a revolution in air-conditioning technology—or, indeed, anything else.

At Benson, like at all colleges, faculty are the sacred cows; during lean times, in other words, you don't get to kill them for food. When budget crises strike, the ax falls on the support staff—and folks who deal with pipes and lightbulbs rather than live human beings tend to be first on the chopping block.

I mention this by way of explaining why there was a single belea-guered secretary at the front desk trying to cover the whole building. I told her I was looking for Shardik but—what with the ringing phone and the hold lights blinking on her desk like a peep show mar-quee—she was barely listening. She just pulled a pencil out of the hairsprayed helmet atop her head and waved vaguely down the hall, then answered another call.

"Facilities management," I heard her say, her voice a delicate bal-ance between boredom and stress. "No, I'm not sure when it'll be fixed. Yes, I know it's been two weeks. Yes, I know it's supposed to rain tomorrow. Have you thought about getting a bigger bucket?"

I kept walking. Shardik's office was at the end of the hall, a private closet amid a warren of partitioned cubicles. The whole place was de-serted; he and his staff were probably off at some meeting on how to salvage their $150 million mess.

Shardik's tiny room had space for his desk, a filing cabinet, and two chairs, period. I sat down in the visitor's chair and tried to decide if there was any point in waiting for him. Since I had no idea when he'd be back, I decided to leave him a pleading note about how I needed to talk to him ASAP. I scribbled it on a sheet of paper from my reporter's notebook and dropped it on his desk, pausing to appre-ciate the fact that, at least judging by the work of the Sears Portrait Studio, Shardik's kids were going to turn out as hairy as he was.

I was just about to pack up and go, when my eyes alit on a fax cover sheet from the Gabriel Police Department. It was perched atop the mound of paperwork on the desk—Shardik apparently being as well organized as I am—so I almost missed it. But there it was, the department crest reproduced in grainy black and white.

And since (like every other reporter I know) I can read upside down without breaking a sweat, I can tell you what it said, typos and all:

TO: **Glen Sherdick, Benson Facilities**
FROM: **G.P.D. Forensics**
RE: **D.L.C. H$_2$O analysis**
PAGES W/ COVER: 2

I stood there for a minute, not so much wondering whether I should read it as whether I was at all likely to get caught. Deciding the danger was slim, Miss Journalistic Ethics grabbed the papers and started copying down a list of chemicals that sounded like they'd eat your innards clean through. Then I put the pages back exactly where I'd snatched them—as though he'd noticed the difference in all the mess—retrieved the note to Shardik by way of covering my tracks, and hightailed it out of there.

By the time I got back to the newsroom, I was positively giddy. Mad was doing a phone interview with some Bessler prof, and I stood there practically hopping up and down until he hung up. Then I grabbed him and dragged him into the library.

"Bernier, what's so—"

"What would you say if I told you I just lucked into getting my grubby hands on the analysis of the Deep Lake Cooling water?"

"I'd say you've been a very bad girl."

"And?"

"And then I'd say you better tell me."

I brandished my notebook. "You ready?"

"Give it to me, baby."

"Okay, check this out." I cleared my throat. "Adipic acid, disodium phosphate, fumaric acid . . ." I looked up at Mad, who had a weird expression on his face. If I was looking for horror, I didn't get it. "Whaddaya think? Sounds pretty awful, huh?"

"Yeah . . ." He sounded distracted. "What else?"

"Um . . . sodium, ace . . . acesulfame potassium, malodextrin, glucose—"

"Hold on," he said, and started digging through one of the filing cabinets. After a minute he pulled out a clip and scanned it.

Then he busted out laughing.

"What's so funny?"

He kept on laughing.

"Come on, Mad, what's up?"

"Might that list include . . . gelatin by any chance?"

I checked my notebook. "Er . . . yeah. Why?"

"Adipic acid rang a bell," he said, waving the square of newspaper at me, "so I grabbed this here story I did when Benson won that big food-science competition."

"And?"

"And the hideous substance that shut down the Deep Lake Cooling plant," he said, "is better known as strawberry Jell-O."

CHAPTER *16*

"Strawberry Jell-O? Are you kidding me?"

"Maybe it's raspberry, I don't know." He was still chuckling, damn him. "You said it was red, right?"

"That's what Shardik told me. But, come on . . . killer Jell-O? What kind of crazy shit is that?"

"Hey, it sort of fits. Those tree-hugging Save the Lakers wouldn't really dump something toxic, now would they?"

"I guess not, but . . . come on. I mean, it was bad enough when those anti-G.M.O. morons dumped a load of transgenic potatoes in the middle of Route Thirteen, but this is a whole new level of stupidity."

"Why's it so stupid? They managed to shut down the system for the better part of a week without hurting the lake or hitting anybody over the head. Sounds like a solid plan to me."

"Way to go, Mohawk Warriors."

"Who?"

"The group that claimed responsibility for it."

"Right."

"So"—I cleared a space on the librarian's desk and sat down—"what do we do now?"

"Write up the story for tomorrow's paper. What else?"

"I'd love to. But where exactly am I supposed to attribute the information? 'According to a fax ripped off Glenn Shardik's desk, the water contained—'"

"Don't sweat it," he said. "I bet they're gonna release the findings any second."

"And why's that?"

"Because it's goddamn strawberry Jell-O, for chrissake. It's harm-less."

"I get it. Which means they can turn the system back on pronto."

"I bet you a buck," he said, "that they already have."

He was right; we'd barely gotten back to our desks when the fax machine cranked out a press release from the Benson news service announcing that the stuff in the cooling pool was, quote, "a common commercial flavored-gelatin food substance."

The overwrought language was, no doubt, something the Benson lawyers had concocted to avoid getting the pants sued off them by the Kraft Foods corporation—three guesses where Shardik and his staff had been when I came calling.

And speaking of lawsuits . . . I'd pretty much forgotten about the other story I was supposed to be writing, the one about the music festival getting sued for not paying its bills. We'd gotten tipped off to it by one of the irate creditors, and although I would've been happy to hand it off to the business reporter, the bosses had decided that I was now Queen of All Things Melting Rock. So although I'm not one to balance my checkbook, I called up the injured parties and let them vent about how the festival was run by a bunch of stinking deadbeats.

"I tried doin' this the nice way," said one pissed-off purveyor of Porta-Johns, "but those hippie bastards won't even answer my god-damn phone calls. Well, now they can talk to my freakin' lawyer."

I got a similar sentiment from the local companies that made the festival's T-shirts, printed its tickets, and supplied its overpriced water bottles. Melting Rock, apparently, was stiffing everybody.

I tried the festival office, but all I got was an answering machine telling me how great the bands were going to be at . . . Melting Rock Lucky Thirteen. When I tried to leave a message, it hung up.

Stymied, I went back to the darkroom, where Melissa was tinkering with the new photo computer.

"Hey," I said, "if you wanted to find somebody in charge of Melting Rock, where would you look?"

"At their office down the street."

"No answer."

"Did you try . . . what's her name from the fest? Jo something?"

"Jo Mingle. She's not in the book. But she lives with somebody from that band you like—Larry the Lizard or something."

"That's Stumpy the Salamander."

"Big diff. So you know where I can find these reptiles?"

"Which one is she with?"

"The drummer."

Melissa cracked a smile. "*Phew.* Glad to hear it's not the guitarist. He's a *babe.*"

"So how do I find this guy? I think his name's Ford-something."

"Trike Ford. They call him that 'cause he has one of those three-wheeled ATV things. He even wrote a song about—"

"Terrific. Do we know his real name?"

"I think . . . Wayne maybe. Or Dwayne."

"Is he in the book?"

She shrugged, asked me to let her know if I heard anything about the guitarist's relationship status, and turned back to the oversize computer screen. I went back to my desk and found one Dwayne Ford in the phone book. I called and got Jo Mingle—or what I could hear of her over the screaming baby in the background.

When I told her why I was calling, she sounded like she might bawl herself.

"Uh . . . I don't really know anything about the financial stuff," she said.

"But you run the festival."

"Yeah, but, like . . . I don't deal with numbers. I just do the creative stuff, signing up bands and all. . . ."

"Did you know there's eight different suppliers about to sue Melting Rock to get their money?"

"Huh?" The baby cranked its wailing up a notch. "Can you talk a little louder? Happy's kind of having a fit right now."

"I said, did you know there's eight different suppliers about to sue Melting Rock?"

"Um . . . I'm sure it's all just, like, a big misunderstanding."

"They don't exactly see it that way. They say you guys owe them over forty thousand dollars all together."

"That much?" *Scream, wail, howl.* "Can't be. It's gotta be a big mix-up, you know?"

"Well, if you don't run the business, who does?"

"Trike. He knows all that stuff. He manages Stumpy and all, so he's really good at—"

"Can I talk to him?"

"He's on the road. Won't be back for, like, a couple weeks or something."

"Well, is there anybody I can call for comment? Does the festival have a lawyer?"

"Why would we need a lawyer?"

"Because you guys are getting sued."

There was a long pause, filled entirely by infantile caterwauling. "Jesus," Jo said finally. "Melting Rock is a total goddamn mess."

I didn't argue with her, just got off the phone and wrote up my piece on the impending lawsuit. To be charitable, I included a line about how Melting Rock organizers thought it was all just a big misunderstanding. Then I turned my attention back to Deep Lake.

It was at the afternoon editorial staff meeting, in fact, that somebody pointed out that although we now knew what was in the cooling pool, nobody seemed to be talking about how it got there.

To be specific, how exactly did the so-called Mohawk Warriors break into the facility—a relative fortress by Gabriel standards—to dump it in? And come to think of it, how do you haul around enough powdered Jell-O mix to muck up fifty thousand gallons of water?

This, by the way, is not a question I ever anticipated having to consider in my lifetime.

When it came to trying to address such issues, there was only one place I could think of to start. I was reasonably well acquainted with several members of the anti–Deep Lake lunatic fringe—as opposed to the calmer types who seemed content with legal action. One of them was about to go up the river on drug charges; I went out onto the Green in search of the others.

I found one sitting on the pavement outside Café Whatever, strumming a guitar with what could either be described as artistic passion or extreme hysteria. He had a paper cup with the coffee shop's logo on the ground beside him, stained around the edges and containing what looked to be less than a buck in change.

I can't really say whether he had much musical talent. His playing and singing sounded to me like somebody was strangling a monkey— but based on my Melting Rock experience, I was fairly sure I wasn't the target audience.

He didn't seem to notice me standing there, just kept strumming and howling. Then I dropped a dollar in his cup, and he acknowledged my existence with a solemn nod, like I'd just paid proper tribute at the temple gates. After what seemed like several hours, the song ended with a yowl that (I think) translated into *Oh, girl, come back to meeeeeeeee.* Before he could start singing again, I offered to buy him a cup of coffee.

"Whatcha want?" Axel said, looking at me warily from his cross-legged pose.

"Fine. If you don't want any coffee, I'll just—"

"Nah. Hold on. I'd dig some, yeah. Just . . . what gives?"

"I want to talk to you."

He seemed, if it was possible, even warier. "'Bout what?"

"Deep Lake."

"Oh." He sprang to his feet in one fluid motion. "That's cool."

He picked up his guitar and the meager cupful of change and followed me into the coffee shop, where he ordered an extra-large mug of the strongest stuff they had. I was just about to pay when I noticed him staring at the pastry case with something beyond longing.

"Axel," I said, "when was the last time you ate something?"

He shrugged and looked down at the dirty toenails sticking out of his Birkenstocks. "Got no dough," he said.

"You want a bagel?"

"Really?" He turned a pair of pleading eyes on me, and I was instantly reminded of Cindy Bauer. "You mean it?"

"Sure."

He asked for a pumpernickel bagel with extra cream cheese, and I got one of the café's signature cookies for myself—a chocolate-frosted question mark known as a "Whatever." The place has some tasty treats, but sometimes it's too cute by half.

I expected him to want to sit in the back, but he went straight for a table in the window. We'd barely sat down, when he jammed half the bagel into his mouth and kept pushing and chewing until it was all gone. Then he wiped his mouth with the back of his hand and guzzled down most of the coffee—never mind that it was still steaming.

The calories and the caffeine had a downright transformative effect on him. When he finally said something, he no longer sounded like a Dickensian waif; the confident fellow from Melting Rock was back with a vengeance.

"So . . . *lady*," he said, speaking in a funny singsong voice that was probably supposed to sound supercool. "So . . . newspaper *lady* . . ."

"Um, yeah?"

"Why does newspaper lay-dee want to talk to little old Axel Robbee-nette?"

"She's wondering how the hell somebody dumped a ton of strawberry Jell-O into the Deep Lake Cooling pool."

He started laughing so hard he grabbed his gut and doubled over. His greasy hair trailed into the other half of his bagel, so when he finally sat up there was cream cheese on his head.

"Cool, huh?" he said. "I bet those corporate dopes never even knew what hit 'em."

"Axel, Benson is a university, for chrissake. It's nonprofit."

"Ooh, *nonprofit*," he parroted back at me before biting off a quarter of the remaining bagel slice. "Like big business doesn't run the fuckin' show up there."

"Look," I said, "I'm doing a story for tomorrow's paper on the Jell-O thing. I'd really like to be able to say how you did it."

"Hey, lady, I never said I did anything," he said with a laugh. "Don't go misquoting me, or I'll sue your ass." More chuckles. "I'll *sooooo . . .*"

"Fine, let me rephrase the question. I'd really like to know how it was done. I mean, the heat-exchange building is like a fort—big fence, barbed wire, the whole thing. So did somebody let you in or what?"

He smirked at me. "More than one way in there."

"Meaning?"

"Meaning why should I tell you?"

"Because whoever did it is probably dying to brag about it."

He chewed on that for a while. "So why should I tell you instead of"—he looked up to make sure I was paying attention—"Mr. Gordon Band of the *New York Times?*"

That got me. "Gordon called you?"

"Talked to me on the Green yesterday. I got no phone."

"And what did he want?"

"Guess he got my name from that cool-ass story you wrote. Wanted me to tell him what got dumped in the fuckin' pool, ya know?"

"What did you tell him?"

"I told him, 'You want to know the dope, you gotta show me the green, man.'"

"Huh?"

"He wants the facts, he's gotta pay up. A guy's gotta eat, ya know."

"And what did he say to that?"

"He offered me *one thousand dollars,* baby."

"He did *not.*"

"Did so."

"Axel, Gordon Band is a friend of mine. And although he may be the most competitive reporter who ever lived, there's no way he'd ever pay off a source to get a story. It's what you'd call a big ethical no-no."

"Well," he said, "them's the facts, Jack."

He squirmed in his seat and stared at the tabletop. Axel Robinette was, in short, a very bad liar.

"Look, Axel, if you're not going to tell me the truth, I'm just wasting my time here." I started to stand up.

"Aw, come on, lady. Lighten up." I sat back down. "Besides, what's the big deal? You're sittin' here bribin' me with eats, right? What's the problem with slippin' a guy a little cash?"

"Buying you a snack during an interview and giving you money for information isn't the same thing."

"Yeah, well . . ." He did a little twisty dance in his seat; this, apparently, was supposed to represent moral relativism. Then he ate the rest of his bagel. As he chewed, Guinevere the Psychic walked by the window and waved at us.

"Come on," I said, "you don't have to get your name in the paper or anything. I'm not trying to get you busted. I just want to know how it was done."

He shrugged and favored me with another smirk. So I focused my attention on the cookie, which was shaping up to be a much more charming companion. When I finally looked up again, the expression on his face was, of all things, blatantly lascivious.

"You're kind of a fiery little bitch, aren't you?"

"Excuse me?"

He raised a guitar-callused hand. "Hey, no offense meant, baby. I'm just saying, you're kind of a hottie. For an older chick, I mean."

"Great. Thanks."

"So, come on . . . Can you spot me some dough?"

"No."

"But I really *need* it."

He stretched both arms out for emphasis. Unfortunately, the reptile tattoos snaking their way around both biceps didn't exactly inspire charity.

"Have you thought about maybe getting a job?"

He gave me a smile that probably would've made me swoon, if I had a crew cut and my name was Dorrie Benson. "But then," he said, "I couldn't have any *fun.*"

"Poor baby."

I'd meant it sarcastically. This clearly escaped him.

"Hey, you wanna hear a secret?" He leaned in like I was his unindicted coconspirator. "Well, do ya?"

"Sure."

"Minute I get some cash together, I'm gonna blow this town."

"Really? Where are you going?"

He winked at me. "Santa Cruz, man. It's warm there twenty-four seven. Besides, I gotta get closer to L.A. if I'm gonna get me a music deal, right?"

"Well . . . good luck."

"So will you spot me some dough?"

"Definitely not."

"Aw, come on . . ."

"Look, if you don't want to talk about Deep Lake, how about you tell me a few things about your friend Rob Sturdivant?"

He shook his head, the pseudocharming smile still intact. "No way, baby."

"Were you surprised he made bail? I mean, fifty thousand dollars is a lot of money."

"His folks've got it, so he got sprung. Good for him."

"Axel, the guy got charged with possession with intent. He's under investigation for selling the drugs that killed those kids. Doesn't that bother you?"

"Ain't no business of mine."

"Did you know he was dealing?"

Another shrug. "Who gives a fuck?"

This was starting to get tiresome. "Look, Axel, I gotta get back to work. If you're not gonna tell me anything about Sturdivant or Deep Lake . . ."

He laid a tattooed hand on my arm. "Come on, baby. Don't go getting all huffy, okay?"

"Are you gonna tell me how it was done or aren't you?"

He ran a dirty finger up and down my wrist. "Play your cards right, and I'll do more than tell you."

I yanked my hand away, quelling the urge to run to the ladies' room for a hefty dose of antibacterial soap. "What's that supposed to mean?"

"Meet me at Deep Lake tomorrow night," he said, "and I'll show you."

IT GOES WITHOUT SAYING that I shouldn't have done it. I mean, meeting some scuzzy street kid in the middle of the night? Going alone, without even telling anybody what I was up to? Trespassing?

Well, okay—I do that last one on a fairly frequent basis. But the rest of it was downright moronic.

Still, there I was—hiking to the cooling facility at quarter after midnight, hepped up on caffeine and dressed like a goddamn cat burglar. I was running late, in fact, because I'd gone home after deadline to change into an all-black outfit: boots, turtleneck sweater, and my new low-rise Guess? jeans. If I made a fool of myself, at least I was going to do it in style.

So I'd parked the car down the road and walked back to the heat-exchange building—slowly. I figured inching my way by flashlight was better than tripping on something and tumbling into the lake.

I'm not sure what I'd expected; I guess I thought Axel would be waiting for me out front. But when I got there, I saw nothing resembling a tattooed guitar player. Just a barbed-wire fence, with its front gate ever so slightly ajar.

There was just a sliver of a moon out that night, and the whole place was incredibly dark. Actually, it was *unnaturally* dark; it took me a minute to realize that the outside lights weren't on.

"Axel?" I whispered into the void beyond the front gate. No answer.

I tried shining my flashlight through the chain-link; the beam was broad and bright, but I couldn't see anyone. "Axel?" I said, a little louder this time. "Hey, Axel. Are you here?"

Still nothing.

I ventured forward, shining the flashlight beam around the parking lot. There were no cars except an official Benson service vehicle, which may or may not park there all the time. Still, the possibility that someone might be there made me hesitate for a few minutes. Then I figured that even if I ran into a Benson facilities worker, I could probably talk my way out of it—that's always been a particular talent of mine—so I kept going.

I crossed the parking lot to the main door, a reinforced-steel affair that didn't exactly invite one to come in and stay a while. Then I noticed that, like the fence gate, it was slightly ajar. I reached for the handle but—after several years of covering crime and one of sleeping with a cop—it occurred to me that maybe I didn't want to leave any fingerprints. So I used the butt of the flashlight to open the door, and found that the building was just as dark inside as out.

"Axel?" I whispered again. Zippo.

But the fact was, even if he was there, he probably couldn't have heard me. The Deep Lake Cooling system was on, and the cavernous room was filled with the whooshing of water through pipes and the thumping hum of pumps forcing the chilled liquid back up the hill to Benson. The whole place felt alive, like you were standing inside some gigantic body, lungs breathing and heart pumping blood in an endless circuit. I half expected to feel the ground shift, like I was trapped in the gut of some sci-fi monster.

If you're wondering if I was scared, well . . . the answer would be *hell yes*. I'm generally terrified by campfire ghost stories; poking around a deserted industrial building in the pitch dark had me more than a little freaked out. I was glad for the weight of the flashlight in my hand. The hefty red Maglite was Cody's idea of a Valentine's Day present; it takes four D batteries and could work nicely as a bludgeon, should the need arise.

I shone the light across the room in a slow arc, and the beam illuminated the far wall a good hundred feet away. Huge teal blue pipes emerged from the darkness like tentacles—an analogy that immediately struck me as counterproductive to my own peace of mind. The light glinted off innumerable dials and other assorted gizmos that kept the place running, but it revealed not the slightest bit of Axel Robinette.

Cursing myself for being sufficiently idiotic to be there in the first place, I forced myself to do a sweep of the entire floor. I paced around doing some lame impression of bravery, trying not to jump every time the light cast creepy shadows off the twisted piping—and, for the record, not having a whole lot of success.

I knew from my tour at the open house that the heat-exchange facility had three floors: the main one I was on, an upper gallery with an office and a lot of computer equipment, and a lower level housing the huge pumps and the intake pool. Because the upstairs struck me as less icky, I opted to check that out first. The office was locked up tight, computer screens and other monitoring equipment blinking through a long window; otherwise nothing.

So I went back down to the main floor and made my way to the narrow metal staircase that led to the bottom level. The temperature dropped after just a couple of steps; the air was cold and clammy, like the inside of a cave. On the tour Shardik had told us that because the water was drawn from deep at the bottom of the lake, the pool was a constant 38 degrees.

"Don't fall in," he'd told us, leaning out over the waist-high metal railing. "Unless somebody fishes you out, you'll die in three minutes."

Shardik had been laughing when he said it, like he was enjoying giving the shiny-suited dignitaries a little scare—*you'll die in three minutes, har-har-har*—and we'd all laughed along with him. But his little joke didn't seem so funny as I inched down the stairs, one hand on the flashlight and the other on the chilly metal railing. When I got to the bottom, I swept the light across the room. Unless somebody was hiding behind the massive pumps—and I really hoped no one was—I was all alone down there.

I was just about to go back upstairs when the sensible part of my brain said, *Look in the pool.*

Hell no, said the rest of me.

Come on, you big chicken. Just turn around, aim the goddamn flashlight, and look in the pool.

So I did.

And guess what: I immediately wished I hadn't.

CHAPTER *17*

The body was facedown, arms and legs floating freely in the
black water. Because I spend way too much time at the
movies—and, more to the point, because I was in the process of flipping out—my brain flashed the opening scene of *Sunset Boulevard,*
when William Holden is lying dead in Gloria Swanson's pool, but he
goes ahead and narrates the whole rest of the movie anyway.

Now, I'm sure a more normal person wouldn't have thought of
that. In fact, a sane human being might very well have had the presence of mind not to go to an empty industrial building alone in the
middle of the night in the first place.

But there I was, standing there in the dark, my flashlight trained
on a corpse lolling in the jet-black water. My first instinct, in case
you're wondering, was to get the hell out of there as fast as was humanly goddamn possible. But I managed to ignore it; I even talked
my foot into taking half a step toward the pool.

Was it Axel? That seemed the most likely thing, didn't it? I took
another half step forward to get a better look at the body, but I
couldn't see much. The waterline was about four feet below the floor,
and the face was completely submerged. Since he—or, I suppose,
she—was wearing a baseball cap, I couldn't even tell what the hair
looked like.

I was just steeling myself to go all the way to the edge of the pool
when I heard something. In retrospect, I think it was just some ven-
tilation system going on, but anyway it scared the hell out of me. I
turned tail and ran up the stairs—flashlight bobbing every which way,

boots clanking on the metal steps, fight-or-flight instinct set firmly on *flight.*

I ran up the stairs and out the front door, suddenly terrified that the fence gate was going to be locked. If I hadn't lost it before, I sure as holy hell did then.

What am I going to do if I'm locked in here? And what if whoever shoved whoever's in the pool into the pool is still here—assuming it wasn't an accident, right? And what if I can't get out, and I'm going to get killed because I left my goddamn cell phone in the car because I'm a moron and I don't know enough to . . .

The gate was open. I was too relieved to feel stupid.

I ran toward the car, vaguely aware that—considering that I was dressed like a bloody ninja—the bobbing flashlight was the only thing keeping me from getting run over. And though it was probably just the fear talking, the whole time I had this incredibly creepy sense that somebody was watching me.

I've never been much of a runner, but—darkness be damned—I booked down the road like I was in the goddamn Olympic relay. After what felt like ten or twenty miles, I made it back to my car, hand shaking as I tried to dig the keys from the pocket of my fashionably snug jeans. Once I finally retrieved them, I had to go through a whole other shaking thing as I scrambled to slide the key into the lock.

Then the car alarm went off.

It sounded like a bloody air-raid siren—to me, anyway—and I jumped back so far I wound up in the middle of the road. Luckily, no one chose that particular moment to run me over, because I spent a fair amount of time just standing there trying to calm down enough to remember which little button I had to push on the key chain to stop all the flashing and honking. I fumbled with the gizmo for what seemed like forever until I finally got the thing to shut up. It wasn't until I jumped into the car and locked the doors that I achieved something approaching normal breathing. I started the engine and, the Beetle having a snug little turning radius, pulled a one-eighty and headed back toward town along East Shore Drive.

When faced with dead bodies—something I've encountered far more times than a girl would like—I've been known to go running straight into the manly arms of Detective Brian Cody. And, well . . . this time was no different.

Okay, call me a wimp. But where the hell else was I gonna go?

He answered the door in a pair of navy sweatpants flecked with white dog hair. Don't ask me how I remember that, but I do. Also, please don't ask me to defend the following conversation, which was utterly nonsensical:

"Alex, baby, what the—"

"Remember how I told you I had to work late tonight?"

"Uh . . . yeah."

"There's a dead body in the Deep Lake Cooling pool."

"What?"

"Somebody's floating in the Deep Lake Cooling pool."

"In the . . . ?"

"It's really cold in there. You die in three minutes."

That's when he grabbed me by the arm and walked me over to the couch.

"Just sit down, okay?"

"I don't need to—"

He pushed me down on the couch, then went away and came back with a glass. I sniffed at it.

"Tell me that's not whiskey."

"The medicine of my people."

"Do you seriously expect me to—"

"Bottoms up."

I did as I was told.

"You know," I said a minute later, "you giving me whiskey is what we writers call a creaky stereotype."

"And it's obviously working."

"Huh?"

"You already sound more like yourself."

"Oh."

He was sitting at the opposite end of the couch, looking at me like the proverbial bug under the microscope. "You feel ready to talk now?"

"I was ready to talk before."

He let that one pass. I sat up and told him about my evening's adventures, which took all of five minutes. (Granted, I saved some time by editing out the part where I ran out of the building like terrified poultry.) Then he spent a while berating me for being dumb enough to meet Axel at the Deep Lake Cooling plant by myself in the middle of the night. He seemed inclined to continue in this vein for quite a while, but eventually he had to stop reading me the riot act and report the body.

If I was hoping to spend the rest of the night soaking up sympathy, I was out of luck; Cody told his dog to keep me company and headed off to the scene of the crime.

Knowing the man as I do, that much was fairly predictable. What surprised me was that he was back inside of an hour. And he was looking at me funny.

"Um, Alex . . ."

"Yeah?"

"You didn't happen to stop at the Citizen on your way to Deep Lake, did you?"

I had the feeling there was an insult in there somewhere. I stood up because it seemed like the thing to do. "What the hell is that supposed to mean?"

"Nothing. It's just—"

"What, do you think I've been drinking and driving or something?"

"No, I—"

"Are you nuts?"

"Listen, just calm down for a second—"

"Christ, you know I *hate* it when you tell me to calm down."

"Alex—"

"Come on, tell me what you guys found. Who the hell was it floating in there? Was it Axel?"

"Er . . ."

"Come on, Cody. Would you just tell me already?"

"It was nobody."

"What?"

"Alex, there was nobody in there."

"Are you crazy? Of course there was. I saw it."

"Baby, I know what you think you saw, but—"

"Think I saw? I know what I *saw.* I went down into that godfor-saken basement with the big-ass flashlight you gave me and I shone it into the goddamn pool and there was a *person* floating in there. And they weren't doing the goddamn backstroke, either. Whoever it was was floating facedown. *Facedown,* okay?"

"Isn't there any way it might have been, you know . . . a trick of the light or something?"

"What *light?* I told you, I looked in the pool and there was a dead body in there. And I tried to see who it was, but then I heard a noise and it scared the crap out of me and I ran out and got into my car and drove straight here, okay? Now do you believe me or don't you?"

"Baby, please ca—" He cut himself off, and just in time too. "Please try and listen to me, all right? I'm not saying that I don't be-lieve you. I'm just saying that we went to the scene just now and the place is totally deserted. We looked in every corner of the building, and there's no body."

"That's impossible."

He shrugged and sat down on the couch. "Honey, I don't know what else to tell you."

"Wasn't there even any evidence?"

"I told you, there was no—"

"Like wasn't the floor wet or anything?"

"Wet from what?"

"From fishing the body out."

For a minute he looked like he wanted to strangle me. Then he just looked intensely perplexed. "It . . ."

I crossed my arms and fixed him with a distinctly uncharitable glare. "Yes? Come on, spit it out."

"You know, the entire place is pretty damp. I mean, with the water coming up from the bottom of the . . . Oh, *hell.*"

"What?"

"All right, now that you mention it . . . part of the floor *was* wet. A little wet, anyway."

"And that didn't clue you in that maybe your girlfriend was telling the truth? Some big-city detective you are."

"Give me a break, all right? When we didn't even find a body in there or any sign there'd ever been one, it didn't instantly occur to me that maybe somebody'd removed it, all right?"

"You just figured it was never there in the first place."

He shook his head and stared at the carpet. "Yeah."

"And you therefore figured I must be a moron."

"Yeah—*no.* Hey, I never said that. I just thought you were, you know . . . mistaken."

"Well I'm not."

"Okay."

"I swear, Cody. There was a body in there."

He shook his head again. "Okay," he said after a while. "Let's work this. If there really was a—"

"*Cody.*"

"Okay, okay. *Assuming* there was a body, do you think you could identify it?"

"You mean, do I know who it was? Hell no."

"Could you at least tell if it was male or female?" I shook my head. "Approximate age?"

"Sorry."

"Don't you remember any details at all?"

I thought about it. "It was wearing a hat."

"Okay, that's something. What kind of hat?"

"I'm pretty sure it was a baseball cap, but I didn't get that good a look at it. So, come on, tell me. What was it like over there? Was the front gate open at least?"

"Yeah, it was open just like you said, and the front door was ajar. There was just no body."

"So what do we do now?"

"*We're* doing nothing. Right now, *you* are getting into a hot bath and going to bed. *I* am going to get my sorry butt back to the crime scene and try to clean up the mess I just made. Jesus, if they ever heard about this back home . . ."

"They'd toss your gold shield in Boston Harbor."

"Something like that."

"Seriously, how are you going to deal with this?"

"After I finish kicking myself, I'm going to try and figure out what happened to our corpse and who the hell it is."

"Sounds like a plan."

"Then, if I manage not to screw up any further, I'm going to try and figure out who killed him, and why the body got moved, and who helped."

"Helped? Why would you automatically assume that—"

"Baby, you don't want to know how heavy a waterlogged corpse is."

I sat down on the couch next to him. "You got that right."

"And there was *some* water back there on the cement, but not a whole lot of it—I'm an idiot, but I'm not that much of an idiot. Even if a single person could drag a body out of that pool, which I really doubt, there's no way on earth they could do it alone without making a mess."

"You mean without getting water all over the place?"

"Yeah. You saw that intake pool. It's got a little railing around it, but the sides are straight concrete three feet down to the water, and there's nothing to grab on to except that little safety ladder. So a guy trying to do it by himself would have to hang on to the ladder, lean down, and drag the body up with one hand. Ask me, it'd be impossible."

"But how could they do it?"

"You mean how could they kill him?"

"I mean, how could they get rid of the body so fast? From the time I left the building until you guys got there it was . . . what? Forty-five minutes?"

"Probably more like half an hour."

"Right. That isn't really much of a window, is it? I had to leave, and then they had to get there, get the body out, carry it to a car, and drive off before you guys got there." Something struck me. I didn't much like it. "Unless . . ."

I looked at Cody. Cody looked at me. I could tell that we were thinking the same damn thing.

"Unless," I said, "they were there the whole time."

T HE WEEKEND CAME AND WENT, and Ochoa did a story on the cops' search for a body in the Deep Lake Cooling plant—but no corpses cropped up in the greater Gabriel area. In fact, not only did the body in question not get found, two other people went missing.

First off, Axel seemed to have vanished—and I mean *poof.* I tried his usual haunts, talked to the greasy-haired weirdos he hung with on the Green, but nobody had seen him since Friday. As far as I could tell, the last person who'd definitely seen him in town was, in a word, me.

And, okay . . . If you're wondering if I was basically assuming that Axel and the Deep Lake Cooling corpse were one and the same, well . . . of course I was. I had, after all, been supposed to meet Axel there—and now he was nowhere to be found.

True, he'd said he was planning on leaving town the minute he got some money together. Maybe he'd somehow gotten the cash, had blown me off entirely, and was presently hitchhiking his way to the West Coast in search of folk-rock stardom.

Or maybe he'd gotten coshed over the head and had died of hypothermia in the Deep Lake pool. Maybe he'd been buried in a shallow grave somewhere in the woods, to be found by some poor schmuck during turkey-hunting season.

Even though Axel wasn't what you'd call an upright citizen, I found myself hoping he was on his way to Santa Cruz—that fabled land of drum circles and astronomical rents. The other version was just too goddamn awful. The more I thought about it, though, the more I had to admit that both outcomes sounded equally likely.

But if he'd really been thrown into the pool, then . . . why? Why would someone want to kill a spaced-out musician whose major crimes (as far as I could tell) were a rotten singing voice and a disdain for chicks with military haircuts?

And then there was his buddy Robert "Sturdy" Sturdivant—for my money, a way more likely target. The Gabriel cops had arrested him for possession with intent to sell, and everyone from the Jaspersburg P.D. to the F.B.I. was working like crazy to pin the sale of the deadly Melting Rock acid on him. His parents—as it turned out, yet another pair of high-profile Benson professors who'd spent way more time on their research than their offspring—had put up their lake home to get him out of jail.

But as we'd report in Tuesday's paper, Sturdivant repaid their parental devotion by jumping bail. He'd shown up at their Benson Heights manse while his parents were at work, ripped off their Bose Wave radio and some of his dead grandmother's jewelry, and hit the road.

The authorities had found out about it when the Feds came by on Monday morning, slavering to interview the housekeeper about Junior's history of misbehavior. What they'd found was a middle-aged lady wringing her hands over how such a sweet little boy could've grown up so bad, and did they really think the family was going to lose their cabin over it?

She'd tried to talk some sense into him when he'd come barging in, she said, but he wouldn't listen to her—not even to her, and she'd practically raised him.

That was Friday. From what the cops could tell, not a soul had seen him since.

What had become of Sturdivant was, of course, an open question.

And maybe, just maybe, the Deep Lake corpse wasn't Axel, after all.

CHAPTER *18*

While Ochoa covered Sturdivant's disappearing act, I spent part of Monday working on a follow-up to my little story about Melting Rock getting sued. Since the first piece had appeared, a half-dozen other creditors had come out of the woodwork claiming that the festival had stiffed them. Even a member of the collective that runs the Ecstatic Eggplant Vegetarian Restaurant phoned to say they hadn't been paid for catering this year's volunteer kickoff dinner. And not paying your debts, the woman told me, is "super-duper bad karma."

Now, as far as I was concerned, the situation wasn't particularly surprising. The festival, after all, had been shut down a day early, and the trauma of the boys' deaths had probably put a major crimp in T-shirt sales. No, what was curious wasn't that the festival was in the red, but how much; the tally of bad debts had topped fifty thousand clams.

I still hadn't been able to speak to Trike Ford, Jo's honey and Melting Rock's financial guru. So I just wrote up a short piece about the new lawsuits, then turned back to the story that had been bumming me out for a week—that miserable "youth drug-culture" piece. Now, I know I should probably have a better attitude, but as far as I was concerned, the whole thing was idiotic. It was one of those over-blown, all-encompassing assignments that sound great to an editor but turn out to be a reporter's nightmare. You have to do a ton of interviews so you can justify throwing around a bunch of generalities, and you usually wind up feeling like you're doing the journalistic equivalent of taking potshots at the carnival ducky.

The story's one saving grace was that Bill and Marilyn had agreed that it ought to have a sidebar on Melting Rock; it was, after all, the site of the adolescent self-medication that had prompted the piece in the first place. As a reporter, I found doing something on drug use at the music festival a lot more appealing—it seemed like an *actual story.* So, admonished by my bosses to finish the package pronto or else, I took the easy way out and started writing the sidebar first.

I had Cindy's reminiscences about Melting Rock's status as some kind of teenage utopia, which seemed a good place to start. My plan was to craft a lead around her riff on *ecstasy* as both drug and state of mind—but I hadn't even finished the first paragraph when I realized the piece was missing something. To wit: the voice of reason.

At the scene of Shaun Kirtz's death, I'd barely had a chance to ask Chief Stilwell about the police's policy on prosecuting drug use at the festival. As far as I could tell, their attitude was one of not-so-benign neglect; it seemed as though the Jaspersburg powers that be let people dose themselves with impunity.

So I put in a call to the chief, and though I rather expected him to give me the runaround, he actually came to the phone. I was armed with all sorts of arguments for why he should talk to me—saving future Melting Rockers from doing themselves harm, yadda-yadda—but I never had to use them. I just told him what I wanted to talk to him about, and he only hesitated a second before agreeing to an interview that very afternoon.

I spent an hour or so dithering over the mainbar, then went out to the Green for a plate of veggie curry and a big hunk of nan. I left plenty of time to get out to Jaspersburg, which turned out to be a good thing. The drive took twice as long as usual because I got stuck behind (get this) a giant thresher. By the time this charming bit of Americana finally turned onto a side road, I'd practically crawled all the way to the village, and I walked into the police station cranky and smelling like stale hay.

Now, when I say *police station,* I don't mean a building entirely devoted to law enforcement. In actual fact, the Jaspersburg cop shop is all of three rooms in an old stone building that also houses the village hall, clerk, part-time mayor's office, animal control, youth program, senior center, and bingo palace. The only thing it doesn't have is the volunteer fire company, which is right across the street.

When I got inside the J.P.D. office, I thought it was deserted. Chief Stilwell must've heard me come in, though, because he called out from a room in the back. I went past the front counter and down the short hall, and there he was—sitting behind a desk that was probably normal size but, since he was such a big bear of a guy, looked like doll furniture.

"Alex Bernier," he said, dragging my name out—*Berrrrn-YAAAAY*—in a way that made me feel vaguely like I was being made fun of. "Have a seat."

He waved a meaty paw at the two fifties-era chairs facing the desk. They were made of curved wood and, like Chief Stilwell himself, looked to be rock solid. I sat in the one on the right and pulled out my notebook.

"Thanks for seeing me," I said. "Like I said on the phone, I—"

"You want to talk about drugs and Melting Rock."

"Um . . . That's right."

He leaned back in his chair, which took his weight without a groan. "Important topic."

"I think so. I'm doing a story on it. It's part of a bigger piece on kids and drugs."

He raised a bushy black eyebrow at me. "You say 'kids' like you're not practically one yourself."

"I'll be twenty-eight next month."

"Ah. I thought you were younger."

"Most people do."

"Anyhow, you're still just a kid from where I'm sitting."

"To tell you the truth, a few days at Melting Rock made me feel pretty ancient."

He stroked his salt-and-pepper mustache. I'm not generally a facial-hair fan, but somehow he managed to pull it off.

"Now, now," he said, deadpan. "You know Melting Rock's not just for kids. It's fun for the whole family."

I searched his face and voice for a trace of irony, but I was damned if I could find it.

"Back at . . . When we spoke at the festival, I asked you about drug enforcement. And you said—"

"I said we arrested three people last year for possession with intent to sell."

I flipped back a bunch of pages in my notebook. "As a matter of fact, that's *exactly* what you said."

"And you said, 'Three out of how many?'"

"Right." He didn't say anything, just sat back in his chair and inspected me so thoroughly I was wondering if a stray bit of hay was sticking out of my ear. "So I wanted to ask you . . . how is it that all these drugs are floating around Melting Rock, but almost nobody gets arrested?"

"Miss Bernier, you might not have noticed this, but I'm a policeman."

It seemed like there had to be a trap in there somewhere, but I couldn't quite figure it out. "Er . . . yeah?"

"And as such, I'm a pretty good judge of people."

"Um . . . okay."

"And right now, I'm judging that you already have a theory about this particular situation."

"You mean about Melting Rock?"

"Unless you've shifted your attention to the Dairy Princess pageant in the past few minutes."

There it was again—that tone that managed to be mocking without exactly *insulting* you. As demeanors go, it wasn't necessarily appealing, but it wasn't totally alienating, either. Something about it made you feel like even though you were the butt of the joke, at least you were in on it.

Yet again, Chief Stilwell was reminding me of Cody.

"Okay, you're right," I said. "Everybody knows that Jaspersburg makes a ton of money off the festival. And if lots of people got busted there, maybe hardly anyone would show up anymore. So, yes, it *has* occurred to me that maybe your office is under a certain amount of pressure to . . . you know, live and let live. Is that an accurate way of putting it?"

He looked me straight in the eye. "I'd say it's dead-on."

I wasn't sure I'd heard him right. "You would?"

"Absolutely."

"Um . . . Are you telling me straight out that you've been discouraged from policing the festival for drug use?"

"I'm telling you that in the past I've been told that it would be best for everyone if my men and I simply looked the other way."

"And you . . . uh, you realize we're talking on the record right now?"

"Miss Bernier, is Chief Hill over in Gabriel what you'd call a fool?"

"No, of course he's—"

"Then I can't imagine why you'd come into my town and treat me like *I'm* one."

"Look, Chief, I'm sorry. I'm just kind of taken aback here, okay? I didn't expect you to—"

"To be honest with you? Would you prefer that I lie?"

"No, I—"

"You asked me a question; I answered it. Go ahead and write it down."

I did. "Um . . . Who told you this?"

"Who told me what?"

"Who told you to, uh . . . to ignore all the drug taking that was going on?"

"I don't think that's important. Let's just say folks around here know what Melting Rock means to the village."

"And so you did it? You just looked the other way?"

He shrugged. "I'd rather say that we just didn't look too hard. And don't get me wrong—I'm not proud of it."

"So why did you do it?"

He clasped his hands church-style and laid his arms across the desk. "It seemed like the right thing to do at the time."

"How so?"

"You have to keep in mind how much the festival means to the town in terms of finances. Jaspersburg doesn't have a great deal of revenue, you know. Melting Rock means a new floor in the school gym, repairs that keep the village fire truck running, money to keep the senior center open. And the feeling was that if Melting Rock was ever considered, let's say . . . a hostile environment for certain things, that revenue would go away and all those important projects would have to be scrapped." He shook his head. "As I said, I'm not proud of it. What I'm telling you is that we didn't do our job."

"Do you mean to say that you feel responsible for what happened to those boys? And to that girl in Baltimore?"

He looked away from me and toward the left-hand corner of his desk. When I followed his eyes, I landed on a framed picture of Trish—much younger, significantly chubbier, and cuddled up to a smiling, open-faced lady.

Chief Stilwell stared at the picture for a while, then looked back up at me like he'd momentarily forgotten I was there. "Of course I do," he said.

"Of course you feel responsible for their deaths?"

He leaned forward, feet on the floor and elbows on the desk. "Those boys were my daughter's friends. And I always thought, before this happened . . . I assumed they were good kids."

"Well, from what I've heard about them, and from what I could tell . . . for the most part, they *were* good kids. They just were stupid enough to take drugs." He barked out a laugh. "You think those things are mutually exclusive?"

His lips formed a tight smile, which contained exactly zero in the way of mirth. "Obviously, you don't have children."

"No. Why?"

"If you did, you'd understand. Nobody who put your daughter in harm's way could be what you'd call a good kid."

I still didn't get it. "You mean—"

"I mean, my daughter was right there. She was a friend of theirs.

If she'd been stupid enough to try that garbage, right now she'd be . . ." He shook his head as though he couldn't stand to think about it.

"Is that why you're telling me this?"

"It can't go on anymore," he said. Pretty melodramatic, I know—and believe it or not, he actually squared his shoulders and straightened his spine as he said it. "They can fire me if they want to, but it just can't go on. It *won't* go on. Not in my town."

"You mean you're going to crack down on drugs at the festival next year?"

"If there *is* a festival."

"You mean there might not be?"

Another shrug. "Who knows? I wouldn't call this year's much of a success, would you?"

"So what are you planning on doing exactly?"

"All I'm talking about," he said, "is doing what we should've done all along—policing Melting Rock like any other public event. I'm not recommending anything radical. We're not going to do random searches or infringe on anyone's civil liberties. But this kind of blatant violation of the law won't be tolerated. Period."

"Would you maybe send in plainclothes cops or something? Drug-sniffing dogs?" He laughed—like he thought I was a very silly creature. "I'm just trying to get a picture of what you have in mind."

"I see."

"And what kind of reaction do you think you're going to get?"

"That's what I'd call a reporter's question."

"I don't think I follow."

"It's the kind of question only a reporter would ask. A stupid one with an obvious answer."

"Look, I was just wondering how you thought this . . . policy shift was going to be received."

"And the obvious answer is, some people will be glad, and other people will be furious."

"Who do you think will be glad?"

"Parents."

"Okay, and who do you think will be furious?"

"Everyone else."

"And that would be . . . ?"

"Kids. Drug dealers. People who make a lot of money selling pizza to teenagers when they're as high as a kite. You name it."

"What do you think the village council will say?"

"I don't really give a damn."

"How do you think Trish will feel about all this?"

It was an out-of-bounds, below-the-belt sort of question, and I'm not quite sure why I asked it. I also have no idea why he answered.

And at first, he didn't—just spent some more time staring at the photo of his daughter and his dead wife. Finally, he shook his head.

"Trish can be a very confused young lady," he said.

"She's a nice kid," I said. "She's just at a pretty awful age. I'm sure she'll turn out just fine."

A new expression parked on his face all of a sudden. One second he was looking all macho and judgmental, and the next he was, well . . . desperately hopeful. "You really think so?"

"Look, Chief, I've spent a fair amount of time with Trish and her friends over the past couple of weeks. And I'll be honest with you— they're not necessarily the kind of kids I would've hung out with when I was in high school. But Trish and Cindy and Lauren . . . their hearts are obviously in the right place. And you've got to remember that adolescence is a lot less fun than people make it out to be. Maybe it's because adults are bummed because they missed out on some great time they think they were supposed to have had. I don't know. But the way I remember it, being a seventeen-year-old girl is no picnic." I glanced back at the photograph. "And I'd imagine that—"

I'd been about to say something too intrusive even for me, but I managed to stifle myself. It didn't get past Stilwell.

"Especially," he said, "if you don't have a mother."

"Um . . . right."

"My wife died when Trish was twelve. I know there's never a good time, but . . . it's hard for me to think of a worse age."

"I'm sorry," I said, because I couldn't think of anything else. To tell you the truth, Stilwell's shift from Burt Reynolds to Phil Donahue was starting to freak me out.

He didn't say anything for a while, and the silence grew until it got downright uncomfortable. I wasn't sure whether I should just stand up and end the interview, or whether he was expecting me to say something else.

This intermission, while definitely weird, at least gave me a chance to take a long look at Stilwell, who was shaping up to be one strange fellow. In some ways the guy was a study in machismo, but when it came to his daughter, he was starting to look like a big softy. He obviously wanted to be a good cop, but he'd let his bosses strong-arm him into ignoring the law. He was fairly uptight, but he also had a major ironic streak that he pulled out when you least expected it. I knew he'd been to war, but for some reason I couldn't picture him there—although, truth be told, I could say the same thing about Brian Cody.

In short, I'd spent the past year wondering how a guy like Cody gets to be a guy like Cody; now I was pondering the same question about Steve Stilwell.

Finally, my reporterly survival instincts kicked in, and I opened my mouth and asked the first question that came to mind.

"What happened?"

He blinked, like he needed to drag his mind back from wherever it'd been. "Cancer," he said.

"Oh." More uneasy silence.

"Listen, Chief," I said finally, "I kind of had a talk with Trish recently, and it seemed to me that . . . maybe she's on the mend."

That *please-God-let-it-be-true* expression moved across his face again and parked there. "Do you really think so?"

"She told me how she'd gone into treatment, and how she wasn't doing any drugs or anything. Those seem like good things, right?"

He chewed on that for a while. The next thing that came out of his mouth totally took me by surprise.

"She likes you," he said.

"What?"

"Trish told me that. She said you were one of the only adults she'd ever met who really listened to her."

"I'm flattered."

"She also told me that I shouldn't give you a hard time." He cracked a hint of a smile. "She said I give everyone a hard time, and I should cut you some slack."

"Is that why you said you'd see me today?"

The smile got ever so slightly bigger. "Could be. Partly."

"The other part being a desire to get the word out about Melting Rock?"

"I guess you could say that."

"Listen, Chief, you're being straight with me, so I'll be straight with you. If there was an overt decision to allow drugs at Melting Rock, it's a pretty huge story."

He raised a hand. "I never said that there—"

"Okay, maybe not overt. But what you're telling me is that at the very least the powers that be in this town were willing to look the other way, to maybe put kids at risk for the sake of making money. People are gonna be furious. And one of the people they're gonna be furious at is you."

"I guess maybe they have a right to be."

"What about Rosemary Hamill?"

"What about her?"

"Is she one of the people who wanted you to—"

"I told you, who wanted what isn't important."

"I can guarantee you, most people aren't going to feel that way."

He shrugged yet again. "That's not my problem."

"Chief, I'm not trying to be rude. But this stuff you just told me's going to be in the paper tomorrow. Once it hits the streets, your phone is going to be ringing off the hook."

"A person does something wrong, it seems to me he ought to face the consequences. That's what I've tried to teach Trish, anyway."

I started to get up. "Fair enough."

"Let me ask you something," he said. "Do you know what they say is the single biggest influence on a kid?"

"Um . . . their parents?"

"You'd think so, wouldn't you? But it's not. And it's not their teachers, either. It's their friends—the people they hang around with every day. That's what makes all the difference. You gravitate toward the A students, you're probably going to be an A student. You fall in with the wrong crowd . . ."

He didn't finish the sentence. Not that it really needed finishing.

"Peer pressure," he said. "That's what it all comes down to."

"I guess that makes sense."

"And you know what?" he said. "It damn well doesn't stop when you turn twenty-one."

CHAPTER *19*

When it came to the reaction to my story about drugs and Melting Rock, "furious" proved to be one mother of an understatement. But as it turned out, said fury kicked in long before the paper was even printed. When I called Rosemary Hamill for commentary about what Chief Stilwell had said, she went so ballistic I was fairly sure that if she could've reached through the phone line and throttled me, she would've done it. As it was, I had to hold the handset a foot from my head to avoid popping an eardrum.

Predictably, she categorically denied that anyone would even *suggest* ignoring drug use at the festival; what was a tad surprising, though, was that she'd have the chutzpah to argue that there were hardly any drugs there in the first place. I'd barely gotten off the line with her when I heard the phone ring in the managing editor's office. Sure enough, it was Mrs. Hamill threatening all manner of doom if we printed the story.

Predictably, Marilyn told her to go to hell. Then, just as predictably, Mrs. Hamill promptly called downstairs to the publisher's office. But, it being a whole two minutes after five P.M., he'd already flown the coop.

The story ran the next day.

The good news was, with the Melting Rock sidebar metastasized into a giant story of its own, I appeared to be off the hook for the ever-vexing mainbar, at least for the moment.

The bad news was, people were, well . . . *furious.*

Now, this didn't really impact negatively on yours truly, controversial stories generally being the most fun to cover. But it did have the good people of Jaspersburg beating their bosoms and rending their garments—though why it was so traumatic to have the facts about drugs at Melting Rock go from blatantly obvious to merely confirmed was beyond me.

Such a hot potato of a story, naturally, demanded a whole slew of follow-ups. I ran around interviewing irate parents and embarrassed officials. Meanwhile, the editorial-page editor cranked out a column condemning what he called "an ends-justify-the-means mentality." The letters on the Op-Ed page were running three-to-one in favor of Chief Stilwell, who (to my surprise) got more praise for blowing the whistle than condemnation for turning a blind eye to the drugs in the first place.

Two days after the big story came out, Marilyn and Bill decided it was a perfect opportunity to satisfy Chester's edict that the *Monitor* be, quote, "a moral leader." So they assigned me to do one of those tortured debate pieces, the subject of which was the future of Melting Rock. Considering all that had happened over the past few weeks— the boys' deaths, the lawsuits over bad debts, and now the revelations about lax drug enforcement—I was supposed to go out and take the people's pulse about whether the festival ought to be scrapped for good.

It may sound straightforward, but my interview list was a couple of dozen names long. I needed to talk to musicians, fans, average J-burg residents, antidrug folks, festival organizers, vendors, town officials, et cetera, et cetera. When Marshall suggested at an edit meeting that it might be nice to add a sidebar on whether Melting Rock was financially feasible in the first place, I could've strangled him.

Naturally, Bill thought it was a smashing idea. So there I was, twenty minutes later, stuck in the basement of city hall going over the festival's stupid budget numbers. They were on file down there because Melting Rock had gotten some kind of city arts grant that required financial disclosure. And although maybe a mathematically gifted human being—or an investigative pit bull like Gordon—

might've been able to make some sense of it all, to me it was just a mess.

Periodically sneezing from the gobs of dust and mold lurking in the corners, I tried to force myself to look at it piece by piece. According to the papers, the festival made a little over $100,000 on admission fees, which seemed right. About twelve thousand people showed up, and a four-day pass cost $100; a single day was $30. Then there was income from campsite rentals, revenue from T-shirt sales and the like, and a whopping $65,000 in vendor fees; thus explaineth the $4 hot dogs.

It all sounded like Melting rock ought to be in the gravy—if only its expenses weren't equally titanic. There were the costs of insurance, garbage hauling, program printing, sound-system installation; the list went on and on. The festival had broken even the previous year, but just barely.

I took some notes and fled the basement while I still had working sinuses. Then I went back to the paper, where I pulled out my folder on the vendor lawsuit story and tried to figure out which one I should call for comment. But when I got to the ticket printer, I noticed that something didn't jibe.

A & S Printing was complaining that Melting Rock had stiffed it for printing seventeen thousand tickets—two thousand day tickets and fifteen thousand all-fest passes. I called the guy, and he confirmed it; they'd filled the same order as in the past two years, only this time they didn't get paid.

Now, I may not be anyone's idea of a C.P.A., but this sounded funky to me. Melting Rock consistently paid to have seventeen thousand tickets printed, but whenever it announced its attendance figures, they always hovered around twelve thousand. Overprinting one year could be chalked up to optimism, but *three?* And by an organization that had always operated just barely in the black?

No, it seemed to me that there was a far more likely explanation, which was that Melting Rock was selling a lot more tickets than it was copping to. And if that was true, it meant that it was pulling in—

what?—as much as fifty thousand dollars more than what was reflected on its financial statements. And that was assuming that it
wasn't also cooking the books in other places.

So where was all the money going?

It was a good question. And within a couple of hours, I had a
pretty good answer.

NOW, I'm sure this isn't what Mrs. Hamill wanted to accomplish
when she called Marilyn that afternoon, her tactics having changed
from stonewalling to spin control. Since we'd been irresponsible
enough to run the story, she said, she positively *demanded* that she be
allowed to give her side of things.

So I drove out to Mrs. Hamill's house, which turned out to be one
of those "painted lady" Victorians. The place had been restored to
within an inch of its life, with so many contrasting colors and
painstaking architectural details it looked like some architecture magazine's version of a centerfold; call it preservationist porn. Sitting on
the front porch waiting to be installed was a hand-painted sign that
said CUPID'S CUPOLA BED & BREAKFAST.

I rang the antique bell, and Mrs. Hamill answered—wearing a
typically hideous flowered skirt-and-sweater combination and an utterly wrathful expression. She showed me inside, and the interior
turned out to be equally overdone, with doilies on every available sur-
face. There were also little angels and cupids everywhere, so many that
if they ever decided to rise up in a winged army, Mrs. Hamill wouldn't
have a chance.

She put me on a couch that looked like it belonged in a French
Quarter bordello; it had an intricately carved wooden frame and hot-
pink velvet cushions. She sat in a doily-laden armchair opposite me,
and though there was a glass plate of lacy chocolate cookies on the
table, she didn't offer me one. She just looked me up and down,
pursed her lips, and said, "Why are you doing this?"

"Doing what?"

Her lips puckered even more, like she was sucking on an invisible lemon. "Why are you trying to destroy Melting Rock?"

"Er . . . I'm not."

"Of course you are."

"Really, Mrs. Hamill, all I'm doing is covering a story. I went to interview Chief Stilwell about drugs at Melting Rock, and he told me he'd been instructed to look the other way."

"Instructed by whom?"

"He wouldn't say."

If she was relieved, she didn't show it. "In any event," she said, "the man is mistaken."

"Are you telling me that the Jaspersburg chief of police somehow misunderstood the fact that he was supposed to ignore drugs at the festival?"

"That's precisely what I'm saying."

"No offense, but that doesn't sound very plausible."

"Of course it does," she said. "Some . . . well-intentioned person could have mentioned to the chief how arrests might tend to make people uncomfortable, and he simply took it the wrong way."

"Are you serious?"

"It certainly could happen," she said, cracking something resembling a smile. "Who's to say it didn't?"

I'm not going to bore you with the rest of the conversation, which consisted entirely of the same crap being shoveled for another forty-five minutes. Suffice it to say that by the time I left, I felt like I needed to take a shower to get the slime off. But, instead, I went back to the paper and dutifully added a couple of Mrs. Hamill's lame quotes to the story. I also spent a fair amount of time bellyaching to anybody who'd listen about what an insufferable battle-ax she was.

"What's this chick's story, anyway?" Mad said. "Sounds to me like the lady needs to get laid."

"You say that about everybody."

"And it's usually true."

"Well, I have no idea about the state of the woman's sex life, and I'd just as soon not find out."

"Is old Mr. Hamill still in the picture?"

"I don't know. Her house sure as hell didn't look like someplace any self-respecting man would want to live."

"Maybe she killed'm and ate'm."

"I wouldn't put it past her," I said, and went back to the story.

But as I was typing in Mrs. Hamill's quotes, it occurred to me that I really didn't know a damn thing about her—beyond a generalized desire to smother her with a pillow every time she opened her mouth. Partly out of curiosity and partly out of old-fashioned procrastination, I went back to the newspaper's library to see if there was a file on her. There was, though all it contained was a four-year-old profile from when she became the first woman to head Jaspersburg's town government.

The story had been written by a former towns reporter, a position now filled by the ever-annoying Brad. Much as I hate to say it, though, Brad would probably have done a better job of it. The clip I was holding had a lame lead—"On the Jaspersburg town council, the right man for the job is now a woman"—that, come to think of it, made its subject sound like she'd undergone gender reassignment surgery. The quotes were mediocre, and the reporter apparently hadn't bothered to ask Mrs. Hamill anything about actual issues facing the town government. It was, in short, a puff piece.

The story did tell me a few things, though. Mrs. Hamill was way older than I'd thought; she was fifty-one when the story was published, making her fifty-five now. She was a widow living on what she called her husband's "modest life insurance." And although she lived in the same house as she did now, back then it was a dilapidated mess.

I photocopied the story, put the clip back in the folder, and slammed the file drawer shut with something akin to satisfaction.

I'd been wondering where all that Melting Rock money had gone. What, I thought, were the odds that a fair amount of it had gone into bankrolling—the name alone made me want to hurl—Cupid's Cupola?

• • •

"You know," Cody was saying from the other side of the pillow, "that's a pretty serious accusation."

"Well, her house is pretty seriously ugly."

"I'm not sure that's a crime in this county."

"Honestly, Cody, the woman's gotta be on the take. Where else could she have gotten all the money to restore her place? I've done stories on people who've done stuff like that in Gabriel. It can cost, like, hundreds of thousands of dollars. And her house is *huge.* Plus, I'd bet dollars to doughnuts the woman's had a face-lift."

"Maybe she inherited the money or something."

"Jesus, do you always have to think the best of people?"

"It's a weird habit for a cop, I know. Now, tell me again about what you found in the Melting Rock financials."

"Hey, weren't you even listening before?"

"I was busy trying to get your jeans off you."

"The button fly is something of an impediment to romance."

"And about Melting Rock . . . ?"

"Like I said, I really think they're making more money in ticket sales than they're copping to. And if they're doing it with the tickets, who's to say they're not also doing it with everything else—vendor fees and camping passes and merchandising and all that?"

"How much money do you think we're talking about?"

"I guess it depends on how long it's been going on. Potentially . . . Jesus, I don't know. If they're skimming a hundred K or so a year, it could definitely add up."

"And you think all the money's going to Mrs. Hamill?"

"Not necessarily all of it. I mean, I've gotta think that the people who run the festival have to have their hands in the till too. Like, apparently the band that one of the heads of it is in just put out a double CD. Time in a recording studio isn't cheap, and from what I hear, none of them have day jobs that pay anything."

"So you think this guy . . . What's his name?"

"Trike Ford. He's the drummer for Stumpy the Salamander."

"You think he's embezzling Melting Rock money to fund the band?"

"It occurred to me."

"Have you talked to him about it?"

"Tried. Apparently, he's on the road."

"Oh."

"Are you about to tell me I should stay away from him in case he's a big meanie?"

"I was thinking about it."

"Come on, we've been through this a—"

"Baby, if there's really that much money at stake, I doubt the guy's gonna be too pleased about you nosing around."

"I can take care of myself."

"Nobody's saying you can't."

"Fine. Then presumably you won't mind me doing my job."

"I didn't—"

"Because this could be a pretty big scoop, you know. If Melting Rock is really cooking the books and paying off the town council to get them to keep the police from busting drug dealers, I'm damn well going to be the one to break the story."

"And nobody's saying you aren't."

"Fine."

"But, Alex . . . I really have to look into this."

I pushed myself off his chest and sat up. "Hold on. We have a deal, remember? Anything you tell me doesn't go to the paper, and anything I tell you doesn't go to the cops." He didn't say anything. "Remember?"

"Baby, I know. But I think maybe this is going to have to be an exception."

"Why?"

"Because three boys are dead."

"What does that have to do with it?"

"I don't know. Maybe nothing."

"What are you—"

"All I'm saying is, anything connected to Melting Rock—particularly to drugs at Melting Rock—is potentially connected to the murders. Now that I know about this, I can't just ignore it. You've got to understand that."

"But once you start nosing around about it, goddamn Gordon'll find out and that'll be the end of my scoop."

"I'll keep things low-key."

"The man is a bloodsucking creature of the night."

"I thought he was a friend of yours."

"The two things," I said, "are not mutually exclusive."

CHAPTER 20

As it turned out, I ran into the aforementioned vampire the very next evening. After a long day of trying to chase down more information on the Melting Rock embezzlement story, I decided a girl was entitled to skip her workout and go straight to the Citizen Kane. With Mad off pumping iron, I was thoroughly prepared to drink alone, but when I went to the bar to pick up my bourbon and ginger ale, I noticed a familiar pair of squinty eyes peering through a just-as-familiar set of wire-rimmed glasses. I carried my drink to the rear-most booth and sat down.

"What are you doing here?" I said.

"You know," Gordon replied, "you say that every damn time you see me."

"Maybe that's because you always look like a fish out of water up here."

"And the day I fit in is the day I pour gasoline over my head and light a match."

"Just make sure you send us a press release first so we can assign a photographer."

"Har-har."

"Seriously, what are you doing here?"

"I like sitting in the back. Less chance somebody'll come over and bother me."

"I meant, what are you doing in Gabriel?"

"None of your damn business."

"Jesus, do we have to go down that road again?"

"Apparently."

"Come on, Gordon, don't be such a prick. It's just a friendly question."

"In our business there's no such thing."

"Yikes. I guess you can take the boy out of the city, but you can't take the city out of the boy, huh?"

"I hope the hell not."

"Come on, be a pal."

"I have never been a pal in my whole miserable—"

"Given."

He let out his signature strangled groan. "Can't a guy just have a drink in peace?"

"You know, I'd assume that if a guy really wanted to drink alone, he wouldn't go to the bar that all his friends go to."

"Friends? What friends?"

"You are *so* infuriating sometimes."

He smiled like it was the first thing that had made him happy all day. "Okay, okay," he said. "I'll be a nice guy for five minutes. To answer your question, I'm here because a certain drug suspect has jumped bail. Or don't you read the papers?"

"I thought you were going to be nice."

"Right. Forgot."

"So you're doing something on Sturdivant. What's the angle?"

"Who he is, what kind of case the cops've got on him. You know—the usual."

"And?"

"And the rest is well and truly none of your beeswax."

"Lovely."

"You got anything juicy on him?"

"Let me get this straight. You're going to tell me practically nothing about the story you're covering, but you want me to open my mouth and give you whatever I know."

"Works for me."

"Well, unfortunately for you, I don't know anything."

"Aw, come on. You hung out at that freak fest for three days—"

"Practically four."

"Practically four. Didn't you even meet the guy?"

"Yeah, I met him."

"And?"

"And nothing. He was pretty unremarkable."

"A pretty unremarkable guy who helped kill four people."

"Four? Do you mean that girl in—"

"Nah, not yet. But ten bucks says she croaks within the week."

"You sentimental fool you."

"So fine, three people. He's clearly still a scumbag."

"Assuming he knew."

"You don't think he did?" Gordon's eyes narrowed. "What, did your buddy Cody tell you something?"

"Jesus Christ, would you stop pumping me like I'm some damn source? No, Cody did *not* tell me anything. And as you're fond of saying, if he did, I damn well wouldn't tell you."

"Okay, fine. I'm sorry."

I glared at him. "You are not."

"Okay, you're right, I'm not. I've done it before and I'll do it again. Satisfied?"

"Slightly."

"Good. Now, what do you say we have a little fun for old time's sake?"

"Meaning?"

"Meaning this story's driving me crazy."

"You mean Sturdivant?"

"I mean the whole thing—him and the three deaths and that girl in Baltimore. It all just seems so . . ."

"Random?"

"Yeah," he said. "How did you know?"

"It's kind of been on my mind lately."

"I mean, I can understand wanting to kill somebody you know. Like, if I thought I could get away with—"

"Yeah, yeah. You'd as soon off your editor as look at him. I'm fully aware."

"But the idea of whipping up that poisoned acid and just putting it out there to get taken by any poor bastard that comes along . . . that's pretty evil, don't you think?"

"Yeah." I took a hefty slug of my drink.

"But what if it wasn't random?" he said. "That's pretty evil too."

"Sure, but, come on . . . that's nuts."

"What makes you think so?"

"Gordon, I met them. They were three perfectly harmless, slightly idiotic teenage boys. Who'd want to kill them? And, more to the point, who could possibly want to go to such crazy lengths to do it?"

"I don't know. You tell me."

I swallowed some more of my drink, which was damn tasty. "Oh, hell," I said, "why does anybody kill anybody? Money, jealousy, revenge, lust—"

"Because they got shafted with being somebody's goddamn upstate correspondent . . ."

"I'm not sure that last one's in the Bible."

"Okay, seriously," he said. "Let's just say for the sake of argument that somebody did kill those three guys on purpose. Why do you think they'd do it?"

"How would I know?"

"You spent a hell of a lot more time with them than I did, which is none."

"Yeah, but—"

"Hey, come on, where's that girl I know? The one who just *lives* for wild speculation?"

His tone was smarmy but effective. "Oh, hell, all right. Let's think about it from the beginning. So . . . you've got these three guys. They're all friends. They hang out at school and they go to Melting Rock together every year. Maybe . . . I don't know. Maybe somebody just hates their guts or something."

"Oh, yeah, *that's* pretty damn convincing. How about we start over?"

I wrinkled my nose at him. "Okay, fine. So there's these three . . . No, there's four—" I cut myself off, then spent some quality time staring into space.

"What?"

"I . . . Nothing."

"You just thought of something."

I drained my glass and stood up. "I gotta go."

"Hey, come on, sit down. Let me buy you a drink."

"I'm a moron."

"What are you—"

"God, I don't know why I've been so obtuse lately. I guess all this stuff has been kind of dribbling in and I've been covering it in bits and pieces. I haven't really had a chance to think about the big picture."

"Which is?"

I finished putting on my sweater and shrugged into my backpack. "Never you mind."

"Hey, come on. . . ."

"Look, I may have been an idiot for the past couple of weeks, but I'm not so dense I can't see my damn nose in front of my face."

"Huh?"

"Give it up, Gordon. I know you too well."

"What's that supposed to mean?"

I leaned down to peck him on the cheek. "What that's supposed to mean," I said, "is that as far as I'm concerned, there's no way you dropped in here by accident."

I WENT STRAIGHT from the Citizen to Mad's apartment and found the occupant recently emerged from his postgym shower.

"Yo, Bernier. What's up?"

"I was just over at the . . . What's that smell?"

"What smell?"

I sniffed the air. "It's like . . . flowers or something. Lavender." I took a step closer. "It's *you*."

He tightened the towel around his waist. "It is *not*."

I leaned in and sniffed him. "It is *so.* Lavender and . . . rosemary."

"I don't know what you're—"

"Have you been shopping at Centered Scents or something?"

"What?"

"The aromatherapy store on the Green."

"No. *Hell* no. I . . . It was a gift, okay?" He went into the bathroom and emerged with a tin whose hand-lettered label said RELAX-ME-TALC. "It makes my skin feel good, all right?"

"Jeepers, Mad, who gave you that crap?"

"Nobody."

"Come on, who?"

"A chick."

"What chick?"

"Just a chick, okay?"

"You are such a— Oh, my God. Tell me you didn't get that from Lauren Potter." He didn't answer, which was proof enough for me. "Christ, I should've known. That hippie junk is right up her alley."

"You wanna tell me what you came over here for?"

"Jesus, Mad, do I have to remind you that the girl is only seventeen? You're practically old enough to be her—"

"She's eighteen. Just turned."

"Please tell me you weren't her birthday present."

"Are you gonna say what you came over here for or aren't you?"

I sighed and flopped down on the lumpy couch. "You got any snacks? I'm starving."

"Fat-free chips and salsa."

"The yucky hot kind that burns my tongue?"

"Yeah."

"Okay."

He went into the bedroom to put on some shorts and a T-shirt while I sussed out the food—not hard because Mad's kitchen contains fewer provisions than a U.N. relief kit. We rendezvoused back on the couch, where he drank red wine out of an old jar and I sipped one of his diet Sprites—Mad being the only guy I know who's secure enough in his masculinity to admit to drinking diet soda.

"So," he said, "you ever gonna tell me why you came over here?"

"I was thinking."

"Dangerous habit. About what?"

"Okay . . . I went over to the Citizen to, you know, wet the old whistle after work, and there was Gordon—"

"Band? What the hell was he doing there?"

"My question exactly. And I'm pretty sure the answer is that he was hoping I'd show up so he could pump me for information about the Melting Rock story."

"What information?"

"Damned if I know. But Gordon obviously figured that since I was stuck in that hellhole for three days and I've been covering the thing so much ever since, I must know *something*."

"Weaselly little bastard."

"Yeah, but at least he's consistent. Anyway, it kind of hit me that, well, maybe he's right. Maybe I *do* know something—or maybe I *should* know it, anyway. . . ."

"What are you talking about?"

"I'm not quite sure. But while I was sitting there talking to Gordon, one thing did hit me over the head."

"Which is?"

"Four." I held up the appropriate number of fingers.

"Four what?"

"Okay, listen. . . . This whole time, everybody's been marveling at the fact that besides the three kids who died, only one other person has gotten sick from that stuff—the girl from Baltimore. Everybody's been wondering where the rest of the drugs are, when the other shoe's going to drop. Right?"

"Right. So?"

"So maybe there *is* no more. Maybe all there ever was was those four doses. Four doses, four guys."

"Four? But only—"

"First Tom Giamotti dies. Then Shaun Kirtz, then Billy Halpern. Maybe it's because they're buddies and so they just happened to share the same batch of bad drugs. Or maybe it's because they were targeted in the first place."

"Are you serious?"

"Now, as far as we know, four tabs of the killer acid were sold at Melting Rock. The fourth one went to Norma Jean Kramer. But what if it was supposed to go to somebody else?"

"And who would that be?"

"I was thinking about that when I was walking over here. And my first thought was, who's the most obvious person? I mean, there were four guys in that little Jaspersburg High enclave, and only one of them is still breathing."

"The jock, right? What's his name . . . ?"

"Alan Bauer. And if I'm right, we've got to warn him. I mean, if somebody tried to kill him once, who's to say they aren't going to do it again?"

"Wait a minute. Why do you think he didn't take the acid along with the others?"

"I'm not sure. I know he was indulging in various, you know, *substances,* but he was also counting on getting a soccer scholarship. Maybe he didn't want to take the chance."

"Or maybe he knew."

"*What?*"

"It's just a thought. Maybe he didn't take it because he didn't want to get dead."

"So you mean maybe he was in on it? Jesus, I guess it's possible, but . . . I really doubt it. As far as I knew, they were all friends."

"You got any other ideas?"

"Yeah, maybe this is totally out of left field, but . . . what if that fourth tab really wasn't meant for Bauer, after all?"

"What makes you say that?"

"Think about it," I said. "Bauer's alive and well right now, but somebody else isn't."

"And who would that be?"

"Whoever I found in the goddamn Deep Lake Cooling pool."

"Couldn't that be Alan Bauer?"

"What? God, that never even occurred to me, either. But, come on . . . I saw that hideous thing four days ago. If Bauer's been missing since then, don't you think somebody would've said something?"

"Yeah, I guess. So, if it's not him, who do you think was supposed to get tab number four?"

"Well, who do we know is missing right now?"

"The bail jumper with the earring fetish."

"Robert Sturdivant. You got it. Not to mention his buddy Axel Robinette."

"But wait a second," Mad said. "Sturdivant is the guy who sold the drugs to those kids in the first place. How could he be a target?"

"I was thinking about that on the walk over here too, and—"

"It's only a block and a half, you know."

"Yeah, well, I think fast. So, like I was saying, I was thinking . . . what if he wasn't just supposed to sell the drugs, he was supposed to *take* them too? What if whoever set this whole thing up gave him four tabs and said, 'I want you to sell three of them to Tom and Shaun and Billy, and, by the way, here's a freebie for your trouble'?"

"So the killer, whoever he is, gets rid of those three guys and the delivery boy all in one fell swoop. Convenient."

"Yeah, but maybe Sturdivant gets greedy. Maybe he'd rather have the money than the high, so he sells it to that girl from Baltimore. He obviously hasn't been told that the acid is bad, or he'd never take it himself, right? Which means that Sturdivant is just a patsy."

"Like Lee Harvey Oswald."

I stared at him over my Sprite can. "Where did that come from?"

"Hey, the government knows what really went down. It's all in files in the basement of the Pentagon, believe me."

"Whatever. So the question is, how does Axel Robinette figure into all of this? Was *he* really supposed to get the fourth tab? I mean, the guy was definitely jittery when I talked to him the day before he disappeared. He clearly needed money so he could blow town. Maybe he knew he was in danger or something. What do you think?"

"I think," he said, "that in all this cogitation you're skipping over the most important part."

"Which is?"

"Jesus, Bernier, how many times have you had to talk to the journalism club at Benson High?"

"Too damn many. What's your point?"

"What do you always tell them about the five *W's?*"

"I'm not following you."

"You've got your *who,* your *what,* your *where,* and your *when,*" he said. "But nine times out of ten, the most interesting part of the story is the *why.*"

CHAPTER *21*

You're wondering about the motive," I said.

"Damn right I am," Mad shot back. "Aren't you?"

"Yeah. I just . . . God, I just don't know. I mean, let's set aside the possibility that maybe these three guys *weren't* the intended victims—that the whole thing was random or the acid was meant for somebody else. If we assume for the moment that those four tabs were meant for Tom, Shaun, Billy, and whoever else, then . . . why?"

"I think I just asked you that a second ago."

"Why would somebody want to kill them? How could somebody hate three clueless teenage boys enough to want to pull this off?"

"Maybe somebody just wanted to shut down Melting Rock."

"What?"

"I mean, that's what happened, right? Maybe that was the point all along."

"Why would someone want to do that?"

"Because the place is a goddamn smelly mess."

"Come on, be serious."

Mad shrugged, then coated a tortilla chip with an obscene amount of salsa. "Who knows why? Maybe it's a political thing. I mean, if there's no Melting Rock, the village of J-burg is pretty much in the crapper, financially speaking."

"You've got a point there."

"And, hey, think about it. What did those three kids have in common?"

"They were all male; they all went to the same school. . . ."

". . . and they were all hometown boys."

"So you're saying . . . what? That the killer was hoping that if a bunch of local kids died of bad drugs, people'd want to shut down the festival for good? Do you really think that makes any sense?"

"Hey, you wanted me to play ball with you, I'm playing ball. That's all I've got."

"So shutting down the festival—maybe just for a day, maybe for good—either it was the whole point of the killings, or it was just a fringe benefit."

"I guess."

"And if it *wasn't* the point—if killing them was an end in itself, then . . . why?"

"Here we go again."

"I mean, come on," I said. "How does a bunch of high-school kids piss somebody off enough to want them dead? Is it just . . . jealousy? Some nerd deciding to get one over on the cool kids?"

"Nah. I think they usually just cut to the chase and shoot up the lunchroom."

"Okay, so what else could it be? I mean, most murders are about money, aren't—holy shit."

"What?"

"There's, um, this story I've been working on. . . ."

I filled him in about the Melting Rock budget snafu and Mrs. Hamill's pricey Victorian hellhole.

"And you think . . . what? That the boys were killed because they knew about it?"

"I don't know. I was just saying how most murders are about money, and it occurred to me that there's actually a lot of money at stake."

"But how could they know about it? They were just a bunch of teenage kids."

"Right, but they were a bunch of kids who went to Melting Rock their whole lives. And, in fact, when I first met them, Lauren said they were involved in organizing it too. She said"—I hunted for the details—"that Shaun Kirtz had worked on the festival's Web site and Tom Giamotti had volunteered in the office. Plus, she and Billy had manned some promo table on the Green. Maybe one of the guys stumbled onto the financial racket, and either they threatened to go to the cops or they—"

"Wanted a piece of the action?"

"Yeah."

"It's definitely worth looking into."

"You know, Cody said the embezzlement could potentially be connected to the murders. I just don't think he meant this directly."

"You told Cody?"

"Pillow talk."

"So what's he gonna do about it?"

"Look into it. Subtly."

"And goddamn Band's gonna—"

"Cody promised we'd get to break the story one way or the other."

"Jesus," he said, "you really think the money's the motive?"

"It's the best one I've heard so far."

"Yeah, but if you ask me, somehow it just doesn't jibe."

"Why not?"

"I guess . . . I don't know, it's just the way they were killed. The whole thing seems so . . . ."

"Sneaky and psychotic?"

"Not the words I was looking for," he said, "but I guess they'll do."

"And you're thinking that if somebody was really doing this over money, they would've done something more . . . straightforward?"

"More or less."

"It could be they wanted it to look like an accident all along. Maybe they thought nobody would figure out it wasn't just an OD."

"Yeah, but . . . I don't know, maybe it was really just your regular, old-fashioned crime of passion. Teenagers definitely have plenty of *that*."

I thought about the tin of Relax-Me-Talc, and decided not to go there.

"Fine," I said. "So if that's really the story here, then what prompted it? What kind of, you know, *passions* did these kids stir up that made somebody want to kill them?"

He repeated his shrug-and-dip-the-chip maneuver. "Maybe somebody got sick of looking at a bunch of scruffy little creeps."

"Would you be serious?"

"Okay, okay," he said. "So what are you asking exactly?"

"What I'm wondering," I said, "is just what the hell these guys did. And more to the point, who did they do it to?"

THEY WERE LOVELY QUESTIONS; unfortunately, it didn't look like I was going to find answers anytime soon—if indeed there were answers to be had.

With Labor Day weekend just days away, much of the population of Walden County appeared to have blown town in search of a few final days of summer vacation. My attempts to talk to Alan Bauer, therefore, were foiled by the fact that his entire family had decamped to Hershey, Pennsylvania, for some sort of amusement-park-related healing. I tried to picture purple-haired Cindy riding a Ferris wheel shaped like a chocolate kiss, and couldn't.

Although I would've been more than happy to flee the 607 area code myself—particularly if it involved a homicide detective and a hot tub—it was sadly not an option. At the beginning of the year, we reporters divide up the holidays, and to make sure I'd get to go home for Christmas, I'd volunteered to work on New Year's, Thanksgiving—and Labor Day weekend.

So there I was, covering the cops beat for three days straight and writing the usual fluff about back-to-school plans and the Gabriel Workers' Alliance Solidarity Barbecue. I was also feeling fairly sorry for myself, though I was somewhat mollified by the fact that I'd at least get to make an appearance at the newsroom picnic—which, by the way, was happening in my own backyard.

Unfortunately, the chance to have a veggie burger and pet my dog for an hour was just about all the consolation I was going to get; with the search for Sturdivant at a standstill, Cody had taken the three-day weekend to drive his mom back to Boston to visit his sisters and their frighteningly well-behaved kids.

That left me to make my own fun on Friday and Saturday night. I saw a delightfully stupid action movie for my column, split some veggie sushi with the still-heartbroken Melissa, and spent a good hour reading *Dog Fancy* in the bathtub. Labor Day itself turned out to be gorgeous—the kind of blue-sky-perfect weather that we rarely see here in the cloud capital of upstate New York. This, as you can imagine, inspired me to thoroughly research my piece on the Solidarity Barbecue. And I mean *thoroughly.*

The yearly event, which pretty much takes over the big park at the edge of Mohawk Lake, is a major fund-raiser for the Workers' Alliance—a nonprofit group that promotes union membership, lobbies for living wages and fair working conditions, and generally tries to keep the little guy from getting screwed by the Man. There's always a bunch of speeches by politicos and union agitators, plus games of horseshoes, softball, volleyball, and the like, with many a beer bet riding on the outcome.

And speaking of beer, the local Budweiser distributor traditionally parks a truck on the grass and sticks a tap in the side of it; suffice it to say, everybody has a damn good time.

But for a lot of the people, the real draw is the barbecue itself, which is an orgy sufficient to bring about the fall of Rome. In addition to the various creatures dipped in sauce and grilled over a spit, there's also a ton of distinctly unhealthy vegetarian food: butter-laden corn on the cob, delectably mayonnaisey potato salad, that sort of thing. Yours truly got a complimentary media ticket, which garnered me a blue plastic OVER-21 bracelet and the freedom to eat and drink till I keeled over.

Between the weather and the comestibles, I spent a good three hours at the barbecue. I was just about to bow to the inevitable and go back to the paper for another round of cop calls when I figured I should have more to show for myself than a couple of measly quotes, so I made another loop around the park.

I was interviewing a Benson janitor when the screaming started.

It came from the water, which is where a bunch of future union-dues payers were playing, and at first everybody seemed to take it for the usual kiddie screeching. But it didn't take long for people to realize that there was something wrong. The natural assumption, of course, was that some poor kid was drowning. What seemed like the city's entire union membership ran en masse to the water's edge, and I had to dodge my way through a crowd of very solid men to get a look.

By the time I got through the clutch of people, it was too late—for the victim, anyway. The body was floating facedown, gliding back and forth with the motion of the water. The way it was moving implied a weird sort of purpose—it came close to shore, then slid back toward the open water, hovered at one particular spot, and slid back in again. It was an illusion, of course; the person lying facedown in Mohawk Lake no longer had any free will, nor would he ever.

It only took a second for me to realize that I'd seen this body before. I'd seen it in exactly the same position, glimpsed by flashlight, floating in a near-freezing pool.

The truth of it was still sinking in when a couple of guys waded into the water, sneakers and all. They grabbed the body as though there were some hope of reviving it, turned it over like they could drag it to shore and give it mouth-to-mouth and maybe everything would be okay.

But they'd barely flipped it on its back when they dropped it again. The horrified sounds they made were decidedly unmacho, but nobody could blame them—no one, at least, who saw what they'd seen. And touched.

It was a body that had been underwater for more than a week—discolored, decomposing, dehumanized. A collective gasp went through the crowd, hands clasped to mouths, mothers (literally) covering their children's eyes.

There's probably a psychological study to be done about who keeps watching at moments like this and who looks away. I don't know what it says about me. I couldn't drag my eyes from the corpse's face. It was bloated, distorted—and familiar.

ON HOLIDAYS, the Gabriel Police Department—like the *Gabriel Monitor*—runs on a skeleton crew. Maybe big-city law enforcement schedules a full complement of officers 365 days a year, but around here the mayhem level is generally low enough to allow most of our men in blue to toss around a football on Labor Day.

It just so happens, though, that the Gabriel police union is a major sponsor of the Workers' Alliance; therefore, nearly every guy who wasn't in uniform was roasting weenies in Mohawk Park. The crime scene, in other words, was already crawling with cops—including the chief himself.

Wilfred Hill had been at the far side of the park when the body washed up, so it took him a couple of minutes to get to the shore, but once he did he was all business. He assigned a few cops—presumably, the ones who smelled less like the floor of a frat house—to secure the scene, then pulled a cell phone from a voluminous front pocket of his plaid Bermuda shorts.

I guess he was trying to track down the coroner, but he didn't seem to be having much luck; he dialed four or five different numbers before he flipped the phone shut and jammed it back into his pocket with a scowl.

I approached him because I didn't have much choice.

"Excuse me . . . Chief?"

He turned around, and if there existed someone he was less in the mood to see, well . . . I pity them.

"How did you get here this fast? You people are *unbelievable*."

"I was already here. Covering the picnic."

"Oh."

"Listen, Chief, can I talk to you for a second?"

"Come on, Alex. You have to know better than that."

"But I just—"

"We've been on the scene five minutes."

"I know, but—"

"*No,* we do not know who the victim is. *No,* we do not know how he died. *No,* we do not know how he got here. Are you satisfied?"

Since the chief is usually the epitome of levelheaded, this lakeside freak-out was definitely out of character. The reason why made itself clear when Mrs. Chief came over two seconds later to inform her husband that she was taking the children home.

"Your family's here, huh?" I said once she'd gone.

This comment sounded, if you can believe it, even lamer than you might think.

"If you're even *thinking* about putting that in the paper, I promise you'll regr—"

"What? That wasn't what I—"

"Now, please do me a favor and go away. We'll let you know if there are any developments."

Yeah, right. "Listen, Chief, I—"

The expression on his face said he wished he'd had room in the damn Bermuda shorts for his .357. "Do you want me to have you removed from the scene?"

"No, I—"

"Donner," he called to one of the relatively sober cops. "Do me a favor and escort Miss Bernier to her car."

"Wait," I said. "I'm not trying to be a pain, it's just—"

"Do you want to get yourself arrested for interfering with an investigation?"

"I recognized him."

"You *what?*"

"The body. I know who it is."

"Jesus, why didn't you *say* something?"

Yeah, I know; it sounds like something out of a goddamn sitcom. And it might've struck me as funny—except for the rubbery corpse lying twenty feet away.

"Come on," he was saying, "who is it?"

"It's this kid I met at Melting Rock. I didn't know him that well, but I interviewed him a couple of times. He's been missing since last week. I was supposed to meet him someplace, but he never showed up, so I thought maybe he left town, and—"

"For God's sake, Alex, out with it," he said. "What's his name?"

"It's Axel," I said. "Axel Robinette."

YOU WOULDN'T HAVE THOUGHT that a picnic for a few thousand union workers would have much (or, in fact, anything) in common with the Melting Rock Music Festival. But this year, it did. At both events people were having a perfectly good time—just whooping it up and minding their own business—when somebody's corpse came along and ruined everything.

If the death of Shaun Kirtz wasn't enough to immediately shut down Melting Rock, the discovery of Axel Robinette's body was plenty to derail the Solidarity Barbecue. Amid the wails of children upset by a glimpse of the decaying Axel—and others simple traumatized by the cancellation of the make-your-own-sundae bar—everyone packed up their chairs and blankets and boom boxes and headed for the exit.

This exodus caused a mother of a traffic jam, alleviated only when some of the off-duty cops donned orange vests and directed the parade of cars and trucks onto Route 13 in batches. Chief Hill continued to look pissed and weary in his Bermuda shorts and ugly white golf visor, and his mood only improved when two things happened: He finally got the coroner on the phone, and he watched his family station wagon drive out of Mohawk Park.

As for me: Once the chief finished peppering me with questions about Axel and that night at the Deep Lake Cooling plant, I called the photo editor and told him to get back to the park pronto. Wendell had already taken pictures of kids running the potato-sack race; now he had to snap some of Axel being hauled away in a body bag. He found the task, quote, "very uncentering."

Instead of going back to the paper, I went home—where, conveniently, most of the newsroom was grilling hot dogs and getting companionably drunk. I found Ochoa presiding over the sangria pitcher, and five minutes later, most of the cityside staff was having an impromptu editorial meeting in my kitchen.

The overtime budget being smaller than a bad kid's allowance, it was decided that I could cover the breaking news all by my lonesome. After all, Marilyn said, it was really just a matter of writing about the discovery of the body, plus a reaction piece based on interviews with whichever of Axel's friends might be slacking around the Green on a national holiday. That, and maybe a short summary of all the recent mayhem—basically, a roundup of how the county's youth was dropping like flies. If I had the chance, I could put together a little time line of events, going back to the start of Melting Rock 13. No pressure.

Hours later, when I was putting the hateful time line together— Chester just *lives* for devices that reduce the news to Tinkertoy chunks—it occurred to me that I ought to call Baltimore. I was writing up a bit about Norma Jean Kramer going comatose on the stuff that had killed the three Jaspersburg boys, and I figured I should go through the motions of updating her condition for the next day's paper.

So I called and got the poor P.R. underling who'd been assigned to work on Labor Day. The guy put me on hold for a good five minutes; I was about to hang up and dial again when he picked up.

"Um . . . I'm sorry that took so long," he said. He sounded barely old enough to drive.

"That's okay," I said, doodling a pair of pointy dog ears in my reporter's notebook. "So her condition's unchanged?"

"Uh . . . That's just it. I mean, that's what took me so long. I, er . . . I needed to get confirmation."

"Confirmation for what?"

"I called up to the eighth-floor nurses' station, and they told me . . ."

"Yeah?"

"Apparently, Miss Kramer is awake."

CHAPTER *22*

I wanted to run down to Baltimore and interview Norma Jean Kramer the minute I found out she was conscious. Unfortunately, though, when I called the hospital back to ask about setting something up, the P.R. guy laughed at me, said, "You gotta be kidding," and hung up.

That left me with nothing to do but rehash the stories that had run on her when she'd first gotten sick, with a lead about her miraculous recovery slapped on top. When I was done, I felt badly in need of a drink but in no mood for the Citizen—nor was I inclined to go home and face the postpicnic disaster. So I went over to Mad's and found him in his usual pose on the couch, sipping midpriced red wine out of an old salsa jar and watching a documentary about mummies on the History Channel.

"You know something?" I said. "The only person who has uglier furniture than you is Mrs. Hamill."

"Mine's what you call 'shabby chic.'"

"It's what you call 'garbage-dump.'"

"You want a drink?"

"More than you know."

He got me a jar of my own, and I told him about Norma Jean waking up—and how Marilyn had gone mildly ballistic when I told her we weren't getting an interview anytime soon.

"She's gotta be psyched about the Axel thing," he said. "Since he doesn't seem to have any family for the cops to notify we're gonna have it on the streets first thing in the morning. Only guys who could maybe scoop us is drive-time radio."

"True."

"Must've been a hell of a scene at the picnic."

"You said it."

"Cody there?"

I shook my head, which was already starting to feel pleasantly groggy. "Took his mom to Boston for the long weekend to see his sisters."

"No wonder you're here drinking with me."

"Since when do I need an excuse?"

"You want a refill?"

The image of Axel Robinette's bloated body flashed across my brain. "Dear God yes."

We sat there like that for an hour, talking about the ridiculous number of stories we'd been covering and getting happily smashed. When we got to the Melting Rock embezzlement, Mad slammed his jar down on the coffee table and said, "You know what?"

"No," I said, still sober enough to be aware of the slur in my voice. "What?"

"We gotta break this goddamn thing before goddamn Gordon Band breaks it for us."

"Cuh-lear-ly."

"Which means we got to get ourselves some proof of what the hell's been going on."

"Ob-vee-ous-ly."

"We gotta get our goddamn hands on the real numbers."

I waved my jar at him in a boozy salute. "You said it, sister."

He stood up. "So let's go."

I squinted at him. "What the holy heck are you talkin' about?"

"Let's go get it."

"Go get what?"

"Proof. Evidence. Incontrovertible"—he sat back down and poured more wine, most of which actually ended up in his jar—"stuff."

"Where?"

"I dunno. Where d'ya think?"

I stretched out on the couch. "If I thought you were serious, which I seriously do *not,* I'd say the place to look would be the Melting Rock office."

"Which is where?"

"Back of Groovy Guitar."

"Like the store a couple doors down from the paper?"

"Just like that."

He stood up again. "So let's go."

"Let's go where?" He waggled his eyebrows at me. "Let's do what? Break into the place?" His face broke into a diabolical smile. "You . . . are . . . insane."

"Come on," he said, "it'll be fun."

"Actually," I said, "it'll be a felony."

"Only if we get caught. Which we won't."

"And how the hell do you know that?"

"Because we'll go in all sneaky-like."

"Mad, the last time we tried to go someplace 'all sneaky-like,' we almost both got very killed. 'Member?"

"Hey, baby. Horseshoes and hand grenades."

"You're drunk," I said. "An' come to think of it, so am I."

"Chicken." He flapped his elbows at me and clucked like poultry: *brawk-brawk-brawk-brawk.* "Alex Bernier is a big *chicken.*"

"Alex Bernier," I said, "doesn't feel like getting arrested for breaking and entering."

But there was no talking him out of it; within two minutes he'd pulled on a pair of khakis over the boxers he'd been lounging in, grabbed a flashlight, and headed out the door. So . . . I followed.

Since the newspaper is less than a block from Mad's apartment, we got to the guitar store in under a minute—not nearly enough time to convince Mad he was well and truly out of his mind.

Finding the street deserted, he declared his intention to, quote, "case the joint." Since the building that houses the music store abuts its neighbor to the left, that meant walking down the narrow alley to the right. And since Mad had the only flashlight and didn't seem inclined toward chivalry, I picked my way in the dark, trying not to trip over broken bottles and discarded pizza boxes. He shone the light on the wall, which proved to be solid brick—no windows. Hopefully, Mad's burglary career was going to be over before it started.

At the back there was a door that didn't look particularly solid—not steel reinforced or anything—but though Mad tried twisting the handle and pulling hard, it didn't budge.

Unfortunately, though, there was also a window. And to my even greater chagrin, the damn thing was cracked open.

Mad made some happy-little-girl sound (*"Ooh-hoo-hoo!"*) and shone the light inside. The first thing we saw was a promotional poster for Stumpy the Salamander.

"What do you think's in there?" he asked.

"I'd . . . rather not say."

"Don't be such a pussy."

"Fine. If you gotta know, I think it's the goddamn Melting Rock office."

"Excellent." He made a move to open the window all the way.

"Hold on just one sec," I said. "How do you know there isn't a"— I struggled for the term—"burglar alarm or something?"

"Bernier, the place is called Groovy Guitar. You really think they got an alarm system?"

"They might."

"Besides, the window's kinda cracked open. Even if there's an alarm, it can't be set, right?"

I never got a chance to answer because Mad proceeded to slide the window open and pull himself inside in one surprisingly fluid motion. Lacking much in the way of upper-arm strength, I just stood there whispering at him to get his drunken ass back outside.

"I'm just gonna have me a little lookee-look around," he said. "Now, do you want in or don't you?"

"Oh, hell. In."

He reached down and gave me a hand up—which basically amounted to hauling me bodily over the sill.

"Jesus, that was easy," he said. "Music folks ain't too security conscious, eh?"

"Like you don't leave your windows open all the damn time."

He stuck his tongue out at me, eyes vaguely crossed. "*Yuh,*" he said.

There was a crooked shade atop the window, and Mad pulled it down before he turned on the flashlight. Then he hunted around for a light switch, finally figuring out that you were supposed to pull a string hanging from the ceiling. The single bulb didn't do a great job illuminating the room, but at least we could see enough to read.

There was one whole bookshelf filled with multicolored volumes; even in the context of Melting Rock—and, more to the point, the context of my booze-addled brain—I tended to doubt they were financial statements. So we pawed through the piles of papers clogging the place; a lot of it turned out to be promo stuff from unknown bands hoping to play at the festival.

Finally, when Mad was starting to sober up enough to think that maybe it was time to leave, I came across a three-ring binder in the bottom left-hand drawer of the desk. It looked like something a seventies-era junior-high student would've brought to school—denim cover, blue-lined paper inside.

But . . . I seriously doubt that some middle schooler was inclined to give thirty thousand bucks to Rosemary Hamill.

At least that's what I assumed this entry meant: *R.H.—$30K.*

There were about two dozen other ones too—most of them initials with amounts of money. But Mrs. Hamill was clearly getting the most, followed by one T.F., who I assumed to be Trike Ford; he appeared to have raked in twenty thousand clams himself. Some of the entries had the initials M.A. in the margin, whoever that was. I flipped through more pages and found another, shorter list of amounts, presumably from a previous year. But if it was, the recipients had completely changed; none of the initials were the same, not even

T.F. himself. The amounts were a lot smaller too, most around a grand and none topping five thousand.

"Whatcha got there?" Mad asked.

"Your basic smoking gun. At least I think so." He peered over my shoulder and I flipped back to the first list. "Looks here like Mrs. Hamill got thirty grand. The guy who runs the Melting Rock finances got twenty."

"Who's M.A.?"

"Damned if I know. Can you think of anybody?"

"Just Mayor Marty."

"*What?*" Martin Anbinder is Gabriel's crusty-but-lovable chief executive, a retired Benson engineering professor whose politics make Karl Marx look like Ronald Reagan. "You can't seriously think he'd be on the take."

"Nah. You just asked me if I recognized the initials."

"Oh."

"So if we're really seeing a list of payoffs, which I sure as hell think we are, then what do you think it's all about?"

I scratched at my scalp in a vain attempt to get some of the alcohol out of my cranium. "Um . . . drugs?"

"You think Rosemary Hamill is buying dope?"

"Nah, not buying it, maybe just . . . making sure Melting Rock doesn't have, you know, a hostile atmosphere. Maybe it's a cover-up to keep people quiet about all the cash they're skimming. Or maybe it's just plain-old kickbacks. The festival generates a ton of money. Maybe this is a way of letting the powers that be . . . What's the Italian phrase? 'Dip their beak.'"

"Oh. I get it. I think."

I turned to the page with the smaller amounts. "What do you make of this other list?"

"'A.G., M.L., A.R., R.S., A.W.,'" he read off from the top. "Anything ring a bell?"

"Um . . . Actually, yes. A.R. could be my old pal Axel Robinette. R.S. could be Rob Sturdivant. I don't recognize any of the others."

"Any idea why they'd be getting payoffs?"

"Not off the top of my head." Mad pulled open a filing cabinet and started riffling through the folders. "What are you looking for?" He didn't answer. "Come on, we found what we were after. Don't you think we'd better get out of here?"

"Just give me a minute."

"What are you looking for?"

"The budget."

"I told you, it's on file over in city hall. That's how I found out that—"

"I mean the *real* budget."

"You really think they'd be stupid enough to write it down?"

He looked through the rest of the folders and shook his head. "I guess . . . Wait a second."

"Did you find it?"

"Something else." He pulled out a file and handed it to me.

"'Mohawk Associates, Inc.,'" I read off the tab. "M.A."

"Right-o."

I opened it up. "All there is in here is a receipt for a post office box in Gabriel."

"What do you think it means?"

"I have no idea."

"Do you recognize the name?"

"It sounds sort of familiar, but I can't place it."

"Well . . . are we looking for anything else in here?"

"I think we've broken enough laws for one night, don't you?"

"What about those?"

Mad gestured toward the albums on the bookcase, and I pulled one at random. They turned out to be scrapbooks of past Melting Rocks, laden with photos of dazed-looking dancers. "Nothing useful," I said.

"Then let's get out of here," he said, tucking the denim binder under his arm and tossing a leg over the windowsill.

"What are you doing? We can't just take that."

"Why not?"

"Isn't it . . . I don't know, tampering with evidence or something?"

"We're preserving it," he said. "Who's to say when that Trike guy gets back into town he doesn't destroy it to cover his tracks?"

He had a point. So I stopped arguing and followed him out the window, whereupon we went back to Mad's and hid the binder in his bedroom closet. Then we repaired to the living room for a celebratory drink, only to discover that there wasn't a drop of liquor left in the whole damn place.

I WOKE UP THE NEXT MORNING with a nasty hangover and a vague sense that I'd done something very, very stupid. It took me a couple of minutes to piece it together—the sight of Axel Robinette's body washing up on shore, the news that Norma Jean Kramer was awake, the red-wine bender in Mad's apartment. And then—this was the thing that finally sent me retching to the commode—the two of us breaking into Groovy Guitar to steal documents from the Melting Rock office.

Had I actually been drunk enough to go along with it? Was there really enough alcohol on the whole damn planet to get me to do something that intrinsically stupid?

Apparently, the answer was yes. I was definitely in no hurry to share this news with Cody.

I gave my teeth a halfhearted brushing and flopped back onto the mattress. I had the day off as payback for working Labor Day, and I'd planned to get stuff done—like, maybe do laundry for the first time in a month. At the moment, however, I was busy lying in bed with the shades drawn and a facecloth on my forehead.

But Shakespeare was determined to go outside and powder her snout. So after her whining hit a fever pitch, I put on some sweats and took her around the block. Although the thought of breakfast didn't appeal, I made myself gag down a piece of toast in the hopes of set-tling my stomach.

It was a quarter after three.

I was on my way back upstairs when I noticed the answering-machine light blinking. The first message was from Cody, who'd called the night before to say he was back in town and that he was going to come over and get Zeke. The second must've come in while I was walking the dog. It was from Ochoa, who wanted me to call him at the paper ASAP.

Since this duty could be performed from the boudoir as well as anywhere else, I crawled back into the sack with the cordless phone. He answered with his usual bark.

"Newsroom. Ochoa."

"It's Alex."

"Good. I needed to—"

"Could you maybe not talk so loud? I've kind of got a hangover issue going."

"It's about Band. Madison thought we ought to give you a heads-up."

"What about him?"

"The bastard's up to something."

"Up to what?"

"I'm not sure. But Madison and I were going past the library on the way to grab lunch, and out came Band looking like the cat that ate the goddamn canary. Bastard was grinning ear to ear."

"Son of a bitch."

"That's what Madison said. I didn't think anything of it myself, but he seemed to think it was bad mojo."

"Gordon's not what you'd call the jolly type. If he's all smiles, it means he's about to scoop somebody but good."

"So I hear."

"And you said he was coming out of the library? Any idea what he was doing in there?"

"Madison went in and sweet-talked the lady at the reference desk. Apparently, he checked out the Deep Lake Cooling file for an hour."

"Deep Lake? What the hell for?"

"That's the question. We looked through the file ourselves and we couldn't find anything."

"Gordon's scary with documents. He's like the Amazing Kreskin of paper pushers."

"So we were thinking . . . You've been covering Deep Lake more than anybody. Maybe you could go over there and take a look for yourself."

"I suck at that stuff." I readjusted the rapidly warming facecloth on my forehead. "And besides, I feel like hell."

"Alex, I don't think we've got a lot of time here."

"Oh, screw Gordon. Let him have his stupid scoop."

"You really want to let him nail you on your own turf?"

That got me. He knew it would, and it did. "Oh, *fine,*" I said, and made myself get vertical.

Not twenty minutes later, I was over at the library checking out the Deep Lake Cooling folder myself. The reference lady made some crack about what a popular item it was, and I hauled it over to a table in the corner.

I say "hauled" because the file was four inches thick; as part of its effort to convince people that Deep Lake was a good idea, Benson had been incredibly forthcoming about its plans. From the project's inception, the university had made all manner of information available to the public. Now that it was up and running, the folder contained the final Environmental Impact Statement, construction specs, budget information, bios on the major players, et cetera, et cetera. Reading through it was going to take the whole damn day.

I went through the EIS first, figuring Gordon would just love to break some scandal about the project threatening an endangered species of mollusk. But though I scrutinized the pages until my eyeballs hurt, nothing particularly naughty jumped out at me. Then I tried the construction papers, but I only lasted ten minutes; all the technical stuff might as well have been in Esperanto. That brought me to the budget documents, which were at least in my native tongue. I flipped through page after page of expenditures, of which there were plenty; it was, after all, a 150-million-dollar project.

I can't swear that I would've noticed it if the page hadn't been manhandled. But with the paper a bit wrinkled and the corner slightly dog-eared, I gave the page extra attention. And there, about three-quarters of the way down, was the following entry: *Mohawk Associates, Inc.—consulting fees—$47,355.*

The entry dated from three years ago, when planning for the cooling project was kicking into high gear.

So . . . what did it mean? Why did a firm listed as a consultant for Deep Lake have a post office box paid for by somebody connected to Melting Rock? A bunch of the names on the Melting Rock payoff list, including someone I assumed was Mrs. Hamill, had M.A. in the margins. Why? Were they somehow getting money through the company?

And—as far as I was concerned, an equally burning question—what did Gordon know about it? Was he somehow on to the Melting Rock connection? Or was he looking at Mohawk Associates solely because of Deep Lake?

Whatever the answers, Gordon was obviously on to something big; at least he thought he was. Maybe it was my imagination, but I could swear—yep, there it was—the paper had a bumpy patch where it'd gotten wet and then dried. Gordon had, in all likelihood, actually drooled on it.

CHAPTER 23

That night, Mad, Ochoa, and I convened our version of a war room, which consisted of sitting around Mad's coffee table and drinking Crystal Light pink lemonade—our host having decided that even he was in no mood for a hair of the dog that bit him. The guys were eating giant gyro wraps from Yanni's, downtown Gabriel's primo Greek diner, while I was sitting there starving and trying not to pinch too many of their stuffed grape leaves. After not seeing each other over the long weekend, Cody and I were scheduled for a romantic Indian dinner, followed by a post-kheer booty call.

"Jesus, Bernier," Mad was saying. "Would you stop checking your watch already? You're driving me nuts."

"Sorry. I just don't want to be late."

"What time is your hot date?"

"Eight."

"And what time is it now?"

"Five after seven."

"Then relax."

"Fat chance."

Ochoa squeezed some lemon juice onto a grape leaf and popped it into his mouth. "What are you so wound up about, anyway?"

"Christ, what do you think? Goddamn Gordon's about to break some huge story, and we have no bloody idea what it is."

"Sure we do," Ochoa said with his mouth full, "Mohawk Associates."

"Which is what?" They both turned their attention to their food. "See? We're gonna get totally screwed here."

"Okay," Mad said. "Let's think. What do we know about this thing?"

"You mean Mohawk Associates?"

"Yeah."

"Not a whole hell of a lot."

"But what *do* we know?"

"Okay," I said, "we know that it's probably being run by somebody at Melting Rock because they had the receipt for the P.O. box. And since Jo said she—"

"Who?" This from Ochoa, still talking through his food.

"Jo Mingle. She runs Melting Rock, but she says she doesn't have bupkis to do with the finances."

"And you believe her?"

"Yeah, I kind of do. She doesn't strike me as a liar."

"So if not her, then who?"

"Her boyfriend, this guy named Trike Ford—"

"You mean the drummer from Stumpy?"

"Right. He's her boyfriend, and she says he handles all the money stuff. I tried to talk to him when the story broke about Melting Rock getting its ass sued off, but I guess he was away on tour."

"Yeah, but they gotta be back by now. They've got a big show this weekend. Release party for their new album is Friday night."

"All right, let's try and get all this straight. For some reason, Deep Lake Cooling paid Mohawk Associates nearly fifty thousand dollars in so-called 'consulting' fees. Meanwhile"—I picked up the pilfered binder and flipped it open—"a bunch of people are apparently getting payoffs, and they've got the initials M.A. next to their names."

"I can't believe you guys actually lifted that thing," Ochoa said.

"We were pretty ballsy," Mad said.

"Actually," I said, "we were pretty sloshed."

"Are you gonna put it back?"

Mad shrugged. I shook my head. "Ain't no way I'm goin' in there sober," I said.

"Okay," Ochoa said, "so if these people have the initials next to—"

"Hold on a second," Mad said. "Before we get into this, let me ask you guys something. Am I the only one who thinks this is one hell of a coincidence? I mean, Bernier and I find that Mohawk Associates file one night, and by the next afternoon, Band is over at the library digging through the Deep Lake papers and finding—*badda-bing!*—Mohawk Associates listed in the damn financials. Doesn't that strike you as kinda weird?"

"Er . . . You're right," I said. "Guess I'm even more hungover than I thought."

"So what's the deal?"

"I don't know. Let me ponder." I reached for another dolmadakia, and Ochoa swatted my hand away. "Seems like what you're saying is . . . What? That our swiping the file somehow triggered Gordon's trip to the library?"

Mad shrugged. "I guess."

"But how?"

"Damned if I know."

"All right," Ochoa said, "let's concentrate on what we've got in front of us, okay? So like I was saying before, if these people have M.A. next to their names, it stands to reason that maybe they're getting their money through this phantom company, right?"

"Yeah," I said, "but there's something I don't understand."

"Which is?"

"It seems like . . . I don't know, like a weird combination of being sneaky and being aboveboard."

"How do you mean?"

"Well, if you're going to take a payoff, why not just take it in an envelope full of small, unmarked bills? Why go through all the trouble of setting up some company? I mean, wouldn't that make it more likely you'd get caught?"

Mad refilled his glass, having previously explained that there was nothing unmanly about drinking diet pink lemonade. "I've been thinking about that," he said, "and I've got two things for you. One's a credit thing; the other's a debit thing."

Ochoa gave me a querying look, so I filled him in. "Mad went through this phase where he was sleeping with M.B.A. students," I said. "They generally fled once they got a look at his net worth."

"Don't knock it," Mad said. "Those finance chicks are *wild*."

"You were saying about credits and debits?"

"Okay. So in terms of payouts, Deep Lake Cooling has to balance its budget, right? A university project can't just charge off fifty grand to 'miscellaneous expenses.' It'd need a bona fide company to make a payment to."

"A payment for what?"

"Damned if I know. I'm just talking about the system here, okay?"

"Okay. Was that the debit or the credit?"

"The . . . Oh, hell, I don't know," Mad said. "But now let's look at it from the other side. Somebody, say that J-burg lady Rosemary Hamill, wants to take a payoff. Maybe she's getting bribed for something. She's breaking the law, so she's obviously not too concerned with doing the right thing. But what's the one bunch of people she doesn't want to mess with?" Ochoa and I swapped clueless glances. Mad looked like a teacher disappointed in his class's abject stupidity. "The I.R.S.," he said. "Get it?"

"No," said Ochoa.

"Not even a little," said I.

"Okay, look," Mad said. "It's one thing to make money you don't deserve. Cheating on your taxes is a whole other ball game. It's like this hooker I knew once." More gaping stares from me and Ochoa. "Hey, I'm a reporter, okay? I meet people. Once when I was in college, I did this story on certain . . . ladies who earned their living by non-traditional means. And I remember this one told me she reported all her income to the I.R.S. 'cause she didn't want to get in trouble with the taxman—said it was way worse than the vice squad. So she'd file it all on her taxes as 'public relations.' Clever, huh?"

"Let me get this straight," I said. "You think these people took money, but they wanted it . . ."

"I think," Ochoa said, "that the word you're looking for is *laundered*."

"Right," I said. "And if there's really that much money at stake—I mean, it looks like we could be talking about hundreds of thousands of bucks over the years—then are we safe in assuming that maybe it has something to do with those boys getting poisoned? Not to mention Axel getting dead?"

"Hell yeah," Mad said. "I'd kill for half that much."

"It's like you were saying before," Ochoa said. "Most murders are about money, right? So here we've got some money, and we've definitely got some murders. What are the odds they aren't connected somehow?"

"Okay," I said, "then who had the most to gain? Or maybe I should say . . . to lose?"

"Top of the list," Ochoa said as he flipped through the binder, "is our friend R.H."

"Rosemary Hamill," I said. "Owner of one very ugly and expensively restored B and B."

Mad plucked the last grape leaf out of the aluminum take-out box. "So waddaya think?" he asked. "Can you picture her mixing up some nasty-ass acid and offing those kids?"

"In a word . . . no."

"Why not?"

"I don't know. She's just . . . way too prissy. But maybe I can picture her hiring somebody to do her dirty work for her."

"Okay," Ochoa said, "what about the rest of the people on the payoff list?"

"Good question," I said. "Unfortunately, we have no idea who they are. We better copy them down and start comparing the initials to . . . well, I guess to everybody who's anybody in Jaspersburg."

"You know who might be able to help us with this?" Mad asked. "Brad. It *is* in his beat, ya know. Maybe he's—"

"That little moron?" I said. "No way."

"He's not so bad."

"The hell you say. First off, he's a total loose cannon, so God knows who he'd go drill. He'd probably blow the whole damn story. Plus, J-burg is one of half a dozen towns he's covering. He's hardly been on the beat long enough to know his ass from his elbow anyway."

"Okay," Mad said, "I'm getting that the answer is no."

"*Hell* no," I said. "And if you breathe a word to him about this, I'll wring your neck."

"Nobody's wringing anything," Ochoa said. "Let's just concentrate, okay? What about this other list?" He held up the page with the smaller amounts. "Any idea what's up?"

I broke off a corner of their baklava in the interest of calming down. "It's got the initials A.R. on it, which I figure has to be Axel Robinette. It's also got R.S., which is probably our buddy Sturdivant."

"So what are they getting paid off for?" Ochoa mused. "And if they *are* getting paid off, why are they on a separate list?"

"And speaking of which," Mad said, "why is Deep Lake paying fifty grand to Mohawk Associates in the first place?"

"The budget said 'consulting fees,'" I said, "which could mean just about anything."

"Yeah, but obviously Mohawk is in bed with the guys who run Melting Rock. What could they have to do with Deep Lake?"

"Specifically," Ochoa said, "what could Deep Lake want from them that would be worth the fifty thousand clams?"

I looked at my watch again. It wasn't even seven-thirty yet, and I was starving-hungry. "Okay," I said, "let's look at this another way. Assuming this phony company is really laundering payoff money, how do we figure out who's in charge of it? I mean, doesn't a company have to have officers or something?"

"I guess," Ochoa said. "This isn't really my beat."

"Mine either," I said. "I hate to say it, but this is the kind of crap that Gordon is goddamn great at."

"So let's ask ourselves," Mad said, "what would Gordon do?"

"W.W.G.D.," I said. "Not likely to appear on a bracelet anytime soon." Mad raised an eyebrow at me. "It's a Bible-thumping thing. Never mind."

"Fine," Mad said, "so how would Band tackle this?"

"He'd dig through piles of documents. Probably dig up the articles of incorporation, or some damn thing."

Ochoa tossed the binder on the coffee table. "And where do you find articles of incorporation?"

"How the hell do I know? Doesn't that have to be filed with the state or something?" Four shoulders shrugged. "Wonderful. So how are we gonna figure out what's going on?"

We sat there pondering the question for a while. I answered first. "Christ, we're reporters, aren't we?" I said.

"Er . . . yeah," Mad said. "So?"

"So," I said, "let's ask somebody."

WHILE THE GUYS SETTLED in for an evening of watching extreme sports on ESPN-2, I went off to meet Cody at Delhi Delite, which is a lousy name for a very good Indian restaurant. An hour of eating like pigs was followed by another of you-know-whatting like rabbits, after which we fell asleep in the company of two dogs.

And just for the record . . . at no point was I even remotely tempted to tell him that my holiday weekend had included breaking into Groovy Guitar, removing potentially valuable evidence, and stowing said evidence underneath Mad's scuba fins.

I did, however, fill him in on what he'd missed by blowing off the union picnic; although he obviously knew about Axel's body washing up onshore, he'd missed the gory details. And although I'd expected him to get all concerned about my delicate sensibilities, apparently he was starting to give me credit for being a fairly tough cookie—though frankly poor Axel had looked so gross I could've used a little sympathy.

The next day, I followed my own advice and did some asking. But what I found out was something wholly unexpected.

Which is: Nearly dying of poisoned LSD turned out to be the best thing that ever happened to Norma Jean Kramer.

CHAPTER 24

How, you may ask, can this possibly be?

Well, her two-week coma proved to be something akin to a health spa. Her parents may have been scared silly, but when she finally woke up, her weight was the lowest it had been since junior high.

Granted, this still put her over two hundred pounds. But for Norma Jean, it was a step in the right direction. After her brush with death, she was determined to give up drugs, go to junior college, and get down to a size ten.

At least that's what she told me.

I met Norma Jean three days after she awoke, by which time the American health-care system had already sent her home to the two-bedroom bungalow she shared with her parents. And although I had plenty to worry about back home in Gabriel, when the opportunity to talk to her suddenly manifested itself, I had no choice but to drive south with all deliberate speed.

The terminus of my six-hour trip was the Kramers' house. It was located in a working-class section of Baltimore, with gray aluminum siding on the walls and a Virgin Mary shrine on the front lawn. The family appeared to be nothing if not thrifty; the shrine was made from an old bathtub, the planters alongside the driveway fashioned out of recycled tires spray-painted silver. Next to the house was a postage-stamp garden, the tomato plants staked with sawed-off hockey sticks.

Now, you may be wondering why Norma Jean Kramer agreed to talk to me—why, in fact, I'd been invited to her family's front door. The answer is simple: Norma Jean was talking to everybody.

When she woke up, you see, Norma Jean found that not only was she slimmer, she was also a minor celebrity. Every news organization east of the Rockies seemed to want an interview with her. Suddenly, the girl who couldn't get a date to the senior prom was that most elusive of things: She was *popular*.

If we'd known all this beforehand, I might not have been the one to make the six-hour drive from Gabriel. Yes, Norma Jean had agreed to meet with a reporter, but since we hadn't yet seen the spate of stories in media from the *Baltimore Sun* to CNN, we had no idea just how chatty she'd be. The whole reason for sending me (rather than, say, Ochoa) was that, as the possessor of my very own set of ovaries, I might make her more comfortable—and, therefore, more likely to spill her guts. As it turned out, though, she was so talkative we might just as well have sent her a tape recorder via Federal Express.

I pulled up to her house just as a CBS news van was driving away. Norma Jean's mother answered the door wearing a burgundy sweat suit, the velour kind with the zip-up jacket and matching pants that you never actually see in a gym—only on out-of-shape types who crave the elasticized waistband. She led me into the living room, where Norma Jean was lying on the couch, clad in a warm-up suit of her own. Her face was made up, and not particularly well; mascara clotted her eyelashes, and her cheeks were striped with cotton-candy pink blush.

The room was a riot of get-well flowers, which looked cheery but saturated the air so the place smelled like a funeral parlor. Mrs. Kramer settled into an easy chair, a happily expectant look on her face, and I got the feeling that she was enjoying the spectacle every bit as much as her daughter was.

The first thing Norma Jean did was offer me a glass of instant lemonade, which I took just to be polite. Then she told me to call her "Jeanie" and indicated a tin of expensive-looking chocolate-dipped cookies, which she said had come in a gift basket from the mayor's office. These, I accepted with genuine enthusiasm.

We spent the next two hours going over the life and times of

Norma Jean Kramer. And although she turned out to be extremely sweet and surprisingly funny, I'll spare you most of the details. She did mention that she was thinking about getting an associate's degree in mass communication, that the local Weight Watchers franchise had offered her a free membership, and that her dream was to be a spokesperson for the company, "just like Fergie."

But the really interesting part of the conversation didn't come until the end.

"Jeanie," I said, "before I go, I was wondering if you'd mind telling me about the circumstances of your buying the LSD." Her face took on a blank, slightly confused look, which kind of threw me. "You did buy it, didn't you? Or did one of your friends buy it for you or something?"

"No, I bought it," she said. "It's just that . . . none of the other newspeople asked me that before."

"Oh. Well, I guess for most of them the story is really about you being the only person to survive taking one of those poisoned tabs. And besides, since Robert Sturdivant is obviously going to get charged with—"

"Hey, who is he, anyway?"

"Sturdivant? He's . . . Well, he's the guy who sold you the drugs. Isn't he?"

"Gosh, I . . . I don't really know."

"You bought the drugs from a total stranger?" She nodded. "Didn't you even get his name?"

"Yeah, it was Robbie-something. I guess it could've been that Sturdivant guy. I just don't know for sure."

"Listen, Jeanie, I'll be right back, okay?" I went out to my car, retrieved a stack of newspapers from the backseat, and dug out a story that Ochoa had done on the continuing search for the bail-jumping Sturdy. "Was this the guy?" Jeanie squinted at the photo. "Does he look familiar to you?"

"Um . . . yes and no."

"What do you mean?"

"He isn't the guy who sold me the tab, but . . . I think I saw him one time."

"When was that?"

"When I was still in the hospital, some nice people from the F.B.I. came by and showed me some pictures—a bunch of little black-and-white pictures, like six of them together. I'm pretty sure this guy was in one of them."

"They showed you a photo array and asked you to pick out the person who sold you the drugs?"

"Yeah, I guess. And then they asked me if I knew somebody named Sturdivant, but I told them I wasn't sure—all I knew was that I bought the stuff from somebody named Robbie."

I handed her the paper. "And you're sure this isn't the guy?"

"Nah. He was a lot smaller, and he had way more hair. And this Sturdivant guy looks, I don't know . . . *mean.* The other guy was kinda cute."

"Okay, well, thanks for—"

"Hey," she said, "there he is."

She'd unfolded the paper and was looking at a story on the facing page.

I followed the direction of her eyes. "Are you sure?"

"Yeah. There's the guy. Omigod, that's *him.*" She was starting to get upset, and her mother came over to pat her on the back. "That's the creep who sold me the stuff that almost killed me."

She pointed a pink fingernail at the newsprint—hard enough to poke a hole right through the photo of Axel Robinette.

I WROTE UP THE PIECE on Jeanie Kramer in my Super 8 motel room, fueled by a mushroom-and-onion pizza and a six-pack of Tab. When I was done, I made yet another call to Alan Bauer—and, for the fifth time, got the family answering machine. I left another message telling him to call me on my cell, that it was *important*, but something told me I was wasting my time. If I talked to Bauer, it was going to have to be in person.

Then I tried Glenn Shardik again, this time at home. His wife answered, said he was out, but she'd be glad to give him another message.

The headline to my page-one piece (ROBINETTE SOLD DEADLY DRUGS, SAYS VICTIM) blared out of the *Monitor* vending boxes as I drove into town the following afternoon. I made it to the newsroom just in time for the afternoon editorial meeting, during which I got a slightly malevolent stare from Ochoa and high fives from everybody else.

Five hours later, when we'd repaired to the Citizen Kane, the reporter in question was still mouthing the phrase *sob sister* at me.

"Oh, piss off," I said. "And while you're at it, how about you buy me a drink?"

"Fat chance."

"Don't be such a sore loser. Besides, all I did was interview the Kramer girl. Robinette's death is completely in your beat. And as far as I'm concerned, you can have it."

"Since when are you so generous?"

"Since I saw his goddamn body floating in the water. *Twice.*"

"Yeah, well, right now I'm as stalled as the cops are."

"Meaning?"

"Meaning I've been nosing around for a week and I've hardly been able to find out anything beyond what the cops released."

"Which is that he died of hypothermia from falling into the Deep Lake Cooling pool."

"Right. Whether it happened accidentally or on purpose—according to my buddy in the coroner's office, they're not having much luck nailing it down."

"And if he was pushed in on purpose," I said, "which I assume that he damn well was, did it have anything to do with the fact that he sold the drugs to Kramer? Or was it about Deep Lake somehow? And what's the connection to Mohawk Associates?"

"Goddamn Robinette," Mad said. "Seems to me like the son of a bitch is at the middle of everything. Too bad he's in no shape to talk."

"The Axis of Axel," I said, mostly because it sounded so clever.

"Let's count them up. First, he was at Melting Rock. He was the one who sold the drugs to Norma Jean, and presumably to the boys as well. His initials were on one of the payoff lists in the festival office, but there's no M.A. next to his name. He was one of the demonstrators on opening day at Deep Lake—in fact, he's one of the people who shut down the system with goddamn Jell-O. And to round out the list, one of the J-burg girls has a massive crush on him, and he's best buddies with our missing drug dealer, Rob Sturdivant."

"And while we're on the subject," Ochoa said, "where the hell is he?"

"Rob Sturdivant," I said. "Goddamn Axel Robbee-nette. I was thinking about it on the whole drive up, how Axel pronounced his name that way when I talked to him at Café Whatever. That's even how some of his stupid slacker friends said it when I interviewed them for his news obit."

"And?"

"And the only evidence that Sturdivant sold the drugs to those boys was double hearsay—Cindy said that Shaun told her he did it. But Shaun was dying, and Cindy was hysterical, and maybe . . ."

Mad raised an eyebrow. "And maybe," he said, "she misunderstood him. He said 'Robinette,' and she heard 'Rob Sturdivant.'"

"People must've known he was a dealer, so it was probably a natural mistake."

"Sturdivant swore up and down he hadn't sold the acid to those kids," Ochoa said. "Maybe he was actually telling the truth."

"It's what I've been thinking," I said. "I mean, I suppose it's possible that Sturdivant sold three tabs and Axel sold the other—after all, they were buddies and everything. And to tell you the truth, I kind of hope that was the case. Otherwise . . ."

"Otherwise," Ochoa said, "the only person we can directly connect to the drugs is Axel, and he's dead."

"Exactly," I said. "Jesus, it would be nice if somebody in the coroner's office could figure out just what the hell happened to him."

"Right now, all they know is that Robinette fell into the pool, where a witness"—Ochoa's eyes rotated toward me—"sees him floating dead. Eventually, his wet clothes drag him down to the bottom of the pool, where he gets sucked into the outflow pipe and goes shooting out into the lake. The cops are looking for a body, and they have the Benson engineers check the pipe, but of course by then it's all clear. They send down some divers, but it's damn deep and dark, and they don't find anything, so they figure somebody fished it out of the pool and buried it someplace. But after a while, the body gets dislodged from whatever it was snagged on, and between that and the decomposition gases, he pops up to the top. End of story."

"Except," I said, "that they have no idea how he got into the pool in the first place."

"From what my source tells me," Ochoa said, "all the damage they found on the body was postmortem, from getting banged around on the trip through the pipe. They didn't find any evidence that anybody beat on him or anything."

"So maybe it really was an accident," Mad said. "Could be he was there waiting to show Bernier how they doctored the water with goddamn Jell-O, and he fell into the pool in the dark. Couldn't see to climb up the safety ladder, and three minutes later, *poof*—the guy's a goner."

"Okay," I said, "so how did they do it?"

Mad stopped tilting the beer pitcher in midpour. "Do what?"

"How did they doctor the water?"

"What difference does it make?"

"And come to think of it, how did Axel get into the Deep Lake building in the first place?"

Mad shrugged. "Probably had somebody on the inside, don't you think? I mean, somebody had to give him the key, or at least open the place for him, right?"

"Yeah," I said, "but presumably the cops've looked into that, and if they'd nailed somebody, whoever it was would've been canned in a minute. You heard anything about one of those guys getting fired?" Mad shook his head. "Me neither."

"Okay," Ochoa said, "so the question is, how does a lowlife like Axel Robinette get his hands on a key? It's not like he had the money to bribe anybody."

"True," Mad said, "but we're not just talking about him. We're talking about all the goddamn Mohawk Warriors, whoever they are."

"Yeah," I said. "But the night he died, it was Robinette who got in there. And think about *why* he was there—to show some reporter how they did their trick with the intake pool. Do you really think if some halfway-sane person in the group had the key, they would've given it to him for *that?*"

Mad finally finished pouring his beer. "Hey, the guy was no prince. Maybe he lied about why he needed it. What difference does it make?"

"Yeah, but—"

Ochoa held up a hand. "There's something else," he said. "Another detail I got from this chick in the coroner's office that I, um . . . hadn't really wanted to mention." There was a funky tone in his voice, though I had no idea why. "Er . . . okay. If he was really there to show Alex how they filled up the pool with Jell-O mix, how come he didn't have any on him?"

"Good question," I said, "and maybe the answer is obvious, which is that it got washed down the outflow pipe along with him."

"Maybe," he said, "but anyway, they never found any trace of it. But, well . . . they *did* find something else. Something in his pockets which might, um . . . indicate what his plans were."

"Which is?"

"A whole lot of, well . . . condoms."

It took a second for his meaning to sink in, and when it did, I thought I might toss my Beer Nuts.

"Are you telling me that Axel's whole point in meeting me at Deep Lake in the middle of the night was that he thought he was going to get *lucky?*" Ochoa nodded. Surprisingly enough, he didn't seem to be enjoying this as much as I would've expected. "God, I . . . *yuck.*" I took a slug of red wine to try to get the nasty taste out of my mouth. "That little prick did consider himself quite a goddamn ladies' man. Far as I could tell, the only person who ever agreed with him was—*holy shit.*"

"What?" Mad said. "Yo, Bernier, are you okay?"

"I'm fine. I just . . . I think maybe I know where Axel got the key."

"And . . . ?"

"There was this girl he had wrapped around his finger," I said. "And her last name just happens to be Benson."

I WAS SITTING AT OCHOA'S TERMINAL the next morning, subtly gloating about my Norma Jean scoop while ostensibly helping him with a follow-up to the Axel story, when the photo editor appeared at my shoulder.

"Hey, Alex," Wendell said, "do you know where Melissa's at?"

"Er . . . no. Why?"

"She's late. Way late."

"Well, she's not much of a morning person. . . ."

"Like I don't know it. Late's no big deal, but it's not like her to screw up an assignment."

I stood up to face him. Since he's as short as I am, we were nose to nose—though his Gene Wilder hairdo gave him an extra three inches on me. "What did she miss?"

"She was supposed to shoot an enterprise thing at the high school—metal-shop kids made a car. Page-three stand-alone for tomorrow."

"And she didn't show up?" He shook his head. "Maybe she got the time wrong or something. Did you try her on her cell?"

"Cell, home phone, yeah. No answer. So I was wondering if she said anything to you this morning about—"

"Uh . . . I didn't actually stay at home last night. Shakespeare and I were at Cody's."

"Oh."

"Look, she probably just slept through her alarm again. I'll go home and get her, okay?"

He thanked me, mumbled something about how such positive karma always gets repaid by the universe, and went back to the darkroom. I told the newsroom secretary what I was up to, then went down the back stairs and wiggled my car out of the lot.

The drive home took all of three minutes. I unlocked the front door and yelled for Melissa; there was no answer.

Two steps later, I was yelling for help.

CHAPTER 25

The place had been trashed; there was no other word for it. Every single thing that Melissa and I owned appeared to have been rifled, manhandled, busted up, and/or thrown on the floor. The house didn't look like it'd been hit by thieves. It looked like it'd been raided by goddamn Visigoths.

I hollered for Melissa again, but there was still no answer. I was halfway up the stairs when I was struck by the painfully obvious: Whoever had blitzkrieged the house might very well still be there.

I froze on the step, trying to calm my breathing so I could actually *hear* something. I thought I caught a sound from upstairs—but what the hell should I do? Go running out the front door and call the cops? Try and hide under the upturned couch?

There were definitely steps coming toward me, light and way too fast for me to get away. I braced myself for God-knows-what—at which point Melissa's cat came flying down the stairs and started rubbing against my ankles.

I tried to shoo the cat away, but he wouldn't go, just kept snuggling and yowling at me. Did this mean the coast was clear? Probably—at least I hoped so. I went upstairs and headed straight for Melissa's bedroom.

I found her lying on the bed, looking as close to dead as a live person could get. Her breathing was so shallow, in fact, that at first I was afraid it was too late. But then I felt her neck and found a pulse, which sent me scrambling for the phone at her bedside. But there was no dial tone; the line had been ripped out of the wall.

I ran down the hall, hoping like hell that the cordless in my room was working. It was. I dialed 911 and tried to sound coherent as I asked for an ambulance.

When the operator asked what kind of medical emergency it was, I said that a woman had been attacked and beaten. But to tell you the truth, those two words didn't come anywhere near describing what Melissa had gone through.

Her face was black and blue, with blood caked around her nose and mouth. Both eyes were swollen shut, and what looked like cigarette burns dotted one arm. Except for the scrap of bedsheet across her stomach, she was naked; I'd tell you how many bruises were on her body, but I lost count.

I stood there staring at her, wanting to do something comforting but afraid to touch her. But she must've sensed that somebody was there, because her eyelids started to flutter and she made a low moaning sound.

"Melissa?" I said. "It's me, Alex, okay? You're gonna be all right, sweetie. There's an ambulance coming."

She half opened one eye, focusing not on me but on the cat, who'd leaped onto the bed and started yowling again. I grabbed him before he could crawl on her, and she lifted a hand weakly in his direction.

"Zoo . . . ," she mumbled, sounding only marginally coherent. "Z-Zeus . . . He's . . . h-hungry. . . ."

Her eyes fluttered shut just as the cat jumped back on the bed. I picked him up again and—vaguely relieved to have an excuse to go downstairs—went into the kitchen. I was still hunting for his kibble when I heard the sirens.

The guys from Sand's Ambulance came in first, hustling up the stairs with their red plastic cases. They'd barely gotten into the bedroom when a pair of uniformed cops ran in behind them, and I'd barely started to tell *them* what I'd found, when Brian Cody came rushing up the stairs too.

He'd heard the call on the police radio and—hearing the address and whatever the cop code is for an assault—was terrified that something had happened to me. He took in the state of the house and the condition of my roommate, and all at once, he looked angry enough to put a fist through the wall.

We followed the ambulance to the hospital in his unmarked cop car, and on the way I called the newsroom on my cell to tell them what was going on. He sat with me in the waiting room while Melissa was being treated in the E.R., and after what felt like a week, a gray-haired lady doctor came out and told us she was being admitted upstairs.

"Did you do a rape kit?" Cody asked her, and when she seemed inclined not to answer, he flashed his badge.

The woman nodded. "There were no fluids present, but considering the shape she was in, we did one anyway."

"Is she going to be okay?" I asked. "When can I see her?"

"She'll be all right," the doctor said. "She has a broken jaw, but there don't appear to be any serious internal injuries. We need to keep an eye on her spleen, but . . . it's quite a miracle, actually."

"When can I see her?"

"And who are you?"

"Her roommate."

The doctor didn't seem impressed. "She can have visitors tomorrow at the earliest. She needs to rest now."

Cody seemed to be calming down, but slowly. "But she's awake?"

"Barely."

"We need to get her statement," he said. "I'll be in and out in five minutes, I swear."

I expected her to argue with him, but she just said, "You'll have to wait until she's upstairs."

"All right," Cody said. "Thank you."

Half an hour later, I was still waiting—only I was on a bench outside the hospital, while Cody was interviewing Melissa. True to his word to the doctor, he was gone less than ten minutes. And though I would've bet there was no way he could possibly have looked any angrier, I was wrong.

"What did she say?" I asked. He shook his head. "Come on, Cody, tell me."

He didn't answer, just kept shaking his head. After a minute he sat down on the bench next to me and started rubbing his temples. When he finally took his hand away, I could swear there were tears in his eyes.

"Jesus, Cody, what the hell is going on? What did she tell you?" More head shaking. Finally, he reached into the pocket of his suit jacket and pulled out a crumpled pack of cigarettes. "Since when did you start smoking again?"

When he spoke, his voice sounded gritty and raw.

"Emergency stash," he said.

"Then, for God's sake, give me one."

He lit a pair of misshapen Marlboros and handed one over. We sat there smoking for a while, in flagrant violation of the sign outside the hospital entrance.

"You have to tell me," I said.

"I know," he said. "But I don't want to."

"At least tell me how she sounded."

"Messed up," he said, then cracked a humorless smile. "Can you blame her?"

"Did she say what happened?"

"Did you try and call her family?"

"I told you, she doesn't have any. Both her parents are dead. And stop changing the subject."

He took another long drag on the limp cigarette, followed by an even longer pause.

"She was asleep," he said. "When she woke up, there were two guys in her room. Big guys wearing ski masks. She said they kept asking her for something, but she's not sure what it was. When she didn't give them the answer they wanted, they started beating on her. One of them held her down while the other one hit her. She said she was knocked out for part of it, which is why everything's so hazy. But she . . . she had a damn good memory of them saying, 'Where is it? Where is it?' and putting out cigarettes on her arm."

"Oh, my God," I said.

"Yeah," he said.

"Hold on. There's something you haven't told me. I can tell just by looking at you." He bit his lip, but he didn't try to deny it. "Come on, Cody. What is it?"

"It's . . . something else she remembered."

"Which is?"

"What the two guys called her."

"And what did they call her?"

"'Alex.'"

"*W*HAT?"

"Now can you understand why I didn't want to tell you?"

I practically leaped off the bench. "They thought she was *me?*"

"Alex, honey—"

"They beat the shit out of Melissa—they fucking *tortured* her—because they thought she was me? Oh, my God. . . ." Cody stood up and tried to touch me, but I shook him off. "Son of a . . . How could . . . How can I ever . . ."

"Baby, it's not your fault—"

"What did she say? I mean, what did she say exactly?"

He reached into his pocket and pulled out his little black notebook. "She said they told her"—he flipped to a page—". . . They said, 'We know you took it, bitch, and we want it back.' Do you have any idea what they might have—"

"Oh, my God. Oh, no . . ." My knees felt in actual danger of buckling, but I managed to make it back to the bench before I keeled over. "It's all my fault. It's all my goddamn fault. . . ."

"What is it?"

"It's the list. They wanted the fucking list."

"What list?"

"Monday night, Mad and I got all liquored up and broke into the Melting Rock office looking for some kind of proof that they were making payoffs. We found this binder filled with lists of initials and amounts of money, and . . . we took it." He started to say something, but I waved him off. "I know it was stupid. But we were just really drunk, and neither one of us was thinking straight."

"And you think that's what those bastards were after?"

"It has to be."

"But how would they know it was you? Did anybody see you break in?"

"I don't think so, but . . . I've been asking lots of questions about the Melting Rock finances, and I broke that big story about the cops being told not to make drug busts at the festival. I guess . . . when somebody noticed it was missing, it would've been easy for them to put two and two together."

"Where's this binder now?"

"Mad has it."

Cody stood up. "Then let's go find him."

"Why?"

"If somebody wants to get it back this badly," he said, "then there must be something seriously incriminating in there."

In the car I told him everything we knew, or thought we knew— the details about Rosemary Hamill, Mohawk Associates, and the connection to Deep Lake Cooling. When we pulled into the newspaper parking lot, I stopped him before he got out of the car.

"Tell me straight, Cody. Did they . . . did they rape her?"

"It doesn't look like it."

"What's that supposed to mean?"

"The doctor said there was no specific physical evidence, and Melissa said she had no memory of a sexual assault."

"Then why can't you just say no?"

"Because of the way they found her, without any clothes on . . ."

"Oh."

I went to open the car door, but this time Cody stopped me. "Were you ever going to tell me?"

"Tell you what?"

"About that notebook."

"You mean, was I going to tell my boyfriend the cop that my best friend and I got stinking drunk, broke into a record store, and stole a piece of evidence?"

"Yeah."

"No."

"I see," he said, and got out of the car.

Cody, Mad, and I parted company fifteen minutes later, with the former in possession of the blue binder that'd nearly gotten Melissa killed. And though I was clearly in the doghouse, the cop in question told me that I was damn well spending the night with him, for my own personal safety. Considering the condition of both my house and my roommate, I was in no mood to argue with him.

What I *was* in the mood for, though, was ending this insanity once and for all—figuring out what the hell was going on, who was after me, and what they were really up to.

So I told Bill I was taking the rest of the day off out of posttraumatic stress. Then I walked over to Café Whatever and ordered myself a double espresso. I sat down at a back table, called a certain Benson law professor, and asked him how a person could find out who was in charge of a New York State corporation. Two minutes later, he'd offered to track down Mohawk Associates for me himself.

I drank my espresso and ordered another, the usually attractive contents of the dessert case making my stomach turn. Within fifteen minutes my phone rang.

"I called in a favor at the secretary of state's office," Joe Kingman said, "and what I've got for you is a list of names and addresses of the officers of Mohawk Associates, Inc."

"I'm all ears."

"But there's something fishy."

"There is?"

"For you, I thought I'd go the extra mile and do a LexisNexis on these people, but . . . Well, it seems that all the names and addresses are fake. I Googled them and looked through the crisscross directory, but none of the addresses match up. And the names . . . they're all supergeneric—Mary Brown, Jeff Smith, that sort of thing. So I'm afraid I flunked."

"No—you didn't," I said. "Thanks a lot for trying."

"Anytime. I mean it. Like my wife and I told you, anything, anytime. You saved our daughter's life. We owe you the whole damn world."

"Thanks, I . . . Wait—let me ask you something else. How hard would it be to fake this kind of thing—to basically make up an untraceable dummy corporation?"

"I hate to say it, but . . . not too hard. When you file your articles of incorporation, you have to list who your officers are, but it's not like anybody checks your ID or anything."

"What about opening a bank account, like so you could write checks?"

"You'd have to apply for an employer ID number, but again it's not like you have to prove your identity at any point in the process."

"Is it just me, or is that a little crazy?"

"You know how I feel about big business," he said. "Thieving bastards love it like this."

"Like what?"

"Ain't nobody guarding the henhouse," he said, "excepting the fox."

By the end of my second double espresso, I was pretty much bouncing off the walls. All hepped up on caffeine and guilt, I sat there in the back of the café feeling desperate for something to do but having no real clue what. Not knowing a whole lot about corporate law, it hadn't occurred to me that I wouldn't be able to figure out who was really behind Mohawk Associates. But now I needed a Plan B, and fast.

I pulled out my reporter's notebook and spent some quality time bouncing the end of my pen against the paper, *whack-whack-whack*. When I finally wrote something down, it all came out in a rush:

Mohawk Assoc. Sources
- R. Hamill—doubtful
- Trike Ford—scary?
- Jo Mingle—also doubtful
- Glenn Shardik
- R. Sturdivant—where is he?
- Lauren—via Tom, etc.?
- Alan Bauer—still blowing me off?
- Gordon—?

I'd barely written down the last name when I crossed it off; appealing to Gordon's sense of humanity seemed like the dictionary definition of pointless. I scanned the rest of the list, finally settling on the one name that didn't have a question mark or "doubtful" attached to it—Glenn Shardik. Shardik was also the only one who wasn't involved with Melting Rock; his connection to Mohawk Associates came through Deep Lake Cooling.

And speaking of Deep Lake . . . That was where Axel—whose initials (I was pretty sure) were on the list in the Melting Rock office—had gotten himself killed.

So why had Deep Lake paid Mohawk Associates fifty thousand dollars? And how had Gordon gotten onto the story in the first place?

Those two questions prompted me to do two things: (1) call and leave a message for Glenn Shardik that I wanted to set up an interview with him and (2) go back to the library.

This time, though, I didn't head for the Deep Lake file; I went over to the stack of recent copies of the *New York Times* and waded through the entire past month in search of Gordon's byline. There were nearly a dozen of them, of which several had datelines within Walden County. Since I couldn't rip out the clips, I jotted down the headlines in my notebook, in order of publication date:

- THREE TEENS DIE IN APPARENT OD AT MUSICAL FESTIVAL
- IN GABRIEL, PROTEST CULTURE IS ALIVE AND WELL

- BENSON UNVEILS "ENGINEERING MARVEL" OF DEEP LAKE COOLING
- SUSPECT IN MELTING ROCK DRUG MURDERS JUMPS BAIL
- AT UNION HOLIDAY PICNIC, AN UNWELCOME GUEST

I read through each of the stories twice, but my bright idea was starting to look like a dud. I'd thought that maybe if I saw what Gordon had been covering recently, I might be able to figure out who or what had sicced him on his big scoop, whatever it was. Unfortunately, the five stories looked pretty innocuous. The first was a combination of spot news and the feature he'd been working on when I ran into him at Melting Rock; the second an enterprise thing about Gabriel's surfeit of civil disobedience; the third a straightforward feature on Deep Lake; the fourth a news story on Sturdivant vanishing; the fifth a short piece (with, if you ask me, a rather snarky headline) on Axel's appearance at the park. Any of them could have led Gordon to the Mohawk Associates thing one way or another, but I was damned if I could figure out how.

It was on the third pass that I finally noticed something. It was the lead of his Deep Lake story—not particularly noteworthy in and of itself, but odd coming on the heels of the previous piece.

> To the sounds of a student chorus singing songs about *cool,* Benson University today turned on its Deep Lake Cooling system, $150 million and three years in the making. The flipping of the ceremonial "on" switch was greeted with surprisingly little opposition in this upstate college town, home to innumerable action groups and protest movements over the past several decades.

He was right; practically from the beginning, the Deep Lake protests *hadn't* amounted to much. And to be honest, I hadn't really thought about it beyond a vague sense of relief at not having to cover more chanting sign-carriers than I already did. And if I had considered it, I probably would've chalked it up to the university's concerted efforts to prove the cooling project was kosher.

But coming as Gordon's Deep Lake story did—directly after the one about the Gabriel protest scene—the contrast was pretty damn striking. I mean, even if Deep Lake was the most environmentally sound project in the history of the planet, the local reactionaries would probably have agitated against it anyway. And as it was, the Benson name alone was enough to make people oppose the plan. But every time the protesters had raised an objection, the university had won them over to its side in record time.

The whole process, in other words, had been conducted in a perfectly sane and reasonable manner.

In Gabriel, though, that was the weirdest thing of all.

CHAPTER 26

An hour later, not having sussed out some clever way to penetrate the Deep Lake weirdness, I headed back to Jaspersburg. But just inside the Gabriel city limits, I pulled a spontaneous right turn and wound up exactly where I'd been that morning: the hospital parking lot. I made a pit stop at the gift shop and, in flagrant violation of doctor's orders, headed upstairs.

I'm not sure what I expected, but it definitely wasn't what I found—which was Melissa propped up on pillows, eating a blueberry yogurt, watching a rerun of *Ally McBeal*.

"Hey," I said from the doorway. "How ya doin'?"

She gave me a weak smile, licked the back of her spoon, and said, "Pretty okay."

"I'm glad."

"Whatcha got there?"

I eyed my gift shop swag. "Er . . . I think they call it 'overcompensation.'"

Her smile got a little stronger. "Then bring it over here."

Shutting the door to avoid trolling nurses, I dropped the booty on the tray table: stack of magazines, bouquet of carnations, giant stuffed cat, balloon proclaiming GET WELL SOON.

"Jeepers," she said, pulling the gray kitty onto her chest and kissing it on the nose. "When you overcompensate, you don't mess around, do you?"

I sat down on the edge of the bed. "You look really good," I said. "I mean, I expected you to be—"

"All messed up?"

"Um . . . yeah."

"Well, I sure look like hell, and I hurt all over. But I guess I'm . . . I'm just kind of in a good mood or something."

"What? Why?"

"'Cause last night I really thought I was a goner," she said. "And, holy shit—here I am, still breathing." She waved the plastic Dannon cup. "I'll tell you, goddamn yogurt never tasted so good. Is that weird or what?"

"Melissa, I'm . . . I'm really glad you're okay."

"You didn't have to bring me all this stuff, you know."

"Are you out of your mind? You got the shit beaten out of you because somebody thought you were me."

"Yeah, but that's not your fault."

"It goddamn well is," I said, and told her about the break-in at Groovy Guitar.

"So *that's* what those assholes were after," she said. "I just . . . They kept hitting and hitting me, saying, 'Where is it? Where is it?' And now that I think about it, they might even have said, 'Where's the file?' But I just had no idea what they wanted."

"Listen, I don't want to upset you or anything, but I just need to ask. Are you sure you weren't, um . . . sexually assaulted?"

"No. I mean, yes, I'm sure. It was close, but no."

"Jesus, Melissa, what the hell happened? No, wait. You don't have to—"

"One of them wanted to. The other one didn't. End of story."

"Oh."

"They sort of started to argue about it, and they got spooked—I think it was some headlights from across the street. Anyway, I'm pretty sure that's when they bolted."

"Melissa, I'm just so . . . I'm really sorry this happened. I swear, I wish . . . I wish I'd been there. I wish it'd happened to me instead of you."

"No offense," she said, "but that makes two of us."

•   •   •

JASPERSBURG HIGH ISN'T MUCH to look at. It's one of those bland, no-nonsense academic buildings that went up in the late sixties, replacing something made of brick or stone that had less space but a hell of a lot more character. It's located on the main Gabriel-Jaspersburg road, next door to the equally ugly junior high. Out front is a rusting metal sculpture of the school mascot made from scrap in the vocational machine shop.

I drove past a hand-lettered sign that said GO JAGUARS! and pulled into the last space in the student parking lot. My timing turned out to be pretty good. The final bell rang as I was getting out of my car, and within seconds a tide of adolescence came streaming out of the institutional glass doors.

The buses were already lined up, and some kids got right on. Others wandered toward the queue of idling cars, each with a parental type behind the wheel. But the older ones, the juniors and seniors with driver's licenses and parking privileges, headed in my direction.

I'd come in search of dual prey: I'd take either Alan Bauer or Dorrie Benson, whichever wandered into my clutches first.

Obviously, Bauer was my first choice. I'd been trying to talk to him for over a week, ever since Mad and I had debated the actual target of the fourth acid tab. But the messages I'd left on his family's answering machine had been predictably ignored, as had the e-mails I'd sent him after having sweet-talked his address out of Lauren Potter.

Unfortunately, my lying in wait for him outside Jaspersburg High did no good, either. Although Bauer was one of the first to emerge from the building, he was accompanied by his entire soccer team—which promptly boarded a bus for an away game.

But I did manage to waylay Dorrie for a conversation that would culminate in her smacking me in the kisser.

I'd noticed her in front of the school even before she'd broken out of the pack; her shorn head and multiple piercings set her apart from the JHS mainstream, which was actually pretty conservative. She was clad in a baggy pair of army-surplus pants and a brown work shirt, and since she didn't have much of a figure from a distance, you could've easily taken her for a guy.

She walked out of the school by herself, a black backpack slung over one shoulder, and kept her head down as she made straight for her car, which turned out to be a red Beetle identical to mine. And I thought *I* was spoiled.

"Hey, Dorrie," I said as she opened the door, "can I talk to you for a second?"

She squinted at me, her expression saying I was about as welcome as the SATs. "What for?"

"A couple of things, actually."

She tossed her backpack on the passenger seat. "I don't have time."

"It'll only take a second."

"I have homework."

"Look, Dorrie, I just—"

"Sorry." She climbed in and tried to shut the door; I say "tried" because I stood by the car and blocked her way.

"Hey, what the—"

"Did you get a copy of the key to the Deep Lake building for Axel Robinette?"

Her mouth fell open, revealing the silver tongue stud. Within a couple of seconds, she recovered and tried very hard to glare at me. "I don't know what you're talking about."

"I think you do."

"Well, I *don't.*"

"Give me a break, Dorrie. I saw you at Melting Rock. You were following him around like a goddamn puppy dog. I bet you would've done anything to get him to like you."

Her gray eyes instantly filled up with tears. I felt like a heel, which at the moment I was. "I . . . How would I even get . . ."

"Come on, you've been hanging around that campus your whole life. I'm sure you could figure it out."

Her eyes overflowed in a veritable gush. "Axel's dead."

"I know. I'm sorry."

"No you're *not*."

She was right, but I decided now wasn't the time to agree with her. "Honestly, Dorrie, I'm really sorry. I know you liked him a lot."

She sat there sobbing for a good long while, me standing by the open door like an idiot. Finally, she stopped crying, blew her nose on a pile of Subway napkins, and announced that she needed a smoke. I told her to go ahead, but she informed me that it was against school rules.

"Okay," I said, "let's take a walk."

"Hey, I . . . I never said I wanted to talk to you."

"Christ, Dorrie, look at yourself," I said. "You've gotta talk to *somebody*."

She didn't contradict me, and the two of us set out across the empty athletic fields and down a well-trodden path through the woods.

"Where does this thing go?" I asked.

The hint of a smile formed at the corners of her mouth. "Melting Rock."

"You're kidding."

"Path goes from JHS to the fairgrounds."

"How far is it?"

She shrugged. "I dunno. Half a mile maybe."

"Oh." We kept walking. "So listen, Dorrie . . . have you ever heard of a company called Mohawk Associates?"

"Huh? No."

"Are you sure none of the guys ever mentioned it? Or maybe Axel?"

"Nah. He didn't talk about his business with me. He didn't trust people too much."

"Okay, but about breaking into Deep Lake—"

"I already told you I don't know anything about that."

"I think you do."

"Well, that's not really my problem, is it? And why do you care so much, anyway?"

"I was there."

She stopped walking. "Huh?"

"I was at Deep Lake the night Axel died. I was the one who saw his body floating in the pool."

She stared at me. "What were you doing there?"

"Axel said he'd show me how they pulled that trick with the Jell-O. But when I got to the building, he was already inside, and the gate was—"

"Inside?"

"Yeah. Why?"

"If Axel was really . . . If he wanted to show you how they did it, why would he go in?"

"What do you mean? Are you saying they did it from the outside?"

"Yeah, I"—she looked down at the dirt path, littered with cigarette butts and the occasional beer can—". . . I'm not supposed to tell."

"Come on. What difference does it make?"

"I promised Axel."

I tried to think of a way to weasel it out of her, and after a disturbingly short time, a method occurred to me.

"Look, Dorrie," I said, "I totally respect your loyalty. But Axel isn't around to get nailed for it anymore. Don't you think he'd want people to know how clever he was?"

It was a pretty lame attempt, I know. Funny thing is . . . it worked.

"You . . . you think?"

"Definitely."

She bit her lip, took a long drag of the cigarette, and shrugged. "It was pretty simple, really."

"Oh, yeah?"

"They just sort of dumped the stuff."

"What do you mean, dumped it?"

"He said they got a ton of that Jell-O shit from somebody in a kitchen up at Benson, and somebody else in one of the materials science labs gave them this biodegradable plasticky stuff that dissolves in water after a while. So they did up all these pouches of the powder, and they made some of 'em thicker so they'd take longer to open. At night they rowed out to the buoy that marks where the intake pipe is, and they just tossed 'em down there and like, *whoosh,* a lot of it got sucked up."

"That's it?"

"Yeah, I guess."

"So if that's what Axel was going to tell me, why would he be inside the Deep Lake building?"

Another shrug. "How do I know? Why did Axel do anything?"

"How seriously were you dating him?"

She started walking again. "Who says we were dating?"

"I got the impression that was what you wanted."

"We got together a couple times. That's all."

"Got together?"

"Axel . . . he wasn't really the dating kind."

"Were you supposed to, um, get together with him the night he died?"

"What makes you ask that?"

"Well . . . I heard he had a box of condoms on him." She froze, looking so wounded I could practically see the outline of my knee in her gut. "Some people seemed to think he was hoping to, er . . ."

"To get laid."

"Right, but . . . I've been thinking about it, and I wondered if maybe he had a date later." *At least, I damn well hope so.*

"I wouldn't know anything about that."

"You don't know who he was seeing?"

She started sniffling again. "No."

"Look, Dorrie, I know it's probably none of my business, but I'm really not sure Axel Robinette is worth crying over. He obviously wasn't very nice to you. And, I mean, come on—he may even have been the one who sold the drugs that killed your friends."

She went from morose to irate in a heartbeat.

"No way. You don't know anything. There's no way he would've done that. Axel was . . . He was just really special, okay? He was gonna be, like, a big star someday. He was gonna go out to L.A. and get a record deal and everything. So just shut up about Axel, okay? Just *shut up.*"

"I'm sorry."

"You *should* be."

She pulled another cigarette out of the pack, her hands shaking as she lit up. We kept walking, in not-so-companionable silence.

"Dorrie," I said finally, "why do you think someone would want to kill them?"

She didn't answer.

"I've been thinking about this a long time," I went on, "and I'm pretty sure Tom and Shaun and Billy didn't just die randomly. I think somebody killed them on purpose, and I think maybe you know why."

She stopped short. "Are you crazy?"

"Probably. But all the same, that's what I think."

"Yeah, well, think whatever you want."

"Was there somebody in school, maybe somebody they did something to, either accidentally or on purpose? I mean, kids don't always think before they do things. Maybe someone just flew off the—"

"*Stop* it. Just *stop* it, okay?"

"And what about Alan? There were four tabs of that acid out there, Dorrie. *Four*. What are the odds that the last one wasn't intended for him?" I grabbed her by the shoulder to get her to stop walking and face me. "So why didn't he take it? Was it really meant for someone else? Was Alan in on it all along?"

That's when she slapped me across the face.

Honestly, it was like something out of a bloody soap opera. She just hauled off and smacked me. And although it didn't actually hurt that much, it made a hell of a noise, echoing through the woods like a rifle shot. She stood there for a minute like she couldn't quite believe what she'd done, then turned around and sprinted down the path back toward the school.

Apparently, Dorrie Benson had spent some time on the J.V. track team; at any rate, it was obvious there was no way I could catch up to her. So I walked back to JHS and, to no great surprise, found that there was only one red Beetle left in the parking lot.

I checked my face in the rearview mirror as I drove back to the paper, tracking the development of the red welt that was rising on my cheek. This exercise in vanity must have made me blow through a stop sign or something, because the next thing I knew there was a G.P.D. squad car flashing its lights and hooting its siren at me. I pulled over, hoping that whoever it was behind the wheel was familiar with the banana bread I regularly send to the station house with Cody.

No luck; the cop looked vaguely familiar—okay, they all did—but he didn't seem particularly friendly. "Alexandra Bernier?"

"Um, yeah. . . . What's the problem, Officer?"

"Would you step out of the car, please?"

"Are you serious?"

"Just step out the car, ma'am. Do it slowly, and keep your hands where I can see them."

"Is this some kind of joke? Because if Cody put you up to this, I'm going to—"

"Ma'am, just do as you're told and step out of the car."

The guy sounded like a parody of a drill sergeant. If he was putting me on, he was doing a hell of a job of it.

I followed his orders—not that I had much choice. When I got out of the car, I noticed another police cruiser had parked across the street.

"Listen," I said, "can you please just tell me what's going on?"

"Ma'am, are there any illegal drugs in your vehicle?"

"What?"

"Are there any illegal drugs in your vehicle?"

"Of course not."

"Would you consent to a search of your vehicle?"

"Is this for real?" No response. "Fine, go ahead. Look wherever you want. For chrissake, there's nothing in there."

Now, at this point in the story, I have to pause to apologize to my mother. The woman is a defense lawyer—and a damn good one. And as such, she is deeply ashamed that her offspring would be so stupid as to toss out her constitutional rights like a goddamn gum wrapper.

But give me a break; I knew there was nothing incriminating in my car, right? I knew for sure I was innocent, which means I also knew I had nothing to worry about.

This sentiment proved to be highly inaccurate.

The second I gave him the go-ahead the first cop went rooting around in my car; the other two kept an eye on me like I might make a break for it. The guy looked in the glove compartment, inside the trunk, and under the seats. Meanwhile, I stood there anticipating the delicious moment when they'd have to apologize for acting like fascist morons.

Then he pulled out a bag of white powder the size of a regulation softball.

I really, really hoped it was Sweet'n Low.

"What the hell is that?" I said. "Hey, that's not *mine.*"

The cop eyed the Ziploc bag, and though I expected him to taste it or something, he just nodded at one of his buddies. The next thing I knew, somebody was grabbing my arms behind my back.

"Hey, wait a minute," I said. "You don't actually think that stuff is mine, do you? Somebody must've put it there. Hold on just a—"

"You're under arrest for possession of cocaine. You have the right to remain silent. If you give up that right . . ."

"Look, this is obviously some horrible mistake. Would somebody please just call Detective Cody and—"

". . . anything you say can and will be used against you in a court of law. You have the right to an attorney and to have that attorney present during questioning. If you desire an attorney and cannot afford one—"

"Oh, for chrissake, I know the Miranda. Now will you please just call and tell him somebody planted a bunch of drugs in his girlfriend's car?"

That got his attention. "You're Detective Cody's—"

"Yeah. Now will you take these goddamn handcuffs off me?"

"I can't." The look on his face was, at least, vaguely regretful.

"Why the hell not?"

"You may be Detective Cody's girlfriend," he said, "but right now, you're still going to jail."

• • •

I HAVE ALWAYS BEEN a rabid fan of TV cop shows, from old reruns of *Barney Miller* to the various incarnations of the sacred *Law & Order* franchise.

And it's a good thing too, because the next couple of hours made me feel like I'd just been drop-kicked into one of them.

First I got put into the back of a squad car, head-ducking thing and all. Then I spent the whole ride to the station house—roughly five blocks—protesting that I'd been set up.

I got photographed. I got fingerprinted. I even got to make my one bloody phone call, by which time I'd smartened up enough to swallow my pride and call my mom.

For the record, my mother isn't admitted to the bar in New York State. Lucky for me, though, somebody she clerked with after law school is a big defense attorney in Manhattan—a lady who makes a fortune getting rich people off the hook. Normally, of course, a piddling drug case wouldn't have crossed her radar, unless it involved the dopehead kid of one of her clients. But she and my mom used to be pretty tight; one call got me the fee-free services of a $400-an-hour lawyer.

You're probably wondering where Cody was at a time like this. So was I.

The answer, and a damned inconvenient one too, was that he was at some stupid closed-door meeting with the F.B.I.

He finally showed up about two hours later, just as I was deciding that I'd officially gone insane from boredom. The lady officer who'd relieved me of my purse and jewelry unlocked the cell door and he came inside—officially, the most welcome sight I'd ever seen, *ever*.

For some reason, though, I was also furious with him.

"Son of a bitch, Cody, where the hell have you been? I've been rotting in here for—"

He wrapped his arms around me, so the rest of my tirade was stifled by his shoulder. He held me like that for a good long while, and when he finally let me go, I was no longer in the mood to yell at him.

"Baby," he said, "I'm so sorry."

"What the hell is going on? Nobody will tell me anything."

"Apparently, somebody phoned in an anonymous tip that there was a big drug shipment coming into town today. They gave the plate and model of the car and it was . . . yours."

"I don't believe this."

"Obviously, with everything that's been going on, the department's pretty on edge when it comes to narcotics. And the chief and I were meeting with—"

"I heard. So what the hell's going to happen to me?"

"They're going to arraign you."

"*What?*"

"That's the only way they can set bail so I can get you out of here. I promise, we'll get this thing straightened out as fast as we can, but right now we ought to get you a lawyer."

"I've got one." I told him the details. "But seriously, Cody, what in the hell is going on? How did those drugs get in my car?"

"I was just going to ask you the same thing."

"Jesus," I gasped at him, "don't tell me you think I—"

"Are you crazy? Of course I don't think that. What I meant was, how do *you* think they got in there?"

"Well, obviously, somebody must've planted them on me and then called the cops."

"Right," he said, "but how? And when? And most importantly . . . why?"

"I've been thinking about that, believe me—there's not a hell of a lot else to do in here." I motioned around the goddamn dog kennel I was cooped up in, its only furniture a metal bench welded to the floor. "And obviously, it's got to have something to do with Melting Rock."

"You think somebody did this to get you off the story?"

"Don't you?"

"Yeah, I do."

"So where does that leave me?"

"Baby, I . . . I'm really sorry. I wish I could just make this go away."

"Me too."

"It just doesn't work that way. For now, we've got to go through the system. And unfortunately . . . I'm thinking that if anything, they're going to be harder on you because of me."

"What? Why?"

"The chief has to avoid the appearance of impropriety. Especially with the F.B.I. swarming around . . . he can't have anybody accusing him of playing favorites."

"Great."

"But I swear, baby. When this is all over, your record will be clean."

"*Record?* Oh, my God—"

"It's going to be okay, I promise. I pulled some strings, and they're going to get you arraigned in an hour or so. The bail's probably going to be around twenty, so—"

"I don't have that much cash on me," I said. "And anyway, they took my purse, so—"

"Baby, I meant . . . twenty thousand."

"*Dollars?*" He nodded. "Are you out of your mind?"

"Alex, I'm not sure you realize . . . Do you know how much coke they found on you?"

"I told you, nobody would tell me anything."

"It was a little over a kilogram."

"Is that a lot?"

"The street value is over a hundred grand."

My chin practically hit the concrete floor.

"And somebody put that in my car? What are they, nuts?"

"Even so, they did it. And do you know what that means?"

"That I'm absolutely and completely screwed?"

"It means that to whoever did this," he said, "getting you off the story was worth a hundred thousand bucks."

CHAPTER 27

As everybody learns in civics class, a person is innocent until proven guilty. According to the criminal justice system, at least.

At the *Gabriel Monitor,* however, things work a little differently. Like the denizens of some banana republic, we don't have much in the way of constitutional rights.

Which means . . . the minute I got out of jail, I got suspended.

The long and the short of it was that although nobody really believed that yours truly ran the Gabriel outpost of the Medellín drug cartel, it didn't matter. Chester, our much-detested publisher, has always been obsessed with the "family newspaper" thing—and having one of his reporters get busted with a kilo of coke doesn't make for an image of milk-fed wholesomeness, if you know what I mean.

Marilyn was very apologetic; she said she was sorry I was getting royally shafted, but her hands were tied. Until the whole mess got resolved, I wasn't welcome anywhere near the *Monitor* newsroom. And I wasn't getting paid, either.

Now, normally I would've been just as happy to go running home to Mom and Dad, where I could get lots of sympathy and not have to worry about grocery money. But under the terms of my bail, I didn't get to leave the county. So there I was—stuck at home, with no desire to show my recently incarcerated face in public, and so financially freaked out I was living on Lipton's pasta packets.

Sure, my friends stopped by after work with red wine and newsroom gossip, but I felt like I was already halfway up the river. Cody called me every night, but for some reason I didn't want to see him until this idiotic nightmare was over. I guess I was feeling like Typhoid Mary, and I didn't want my criminal squalor to rub off on him. And to make matters worse, I was living alone—Melissa having gone straight from the hospital to visit friends in Toronto. My only company was my dog and her cat.

After a few days of this, I was ready to chew my own foot off. Although I'm a big fan of hanging around and doing nothing, I don't much enjoy doing it against my will. And even though Cody had promised it would all be over soon—obviously, there was no way I was going to get indicted—even the remote possibility that I was going to spend my next thirty birthdays in Bedford Hills was enough to send me into one whopper of a depression.

Then I got indicted.

If that surprises you, well . . . imagine what a mother of a shock it was to me.

How, you may wonder, could this possibly occur? I mean, obviously, I didn't do it; I've never even *tried* cocaine, much less sold it. So how could the system shove an innocent person such as myself one giant step closer to the hoosegow?

The answer is simple: Somebody lied. According to my lawyer—a sweet, motherly lady who proved to be a goddamn banshee in the courtroom—a guy who'd been picked up on drug charges was told he could cut a deal if he named his supplier.

He said it was me.

The guy even testified to that fact, under oath, to a grand jury. If I wasn't entirely screwed before, I was now.

And by the way: The person who screwed me was named Robert Adam Sturdivant.

They'd picked him up at the Miami airport, where a test of some new facial-recognition software had paid off within the first two hours. Sturdivant's ugly mug triggered a hit from the fugitive database, and the next thing he knew he was on a plane back to New York. After getting interrogated by every law-enforcement agency with jurisdiction over the Melting Rock deaths—not to mention the Gabriel cops—Sturdivant started talking.

Unfortunately, what he told them was that I was the drug queen of upstate New York.

Naturally, Sturdivant's accusations were duly documented in the *Gabriel Monitor*—so in addition to being railroaded and framed, I was also intensely humiliated. My beloved colleagues even took the head shot from my movie review column and ran it on page one under the headline LOCAL REPORTER INDICTED ON COKE CHARGES. Within five minutes the Walden County D.A. was trying to convince my lawyer that I should do myself a favor and flip on *my* supplier in return for a reduced sentence. Overnight, I'd gone from Alex B. to goddamn Josef K.

It was all so ridiculous, it would've been funny. That is, if it were happening to somebody other than me.

Granted, I had a lot more going for me than most people who get shafted by the system. I had a high-priced lawyer, gratis; I had a cop boyfriend who swore up and down he was going to get me out of this, despite the fact that he'd been told to steer clear of my case or else; and I had a couple of friends (Mad and Ochoa) who pledged to defend me like some semi-inebriated Knights of the Round Table.

But I was still pretty terrified.

Finally, three days after the grand jury threw me to the wolves, something good happened. To wit: I woke up mad as hell.

It's true; I was positively furious. After a week of wallowing in self-pity and abject fear, I finally got pissed off. Somebody wanted me out of the way—specifically, I was pretty sure they wanted me off the Melting Rock story—and so far, they were doing a damn good job of it.

Well, as far as I was concerned, that was bloody well over. If somebody didn't want me to figure out what had really happened at Melting Rock, then that was exactly what I was going to do. Although I wasn't officially working for the paper at the moment, I was still a goddamn reporter. And if I had to trick people into thinking I was still representing the *Monitor*—well . . . too damn bad.

Thus jazzed up, I plopped myself on the porch swing with my faithful canine at my feet and tried to figure out just what the hell I was going to do. In an effort to be organized—not something that comes naturally—I decided to make a list entitled *Things to Figure Out in No Particular Order.*

It was depressingly long, but here it is:

1. Who put the coke in my car? Why? How? When? Where did they get it?
2. Why did that jerk testify against me?
3. Who broke into my house?
4. Who killed Axel? Why?
5. Who made the poisoned LSD?
6. Were Shaun, Billy & Tom really killed on purpose? *(Duh.)* Who did it?
7. WHY???
8. Is whoever had me framed the same person who killed the guys?
9. What does Dorrie know?
10. Does Lauren know anything she hasn't told me? Trish? Cindy? Alan?
11. What's up with Mohawk Associates?
12. Did Deep Lake really spend $50K to shut up the opposition?
13. When is Gordon breaking his stupid story?
14. Am I going to jail?

I crossed out that last one because I didn't want to think about it.

I stared at the list for a while, trying to figure out where to start. It made sense to begin with the easiest question and go from there; unfortunately, all of them seemed pretty hard. So I read over the list again and again—and every time I did, my eyeballs stuck on number nine.

What does Dorrie know?

All of my snoopy reporter's instincts were telling me that she was hiding something; I couldn't believe that she'd smacked me across the face purely out of moral indignation. No, I definitely got the feeling that she was agitated about something. But how could I get her to tell me what it was?

Blackmail her, came the answer from the devilish corner of my psyche. *Prove that she's the one who got the Deep Lake Cooling key for Robinette, and threaten to tell on her unless she comes clean.*

That much decided, I went back to the top of the list. Finding out who'd framed me was, obviously, the most pressing issue of all; solving the Melting Rock case wouldn't do me much good if I wound up playing the lead in a chicks-in-prison movie. And in terms of solving question number one, question number two seemed key.

On one hand, it could be that Sturdivant had fingered me just because my arrest had been in the news. But then again, maybe there was something more nefarious going on; maybe whoever had put the drugs in my car had put him up to it, just to make sure I was well and truly screwed.

Considering the situation I was in, my money (and, come to think of it, my entire future) was riding on the second version.

Believe it or not, that struck me as good news. If Sturdivant had really been told to railroad me, that meant he was a link to whoever had ordered it—as far as I could see, the *only* link. If I could get him to talk, then maybe I could find out who'd gotten me into this mess. But how?

For a while I sat there imagining how great it would be if Cody beat the guy senseless until he confessed. Sadly, such an event did not seem likely to occur in the real world.

I was distracted from this happy fantasy by the ringing phone. It turned out to be Gordon.

"Hey, Alex, how are you doing?"

"Astonishingly shitty. How the hell do you think?"

"Do you want to get together for lunch today? I'm buying."

Now, if Gordon Band were a normal human being I might have assumed that he was trying to be nice. As it was, however, the idea never even occurred to me.

"Gordon," I said, "if you think I'm going to give you anything on the record about my miserable predicament, you're out of your nasty little mind."

"But—"

"Listen very carefully. My only comment to you is 'No comment.'"

"Comment? Who said anything about comment?"

"Then what do you want?"

"Can't a friend take a friend out for lunch?"

"And why would you want to do that exactly?"

"I'm worried about you."

"Huh."

"Hey, what's your problem? Are you that pissed about the story?"

"What story?"

"The one in today's *Times.*"

Shit. "Please don't tell me it has anything to do with goddamn Deep Lake Cooling."

"So you saw it, huh?" To be fair, Gordon did seem to be making some little attempt not to gloat. Unfortunately, he was failing big time. "I just live for this kind of—"

"Jesus . . . all right, you win." I scratched number thirteen off the list so hard my pencil broke. "Go ahead, rub it in. How the hell did you get onto it?"

"Wasn't that hard. That town of yours is such a bunch of freaks, it was obvious there was something up when I heard only a handful of people showed up to protest the Deep Lake opening. So I did a little digging, and I finally got a source to tell me the university was doling out fake consulting fees to keep people quiet."

"Somebody who was in on it?"

"Nah. Somebody kind of on the sidelines. I guess some documents went missing from someplace—source wouldn't give me the details— and the people behind Mohawk Associates just immediately went apeshit that they were gonna get caught. She'd had her suspicions be- fore, but that's when she figured out what was up and tipped me off, so I zipped on over to the library and found the company in the Deep Lake papers. Broke the story this morning, and from what I hear, Shardik's gonna be clearing out his desk by noon."

"So who's this source?"

"Like I'm gonna tell you."

"At least tell me how you got the source to talk."

"No way."

"Come on, Gordon. Dazzle me."

"Okay, but . . . I'm only telling you because it's a riot."

"I'm listening."

"Source called me because she had a vision."

"You're kidding."

"Nope. You know how I drive a, er . . . a Volkswagen Vanagon, right?"

"Sure. Sometimes you sleep in it."

"Shut up. Anyway, apparently this person was looking for guidance about who to tell about the Deep Lake racket, and a voice spoke to her. Wanna know what it said? It said, 'Tell the man in the van, man. Tell the man in the van.' Can you believe that shit?"

"Oh, my God," I said. "It was Guinevere."

"Son of a . . . How did you—"

"Small town. So, did you ever figure out who was in charge of Mohawk Associates? Like, who was running the operation?"

"Uh . . . no. But I will eventually, you can bet your—"

"Good-bye, Gordon."

"Hey, wait a second. If you haven't actually seen the story yet, how'd you even know about all this stuff?"

I hung up on him; it was rude, but satisfying. The phone immediately started ringing again, but I ignored it and got back to the porch just in time to see the *Monitor* deliveryman pitching the paper onto the neighbor's lawn. Since the guy had already left for work, I decided to temporarily snag it.

Now, I knew that reading the paper was probably going to upset me even further; being reminded of my suspension from the newsroom was like a punch in the gut. But I didn't anticipate *how* upset—or that the reason for it would be the banner headline stripped across the top of page one: JASPERSBURG TEEN INJURED IN HIT AND RUN.

The subhead said CHAMPION ATHLETE IN CRITICAL CONDITION. The main photo was of an ambulance parked by the side of a rural road. And the name of the victim was Alan Bauer.

ACCORDING TO THE STORY—byline, Cal Ochoa—Bauer had been out on his nightly five-mile run when he'd been struck. If some Good Samaritan hadn't happened along the country road just minutes afterward, the kid would already be dead. As it was, he was barely hanging on.

The car, which had been stolen from a Jaspersburg body shop the night before, had been found abandoned a mile away. "Alcohol," Ochoa wrote, "is suspected to be a contributing factor."

But what the story didn't say—what I'd have to find out directly from the reporter's mouth—was that the '94 Trans Am had been covered in Bauer's blood and stinking of whiskey. They even knew what kind of whiskey; a nearly empty bottle of Jim Beam had been found on the floor of the passenger's seat.

The Jaspersburg cops were calling it a hit and run.

They were calling it a joyride gone awry.

They were calling it another drunk-driving tragedy.

I was calling it attempted murder.

I mean, what were the odds? All along I'd been suspecting that Bauer was meant to be the fourth victim, and now he was next door to dead. How could this so-called "accident" be anything but yet another setup?

I posed this very question to Ochoa when I met him for lunch on the Green a couple of hours later. And yes, I did get a few snarky comments from strangers—but I thought, to hell with it. I was damned if I was going to spend any more time holed up in a cave like I was actually *guilty* of something.

So I waltzed into the Center Gabriel food court and ordered myself a falafel pita, only to be told my "drug money" wasn't welcome there. Then I went over to the Thai take-out stand, whose owners apparently don't keep up on the news.

"You know, Bernier," Ochoa said once we got outside, "everybody in the newsroom knows you didn't do that shit."

"Yeah, well, tell that to King David." I tried a forkful of my pad Thai, which improved my mood. "So, okay," I said, "what's going on?"

"First off," Ochoa said, "I got an update on Bauer's condition just now, and it doesn't look good."

"You think he's not going to make it?"

"The odds are pretty lousy. And even if he does . . . the poor kid got really fucked up. One of his legs was so badly crushed they may have to amputate it."

Suddenly, my food didn't look so appealing. "Holy *shit*. That's . . . Jesus Christ. But how . . . if somebody just ran into him . . ."

Ochoa shook his head, mouth set tight. "Whoever did it didn't just hit him. According to his injuries and the tire tracks at the scene, after he got knocked down, the driver backed up and ran over him again."

"How come that wasn't in your story?"

"Give me a break, Alex. I just got the info this morning."

"And does all that, you know, convince the cops that there's more to this than just your regular drunk-driving accident?"

"Not necessarily. I mean, in a normal situation, why would anybody think that?"

"So then what are—"

"Conventional wisdom seems to be that after Bauer got hit, the driver pulled over; but since he was so loaded, he backed up to see what the hell happened and ran the kid down. Then he panicked, took off, and ditched the car."

"God, I just *knew* I should've warned him."

"What?"

"Ever since we were talking about how he was probably the target for the fourth pill, I've been trying to get in touch with him, to tell him to be careful. But he wouldn't return my calls, and now . . . I kind of feel responsible."

"Jesus, Alex. You didn't run him over with the damn car."

"Yeah, but maybe if I'd said something . . ."

Ochoa reached over and gave my shoulder a little shake. "Come on, *chica*, don't go there. First off, it's not your fault. And second, Alan Bauer's no baby. He's a jock with twice your body weight, and from what you said, he's not stupid. If he and his friends really did something to piss someone off, and then three of them get dead, don't you think the guy's gonna be way on his guard in the first place?"

"I guess."

"Believe it."

"So what's next? In the investigation, I mean."

"Chief Stilwell's holding a press conference this afternoon."

"Oh. Thrilling."

"Yeah, well, I gotta go anyway. Five bucks says all he's gonna do is make an appeal for information—'Please come forward, it'll be easier on you that way,' the usual."

"Poor guy."

"Stilwell?"

"Yeah."

"He's a cop," Ochoa said. "They live for this stuff."

"No, they don't," I said. "Trust me. And Bauer . . . he's another one of Stilwell's daughter's friends. Not a particularly close one, I don't think, but how much trauma can the poor kid take?"

"I could say the same thing about you."

"Excuse me?"

"Come on, Alex. You've been through the wringer yourself these past couple of weeks."

"Yeah, well, it's nothing compared to what's happened to some other people. Melissa, for one."

"I know, but I'm just . . . I'm kind of worried about you, okay?"

"Um . . . okay."

"Look, I know we haven't always been best buddies, but you don't deserve this crap. So anything you need me to do, I'm going to do, *comprendes?* I know there's only so much Cody can stick his nose into without getting up shit's creek, but me . . . I'm not bogged down with a lot of scruples, okay? I'll do whatever needs to be done."

"And then you'll write about it, and eventually you'll get a job at a much better paper than this one."

He flashed his very white teeth. "You say that," he said, "like it's a bad thing."

CHAPTER *28*

As it turned out, Ochoa's lack of scruples began to pay off almost immediately.

He started by going to every bank in town trying to deposit a money order he'd had made out to Mohawk Associates. Most places told him that they couldn't help him without an account number and showed him the door. But at (of all places) the Ethical Vanguard Credit Union, the teller apparently gazed deeply into his big brown eyes and said she wished she could help him, but she wasn't allowed to give out any information about an account holder.

One memorable evening later—I asked Ochoa to spare me the details—she'd changed her tune. Not only did we have confirmation that the bank did indeed have such an account, we had a printout of all the deposits made and checks written since it had been established three years ago.

The bottom line was that there was a lot of activity three years earlier, when the consulting fee from Deep Lake was deposited—and was almost immediately disbursed in varying amounts of cash. Then a full year went by with no action on the account, until cash deposits started to come in, all of them under the federal reporting threshold of ten thousand bucks. The figures seemed familiar, and sure enough when Ochoa and I compared them to the copy we'd made of the lists from the Melting Rock office, they matched up. All the entries that had M.A. next to them corresponded to checks made out for the same amount, while those without the two letters matched with cash withdrawals.

But here was the weird thing: The other list, the one that had Axel's and Sturdivant's initials on it, didn't jibe with checks or withdrawals; they corresponded with *deposits.*

"Son of a gun," Ochoa was saying. "Does this mean that Axel wasn't getting payoffs, he was actually making payments?"

"That's what it looks like," I said. "But what the hell for?"

"Think about it. He and Sturdivant are both on the list. What else do they have in common?"

"They were both drug dealers."

"Exactly. So I'm thinking . . ."

"Wait. I get it. Not only is the account laundering some of the excess cash that the festival isn't reporting, it's also collecting protection money, right?"

"Smart girl."

"The drug dealers pay up, and the town fathers make sure they get to do business without the cops breathing down their necks. Everybody's happy—the dealers, the customers, the people who run Melting Rock. The town makes its nut, and folks like Mrs. Hamill rake in the bucks personally too."

"Nice little racket," Ochoa said, "until you get caught."

"So maybe the four kids—Tom and Billy and Shaun and Alan— they found out about it somehow. Maybe they tried to make a little money off it, or just tried to get themselves some free dope or something, and . . ."

"And to keep their little money-making operation going, somebody killed them."

"But wait a minute. I think I understand all the financial ins and outs, but how do we get from Deep Lake to Melting Rock?"

"Good question," he said. "And I think maybe I have an answer."

"I'm all ears."

"Okay, look at it this way. Three years ago, the powers that be at Deep Lake help set up this shell corporation so they can pay the protesters to leave them alone. Now, obviously, this is a pretty small town, and a lot of those hippie types overlap. The payments get made, but the account is still sitting there. So when the Melting Rock guys need to wash their cash, why bother to start from scratch? Why not just use Mohawk Associates? It worked for them once, why not try it again?"

"I guess that makes sense, but . . . what the hell do we do now?"

"We break the story."

"How can we? We still don't have—"

"We don't have a lot of choice."

"Why not?"

"Something else Chrissy told me."

"Who the hell is Chrissy?"

"The bank teller. She called me up this morning all upset. Apparently, she found out that the cops had also asked for a copy of the same account information."

"Which means they've got evidence of the payoffs, so . . ."

"They're probably going to make an arrest any second. If we want to break the story, it's now or never. Did your buddy Cody really not mention this?"

"Hey, don't look at me like that, okay? God knows I haven't been holding out on you or anything. It's just . . . ever since I got busted, Cody and I have been kind of out of touch."

"I thought he was supposed to be a stand-up guy. Don't tell me he's—"

"It's not him; it's me. I've sort of been keeping him at arm's length lately. And don't bother asking me why, because I'm not sure myself, okay?"

"Hey, it's none of my business."

"I'm glad you realize that."

"So what do you say? Do we break this or what?"

"What do you want, my blessing?"

"For lack of a better word . . . yeah."

"But how are you going to back it up, attributionwise? Are you finally going to interview Trike Ford?"

"Tried," he said. "No go. He pretty much played dumb, then told me asking questions like that could get a guy's ass kicked."

"When was this?"

"Couple days ago."

"Jesus, Ochoa, why didn't you tell me?"

"Figured you had enough to worry about."

"Come on, you saw what happened to Melissa. These aren't the kind of people you want to screw around with."

"I can take care of myself," he said. "Besides, I've got Madison watching my back."

"But if he's denying it, which of course he would, who are you attributing this stuff to?"

"I've got sources of my own in the police department, you know. Between that and all the paperwork—the payoff lists, the account info, the stuff you found from the Melting Rock lawsuits—it ought to be enough to satisfy Bill and Marilyn."

"Not to mention the lawyers."

" 'According to documentation provided to the *Monitor* by anonymous sources . . . ,' " he said with a grin. "Don't you just *love* it?"

OCHOA'S PAGE-ONE STORY ran the next day. And from what I hear, its appearance pissed off not only Gordon—who was apoplectic to learn that he'd missed a big chunk of the Mohawk Associates story—but local law-enforcement officials, who were forced to move on the arrests several days earlier than they'd planned. But sure enough, the following morning's paper featured the banner head ARRESTS MADE IN MELTING ROCK PAYOLA—which, if nothing else, satisfied Bill's long-held yearning to use the latter word in a headline.

The most prominent occupant of the paddy wagon was, of course, Rosemary Hamill. Probably out of spite at the *Monitor*, the county sheriff had tipped off Nine News to the arrests—meaning that viewers of their six o'clock broadcast were treated to the sight of her, gigantic hat askew, swearing up and down that she "hadn't broken any tax laws."

The arrest of Trike Ford was less comical. The Nine News cameras captured him unleashing a torrent of bleeped-out words at the officers as he was taken in handcuffs from the family trailer, with both his infant daughter and Jo wailing on the rickety front porch.

Mrs. Hamill, predictably, hired a lawyer and started fighting the case tooth and nail. Trike, on the other hand, immediately offered to turn in each and every one of his coconspirators—up to and including the two burly Melting Rock security guys who had assaulted Melissa.

A casual observer, therefore, might have assumed that the whole sorry mess was coming to an end. It wasn't.

Because, you see, two things were conspicuously absent from Trike's confession: He didn't admit to framing me, and he swore up and down that the Mohawk Associates scam didn't have anything to do with any of the murders—not of the boys, and not of Axel Robinette.

That he'd lie to avoid a murder rap might seem entirely predictable; the problem was, there was nothing to prove otherwise. In fact, according to Ochoa's cop sources, Alan Bauer swore he'd never even heard about the scam; the female members of the Jaspersburg Eight backed him up, saying that as far as they knew, Tom, Shaun, and Billy hadn't known about it, either.

So . . . were they lying? Were they just mistaken? Or was there something else going on, something nobody even suspected?

And, at the risk of sounding excessively narcissistic . . . what about me?

That was the question I posed to Ochoa, who'd come over to my place to consume vast quantities of pizza to celebrate his big scoop. Melissa, who'd just gotten back from Toronto, had eaten half a slice and pleaded exhaustion; Ochoa and I had camped out in the living room, consuming the rest of the pie and trying to figure out how to keep me out of jail.

"Okay," I said, "here's the bottom line. Raise your hand if you have any idea how I go about finding out who put goddamn Sturdivant up to this."

"Well," Ochoa said, "the way I see it, there are three possibilities. Either he did it by himself in the hopes of staying out of jail, or somebody paid him to do it, or somebody forced him."

"Forced him how?"

"Damned if I know."

"Thanks a lot."

"Well, what does Cody have to say about it?"

"I told you, things are kind of weird on the Cody front lately."

"Let me guess. You're acting like a typical female."

"What's that supposed to mean?"

"You're pushing him away, then getting pissed at him for not being there."

"Jesus, Ochoa, that ex of yours sure did a number on you."

"And I let her. But don't change the subject."

"Okay, fine, I . . . I'm totally humiliated about this whole thing. I got busted, cuffed, indicted, the whole nine yards. And I guess . . . maybe the only thing that'll let me walk upright in the sunlight ever again is to get my own damn self out of it."

"That's perverse."

"Yeah, well, so am I."

"So fine, you're the superhero; what's your plan?"

"I told you, I'm stuck."

"Bullshit. I bet you've got some scheme running around in that twisted little head of yours."

"No, I . . . Well, okay. I have been thinking . . . maybe I ought to go back to the beginning."

"Which is?"

"The thing that got me into this mess in the first place," I said. "Melting Rock."

THE NEXT MORNING, I went back to the scene of the crime—not the one I'd been accused of, but the one I'd actually committed. This time, though, I went in via the front door of Groovy Guitar rather than through a back window. But it didn't matter; even the owner's dog looked at me like I was a felon.

I went in and headed straight for the back, past rows of instruments hanging from the ceiling like sides of beef in an abattoir. I had no guarantee anyone would even be in the Melting Rock office; it's hardly the kind of place that's staffed nine to five. Luckily, though, there was Jo Mingle—still hugely pregnant, and with her other baby whacking wooden blocks together in a playpen.

Jo didn't seem the least bit surprised to see me; she did, however, look completely miserable.

"Look, Jo," I said, "I'm really sorry about what happened with Trike."

"Not your fault," she said, sounding utterly exhausted. "Not anybody's fault but his."

"You really didn't know, did you?"

"Nah."

"I guess that's good."

"Yeah, I guess. At least I'm not going to jail, right? At least my kids'll have one of us to raise them. . . ." I had no idea what to say, so I just stood there. "So," she said after a while, "what are you doing here, anyway? You still writing about Melting Rock?"

"Sort of."

She bit her lip, fingered her thick blond braid. "Then . . . sorry, I can't help you. After what's happened and all . . ."

"Um, Jo . . . I'm not actually working for the paper right now. I just"—I tried to think of a way to explain it—"I was there, okay? I met those guys who died, and I'm just trying to figure out . . . I need to know what went wrong."

"The cops said some sicko sold them bad acid. And Trike . . . he swears he didn't know a single thing about it. And I believe him, okay? He's a bad guy, but he's not that bad."

"Right, but . . . I guess what I'm trying to do is understand the place."

"Understand Melting Rock?"

"Yeah."

"Oh. That's cool, I guess."

"So what can you tell me?"

She shrugged. "I don't know," she said. "Just what I told you at the fest, only it goes double now. It isn't the same place it used to be. It's too bad, too. Back in the day, Melting Rock was really something special."

"Special how?"

"Why don't you have a look for yourself?" She waved toward the lone bookshelf, which was stuffed with albums I'd glanced through when Mad and I broke in, each oversize volume covered in multicolored cloth.

"What are those, exactly?"

"Scrapbooks. There's a couple for every year. Not this year, though. Nobody's got around to it yet. Probably never will, either."

"But what—"

"Oh, *man,* I have to go." She consulted the antique watch hanging from a chain around her neck, then stood up, tummy first. "I have an appointment at the clinic at two. . . . Hey, could you do me a favor?"

"What?"

"If you're gonna stay here and look at the books anyway, could you watch Happy for me? I'll only be gone for, like, twenty minutes. I just have to get my weekly exam. Could you?"

"Listen, Jo, I—"

"She's a really easy baby, no problem. She'll just sit there and play with her—"

"It's not that. I, um . . ." For some reason, I felt the need to come clean. "Look, believe it or not, I just got accused of dealing some ridiculous amount of cocaine, okay? I got arrested and everything. So you probably wouldn't want me to—"

She blinked at me. "Just dealing? Is that it?"

"Um . . . yeah."

"All righty, then," she said. "If Happy fusses a little, there's a box of organic zwieback on the desk. Just give her one. She'll beg you for two, but you gotta—"

"Wait," I said. "You mean it doesn't bother you?"

"Nah," she said. "Drugs ought to be legal anyhow."

With those words and a friendly smile, Jo took off—leaving me with a pile of papers, several rows of scrapbooks, and one very fat baby. The kid watched her mother walk out the door, then screwed up her face like she was fixing to bawl. But she didn't; she just opened her eyes wide and stared at me like I was the weirdest thing she'd ever seen. Then she went back to her blocks.

Thus dismissed, I pulled the first scrapbook from the shelf and settled on the dusty hardwood floor next to the playpen. I flipped through the pages, which brought me back thirteen years—when I was at boarding school, and Melting Rock was just getting off the ground.

Sure enough, there were pictures of ragtag groups of music fans, maybe a hundred or so in all. The only person I recognized was a teenage Jo Mingle, though I did notice that many of the shots included a scraggly-bearded guy handing out thick slices of brown bread and passing around a ceramic butter crock. Fascinating.

I went through a few more like this before it occurred to me that it might be more profitable to work backward instead of forward. So I squatted at the bottom of the shelf and took the most recent volume, which was covered in purple velvet with appliquéd gold stars.

I flipped it open, and right away I saw some familiar faces; Melissa was even there, boogying it up in a crowd shot. Eventually, I came across a photo of Lauren, looking flushed and happy—and, of all things, sitting on the lap of one Axel Robinette. He was holding her around the waist and, in his predictably suave fashion, grabbing one of her breasts.

What the hell was that all about?

A couple of pages later, I hit the jackpot: two full spreads devoted entirely to the group I'd been calling the Jaspersburg Eight. At first I was blown away by my good fortune, but then I figured it wasn't really that unlikely. After all, the reason I'd found the teens in the first place was because Jo had told me they were a Melting Rock institution.

And there they were, looking a lot like they had when I'd first met them—hanging out on the grass, clowning around, giving the general impression that they didn't have a care in the world. They were younger, of course; the difference between sixteen and seventeen can be acute, especially for boys. I noticed that Tom's hair was shorter, and Billy had just started cultivating those ridiculous sideburns; Shaun looked basically the same, skinny and with serious acne issues, though Alan wasn't nearly as well muscled as when I'd met him.

As for the girls: Cindy hadn't changed much from fifteen to sixteen, though the previous year her hair had been electric blue. Lauren seemed as grown-up and confident as ever; Trish, on the other hand, was maybe twenty pounds heavier than she was now—making her almost normal.

But when it came to the prize for Most Transformed, there was no contest: Dorrie was the winner, hands down.

In fact, if she hadn't been with the rest of the gang, I probably wouldn't have recognized her. She looked . . . well, *normal.*

Her hair was still short, but it was nicely styled. She was wearing a sundress akin to the ones that Lauren paraded around in, a flower-print spaghetti-strap affair that showed off her tanned shoulders and budding cleavage. Other than a pair of loopy earrings, there was nary a piercing to be found. On her ankle was a rose tattoo just like Trish's, and I realized I hadn't noticed it before. Every time I'd seen her in person, she'd been wearing pants and long sleeves.

I scrutinized the picture for a while, my first reaction being intense sympathy for Dorrie's parents. Call me uptight, but the idea of a daughter of mine running around looking like an East Village rent-a-boy made me nauseous.

My second thought, though, was even more dramatic.

What the hell happened to her?

What could possibly prompt a girl to make such a dramatic identity shift her junior year of high school? What had made her go from what appeared to be a typical teenager to a morose kid bent on self-mutilation? Was it really just normal adolescent angst? Or was there something else going on?

Those queries prompted me to ask another, one that I'd been pondering for weeks now. Then I put the two together, and suddenly everything seemed to fall into place.

I'd wondered what the boys had done, what could be awful enough to make someone want them dead. I'd thought it was connected to the payoff scam, but it appeared that I was wrong.

And now I was wondering what had happened to Dorrie.

With everything else out of the picture, didn't it make sense to ask, *What had they done to Dorrie?*

And what was the most obvious answer? What was the most likely thing that a group of boys could have done to leave a girl traumatized, maybe even change her overnight? I thought about how I'd found Melissa, naked and brutalized, and what everyone had assumed had happened to her until she told us different.

Oh, my God, I thought. *They raped her.*

OKAY, so maybe I was wrong. Maybe, as my mom would say, I was assuming facts not in evidence. But . . . I couldn't shake the feeling that I was finally on the right track.

I was about to run out in search of more information when I remembered that I was responsible for the well-being of a tiny human. By the time Jo got back fifteen minutes later, I was practically hysterical with curiosity.

I went straight from the Melting Rock office to the Walden County Public Library, where I headed for the reference section. I grabbed the previous year's Jaspersburg High School annual and flipped to the photo of the junior class. It took some searching to find Dorrie in the crowd, but there she was—hair shorn, nose pierced, not having totally adopted her present look, but well on her way.

From my previous incarnation as the *Monitor*'s schools reporter, I knew that student portraits were taken at the end of September, so the kids could give them to their parents for Christmas. That meant that when the scrapbook photos were shot the previous August, Dorrie looked normal; a month later, she'd been transformed. If my theory was right, whatever had happened to her had gone down sometime in the course of those few weeks—maybe even at Melting Rock itself.

Son of a bitch.

So how could I find out more? Asking Dorrie herself didn't seem like a great idea, considering how she'd freaked out and slugged me the last time I'd spoken to her. Trish and Cindy had their own stability issues—which left Lauren, the long-haired nymphet who may or may not be schtupping my best friend.

I called her on her cell just as school was getting out, and she agreed to meet me on the grounds that it was "way more fun than studying calc." So I went over to Café Whatever and read the *Times* while I waited for her, taking some pleasure in the discovery that, even in the wake of his Mohawk Associates scoop, Gordon's latest assignment involved the bitter politics surrounding the closure of an Elmira tampon factory.

Lauren walked in half an hour later, looking rather schoolmarmish in a skirt and lightweight sweater, hair again up in a bun. She ordered an espresso and a thin lemon biscotti, which she dipped into the tiny cup with the precision of a chemist at the bench.

"So," she said through a smile, "how's Jake doing?"

"Um . . . okay, I guess. I haven't seen him that much."

"'Cause you got suspended from the paper?"

"Yeah. How'd you know?"

"It was in one of the stories about you getting busted."

"Oh. Listen, Lauren, I didn't do it, okay? Somebody set me up. They planted those drugs in my—"

"Well, *duh.*"

"You believe me?" Between Lauren and Jo, I was starting to feel like something less than a pariah.

She rolled her eyes. "You're *totally* not the type."

"Oh. Thanks."

"So how come you wanted to talk to me?"

"Well . . . I came across these old photos from Melting Rock last year, and I was kind of wondering about them."

"What photos?"

"Just of you guys, and . . . First of all, there was one of you and Axel Robinette, where you two looked kind of . . . intimate."

Another eye roll. "Yeah, we kind of hooked up that year. Nothing big. Just your typical M.R.F."

"Your what?"

"M.R.F. Didn't you hear that before?" I shook my head. "It stands for Melting Rock"—she leaned in, her smile turning naughty—". . . if you're in front of a grown-up, you'd say 'Fling,' but we've got another word for it."

"I bet you do."

"So, you know, that was that. No big deal. Is that really what you wanted to talk about?"

"That, and . . . Dorrie."

"Dorrie? What about her?"

"Like I said, I was going through some pictures from last year, and she just looks totally different. I checked the yearbook, and it seems like she went for the goth thing practically overnight."

"Yeah, I guess she did," Lauren said with a shrug. "So what?"

"Don't you think it's a little weird?"

"What's wrong with trying something new?"

"Nothing, but . . . In those pictures she seemed so happy, and now she seems so miserable. Are you telling me you didn't notice the difference?"

"Dorrie's always been kinda moody. It's just her style."

"Yeah, but this seems like an extreme."

"So what's your point?"

"Lauren . . . do you think it's possible that something happened to Dorrie?" No answer. "Look, I totally understand if she swore you to secrecy, but this isn't the kind of thing a person should just sit on, okay?"

"What the hell are you talking about?"

"I think something happened to her, maybe at Melting Rock last year. I think . . . maybe she was sexually assaulted."

"Are you serious?"

"So you're telling me you don't know anything about it?"

"What? *No*."

"And you're not just saying that to protect her? Because if you are, I swear it's really not in her best—"

"What the hell are you talking about?" she repeated. "You think . . . what? She got hurt by somebody at the fest?"

"That's what I'm wondering."

"That's nuts. Nobody at Melting Rock would ever do something like that. *Never*."

"Are you sure?"

"Of course I'm sure."

"There's a hell of a lot of drugs floating around that place, Lauren. That doesn't necessarily make for a whole lot of self-control. Who's to say that the guys didn't just lose it or something?"

"Guys? *What* guys?"

"Well . . ."

"Do you mean *our* guys?"

"Um . . . yeah."

She stood up, the shock on her face turning to anger. "Are you telling me you think that Tom and Shaun and Billy . . . They'd never . . . Tom would never . . ."

"Come on, Lauren, sit down. . . ."

"How could you even say that? Tom would never hurt anybody. He was the nicest guy in the whole world, okay? *Okay?*"

"Are you sure about that?"

"*Yes.*"

"Lauren, listen to me. Somebody killed those guys for a reason. Axel probably sold them the drugs. Dorrie's slept with him, for chrissake. Don't you think it's possible that—"

"Oh, my God, you . . . you *bitch.*" She was shouting at me now, and every eye in the place was focused on our little drama. Clearly, it would've behooved me to pick a less public place. "You unbelievable *bitch*. I can't believe you'd even . . . How could anybody even *say* that?"

"Come on, Lauren, I—"

She grabbed her bag and headed for the door. "I never want to talk to you again, *ever,*" she said. "And you know what? I hope they lock you up in jail and throw away the key."

CHAPTER *29*

If you're thinking that Lauren rather overreacted, well . . . so was I.
I mean, obviously, I *was* suggesting all manner of awful things about her closest friends, so I guess she was entitled to flip out. But even so, her attitude still struck me as pretty over the top. Maybe I was full of it, but I got the feeling that the reason she was so mad at me was that . . . well, maybe I'd said aloud something she'd already suspected herself.

Face flushed from my most recent humiliation, I slunk out of Café Whatever with my tail between my legs and a half-eaten question-mark cookie in my backpack. Out of habit I headed toward the paper—until I remembered that I was temporarily jobless.

And speaking of my legal woes . . . I knew I should probably call my lawyer and find out what was going on—but, frankly, I really wanted to avoid thinking about it.

Honestly, the whole thing still had quite the air of unreality about it. Practically every morning since I got arrested, I'd woken up, poodled in bed for a while debating what to wear to work—and then remembered I was in a gigantic amount of trouble.

This prompted me to ponder one Robert Adam Sturdivant; specifically, what the hell was up with him. Assuming he hadn't sold any of the LSD—meaning he wasn't guilty of killing anybody—why would he lie about me? Was I right in assuming that somebody had put him up to it, maybe paid him off?

And, more to the point, were the criminal-justice powers that be really going to take his word over mine? Was there—okay, gotta face it—was there any real chance I was going to prison?

I'm pretty sure it was this last question that prompted my car to go in the direction it went. Now, I'm not arguing that it was a smart thing to do, or even a legal one; I've spent enough time staring at my beloved TV cop shows to know there's such a thing as "intimidating a witness."

But there I was, parked in the Sturdivants' driveway, wondering just how much trouble I'd be in if the cops found out. I knew that Rob himself would almost certainly be home; he was, after all, on an ankle monitor until his plea agreement got approved. Then he'd report for a year in the county jail on drug-dealing charges—charges that had been much reduced, by the way, as payback for fingering me.

That thought was enough to propel me out of the car and up to the front door of the Sturdivants' well-appointed homestead. I'd already rung the bell when I remembered they had a live-in maid, the woman Rob had traumatized when he ripped off his parents' stuff. So I decided to flee—and Sturdivant himself answered the door.

He had a funny expression on his face, eager and sullen at the same time. Then he recognized me, and the combination morphed into disappointed, hostile . . . and sullen. And, come to think of it, maybe even a little bit scared.

"What the fuck do *you* want?" he said.

"To talk to you."

He started to shut the door. "No way."

I stuck my foot out to keep the door open, but it didn't deter him; he just slammed it on my ankle, which hurt. "Do you have any idea how much trouble you're in?"

He stopped trying to amputate my foot long enough to favor me with a nasty smirk. "I could say the same thing about you."

"For the moment."

Now he looked confused. "What the fuck's *that* supposed to mean?"

"For chrissake, Sturdivant, think about it. Sooner or later, you're gonna get found out. Do you know what happens to people who get convicted of perjury?"

"What?"

"Lying under oath, you moron. Let me spell it out for you. *You* are lying. *I* am telling the truth. That means that when this is all over, *you* are going to be in a world full of trouble."

His eyes narrowed. "Hey, it's your word against mine," he said. "You can't prove a fucking thing."

"Jesus, is that the only word you know?"

"Huh?"

I was overcome with the desire to pop him in the snout. "Let's look at it this way, shall we? *I* am a grown-up, taxpaying member of the community. *You* are a low-life drug dealer who pawns his dead grandmother's jewelry for travel money. Maybe the cops are swallowing your crap right now, but do you really think your story's gonna hold water in the long run?"

"Fu—"

"And when it comes out that you lied, you're gonna be in way more trouble than you are now, trust me. So come on, just tell me who put you up to this, and—"

"I don't know what the fuck you're talking about."

I crossed my arms, trying to look all tough and nonchalant. It didn't come naturally.

"You know what?" I said. "I think you know damn well what I'm talking about. I think somebody who wanted me out of commission got you to rat me out. So, did they pay you off, or just strong-arm you into it?"

"I don't know what the—"

"Oh, come *off* it. We both know I didn't sell any drugs to you or anybody else." He glowered at me, and the snout-popping urge increased. "Hey, it's bad enough that you lied to the cops. But until you swear to the plea agreement in front of a judge, you haven't actually perjured yourself."

Now, from a legal standpoint, I wasn't sure this was actually true. I also didn't give a damn.

"You better pay attention," I went on, "because whether or not you're smart enough to figure it out, I'm doing you a favor here. I'm giving you the chance to get yourself out of this before it's too late."

He smirked again, then looked me up and down; I was reminded of the predatory way he'd checked out the girls at Melting Rock. *Yuck.*

"You know something?" he said. "You are one ballsy bitch."

I was momentarily speechless.

Eventually, I recovered myself and said, "Do you really want to end up like Axel?"

"What are you—"

"Use your head. We both know Axel sold the LSD to those kids. Now, maybe he knew what he was doing, but—"

"No way, man. Axel wouldna done that on purpose." He kicked at the doorframe with a house slipper. "That's some fucked-up shit."

"Fine. But if Axel didn't know what was in the LSD, then somebody set him up to do their dirty work, and now he's dead. Somebody set *me* up to get me off the story. And somebody set *you* up to make sure I was totally screwed. What are the odds we're not talking about the same person here?"

"Get—"

"So whatever deal you made to get yourself off the hook, you better believe it was a deal with the devil. And whoever this person is, they're using you just like they used Axel. You really think they're gonna leave you breathing so you can rat on them later on?"

The wisp of fear I'd noticed on his face before came back, and in spades. I decided to exploit it.

"And don't go thinking you're off the hook with the cops, either," I said. "You and I know you didn't sell those tabs, but who's to say the cops won't change their minds and drag you into it again? There's no statute of limitations on murder, you know."

His mouth fell open. *"Murder?* Are you shittin' me? I just *deal,* okay? I wouldn't fucking *kill* nobody."

"Yeah, but who's gonna believe that? Once you get busted for perjury, the cops are never gonna swallow another word you say."

"But—"

"Count on it."

He pondered that for a while, the expression on his face turning petulant.

"This isn't *fair*, man," he said finally. "I'm bored as shit cooped up here all fucking day, and then I gotta go to *jail?* And I never moved *half* the product Axel did. Not half. That dude started selling when he was in fucking junior high."

"And look where it got him."

He shrugged. "Yeah, well, he had a pretty good ride. Got a ton of chicks, hardly ever got busted. Axel was goddamn *Superman*."

"Yeah, right, some— Wait a second. Axel got busted? When?"

"How the hell do I know? It was some juvie thing. Now will you get out of my fucking house?"

"Not until you tell me who put you up to this."

"Get lost."

Sturdivant went to close the door again, and I reinserted my foot. "Were you not even listening to me before? Perjury's a *felony*."

"Fuck you."

I grappled for some leverage, both literally and figuratively. "Did you know that my boyfriend's a cop? A goddamn police detective?"

He eyed me warily. "So?"

"So cops stick together. They had to arrest me when somebody planted the coke in my car, but you can bet your ass that every cop in this town is going to be busting his hump to prove I'm innocent— which means proving you're a liar."

"You've gotta be fucking kidding me."

"His name's Detective Brian Cody," I said. "I understand you've met him."

Sturdivant finally stopped trying to slam the door on my foot. It made me wish I'd played the Cody card to begin with; it would've saved me both time and ankle pain.

"That guy? You're fucking *him?*"

"Watch your mouth."

He leaned against the doorjamb, running a hand over his closed eyes and atop his bald pate. "I am so fucked."

"So tell me who put you up to this." He shook his head. "Come on, Sturdivant, just—"

"You don't get it," he said. "I'm screwed either way. I might as well put a goddamn gun in my mouth and get it over with."

"Listen, whoever's behind this, the cops can protect you from them."

He barked out a humorless laugh. "You don't know shit."

"Oh, yes, I do. I know what happened to Dorrie Benson, for one thing."

"What the hell are you talking about?"

"You mean Axel never told you anything bad happened to her?"

"Goddamn Axel," Sturdivant said. "*Goddamn* that skinny mother-fucker."

"I thought he was your hero."

"Yeah, well . . . I swear, if that shithead weren't already dead, I'd kill him myself."

BACK HOME, I pulled the tape recorder out of my backpack and tossed it on the coffee table; so much for my foray into covert ops. I'd gone to Sturdivant's house hoping he'd at least admit he was lying, but the closest I got was his acknowledgment (more or less) that he'd be in deep trouble if the truth came out. I seriously doubted it was enough to get a grand jury to rip up my indictment.

I also doubted that my assessment of the Gabriel P.D. as my knights in shining armor was particularly accurate. Yes, Cody was obviously trying to get me off the hook, but the truth was that everybody was so hypersensitive about drug offenses at the moment, there was only so far he or anyone else could go on my behalf. Which left me exactly where I was before I went charging over to Sturdivant's. To wit: screwed.

After consoling myself with a frozen mac and cheese, I took Shakespeare for a walk, her leash in one hand and my infamous list of unsolvable questions in the other.

But wait; if I was right about what happened to Dorrie, I could answer number seven—why Shaun, Billy, and Tom were murdered.

And if that was really the motive, then who would've done it? Dorrie herself? How? Could she have somehow cooked up the ingredients herself, then given it to Axel to sell? But that didn't make a lot of sense—unless Axel was in on it after all, how could Dorrie convince him to sell particular acid tabs to her friends? Did she tell him it was some kind of joke or something?

I tried to picture Dorrie as the lone gunman, and couldn't. Somehow, the idea of her getting assaulted and then secretly plotting her revenge over the course of an entire year just seemed . . . well, *crazy*. But if she didn't do it alone, then who helped her? A relative, maybe?

That thought stopped me cold. Dorrie was, after all, a Benson—a member of the richest and most powerful family in the county. Sturdivant had said he was screwed either way; it was obvious he was equally scared of the cops and whoever had made him testify against me. The extended Benson clan would definitely fit the bill.

My thoughts returned to the subject of making the drugs themselves. If what you needed was a laboratory to whip it up in, Benson obviously had about a hundred of them. From what Ochoa had told me, you wouldn't need a Ph.D. to pull it off—a working knowledge of high-school chemistry would do it.

High-school chemistry.

I stopped in midwalk, prompting a dirty look from Shakespeare. But I just stood there and stared at the list, my brain running a mile a minute.

I knew somebody who was good—*very* good—at high-school chemistry.

Somebody who was close to Dorrie.

Whose parents offered easy access to the Benson labs.

Who seemed way more upset at Tom Giamotti's funeral than anyone else's.

Who, in the days immediately following the killings, had stuck to me like glue.

Who'd slept with Axel and could have easily lured him to a rendezvous at Deep Lake.

Who'd recently flipped out at the mention of Dorrie being attacked.

Even someone who, theoretically speaking, was smart enough to find a way to scare the living hell out of a dolt like Rob Sturdivant.

I didn't have a pen on me, but if I did, I would've scribbled down the following questions, again in no particular order:

- What if Tom never hurt anybody?
- What if the four tabs were meant for Shaun, Billy, Alan—and Axel?
- What if Axel messed up and sold them to Tom and Norma Jean?

And here was the big one:

- What if the "mastermind" behind all this was . . . an eighteen-year-old kid named Lauren Potter?

CHAPTER 30

I had to talk to Dorrie. There was just no other way. My entire theory—which, by the way, was seeming more far-fetched with every mile of the Gabriel-Jaspersburg Road—was based on the assumption that the boys had assaulted her. If I was anywhere near right about Lauren, there obviously wasn't a lot of wisdom in interviewing her. And I had a feeling that Cindy and Trish, who'd always seemed the most fragile members of the group, probably didn't know what the hell was going on.

No, Dorrie had to be at the center of everything—didn't she? But how could I get her to talk to me? My recent attempts to get information out of people (Lauren, Sturdivant, Dorrie herself) had been less than successful—unless your definition of success involves getting slapped, yelled at, and summarily evicted. And although I'd previously thought of blackmailing Dorrie by proving that she'd been the one to swipe the Deep Lake Cooling key for Axel, now that I was thinking of her as a victim, I hardly had the stomach for it.

And to top it all off, I wasn't even sure where to look for her. It was eight o'clock on a Thursday night, so I figured she'd probably be home—but the idea of showing up on her parents' doorstep didn't seem very promising. Halfway to Jaspersburg, I pulled over and called her house on my cell; her mother answered, and I tried very hard to sound like a high-school kid. I said I needed to talk to Dorrie to get the math homework; she said she expected her home around nine. I crossed my fingers, said a little prayer to whoever is the patron saint of liars, and told Mrs. Benson I really, *really* needed the assignment right away.

"She's at the Mohawk Nature Center," she said, sounding both patrician and annoyed. "She's having a meeting for . . . some sort of club, I believe."

Score. I thanked her profusely—probably way *too* profusely—and pulled back onto the road. The nature center, a hippie enclave that teaches kids how to spin their own yarn and make tea out of tree bark, is on the far side of Jaspersburg. I'd been there plenty of times when I was on the schools beat. I'd even covered a pagan wedding there once, where the bride and groom had worn nothing but robes made of cloth they'd loomed themselves.

On the drive through Jaspersburg, another thought occurred to me: What if Dorrie and Lauren were in on it together? Wasn't that more likely than Lauren plotting the whole thing on her own?

The answer, it seemed to me, was yes. So should I turn the car around? Somehow, I didn't think so; I still had to find out if I was on the right track. And besides . . . for some reason, I couldn't picture myself being actually *scared* of Dorrie—or, come to think of it, Lauren, either. Was that a pretty solid indication that I was off on some ridiculous head trip?

I was still debating the question when I turned into the center. There were a couple of cars in the parking lot—including Dorrie's own red Beetle—but all the lights appeared to be out. As I went up to the front door, an outdoor safety light went on. I could just make out the words on a handwritten sign taped to the window:

TRI-COUNTY EARTH DAY PLANNING COMMITTEE

7–8 TONITE

RACHEL CARSON LOUNGE

UPSTAIRS

I checked my watch; it was coming up on eight-thirty. I tried the door, but it was locked. The meeting must be over by now, but Dorrie was obviously still here. Deciding to do a loop around the building, I grabbed my trusty Maglite out of the car. I'd just made it over to the right side when I heard some talking and giggling maybe thirty yards off into the woods. Then a voice said, "Shh! Somebody's here!"—plenty loud enough for me to pinpoint where they were. I shone my flashlight in their direction and saw a clutch of kids gathered on the ground; even from a distance, I could smell the pot smoke.

The minute I fixed them with the light, they scattered, amid the snapping of twigs and the crinkling of potato chip bags. I had no idea which one might be Dorrie, so I did the only thing I could think of; I went back to wait in her car, which she'd left unlocked. About fifteen minutes later, she plopped herself in the driver's seat.

"Do you really think," I said, "that you're in any shape to get behind the wheel?"

"Jesus Christ," she said, "you scared me."

"Sorry."

"What are *you* doing here, anyway?"

Her voice sounded odd—not slurred like a drunk, but . . . mellower, a little distracted, maybe vaguely amused.

"I need to talk to you."

"Jesus Christ," she said again. "Can't you just leave me alone?"

"No."

I let the word hang in the air for a while. Finally, she got uncomfortable enough to say something.

"Why not?" The words came out in a whine, which she directed to the steering wheel. "Why can't you just leave me *alone?* Why do you have to keep *bugging* me?"

"Because I need to know what happened."

"What happened *when?*"

"Last year. At Melting Rock."

She squeezed her eyes shut, banging her head dramatically against the center of the steering wheel. Then she struggled to pull a set of keys out of her pocket and stick them into the ignition. I grabbed the ring out of her hand.

"Hey," she said. "What do you think you're—"

"You're in no shape to drive."

She looked around the now-empty lot with a shrug. "My buds already left."

"They're not my concern at the moment. You are."

She let out a beleaguered groan—the kind of sound a person is constitutionally incapable of uttering after age twenty-one—and let her noggin fall back against the headrest.

"Would you please just leave me alone?" I flicked on the overhead light, and she shrank from the glare. "Jesus, what'd you have to go do that for?"

She flicked it off again, but not before I noticed she had a serious case of the bunny eyes. "If you want to talk in the dark, that's fine too."

"I don't want to talk at all. Now would you please get out of my car so I can go home?"

"I doubt very much you'd want your parents to see you like this."

"Like what?"

"Stoned out of your gourd."

"Oh."

She didn't seem particularly offended—just particularly zonked out. True to form, she leaned back against the headrest and closed her eyes.

"I'm not that stoned," she said. Then she let out a manic giggle. "Okay . . . I'm pretty stoned," she said, and giggled some more.

When she recovered from the laughing fit, she took a few long pulls from a plastic water bottle, put it back in the cup holder, and grabbed her backpack from the backseat. She fumbled with the zipper, finally got it to work, and yanked out a bag of blue-corn chips—which she then had a hard time opening. I did it for her.

"Hey," she said after jamming a handful into her mouth. "What do you want, anyway?"

"Just to ask you some questions."

"About what again?"

"Melting Rock."

"What about it?"

"About what happened there last year."

She squeezed her eyes shut, head still reclined against the seat. "I don't want to talk about it."

"You know, you really might feel better if you—"

"No. No way."

If she was starting to get upset, it didn't seem to impede her appetite; eyes still shut, she grabbed some more chips and stuffed them into her mouth. I decided to take a different tack.

"How come you decided to change the way you look all of a sudden?"

She opened one eye. "Huh?"

"I was looking at some old pictures from last year's Melting Rock, and you looked . . . totally different. Your hair was longer; you didn't have any piercings or anything—"

"What's wrong with the way I look?"

"Nothing," I lied. "All I'm saying is that in August you looked one way, and by the time the school pictures were taken a month later, you looked completely different. And I was just wondering . . . what might make a person change so much in such a short time?"

She shrugged. "What do you care?"

"I just do. And I was thinking . . . maybe one reason might be because a person went through some kind of trauma."

Now both eyes were open, and she was looking at me like she'd love to boot me out of the passenger's seat.

"I don't know what you're talking about."

Before she could figure out what I was doing, I reached over and yanked up the sleeve of her sweatshirt to reveal her forearm. What I saw, unfortunately, was exactly what I'd been afraid I might find: a line of horizontal cuts, both new and scarred over, marking the skin at varying intervals.

She jerked her arm away. "What do you think you're—"

"I was wondering why you always wear long pants and long sleeves, even at Melting Rock when it was hot as hell."

"So what if I—"

"Are you cutting your legs too?"

She bit her bottom lip and stared down at her lap. "None of your business."

"You can get help, you know."

She laughed again, but this time there was no humor in it. "Don't even *go* there."

"I had a friend in college who cut herself. I know what it's about—you feel all this pain and the only way you can block it out is to hurt yourself physically. And the only way you're going to be able to stop is if you talk about what—"

"I'm fine, okay? I don't even do it that much anymore."

"Some of those cuts look pretty fresh."

Her sleeve was already covering the marks, but she pulled it down even farther. "Would you just leave me alone?"

"Dorrie, what happened to you at Melting Rock?"

She stared out the driver's-side window. "Nothing."

"I want you to tell me the truth."

"Nothing."

"I know what they did, Dorrie. I know those boys hurt you. I know they were your friends, and you thought you could trust—"

Her head whipped around to face me. "Stop it."

"Jesus Christ, Dorrie. You've got to get this thing out in the open so you can deal with it."

She started crying then, with a hysteria that probably wouldn't have been possible without chemical assistance. "Please," she said, "please just stop it. . . ."

"Somebody killed those boys for a reason, Dorrie. It's taken me a long time to figure it out, but I think I know what they did. And I think I know who they did it to."

"No." The word became a wail. *"Noooooo."*

"Dorrie, please—"

"No. *No.* You don't know what you're talking about. You have no fucking idea—"

"They raped you, didn't they? Something happened, maybe everybody was high or something, but the situation got out of control and they attacked you. *Didn't they?*"

"No." She was crying so hard she seemed in actual danger of choking on her own tears. "No—no—no. You're wrong."

"That's why you did this to yourself. That's why you shaved your head and—"

"No. You don't understand. You don't understand anything."

"Then tell me."

"It wasn't me," she said through the sobs. "It was Trish."

"WHAT?"

"It was Trish. They raped Trish. Not me—*Trish*."

I stared at her, face mottled and wet. "Are you serious?" She just kept crying. "Dorrie, are you telling me the truth?"

"Yeah." Her voice sounded small and faraway.

"Trish? They raped Trish?"

"Y—" She gulped at whatever was running down her throat. "Yeah."

"What the hell happened?"

She turned on me, suddenly furious. "What do you *think* happened? They raped her, okay? The four of them—Billy and Shaun and Tom and Alan—they got all fucked up on E and they gang-banged her."

"They were on ecstasy? But I thought that . . . I mean, I heard that when guys take it they—"

Another humorless laugh. "Can't get up for the party? Sometimes. Not this time."

"Jesus, Dorrie . . . what happened?"

She shook her head and bit her lip again, this time so hard it had to draw blood. Then she grabbed her bag and pulled out a pack of cigarettes. She flipped open the top and offered me one first, like the stress of the situation was somehow making her revert to proper Benson family manners. I took one, she did the same, and she produced a lighter and lit mine first.

She sat there smoking for a while, blowing gray clouds out the open window. When she finally started talking, she was still looking away.

"It was the last night of the fest," she said. "We were having a great time—I mean *great*. Everybody was talking about how it was the best year ever. And the guys, they decided they wanted to go for a swim in the creek. It was kind of cold, so the rest of us blew it off.

"But after a while, Trish decided she wanted to go find them. She . . . she kind of had this thing for Alan back then. She really liked him a lot, but he didn't even notice. Far as he was concerned, Trish was just one of the guys. But she really wanted to hang with him, 'cause it was the last night and all. So even though she didn't really feel like swimming, she went down there anyway. And"—she took a long drag of the cigarette—"she really wanted me to go with her, but I wouldn't go. I just met Axel the day before and I wanted to, you know . . . hang with him. Some best friend, right?"

"You and Trish were best friends?"

"Back then, yeah. Not so much anymore."

"Tell me what happened next."

"Trish went off to find the guys. I went looking for Axel." She exhaled another smoky contrail. "Never found him, though."

"But what happened to Trish?"

"I don't know everything. She wouldn't tell me. I went over toward the creek looking for Axel, and Trish came running up the hill all messed up. She looked *awful*—her clothes were all wet and she was crying like crazy. And she told me . . . She said that all four guys did her. At least she thought they did—she was still pretty high."

"She took ecstasy too?"

"Yeah. And Trish was never as into that shit as the rest of us, probably because of her dad being a cop and all. But I guess she wanted the guys to think she was cool, so she took it. And it must've been pretty strong, because she was all"—she shrugged—". . . I don't know how to describe it. I just never saw anybody on E be so wacked. She was practically . . . What's the word?" She thought about it for a few seconds. *"Catatonic."*

"And that's not normal?"

Her look said I was an idiot. "Of course not. E can make you all manic—you talk a mile a minute sometimes—or else kind of mellow, like you're crazy about the whole world. But Trish was totally . . . just out of it."

"She was probably in shock." Dorrie didn't answer. "And she told you . . . what? That she was attacked by all four guys?"

Her eyes welled up again. "She said . . . I mean . . . I knew . . . Trish never did it before, okay?"

"You mean she was a virgin?"

The word sounded as oddly Victorian as ever, and I immediately felt stupid for saying it. Dorrie didn't seem to notice.

"Yeah. And . . . she said she didn't want to do it, that everything just got crazy and they were all just *on* her, and everybody was laughing and she told them no, but they wouldn't stop. . . ." She squeezed her eyes shut, either to stop the tears or to blot out the image. "She said it was like a big joke to them, that they just laughed and laughed. And she said"—Dorrie finally shifted in her seat to face me—"it was like she wasn't even there, like they fucking raped her, but they still didn't notice her. Can you believe that? Can you fucking *believe* it?"

"Did you take her to the hospital?"

She shook her head again, then pulled some Kleenex out of her backpack and blew her nose. When she pulled it away, there was a bubble of goo stuck to her nose ring.

"She wouldn't go," she said. "I tried . . . I told her she had to see a doctor—that, you know, it would be a good idea if she got the morning-after pill. But she wouldn't even talk about it. And the worst thing was . . . she was just so fucking calm."

"How do you mean?"

"She was talking about all this awful stuff that just happened to her, and she was like . . . like a robot, you know? It was . . . I don't know, just really scary, okay? It was way worse than if she'd been all crying and upset. It was like she was half dead or something."

"Then what happened?"

"She took off."

"What?"

"I tried to get her to come back to our tent, but she was afraid she'd run into Lauren or Cindy—she said she didn't want anybody else to see her like that. And then she said she was really thirsty from the E, so I went to get her some water. When I got back, she was gone. I told her to wait for me, that I'd be right back, but she just . . . left.

"So I spent the whole night looking for her, but I couldn't find her anyplace. And after I got home from Melting Rock the next day, she called me and said the whole thing was a big mistake. She said she wasn't really raped after all, that the whole thing was her fault. And she swore me to secrecy about it, made me promise never to tell anybody what she told me. I didn't see her again until school started."

"And did you tell anyone?"

The look in her eyes turned from anguished to offended. "Of course not."

"Not even Lauren or Cindy? Not anyone?"

"I told you," she said. "Trish swore me to secrecy."

"And did you believe her?"

"About what?"

"Did you believe Trish when she said it was all a mistake?"

"Are you crazy?" Dorrie spat out. "I *saw* her. She was fucking *traumatized.*"

"So why did you let it slide like that?"

Less fury, more tears. "What was I supposed to do? She tells me it didn't happen, and then she hardly talks to me for weeks, and then she practically starves herself to death and she has to go away to some treatment place. . . ."

"Didn't you even try to get her to talk about it?"

"Yeah, a couple times, but she . . . she pretty much acted like she didn't know what I was talking about." She focused on the glowing end of her cigarette for a while, like she found it hypnotic. "And maybe . . ." Her voice trailed off, eyes still on the burning butt.

"Maybe what?"

"Maybe I wanted to believe her," she said. "Maybe I wanted to believe it more than anything in the whole goddamn world."

CHAPTER 31

Y ou mean, it was better than believing that the four of them had . . . assaulted her?"

"Yeah," Dorrie said to her cigarette. "Billy and Alan and Tom and Shaun . . . they were my friends too, you know."

"You know, Dorrie . . . it's pretty obvious that Trish isn't the only one who was traumatized."

She finally looked at me again. "What are you talking about?"

"You see Trish completely messed up. You find out she was raped by four guys she trusted. You can't confide in anybody about it. You don't even know what to believe. And to top it off, you lose your best friend. No wonder you—"

"No wonder I *what?*"

I reached over and pulled her sleeve back up. She pulled it down again and just said, "Fuck you."

"You really ought to see a counselor."

"Like it's any of your business."

"Tell me something," I said. "When it came out that those guys didn't die by accident, didn't you think it might be connected? Didn't you think you should say something?"

She stared down at her lap. "Trish swore me to secrecy."

"For chrissake, didn't it occur to you that maybe the reason they were killed was—"

"I didn't really think about it."

"Well, you goddamn well better think about it now."

"Hey, where do you get off—"

"Dorrie, those three guys are *dead*. So's Axel. Alan's probably crippled for the rest of his life. And what about that poor girl in Baltimore? She almost died too, and she didn't have a damn thing to do with any of this."

She lit another cigarette, hands less than steady. "So?"

"So who the hell is responsible? Lauren?"

"*Lauren?* Are you crazy?"

"Think about it. She's really protective of Trish. She knows chemistry. She can get into the labs at Benson. She slept with Axel. She—"

"She *what?*"

"You didn't know?" Dorrie shook her head. "I don't think it was anything serious, just—"

"For Axel, there was no such thing as 'serious.'" She laughed, again without a trace of humor. "Can you believe I gave it up for that guy?"

"You—"

"He was my first, okay? I thought he was this supercool musician, and . . . this year, right after the fest, I let him fuck me in the goddamn dugout at the JHS baseball field. He said he saw it in a movie once and he wanted to try it in there, said it would be all romantic." Her voice rose an octave. "And you know what? It *wasn't* romantic. It fucking *hurt*. And I didn't even make him use a rubber or anything. I was lucky I didn't . . . I was just lucky, okay?" She shook her head. "What difference does it make? Sex always sucks for girls anyway. And besides, what happened to me was a hell of a lot better than . . ."

She let the sentence dangle. I finished it.

"Than what happened to Trish?"

She took another drag, hand shaking on the way to her mouth. "Yeah."

"Dorrie," I said after a minute, "did you get Axel the key to Deep Lake Cooling?"

She exhaled a plume of smoke. "Fine, all right, yes. How the hell did you know?"

"I figured since you've been around campus all your life, you probably know your way around."

She suddenly flashed a thin smile, and it struck me that it was the only time I'd ever seen her look remotely happy. "I've got a key to the room where they keep all the keys. And Axel . . . he said he found out some people got paid off a while ago not to fight Deep Lake, but he didn't get a penny of it. So he and some of his buddies . . . they wanted to do something really wild, something that'd get everybody's attention even more than the Jell-O thing. So I helped him out."

"Listen, Dorrie . . . about Lauren. Do you think there's any chance she—"

The smile disappeared. "Killed those guys? Are you serious?"

"I'm afraid so."

"Look, Lauren's never been my favorite person, okay? The princess act gets old after a while. And lately . . . she kind of treats me like I'm some sort of sad freak, you know? But I can't picture her ever doing anything like that. I mean, how would she even know about what happened to Trish in the first place?"

"Isn't it obvious? Trish probably told her."

"No way."

"Why not?"

"I told you, Trish is in total denial about the whole thing. She won't even admit it to *herself,* okay?"

"So who—"

"Look, I gotta go."

"But—"

"Christ, I just spilled my guts to you. Do you have to get me in deep with my parents too? My curfew's in, like, five minutes. So can I please have my car keys?"

"Okay." I handed them over and got out of the car. "But we're not done talking about this."

"Maybe you aren't," she said, "but I sure as hell am."

I'd barely shut the door when she peeled out of the parking lot. I went back to my own car and grabbed my cell to call Cody—and was intensely frustrated to discover that this far out in the hinterlands there was no service.

So I headed back toward Jaspersburg. I'd barely gone two miles when I saw flashing lights in my rearview mirror. *Damn.*

I pulled over, rolled down the window, and was summarily blinded by a high-test flashlight beam.

"Hey, what the—"

"Get out of the car."

"What for?"

"Just get out of the car."

I put a hand up to block the glare. "Did I do something wrong?"

The next thing I knew, the car door was being yanked open and I was being hauled out by somebody strong enough to do it with one hand. Before I could even start to figure out what was going on, my hands were cuffed behind my back and I was tossed into the back of a squad car—something that had been happening to me far too often of late.

It wasn't until we were speeding down the road that I recognized the man behind the wheel.

"Chief Stilwell? What's going on?"

"You're under arrest for violating the terms of your bail agreement."

"What? How?"

"The nature center's on the wrong side of the county line."

"But how . . ."

I'd been about to ask him just how the hell he knew where I'd been, but something in his tone made me keep my mouth shut.

We kept going, him never once taking his eyes off the road to look at me—and me starting to wonder if I'd been very, very wrong about Lauren Potter.

Finally, I couldn't stand it anymore.

"Where are you taking me?" I asked.

"To the station."

"In Gabriel?"

"Jaspersburg," he said.

He still didn't look at me, not even a peek at my reflection in the rearview mirror. The icky feeling in the pit of my stomach was starting to spread.

He must've been driving damn fast, because it was only a minute or so later that we got into town. I guess I expected him to pull up in front of the town-hall-slash-police-station, but he drove around the back. He left me inside the car for a second while he unlocked the door, then hauled me up again and propelled me inside.

The place was deserted. Stilwell led me down a hallway, through another door, and down a flight of stairs. We went through yet another door, beyond which was pitch blackness.

He flicked a switch and some fluorescent lights came on, giving the place a sickly greenish yellow glow—and, by the way, revealing a pair of jail cells.

He opened one of the doors, shoved me inside, and clanged it shut behind me. Then he told me to turn my back to him so he could unlock the handcuffs. Since I didn't know what else to do, I complied; imagine my relief when he actually liberated my wrists.

By the time I turned around again, he was gone.

I looked around the cell, which offered exactly one place to sit: the bare mattress of the spare steel bed. I plunked myself down and tried to figure out just what the hell I was supposed to do.

Was there any chance I *wasn't* in the gigantic amount of trouble I thought I was? Could Stilwell have actually picked me up on some stupid technicality? But then . . . how did he know I'd been at the nature center unless—at this point, the icky feeling kicked in again with a vengeance—unless he'd been following me?

The nasty thoughts I'd been entertaining in the backseat of the squad car went shooting across my brain.

It wasn't Dorrie whom those boys raped.

It was Trish.

And who's the most likely person on the goddamn planet to want to punish them for it?

I heard Stilwell's footsteps coming down the hall.

Play dumb, I thought. *If he knows you're on to him, you're screwed.*

As it turned out, I was screwed anyway.

WHEN STILWELL CAME BACK, he was carrying a stack of grayish white linen. He handed them to me, which doesn't sound particularly threatening. But when I went to put them on the bed, he said this:

"Make a noose."

I'm serious. That's what he said—but at first I wasn't sure I'd heard him right.

"Make a what?"

"A noose."

"Like . . ."

"Like what a person hangs himself with. A noose. Got it?"

I stared at him. "Are you kidding?"

"Do I sound like I'm kidding?"

I stared at him some more. Then I said, "No."

"Then do it."

"Uh . . . no way."

A muscle in his jaw twitched. Then he pulled the gun out of its holster, pointed it at me, and said, "Don't make me do this the hard way."

It was such a cliché I would've laughed—if the gun weren't so big and shiny and aimed right at my gut.

I decided stalling was in order.

"I don't understand," I said. I hoped the expression on my face was as stupid as I'd actually been over the past few weeks.

"Take the sheet," he said, jerking his gun in the direction of the bed before aiming it right back at me. "Rip it into strips. Braid them up to make a rope, then tie it into a slipknot. It's called a noose. Then you're going to tilt the bed frame against the wall and tie it on."

"I . . . Why?"

"I think you know why."

"No, I—"

"You're not stupid, Alex, and neither am I."

"But—"

"I'm sorry it's come to this. I can't even tell you how sorry. But at this point"—he shook his head—"right now, it's either you or me. I'd gladly go to prison for what I did, but . . . Trish needs me. After all she's been through, I'm not going to leave her without a father. I hope you can understand that."

"What are you talking about?"

He sighed and sat in a folding chair a few feet from the bars, the gun never wavering a damn millimeter. But though his hand was steady, the rest of his body radiated exhaustion. His eyes were bloodshot, the skin around them saggy and loose, and his Parris Island shoulders were somehow both slumped and tense at the same time. If someone had told me this wasn't really Chief Stilwell—that it was, in fact, his clinically depressed older brother—I would've half believed him.

When Stilwell finally spoke, the misery in his voice made the whole package seem even more pathetic.

"I tried to get you off this," he said. "I thought once you got busted with all that coke, once I made Sturdivant testify against you, you'd get the message—or even if you didn't, you'd have enough to worry about that it'd keep you from digging into it. So why did you have to keep going?" I thought it was a rhetorical question; it wasn't. *"Answer me."*

If there was a point in trying to keep up the pretense, I couldn't see it.

"I . . . guess I had to know why those boys were murdered."

"What difference could that possibly make to you?"

"I was there. I *met* them."

"So?"

"They were just so . . . young."

"Not that young. Not so young that they couldn't"—something dark flickered across his face—"do what they did."

"I know, but . . . why not just have them arrested? Why go through this whole convoluted plan to poison them?"

He seemed to be debating whether to answer. "Just make the noose," he said.

"No."

"Do it."

I lost my temper, probably not the best survival tactic. "What are you gonna do, shoot me?" I said. "How are you going to explain killing an unarmed woman locked in a goddamn jail cell?"

"You wouldn't be found," he said. He sounded detached, but also, weirdly . . . kind of sad. It didn't stop my mouth from going dry. "Now do it."

Since stalling remained the only promising strategy I could think of, I did as I was told. I took the worn top sheet and ripped a six-inch strip down one side. It seemed to placate him.

"You know," I said, "nobody would ever believe I'd kill myself."

"Are you so sure? A woman facing drug charges serious enough to put her away for thirty years gets caught jumping bail, then hangs herself in her cell?"

"Nobody who knows me would ever buy that."

"They're not going to be able to prove otherwise. It's my word against"—he thought about it for a second—"no one's."

I decided to try a different tack. "Come on," I said, "this is completely pointless. You know there are other people out there who know what happened to Trish. Eventually, someone's going to put two and two together, and . . ."

"And?"

"And people may not even blame you for it. Anyone can understand how you'd want to get back at those boys for what they did to your daughter. They could even see why you got rid of Axel—"

"I had nothing to do with that."

"What?"

"I said, I'm not responsible for that little creep's death. I'm not sorry about it, but I didn't do it."

"Then who did?"

"I don't know," he said, "and I surely don't care."

"How did you get him to sell the drugs for you?"

He gave the gun an ominous jerk. "You need to be working right now."

"Not unless you tell me how it happened."

"You're not exactly in a position to make demands."

"If you're gonna kill me anyway, what difference does it make?"

He almost cracked a smile. "That's original."

"It's also true."

He thought about it, then said, "I busted him."

"What?"

"Robinette. I'd busted him before, when he was a juvenile, so I knew what a weak-willed scumbag he was. And I needed someone to sell the drugs, so I tracked him until I caught him with some coke, more than enough to be sale weight. He knew he was up a creek under the Rockefeller laws, so—"

"So you told him to do you this one favor and you'd let him off the hook."

His jaw tightened. "That's right."

"Is he the one who made the LSD?"

Stilwell shook his head. "I had some chemical experience in the service."

I cast about for another topic to keep him occupied long enough for . . . What? The truth was, I had no idea—but talking was a hell of a lot better than hanging.

"There's something I really don't understand," I said. "Why did you admit that you'd been told not to enforce the drug laws at Melting Rock?"

He looked, of all things, confused.

"Because," he said, "it was the right thing to do."

"But I don't—"

"Like I told you in my office, when a person does something wrong, he ought to take responsibility. And I know what you're going to say next, so don't bother. If I could admit what I've done without dragging my daughter into it, I would. I'd be *proud* to. But I can't. And she's . . . she's the only thing I care about. She's the only thing that matters."

Lacking anything in the way of an informed response, I dug in my brain for another question.

"But why put so much ergotamine in the tabs of LSD?" I asked. "Why make it so obvious that it wasn't an accident?"

"It wasn't supposed to be." Stilwell shook his head again. "I didn't mean for it to be obvious. But I had to make sure."

"Make sure of what?"

He looked me straight in the eye. "That they got what they deserved."

"But why do it in the first place? Why not just arrest them for what they did to Trish? Why go through this whole—"

Another definitive head shake. "You wouldn't understand."

"Then make me."

"What difference does it make?"

An idea popped into my head; it was simple, but something told me it had to be the truth.

"She wouldn't testify against them, would she?"

"Just make the noose."

"She wouldn't, would she? It's like Dorrie said. . . . After it happened, Trish tried to convince her it'd all been some big misunderstanding. She said it was all her fault, that—"

"Trish is a very confused young lady." His voice was low, but there was plenty of menace in it all of a sudden.

"Did she approve of what you did for her? Did she thank you for it?"

"Trish has no idea, and she never will," he said. "Now *work.*"

I ripped another strip of cloth, but I kept talking.

"So if Trish wouldn't testify," I said, "that left it up to you to punish them. Is that right? To be judge, jury, and executioner?"

He'd kept his cool up until then; now he lost it.

"You have no idea," he said, springing to his feet so fast he knocked the chair over. "You can't even imagine what it's like to have . . . to have your little girl come to you so . . . so *destroyed.*"

Tears filled Stilwell's eyes, a wildly incongruous sight on a big man with a very big gun.

"It was like she wasn't even there," he said, "like she was *gone.* You think I shouldn't have killed them? Well, they practically killed *her.*"

For all intents and purposes, they *did* kill her. A big part of her died that night—the part that could trust people and think the world isn't full of monsters. And then to have her beg you, to *plead* with you never to tell anyone. To have those bastards just walking the streets, going to school every day, still acting like they're her *friends,* like there's no hard feelings. . . ."

He swiped at his eyes, then looked at me like he actually cared what I thought, that for some reason it was important that I understand where he was coming from.

"Do you know that after it happened, Trish didn't eat for a week? A *week.*" He stepped closer to the bars. "Finally, she fainted, and I had to take her to the emergency room, and . . . Look at her now. Just *look* at her. She looks like the walking dead. I know she does. But she can't even see herself anymore.

"And just when I thought that it couldn't get any worse, she started"—he took a few steps away, as though he couldn't bear to talk about it and look me in the eye—"to bleed, and I had to take her to the hospital again, and it turned out she'd had a miscarriage. One of those sons of bitches got her pregnant and she didn't even know it until it was over."

He strode back to my cell and stuck the gun through the bars. Now it was wavering, which didn't seem like much of an improvement. "So now are you going to tell me they didn't get what they deserved? Well, *are* you?"

I had absolutely no damn idea how to respond. Luckily, Stilwell wasn't done ranting.

"I'm her father," he said. "I'm supposed to protect her. I tried. I had to be a father *and* a mother to her, but I didn't do a good enough job. I never told her . . . I should've warned her about boys, about what they can be capable of. I should've taught her not to trust them. So, you see, this is really all my fault. I failed her, and then I had to make it right."

He stood there staring at me, like he expected me to say something—to agree with him probably. But although I'm rarely tongue-tied, I couldn't think of a single thing that might get me sprung.

The silence filled the concrete hall, until it was interrupted by a single word.

"*Daddy?*"

CHAPTER 32

T rish Stilwell came down the hall, stopping ten feet from her
father. She looked at him, then at the gun, then at me.

"Daddy," she said, "what's going on?"

The expression on his face was goddamn heartbreaking: a combination of fury at the boys, tears at the memory of what his daughter
had gone through, and tenderness at the sight of her.

"You can't be here, Trish," he said. "You have to go home now."

She took a step closer. "Daddy, please . . ." Her eyes were wide and
watery. "Please . . . stop."

"Trishie, what are you doing here?"

"Dorrie came over. She was upset. She said Alex got her to tell
about what happened to me. So I . . . I needed to find you."

"Sweetheart, please leave. This doesn't concern you."

"Doesn't *concern* me? How can you say that? This is all *about me.*"

"Trish, do what I tell you." He was obviously trying to sound all
tough and commanding with her, but he couldn't quite pull it off.
"Please," he said, voice cracking. "Please just turn around and go
home. I'll be there soon."

She shook her head, a gesture so faint I almost missed it. "Daddy,
please. Please let her go. You have to let her go."

"I can't, sweetie," he said. "She . . . did something bad."

"So did you," Trish said, hollow-voiced. "So did I."

His face crumpled. "No," he said. "No, honey. You didn't do anything wrong. It was them. *They're* the bad ones, not you."

"No, I . . . I did. I—"

"Trish, please. You have to go home. Just go home and wait for me, and everything will be all right. I promise. Just—"

"I killed Axel."

Stilwell stared at her. So did I. Then he shook his head and said, "No, honey. Maybe you think you're responsible somehow, but you're not."

"He came to me. He told me he needed money so he could go to California." She sounded disconnected, zombified, and for a second I thought she was on something. Then a worse thought occurred to me, which was that she wasn't. "He said he did you a big favor, but when he asked you for money, you . . . you threatened him. And when I asked him what the favor was, he said you made him sell the acid to the guys. He said he didn't know what was in it when he sold it, but after they died, he knew. And if . . . if he didn't get some money so he could leave, he'd have to sell his story to the newspaper."

She glanced at me. It didn't seem the time for a lecture on how real journalists don't pay for stories.

"He said he was meeting Alex at Deep Lake Cooling to show her how they messed up the water," Trish went on. "He said if I didn't meet him there first and give him some money, he was going to tell her all about . . . about what you did." She looked down at the dingy cement. "So I went there, and I brought him all the money I had, but it was only fifty dollars. And he said it wasn't enough, but if I . . . if I gave him a little something extra"—she choked on the word, sobs racking her skinny little body—"if I . . ."

Stilwell holstered the gun and took a few steps toward her.

"Trish, *no*. You didn't."

"I said I would, and he took me down to the basement. But it was so dark and cold and awful, and I . . . I just *couldn't*." Her voice was still as vacant as her expression; she sounded like the memory was more perplexing than traumatic. "And he got mad and he called me . . . he called me a tease, and he said now you were going to jail for killing those boys and it'd be all my fault."

"Trish, that's not true—"

"And he had me against this railing and I got out from under him and I shoved him as hard as I could and he fell. And he yelled for me to help him, but I . . . I just stood there. I didn't want . . . I didn't want to help him. I wanted . . . I think I wanted him to die."

Stilwell closed the gap between them and wrapped his arms around her. "Sweetie, it was an accident," he said. "It wasn't your fault. Nobody will ever find out what happened, I promise." He pulled away to look at her. "Now, please, just go home. This will all be over soon."

She didn't move. "Daddy," she said, "you have to let her go."

"I can't. She'll ruin our lives."

Trish started crying then—big, fat drops that plopped onto the concrete floor. "I already did that," she said.

"No, you—"

"This is all my fault," she said. "Everything's all my fault."

"You're not responsible for what those boys did to you. You're the *victim*, do you understand? What happened was *their* fault, not yours."

"But I took the E, and I . . . I went skinny-dipping with them. I *wanted* to go. I wanted Alan to notice me. I wanted him to touch me. But then everything all went . . . it all went wrong. And I told them no, but it was like they didn't even hear me, like I wasn't really even there. . . ."

She was sobbing even harder, and Stilwell put his arms around her again.

"Shh . . . it'll be okay," he said. "It'll be over soon, and you'll never have to think about it again."

She pulled away from him. "You don't understand. They never even thought they did anything bad. They never meant to. . . . They thought it was just for fun. And when I saw them at school later, it was like they didn't even *remember*. All except Tom. . . ."

"It doesn't matter," Stilwell said in the same pleading, placating voice. "It doesn't matter what they thought, just what they did. You said no. You didn't consent, and they . . . they hurt you. Trish, honey, please try to understand. I couldn't let them get away with it."

"But what about that poor girl in Baltimore? She didn't—"

"That was an accident. It wasn't supposed to happen. Robinette wasn't supposed to sell it to anyone else. But when Bauer turned it down, he got greedy and—"

"And then when you couldn't get Alan to take the drugs, you ran him over, didn't you? *Didn't you?*"

"Sweetheart, please. I did it for you. I did it so you wouldn't have to think about those bastards every day for the rest of your life."

"And what about *her?*"

Both pairs of eyes turned to me, still clutching the sheets.

"She knows," Stilwell said, as though that explained it all. Then he pulled out his gun again.

"So does Dorrie," Trish said. "Are you going to kill her too?"

He focused the gun on me, and his eyes on Trish. "Dorrie knows what happened, but she doesn't know—"

"She'll figure it out. So will Alan. Are you going to kill both of them because of . . . because of what I did? Daddy? Are you?"

Stilwell didn't answer her. Instead, he cocked the gun and aimed it right at my head. I stood there frozen, the whole world narrowing to that inch of blue-black metal. I remember wondering two things, one of them rather crazy: whether Stilwell was actually going to shoot me in front of his daughter, and why it was that even though the barrel was so short, the hole still seemed goddamn bottomless.

"Make the noose," he said, sounding suddenly desperate. "You have to . . . you have to make it. *Now.*"

"You can't do this," I said, as much to the gun barrel as to him. "If you kill me, Trish will never forgive you. You know she won't."

"Daddy, please," Trish said, taking a few steps toward him. "Please just let her go."

"I'm sorry, sweetheart," he said. "I can't. You have to understand; I just can't. . . ."

He looked right at me, and something in his expression told me this was it. I can't say my whole life passed before my eyes or anything; it was more like a sudden, miserable realization that I was going to die in—of all places—a jail cell in the basement of the Jaspersburg Town Hall.

There was a flash of movement off to my right as the gun went off, the sound roaring and echoing off the concrete walls. It took me a second to assimilate the fact that I wasn't actually dead, and a few more to realize that Trish Stilwell was bleeding on the floor in front of me.

I wish I could report that she said something profound as she lay there dying, maybe some melodramatic words for her grieving father. But she never got the chance. She just lay there on the floor, eyes wide, blood bubbling up into her mouth and dribbling a thin trail down her cheek. Stilwell shouted *"No,"* dropped the gun, and fell to his knees beside her.

It was all over within a minute. From his years in the army, Stilwell must've known it would be; that must be why he never even tried to call for help. He just knelt there next to her, not saying a word—not calling her name or telling her to hang on or any of your other battlefield clichés. He just held her and cried, his sobs filling the hallway as the gunshot had a moment before.

Eventually, he wiped at his face and scrambled backward to lean against the wall opposite me. He sat there for a long time, and since I had no idea what to do or say, I just stood there. Finally, he leaned over and picked up the gun. He pointed it at me and I backed up against the cell wall.

"Please," I said. "Please . . . don't."

He looked back at his daughter's body, and up at me again. Then he cocked the pistol, and for the second time in five minutes, I contemplated the inevitability of my own demise.

I wish I could conjure up the words to describe the expression on his face. It was the most incredibly haunted look I've ever seen, as though he were staring down into some god-awful pit—only the truth is, all he was looking at was me.

The gun moved so slowly, I barely noticed it at first. But eventually I realized that the bottomless hole in the barrel was no longer pointed at me. Then it kept turning, and turning, and turning, until I was staring at Stilwell's hand clasped over the butt.

He opened his mouth.

He put the gun in.

He pulled the trigger.

• • •

CHIEF STILWELL KILLED HIMSELF at approximately ten P.M. The morning shift at the Jaspersburg police station comes in at eight.

If you do the math, you'll appreciate how I spent the next ten hours of my life.

I tried to get out, but it was no use; the keys to the cell were on Stilwell's belt. Even though I tried to get them—which meant leaning across Trish's body—I couldn't reach him. I'll admit that I didn't try too hard. Stilwell's brains had literally been blown all over the wall, and the idea of trying to drag his corpse close enough to unhook the keys was even worse than being locked in there all night.

And locked in I was, the fluorescent lights burning the image of the Stilwells' goddamn Shakespearean tragedy into my brain for the rest of my natural life. I tried yelling for help, but I knew it was no use until morning. My backpack and cell phone were God-knows-where. After a while, I lay down on the bed and covered myself with the shredded sheets, squeezing my eyes shut and willing the hours to go by. I'm not sure whether my watch was a blessing or a curse; I could mark the minutes, but I was also acutely aware of how much time there was to go.

Finally, a good twenty minutes after eight, my hollering finally brought someone down to the cells. It was one of the cops I'd first seen at Melting Rock, a middle-aged Barney Fife who completely flipped out when he saw the bodies. At first he said he wasn't sure he could let me out because it would be disturbing a crime scene—Trish's body was, after all, still blocking the bars—but I finally started screaming at him about lawsuits and emotional distress and he unlocked the door.

With the chief lying dead on the floor—and the rest of the force being better suited to parking tickets than murder investigations—the Jaspersburg cops called in the state police. They showed up with the county sheriff hot on their heels, and twenty minutes later, I was being interviewed by a whole phalanx of guys in Stetsons.

The venue for this conversation was the town hall's all-purpose room, which had been set up for that night's bingo game. So as I sat there spilling my guts about the Stilwell case, I stared at hand-lettered posters offering fifty-cent hot dogs and "doubel-fudge" brownies made by the Jaspersburg Lioness Club. Rather surreal—but, frankly, way better than what I'd been looking at the whole night before.

After an hour of this, during which I told the entire story from the beginning of Melting Rock to the present twice over, the door opened and in walked Brian Cody. He asked the staties to give us a minute, and since he's a rather legendary law-enforcement figure in these parts, they didn't argue. As soon as the door had closed behind them, he wrapped his arms around me and held on tight, and I finally lost it. I cried until I'd soaked the shoulder of his suit jacket, and then I blew my nose on his hankie and cried some more.

When I calmed down, he had me give him the *Reader's Digest* version of what I'd told the state police. By the time I was done, he seemed furious—not even so much at Stilwell as at himself.

"I should've known," he said. "Some goddamn detective, right? I couldn't even figure out that one of our own was—"

"Jesus, Cody, it wasn't exactly obvious."

"Yeah, but . . . after those drugs were found in your car, it should've occurred to me."

"What should have occurred to you?"

"Who could get their hands on that much coke? Drug dealers . . . and cops."

"But, come on, who'd go thinking something like that? Especially somebody like you?"

"What's that supposed to mean?"

"You're incredibly loyal. You'd be the last person to think a cop was breaking the law."

"I'm not sure if that's a compliment or not."

"It is. And listen . . . I know I've been a total freak since I got busted. I didn't mean to blow you off, but I just—"

"It's okay."

"No, it's not. It isn't what you'd call healthy adult behavior."

"We can deal with it later, okay? Right now I'm just glad you're still breathing."

"But—"

"Let's change the subject, okay?"

"To what?"

"I don't give a damn."

"Okay, well . . . how do you think Stilwell got the drugs, anyway?"

"*That's* what you want to talk about?"

"I'm curious."

"You're insane. But to answer you, I assume . . . I wouldn't be surprised if there's exactly that much missing from some state evidence locker somewhere, and Stilwell just happened to be there recently."

"Would it really be that easy?"

"It could be."

"God, Cody, the idea of Stilwell . . . You know, despite everything, I think he was a decent human being who just got totally twisted over what happened to his—"

"Baby, this 'decent human being' that you're talking about is responsible for the deaths of five people, and that's not even counting himself."

"I . . ."

"What?"

"I wonder why he didn't kill me."

"I'm not sure you need to think about that right now."

"No, really, I . . . He could just as easily have shot me and then blown his brains out."

"I guess that's true."

"So why didn't he?"

"Maybe because . . . everything he'd done was about protecting his daughter. Maybe once she was gone, there was no point."

"That could be. But maybe it was because he knew once he was dead, it was all going to come out. Everybody was going to know what he did. But I was . . ."

"You were what?"

"The only person who could explain *why*."

CHAPTER *33*

Explaining why Stilwell did what he did was the central theme of the column I wrote for the paper two days later—by which time Sturdivant had recanted and the *Monitor* had rehired me. Though my fantasies about getting back pay were dashed by budgetary realities, it felt great to be back in the newsroom. My colleagues, not a particularly sappy bunch, expressed their joy at my return with a rash of mock headlines that got taped over my desk. My favorite was BERNIER DRUG RING GOES BUST; SELLS BRAS INSTEAD.

Since the LSD poisonings had been a national story, news of Stilwell's guilt attracted reporters from all the usual places. The *New York Times*, of course, was represented by one Gordon Band, and since I felt guilty about hanging up on him before, I actually gave him a couple of quotes.

The day the column ran, I drove back to Jaspersburg. I can't say I really wanted to, but I didn't have much choice. There was someone I needed to talk to, and there was no way he was going to come to me.

So I drove to a well-kept little house, a Cape Cod bungalow whose quaint facade was marred by the addition of a clunky-looking ramp that ran from the walkway up to the front door. I rang the bell, and after a minute, I heard someone struggling with the handle. I turned it myself, but the door only opened a few inches before it struck something.

That something turned out to be Alan Bauer's wheelchair.

He didn't greet me so much as ask what the hell I was doing there. Then he said, "My parents aren't home."

"I know. I called where they work to make sure."

"You . . . Why are you here?"

"I need to talk to you."

"Talk about what?"

"Trish Stilwell."

He bit his bottom lip. "I . . . You already know about that. Everybody knows."

"They know what happened," I said. "But they don't know how. They don't know why."

"Neither do I."

"You were there, Alan. You're the only one left who was."

"But . . . why do you want to know?"

"Because," I said, "I watched her die."

A melodramatic statement, I know—but an effective one. Alan backed up the wheelchair into a neat three-point turn and headed down the hallway into the kitchen. It was a sunny sort of room, all yellows and whites; there was an empty space on one side of the glass-topped table, and he parked himself there. I took a chair next to him.

"I'm going back to school next week," he said, like he was trying to prove something to one of us. "I get to graduate with my class."

"That's good."

"And . . . I'm having physical therapy three days a week. The doctors say I might be able to walk in three months or so."

"That's good too."

"But no more sports," he said, and this time I got the feeling he was talking directly to himself. "No more sports, ever again."

"Maybe it won't work out that way."

"I don't really care," he said.

I didn't believe him, but I didn't bother to argue.

"That night at Melting Rock," I said. "The night Trish got hurt. What happened?"

"You think I'm going to tell you so you can put it in the paper? So you can get the cops to—"

"It's all over, Alan. There aren't going to be any more stories. And you're not going to be arrested. Without Trish, there's no victim to press charges. You got away with it."

He slammed a fist on the table. "Got *away?* Are you crazy? *Look* at me. I'm fucking crippled for life, okay? My three best friends are dead. I'm sorry about what happened to Trish and all, okay? If I could take it back, I would have—we *all* would have. Don't you think we would?"

"I . . . I suppose so."

"Do you want to hear what happened? If you do, just sit there and shut up and I'll tell you. But don't go saying that I'm not sorry, that we all didn't get fucking *punished* for what we did, okay? Because we did. We *did.*"

"You're right," I said. "I'm sorry."

"And you swear none of this goes in the paper?"

"I swear."

He took a deep breath. "I . . . A bunch of us did some E. And it was . . . We were just really flying. And the four of us, just the guys, we decided we wanted to go for a swim.

"And it was cold, way colder than usual, but we totally couldn't feel it, you know? We were all having fun, splashing around and shit. There was nobody else there, just us, and it was, like . . . perfect.

"I don't know. It sounds stupid. Just some stupid adolescent shit, right? But we were just screwing around, and all of a sudden Trish showed up.

"And she was kind of lit up too, maybe not as much as us, but she said she wanted to go for a swim. And first we told her no, like 'no girls allowed,' just messing around, but she said it was a public place and she could swim if she wanted.

"So she came in, just wearing her bra and underpants, but then Billy said, 'Fine, you can swim, but no bathing suits.' And we all laughed 'cause Trish was always the shy one, and we figured she'd split, but she said it was cool.

"And I knew . . . I kind of knew she had a thing for me, and like I said we were all just having a good time. So I started playing around with her, saying, 'Don't take it off yourself; let me do it for you.' It all seemed like a laugh, you know? But like I told you, she was maybe a little bit lit up, and she came over to me in the water. And she, like, turned around and lifted her hair off her back and said, 'Go ahead.'

"So I did—I unhooked her bra in the back and just kind of threw it in the water. And then she turned around, and all of a sudden she . . ."

He paused for so long I finally prompted him. "She what?"

"She just looked different, you know? Really . . . beautiful. I don't know if it was the E or what, but I never saw her like that before. She was just standing there topless, and I . . . I just wanted to touch her. So I reached out and . . . did it.

"And she didn't push me away. I swear she didn't. She just kind of . . . smiled. And so I pulled her toward me, right there in the water, and I kissed her. And she kissed me back, really deep, and I was like . . . I'd never felt like that before, okay? I'd done E lots of times, but I'd never been, you know, turned on before.

"When I think about it, it feels like it happened to somebody else, you know? I'm not trying to say I'm not responsible; I'm just trying to tell you what it was like—like I was there but I wasn't. And the memory feels weird, like it comes in pieces, but the next thing I remember is laughing. I was laughing; Trish was laughing; the guys were all laughing. We pulled away and Billy and Shaun and Tom were all yucking it up at the sight of us. Then Billy came over and started stroking Trish's back, and we were all just laughing and laughing. . . . First he kissed her on the cheek and then on the mouth and then he touched her . . . her front, and we just all kept laughing.

"And the next thing I knew, Shaun and Tom were there too, and we were all in a circle around her, all touching her and laughing. But after a while, she said, 'Just Alan, I just want to kiss Alan,' and then we kept laughing 'cause it just seemed so funny, this game we were all playing.

"And that's what it felt like the whole time—just a game, just something to do for laughs. But when she tried to get out of the water, I couldn't understand why she didn't want to play anymore. So

I picked her up and carried her to the shore and I started kissing her again, right there on the ground, and she asked me to go back to the tents with her so we could be alone.

"But it didn't make any sense to me. I thought, *We're having so much fun here, why would we want to leave?* And she started laughing again; at least I thought she did. She was making all these sounds and I thought, *Good, she's having fun again.*

"And she looked so beautiful, lying there on the grass, and I thought how much I wanted to see the rest of her. So I started to take off her underpants, but she tried to stop me, and it took me a minute to realize . . . to understand that it was just part of the game too. So I got Billy to hold her down, and we were all just laughing and laughing, and I thought Trish was laughing too.

"And I wanted so much to . . . to be with her like that. It just all seemed so perfect, like this perfect thing to do on this perfect night, all of us together just laughing and laughing. She was lying there, looking so beautiful and perfect, and being . . . on top of her just seemed like the most natural thing in the world."

He paused, and though I should've kept my mouth shut, I couldn't manage it.

"And then you raped her," I said. "All four of you."

"I know . . . how awful it sounds now. But you asked what happened, so I'm telling you. And . . . back then, at that moment, it just seemed, right, you know? Like it was what we all wanted."

"Are you saying she asked for it?"

"No. *No.* I'm not saying that at all. When I think about it now, I know she said no. I know she didn't want to . . . to do it. And I guess she tried to fight back, to yell for help and everything. . . . But then, right then, it seemed like a game, something we all just got caught up in. And Melting Rock . . . it just never seemed like normal life in the first place, you know?"

"Did you ever talk about it afterward? Either with her or each other?"

"We kind of made a deal just to forget about it, the four of us guys.

But later, Tom told me . . . he said once he tried to tell Trish he was sorry, that he knew the whole thing had gotten out of hand, but she pretended like she didn't know what he was talking about."

"And when the other guys got killed, didn't you think maybe this might be the reason?"

"I know you probably won't believe it, but . . . no."

"But how could you possibly—"

"I just thought it was some stupid random OD at first, okay? And then even when the papers said it wasn't, I didn't really believe it. It wasn't until . . . until I got hit by the car that I started to think that it had really happened on purpose."

"Then why didn't you say something?"

"What was I supposed to say? 'Gee, Chief Stilwell, my friends and I gang-raped your daughter and now somebody's trying to kill me'?"

"You never suspected it was him?"

"No. Of course not. Why would I ever—"

"Because it was his *daughter*."

"Yeah, but Chief Stilwell, he always seemed so"—he shook his head—"I don't know how to describe it."

"Try."

"I guess he just always seemed like . . . the opposite."

"The opposite of what?"

"The opposite of anything goes," he said. "The opposite of doing whatever you feel like and not having to deal with it later. I guess what I mean is . . . the opposite of Melting Rock."

THAT NIGHT, after what she said was a fair amount of soul-searching, Melissa told me she was moving out. The bottom line was she felt like she could never feel safe in the house again. And though I hardly felt like dealing with looking for another roommate—or finding a new place to live—I could hardly blame her.

Things with Cody, though weird, appeared to be on the mend; at least he seemed to be having a good time out at the Citizen Kane with the rest of us. We sat there drinking in relative moderation, trying not to rehash the whole Melting Rock thing but managing to talk about nothing else. When I finally got around to recounting my visit to Alan Bauer, the conversation got a little dicey.

It was Melissa—who'd recently suffered through her fair share of male aggression—who asked the questions. Was what happened to Trish an example of aberrant behavior? she wondered. Or did I think that there was some measure of pack mentality lurking in the collective hearts of all human males?

"I'm not sure," I told her. "I mean, some people think morality is really situational. It's not that people are inherently good or bad, it's more a question of how you behave at a particular time."

"Pardon me," Cody said, "but that sounds like a bunch of crap. I mean, call me old-fashioned, but I think a person has to stand for something. The boys that attacked Trish Stilwell might have done it because they were all together or because they were wacked out on drugs, but what matters is they *did* it."

"And you think that makes them fundamentally bad?"

"Damn right," he said. "Anyone who'd be capable of that kind of thing can't call themselves a decent person. To say it's a question of circumstances . . . that just seems to me like a cop-out."

"Here, here," said Mad.

"I'm with you guys," said O'Shaunessey. "Nuns never taught us morality was a part-time job."

"Wait a minute," I said. "Are you telling me you think good people never do bad things?"

"Sure they do," said Mad. "Which then makes them . . . What?" He turned to O'Shaunessey.

"Bad people."

"Fine," I said, "call me wishy-washy or whatever you want. But even if you want to say the other three were a moral wasteland, Tom Giamotti was different. He was a decent guy who got all screwed up on drugs and did something awful. Or didn't the nuns bother to teach you about redemption?"

"Guess they covered that after I got expelled."

"And no offense, Mad, but I'd hardly call you a poster child for the Moral Majority."

"Meaning what?"

"Meaning I know damn well you've been trying to get an eighteen-year-old girl into the sack." Mad began to take a passionate interest in his Beer Nuts. "Son of a . . . You *didn't.*"

"None of your damn business, okay?"

"Tell me you didn't sleep with that child."

He let out a strangled sort of cackle. "*'Child'?* What are you, nuts?" He took a long drink of his Labatt's. "Lauren Potter is a lot of things, but a child is definitely not one of them. Trust me."

"Yo, Madison," Ochoa said. "What did that chick *do* to you, anyway?"

Mad surveyed his audience, then poured some more beer. "Never mind."

"Come on," I said, "you know you're going to tell us eventually."

"And why the hell would I do that?"

"Because every single one of us is a reporter, except for the one who happens to be a cop. That's why."

"Oh, for chrissake, she . . . she turned out to be, um . . . to have been around the block a lot. Or at least on a way freakier block than I've ever been to."

"Oh, really? How so?"

"The chick just scared me, okay? She was a little too . . . out there for my taste."

"So what happened?"

"Come on, would you lay off already?"

"Just spill it. How bad can it be?"

"Pretty bad."

"Would you just—"

"Let me put it this way," he said. "The morning after, I got rid of my most prized possession."

"Mad," I said, "you *didn't.*"

He raised his beer mug in a mock salute. "Damn straight."

"Madison," O'Shaunessey said, "you're breakin' my heart here."

Ochoa shook his head. "If it's true, it's the end of an era."

Cody raised a reddish eyebrow. "Somebody want to let me in on the joke?"

"What I believe Mad is telling us," I said, "is that he sold his signed copy of *Lolita*."

"Sold it?" he said. "I *burned* the damn thing."

"Really? Are you serious?"

"Well . . . no," Mad said. "But I stuck it up on a really inconvenient shelf."